VICTORIA ALEXANDER

THE LADY TRAVELERS GUIDE TO

Deception
with an
Unlikely Earl

HQN™

Recycling programs
for this product may
not exist in your area.

HQN™

ISBN-13: 978-0-373-80406-1

The Lady Travelers Guide to Deception with an Unlikely Earl

Copyright © 2018 by Cheryl Griffin

This edition published by arrangement with Harlequin Books S.A.

For questions and comments about the quality of this book, please contact us at CustomerService@Harlequin.com.

www.HQNBooks.com

Printed in U.S.A.

You always need friends to help you through the desert—in Egypt and everywhere else. This book is for Lizzie, April, Mary, Jenn and Laura with gratitude and thanks for their generous and continuous help navigating the wilderness.

CHAPTER ONE

London, January 1892

"WOULD ANYONE CARE to explain this to me?" Sidney Althea Gordon Honeywell looked up from the newspaper clippings spread before her on the table in her small dining room. "Well?"

Across the table, three of the dearest ladies Sidney had ever known stared back at her, the very picture of elderly innocence.

"Anyone," Sidney prompted. "Anyone at all?"

"I think it speaks for itself, dear," Lady Guinevere Blodgett said in a vaguely chastising manner.

Mrs. Persephone Fitzhew-Wellmore nodded. She and Lady Blodgett had long insisted Sidney call them by their given names—Poppy and Gwen—in spite of the nearly fifty-year difference in their ages as it made them feel terribly old otherwise and they weren't at all fond of that. "I don't really see what needs to be explained."

The third member of the trio, Mrs. Ophelia Higginbotham—Aunt Effie—wisely held her tongue.

Sidney narrowed her eyes. "*You* have nothing to say?"

"Not quite yet." Effie—her grandmother's dearest friend and an aunt by affection rather than blood—smiled pleasantly. "I would rather hear your thoughts first."

"No doubt." Sidney studied the clippings on the table

although there was no need. The words had burned themselves into her mind the moment she read them. "It appears we have a series of letters to *The Times* from—" she picked up a clipping "—the Earl of Brenton in which he alleges that I don't know what I write about. That my stories are total fiction. That I've never been to Egypt. That I am in fact a fraud. And, as we all know—" she blew a resigned breath "—I am."

"Rubbish," Aunt Effie said staunchly. "You never claimed your stories were anything other than fiction."

"It's not your fault that the public decided your adventures were real," Poppy added.

"Regardless, I should have corrected the mistaken impression the moment I became aware of it." It still bothered Sidney that she had allowed herself to be talked out of doing exactly that.

When Sidney had begun writing her *Tales of a Lady Adventurer in Egypt* in an attempt to supplement her modest income shortly after her mother's death four years ago, she had no idea her work would ever be published, let alone become popular. Sidney's father died some thirteen years ago, leaving Sidney and her mother a cozy house near Portman Square and an adequate income from a small trust. Father no doubt assumed Mother would eventually remarry or at least that his daughter would find a husband, but Sidney had not had the opportunity. Mother never recovered from losing the love of her life and her grief took a toll on her health. It was left to Sidney to run their small household as well as care for her mother, a responsibility Sidney neither questioned nor resented.

"Your popularity did take us all unawares. But when your book was published with all of your previously published stories from the *Daily Messenger* it did seem everyone was reading it and clamoring for more of your work. By then it really was too late." Gwen shrugged. "It's hard to undo something like that. No one ever believes it was inadvertent. We know you, of course, and we are well aware that you simply didn't notice the attention your stories were receiving. You do tend to live in your own little world when you're writing, Sidney dear."

In hindsight Sidney felt like something of a ninny but writing did sweep her away to another world altogether. A world of adventure and romance that at times seemed more real than the London she lived in.

"Besides, we thought it was quite thrilling," Poppy said, her eyes glittering with excitement. "Why, you've become famous. The Queen of the Desert and all."

Sidney winced at the title her readers had bestowed upon her.

"And wasn't your Mr. Cadwallender rather pleased that your readers thought your adventures were true?" Poppy pointed out.

"The man was ecstatic. He said it would make the stories more popular and I allowed myself to be convinced." Sidney struggled to keep calm even as her future, her dreams, were crumbling around her. "I should have known it would come to this."

Sidney still wasn't sure how the public misunderstanding had happened. After all, the main character in Sidney's stories was Millicent Forester, a charming young widow and intrepid adventurer who had lost her husband shortly after they arrived in Egypt. A woman confident and courageous and all the things Sidney was not. But while Millicent was nothing more than a figment of Sidney's imagination, her writing was based on the journals of her grandmother Althea Gordon. Admittedly Sidney did take a fair amount of poetic license, and with each new work, her stories bore less and less resemblance to her grandmother's experiences. Sidney wouldn't have known anything about her grandmother at all had it not been for Aunt Effie.

It was shortly after her father's death that Sidney first made Ophelia Higginbotham's acquaintance. She was the wife of a military man who had then become an explorer and adventurer when his days of service to the Crown ended. Effie had met Sidney's grandmother through mutual acquaintances. Years later, Effie would tell Sidney it was as if they'd each discovered a sister they never knew they had. They forged a friendship that would last the rest of Althea's life. Much of that life was spent in Egypt with Sidney's grandfather Alfred, locating and excavating ancient ruins and recovering lost artifacts. Althea regularly wrote her dear friend of their adventures and kept scrupulous records in the form of her journals that she would leave with Effie for safekeeping when she and her husband headed back to the desert.

It was through her grandmother's letters to Effie that Sidney learned of her mother's estrangement from her parents. It had always been something of a mystery and while Sidney was named in part for her grandmother, her mother had avoided further discussion. The Gordons were lost at sea when Sidney was very young and she never knew them. But with each of her grandmother's letters the story of her life unfolded. Sidney's mother had accompanied her parents on their Egyptian expeditions when she was a girl but grew to detest travel in general as well as the climate, the desert and all things Egyptian. When she was old enough, her parents allowed her to stay in England and attend school although, to read Grandmother's letters, leaving her only child behind was a heart-wrenching decision. In spite of visits home to England, Althea and her daughter grew apart. Mother blamed Egypt and she never returned to the land of the pharaohs.

Effie became Sidney's friend and, in many ways, her mentor. Neither woman thought it wise to let Sidney's mother know of their relationship which did seem wrong but also necessary. There was no doubt Mother would not take it well and, given her fragile health, Sidney did want to avoid any upset. What would have been even worse in her mother's eyes was that Sidney fell in love. Passionately, irrevocably in love with the idea of travel, of seeing foreign lands and, most especially, with Egypt.

From then on, Sidney read everything she could about the country, its past and its present. She took night classes at Queen's College on Egyptian history and civilization, hieroglyphics and excavations, and all sorts of other fascinating subjects. She attended lectures and exhibits, often accompanied by Effie and her friends.

When Mother died, Sidney realized her trust would continue to keep a roof over her head but little else. Her dreams of traveling the world and at last seeing Egypt for herself would remain nothing more than that unless she came up with a way to generate additional income. Aunt Effie had not only encouraged her writing, but had brought her initial offerings to the attention of Mr. James Cadwallender at *Cadwallender's Daily Messenger*, the paper that now published her work.

"There's really no getting around it." Sidney shook her head. "His lordship is right. I am a charlatan, a fake, a fraud."

"Don't be absurd." Effie huffed. "The fact that these adventures are not technically yours—"

"Although you *do* own the writing you based them on," Poppy said, "so in the strictest definition of the term, one could easily argue that they do belong to you. Therefore they are *yours*."

"—does not make them any less true, at the heart of it at least," Effie continued. "Really, there are two points to consider here." She held her hands up as if balancing a scale. "On one hand—" she raised her left hand "—you have never claimed you personally had these adventures. On the other—" she lowered her left hand and raised her right "—they are, more or less, true stories."

"Although as Althea was married to Alfred, I suspect there were not quite as many dashing gentlemen in her experiences as Sidney has in her stories," Poppy murmured.

"Millicent Forester is a young widow, Poppy," Gwen reminded her. "It wouldn't be any fun at all if there wasn't the occasional dashing gentleman in her way."

"They're simply not your experiences," Effie finished.

"And therein lies the problem." Sidney sighed and shuffled through the clippings on the table. "Or one of the problems." In her dismay over the earl's scathing comments, she had completely ignored the rest of this disaster. "His lordship's letters are not the worst of it though, are they?"

"They are dreadful letters." Poppy huffed. "Simply dreadful.

Gwen sniffed. "Very nearly rude, I would say."

"And yet—" Sidney's tone hardened "—not the worst of it." She moved several of the clippings to one side. "These are the letters from the earl." She waved at the remaining clippings. "While these responses are allegedly from me."

The ladies wisely said nothing.

"I did not write these." Sidney narrowed her eyes. "Which begs the question of who did."

Gwen, Poppy and Effie traded glances. Effie drew a deep breath. "It's my fault I'm afraid. I started this. When that vile man wrote the first letter I should have ignored it."

"But it really was rather boorish," Gwen added.

"And it did seem he was laying down a kind of gauntlet." Aunt Effie grimaced. "So I picked it up."

"And wrote him back?" Sidney's voice rose. "In my name?"

"It seemed appropriate at the time," Effie said weakly. "But, upon reflection, it might have been a mistake."

Poppy nodded. "As it did seem to incite him. The man obviously has no sense of moderation. As you can see, the second letter was even worse."

"He compares my stories to penny dreadfuls." Sidney drew her brows together. "That's not at all fair. My stories are adventurous but not nearly as far-fetched and melodramatic."

"You're right, he wasn't the least bit fair." Gwen nodded. "You can certainly see why we all felt it necessary to respond to that particular letter."

"We did help Effie write that one. More than help I suppose. You might call it a collaboration." Poppy winced. "As well as the one after that. We really couldn't help ourselves. Someone needed to defend you. Why, the man even criticizes your style of writing."

Effie shook her head. "We could not let that go unchallenged."

"And you never thought to mention this to me?"

"We wanted to protect you, dear." Gwen smiled.

"We did think his lordship would give up." Effie paused. "Eventually."

"But he hasn't given up, has he?" Sidney glared at the older ladies. "No, in fact the man has challenged me to travel to Egypt and prove that I know what I'm writing about. If I fail, he intends to petition the Egyptian Antiquities Society to rescind my membership." Sidney had paid little notice to the praise and attention her stories had received but being granted membership in the Antiquities Society a few months ago was an honor she cherished. Her grandparents were among the founding members of the society and, while she had not yet attended a society event, being a part of that illustrious organization was the very best part of her newfound success.

"Fortunately, we've given this a great deal of thought," Poppy said. "Indeed, we've thought of nothing else since the moment we saw the earl's latest letter this morning."

"And promptly came here to tell you about—" Gwen gestured at the clippings "—all of it."

"Not promptly enough, it's after noon." Sidney blew a long breath. This might well explain why she'd received a note within the past hour from Mr. Cadwallender requesting she come to the *Messenger* offices at her earliest possible convenience. "Mr. Cadwallender wishes to see me and I suspect this is what it's about." She shook her head. "What a dreadful mess this is. What am I supposed to do?"

"You should definitely pay a call on Mr. Cadwallender," Poppy said firmly.

Gwen nodded. "At once, I should think."

"And then?" The most awful helpless note sounded in Sidney's voice. She did so hate sounding helpless.

"And then." Aunt Effie rose to her feet. "Then you shall go to Egypt."

"I THINK IT'S a brilliant idea." Mr. James Cadwallender sat behind his desk in his office in the center of what had always struck Sidney as the sheer bedlam of the world that was *Cadwallender's Daily Messenger*. The office itself was enclosed with walls of paneled wood beneath glass windows that rose to the ceiling, allowing the publisher to observe his domain while saving him from the endless cacophony of noise that was apparently the natural environment of reporters in search of news.

"Brilliant?" Sidney stared at the man. Didn't he realize how impossible this was. "It's not the least bit brilliant. It's dreadful, that's what it is. Positively dreadful."

"Come now, Miss Honeywell." Mr. Cadwallender chuckled. He really was a fine figure of a man with dark brown hair and eyes that were an interesting shade of amber. Sidney had always found him quite dashing although perhaps not today. "How is sending my very favorite writer off to prove she knows what she writes about anything less than brilliant. By Jove, I wish I'd thought of it myself."

"Mr. Cadwallender," Sidney said slowly, "surely you have not forgotten that my work is fiction."

"Of course I have not forgotten but the public believes it's all real. They believe Millicent Forester is a thinly veiled version of you or rather of Mrs. Gordon." He grinned. "And who am I to tell our loyal readership that they're wrong."

Aunt Effie nodded in agreement. She had insisted on accompanying Sidney for the sake of propriety although they both knew propriety was the last thing on the older woman's mind. She simply didn't want to miss what happened next and no doubt had orders from Poppy and

Gwen to report back every detail. "And we would hate to shatter their illusions."

"Exactly," Mr. Cadwallender said.

"Their illusions will be more than shattered when the earl is proved right," Sidney said sharply.

"But he won't be proved right because you won't let him." Mr. Cadwallender leaned forward across his desk and met her gaze directly. "Miss Honeywell, Sidney, you and I both know you have never been to Egypt. We know your stories are loosely based on the life of your grandmother. But all those people out there who read your stories, who clamor for more, who adore every word you write, who've taken Millicent Forester to heart, they don't know you aren't her and have never stepped foot out of England. To them, you have led the life they have always dreamed of living. They count on you, Sidney, to lift them out of their tired, ordinary, everyday lives and bring them to the sands of Egypt. To allow them to take part in the discovery of ancient tombs. To illuminate the sights of that exciting land. Surely, you don't want to deprive them of all that?"

"Well, no, I suppose not. But—"

"People don't care if your stories are true or not."

"Then why can't we simply tell them the truth?" Indeed, that was exactly what Sidney wanted to do when she first realized her stories were being taken as fact.

"Because they will care if they think you lied to them." He shrugged. "It's the nature of things."

"So the lie continues to grow?" Sidney couldn't hide the stubborn note in her voice. This deception did seem, well, wrong.

"Not at all. This earl, in his superior, condescending manner, has challenged your knowledge of Egypt and all things Egyptian. You are one of the most knowledgeable people I've ever met on the topic. Why, you know things most people would never even think to ask. Doesn't she, Mrs. Higginbotham?"

"Oh, she does indeed, Mr. Cadwallender." Effie nodded. "She's spent years taking classes with highly notable personages at Queen's College. I wouldn't dare to count the number of lectures on Egyptology she's attended. Sidney is familiar with every Egyptian artifact on display at the British Museum as well as elsewhere in London. And she reads everything that's printed on the subject." Pride rang in Effie's voice. "I daresay there is no one better versed in anything pertaining to Egypt—past and present—than Sidney."

"Thank you, Aunt Effie." Sidney cast her a grateful smile. "Regardless of my studies and all that I've learned, the fact remains that I've never actually been to Egypt."

"A minor point." Mr. Cadwallender waved off her comment. "If anyone can pull this off you can. I have every confidence in you, Sidney. By the time you return—"

"I don't recall agreeing to go."

"Really, dear." Effie leaned close and patted her hand. "I don't see that you have any particular choice."

"That's not entirely true." Mr. Cadwallender studied her for a long moment. "You have several choices. You can choose to admit publicly that his lordship is right—that you don't know what you're writing about—"

"And allow the beast to win?" Effie straightened in her chair. "Never!"

"In which case there would be a nasty scandal. You would lose your readers who would feel betrayed by you. Cadwallender Publishing and the *Daily Messenger* could not continue to publish your work. We do have a reputation to maintain."

As the *Daily Messenger* did seem to base most of its articles on little more than scandal and gossip, apparently reputation was in the eye of the beholder.

"You're the one who convinced me not to tell the truth when this misunderstanding began," Sidney pointed out.

"Water under the bridge, Miss Honeywell." He waved off her comment. "No sense fretting about what's over and done with. We simply must move forward from here. As I said you have choices. Confess the truth and face the consequences—"

Effie shuddered.

"—or you can kill off Millicent and end the stories altogether—"

Effie gasped in horror.

"—or you can go to Egypt and make the Earl of Brenton eat his words. He started this—beat him at his own game. Prove to him and the world that he's wrong. It would serve him right. Certainly, you've never been to Egypt in person but you can't tell me your mind, your heart, your very soul hasn't been there."

"Her spirit." Effie nodded.

"Exactly. Sidney." Mr. Cadwallender's gaze locked with hers. "Carpe diem. Seize the day. Isn't this the opportunity you've been waiting for?"

"Yes, yes, yes!" Effie jumped to her feet. "She'll do it!"

Sidney could only stare at her.

"Of course she will." Mr. Cadwallender grinned. "I didn't doubt it for a moment."

Sidney's gaze shifted between Effie and Mr. Cadwallender. He was right—she did have a choice. And an opportunity. This was her chance to set things right. To have the adventures, to be the heroine her readers believed her to be.

For the first time since reading his lordship's challenge, the idea of travel to Egypt seemed not only possible but probable. And why not? She was a thirty-two-year-old spinster with no particular prospects for marriage. No family to speak of except for Aunt Effie and her friends. And absolutely no good reason not to at long last follow her heart. She had nothing to lose and at the very least, the adventure of a lifetime to gain.

"Very well, then." She swallowed hard. "I'll do it."

"Excellent." He grinned. "The *Messenger* will pay for all your expenses and we will, of course, send a reporter along."

"A reporter?" Effie sank down into her chair.

Sidney widened her eyes. "Is that necessary?"

"Absolutely. This, my dear girl, will be the story of the year." He paused. "Have you heard of Nellie Bly?"

Sidney shook her head. "I don't think so."

"You do need to get out more, dear," Effie said under her breath.

"Nellie Bly is an American female reporter who attempted to travel around the world in less than eighty days a few years ago. She managed it in only seventy-two." Mr. Cadwallender's eyes sparkled. "It was quite a story. One that captured the imagination of the reading public in America and very nearly everywhere else. I anticipate the story of the Queen of the Desert's return to Egypt to be every bit as profitable."

Sidney's brow rose. "Profitable, Mr. Cadwallender?"

"Profitable, Miss Honeywell," he said firmly. "This story will increase readership and therefore generate greater revenue. Stories like this sell newspapers and books. While our mission is to enlighten and inform our readers, we cannot do so with inadequate funding. Nor can we afford to send our correspondents on trips to Egypt."

"Regardless, don't you think yet another observer watching my every move is dangerous?"

"I have every confidence in you, Miss Honeywell. If I didn't, I would neither finance nor encourage this trip. In point of fact, being accompanied by one of my reporters is in your best interest." He grimaced. "Frankly, if I don't send someone along to document this venture, make no mistake, *The Times* surely will. I suspect you would prefer a reporter who works for me rather than a competitor who would like nothing better than to discredit all of us."

"That makes sense I suppose." Sidney sighed. This was becoming more and more complicated. "Will this reporter know the truth? About my experience with Egypt that is."

"Absolutely not, Miss Honeywell." Disbelief shone in Mr. Cadwallender's eyes. "I would never allow one of my reporters to actively mislead the public."

"Which means it's up to me to *actively mislead* him as well as the earl."

"Oh, the earl isn't going. While he is willing to publicly denigrate your work, he is not willing to see this through personally. He's sending a representative, a nephew I believe, a Mr. Harry Armstrong. Apparently, Mr. Armstrong visited Egypt in his youth and now considers himself something of an expert."

"Wonderful," Sidney said under her breath.

"I strongly suspect the earl's criticism was a direct result of his nephew's prodding." He paused. "You need to prove your legitimacy to Armstrong's satisfaction. If, in his opinion, you do so, he will issue a public apology. If you fail, I've agreed to publish his book."

Sidney widened her eyes. "He's written a book?"

"Of allegedly true stories about his experiences in Egypt." The publisher sighed. "God help us all."

"One moment, Mr. Cadwallender." Effie's brow furrowed. "You're saying that the very man who decides whether or not Sidney is who the public believes her to be, has a great deal to gain if he decides she's a fraud." Effie shook her head. "That's extremely subjective and doesn't sound the least bit fair to me."

"Fair or not, that's the challenge. Refusing it would be the same as admitting he's right." He met Sidney's gaze directly. "You can do this, Sidney. Show the man around Egypt. Take him to the pyramids and maybe a tomb or two. Just enough to establish your expertise. It's not as if you have to discover a pharaoh's treasure."

"But that would be perfect," Effie murmured.

"You have the knowledge and, I have no doubt, the courage to pull off an endeavor of this nature. To be the heroine of your own story. You *are* Millicent Forester. You need to remember that." His tone softened. "We both have a great deal to lose if you aren't successful. My family started Cadwallender Publishing nearly a century ago. I would hate to be the Cadwallender to preside over its demise."

Sidney studied him for a long moment. Did she have the courage to carry off an escapade of this magnitude? Did she have the knowledge to step foot in Egypt for the first time and convince at least two people she did indeed know what she was doing? Still, aside from the deceptive aspect of it all, wasn't this exactly what she had spent years preparing for? Isn't this what she had always wanted? Didn't she owe her readers at least a valiant attempt to be who they thought she was? And apparently, more than just her own future was at stake. She squared her shoulders. "I shall not let you down, Mr. Cadwallender."

"Excellent." Effie beamed. "The Lady Travelers Society will make the arrangements at once. Oh, we will be a jolly little band of travelers."

"We?" Mr. Cadwallender shook his head. "I'm afraid you misunderstand, Mrs. Higginbotham. I will not be going along to Egypt." He scoffed. "I have a newspaper to run."

"Of course you do, Mr. Cadwallender. And no one would expect a man of your responsibilities to abandon his duties even for something as important as this. But I'm afraid you are the one who has misunderstood." The glint in Effie's eyes belied the pleasant tone of her voice. "My friends and I cannot allow our dear Sidney to wander off to the land of the pharaohs without the proper accompaniment. Chaperones if you will."

Mr. Cadwallender's brow furrowed. "Chaperones?"

"Of course. Lady Blodgett, Mrs. Fitzhew-Wellmore and myself will be joining Sidney's party."

"Not necessary, Mrs. Higginbotham," Mr. Cadwallender said blithely. "Why, Nellie Bly went around the entire world completely on her own."

Effie sniffed. "Miss Bly is American. Such things are to be expected from an American. Subjects of Her Majesty do not adhere to such slip-shod standards of propriety and deportment."

"Might I point out that Miss Honeywell writes as Mrs. Gordon, a widow." His lips quirked upward in a subtle show of triumph. "Therefore chaperones are not expected."

"And might I point out that your less than reputable rivals might portray this venture—an unattached female, regardless of whether she is a widow, heading off on a journey of unknown length with a gentleman and a male reporter—as something rife with the possibility of inappropriate activity. Why, the entire venture would be fraught with the suggestion of scandal." Effie shook her head in a regretful manner. "As much as your paper seems to delight in laying out all the juicy details of whatever scandal comes along, I wouldn't think you would want the *Daily Messenger* itself exposed to that sort of thing."

"No." He glared. "I suppose I wouldn't."

"Chaperones will eliminate any hint of impropriety. Furthermore..." She ticked the points off on her fingers. "The other ladies and myself are all the widows of men who each spent a good deal of time in Egypt. They were, as well, honored members of the Explorers Club. Which means that we have a certain amount of credibility as observers. In addition, Sidney will need assistance, support if you will, to carry off this ruse successfully. I daresay we don't want anyone else discovering the truth."

"No, we do not." He drummed his fingers on the desk. "I assume you expect me to finance your trip as well."

"It does seem to me we are doing you a very great favor by accompanying Miss Honeywell." Effie smiled, a triumphant gleam in her eye.

"It seems to me the word *blackmail* is more appropriate than *favor*."

"Semantics, Mr. Cadwallender." Effie waved off the comment. "One word is often just as good as another as long as the end result is the same."

"As long as it's the result you want?"

Effie smiled pleasantly.

Mr. Cadwallender heaved a sigh of resignation. "Very well, then." He turned to Sidney. "How soon can you be ready to leave?"

Sidney thought for a moment. She had nothing to attend to. Nothing keeping her in London. Indeed, she could have her bags packed and be ready to go within a day or so. "As soon as the arrangements can be made, I would think."

"Excellent." He rose to his feet behind his desk, Aunt Effie and Sidney following suit. "I have no doubt this will be an extremely successful venture for you—for all of us, Miss Honeywell."

"Thank you, Mr. Cadwallender."

He opened the door and Aunt Effie swept out of his office, Sidney a step behind. They made their way through the sea of desks, frenzied gentlemen with ink-stained fingers and organized confusion, to the front lobby. Sidney barely noticed any of it.

"That went nicely, I think," Aunt Effie said with a satisfied nod after they'd requested a cab.

"I daresay Mr. Cadwallender has never faced the widow of a colonel before." Sidney grinned.

"Fighting for what you want has as much to do with knowing who you are and, of course, knowing what you want." Effie's lips curved in a satisfied smile. "Being the wife of a colonel is simply the icing on the cake."

Sidney hesitated. "Are you certain you and the others are up to this?"

"Because we are no longer in the prime of youth?"

"Well, yes."

"I assure you, Sidney, we are quite spry." She paused.

"There are two kinds of women in this world, my dear. Those who wave goodbye to others starting on grand adventures and those waving back from the window of a train or the deck of a ship." Effie raised her chin. "It's past time that Gwen, Poppy and I became the latter. We too need to seize the day. Besides, this may well be our last chance."

"And perhaps my only chance."

"Then we shall have to make the most of it." Effie grinned. "As Mr. Cadwallender is paying for it, we should make certain he gets his money's worth."

Sidney laughed. Good Lord! Thanks to a stuffy, arrogant, rude beast of a lord and his nephew she was finally going to Egypt. Certainly, given the amount of deception involved, it was not going to be easy. But it was past time to stop dreaming about what she wanted. Her very future was now at stake. In many ways, it seemed her life—her story—was just beginning.

And she could hardly wait to turn the page.

CHAPTER TWO

"THIS MRS. GORDON is a fraud, I tell you." Harold Armstrong, the new Earl of Brenton, paced the impressive width of the private parlor his predecessors had used as an office in the grand Mayfair house that was now his. Harry was not prone to pacing, or at least he never had been, but everything about his life had changed in recent months and he had a great deal on his mind. In addition, the events of today failed to provide the satisfaction he had expected which cast an unfamiliar sense of doubt over his actions. Harold Armstrong was not used to doubt. "And I intend to expose her for the complete and utter fake she is."

"Try not to restrain yourself, Harry." Lord Benjamin Deane, who had been Harry's friend since their days at Cambridge, lounged in one of the wingback chairs positioned in front of the fireplace. "Tell me what you really think about her."

Harry paused. "This is not the least bit humorous, Ben."

"On the contrary, Harry old boy, it may well be the funniest thing I've run into in a long time."

"Exactly what do you find so amusing?"

"First and foremost the fact that you can't see the humor in it is in itself most amusing. You do seem to be wound tighter than a watch spring these days."

"Nonsense."

"But I suppose when one has abruptly become an earl—an eligible and eminently marriageable earl—without realizing it was even a remote possibility, one does tend to lose one's sense of humor."

"Rubbish, I haven't lost anything." Harry denied it but he was indeed more serious of late. Although, as he'd never been particularly serious about anything in his life until recently, it was perhaps past time. "Indeed, I find the convoluted manner in which I came into this title to be damn amusing."

And completely unexpected. Harry had always known the man he considered his father, Sir Arthur Armstrong, was his mother's second husband and a distant cousin of his natural father, who had died before Harry was born. Harry had heard the story any number of times growing up of how Arthur had fallen head over heels for Harry's mother the moment he met the lovely young widow. Unfortunately, they had only a few years together before she succumbed to influenza. Harry scarcely remembered her and had long suspected the stories of his mother Arthur told were meant to keep her close to both Harry and Arthur.

Both men were aware that they each shared an ancestral link to the tenth Earl of Brenton although it had never seemed of particular importance. Arthur was a scholar of history and long-dead civilizations and a highly regarded expert on ancient Egypt and its artifacts, knighted several years ago in acknowledgment of his scholarly work as well as his efforts in furthering the reputation and collections of the British Museum. He had not raised Harry as a man who would one day be an earl but rather as the son of a man with his nose perpetually in a book and his head more often than not in a long past century. It was only due to fate, death and the fact that there were more females than males in the earl's direct lineage that Harry became the fourteenth Earl of Brenton some eleven months ago.

"And—" Harry flashed his friend an unrepentant grin and, for a moment, felt like the Harry Armstrong of old "—the money doesn't hurt."

"A definite benefit." Ben laughed. As the youngest son of a wealthy marquess, Ben had never been without funds and had in fact financed their first excursion to Egypt nearly twenty years ago.

Arthur had a respectable family fortune of his own although finances had never been particularly important to him, and Harry had grown up in modest surroundings. Now, in addition to the country estate that accompanied Harry's title, he had inherited a large London mansion and had, after much debate, convinced his father to change residences. While Arthur was initially reluctant to uproot his life, he had been lured to the Mayfair house by its grand library and spacious rooms. Arthur's domicile was close to bursting with books, relics and various collections he had accumulated over the years. Besides, Harry had argued, even though he was thirty-eight years of age, a man could always use the company and wisdom of his father.

"Although that entire business about my being eligible and eminently marriageable is somewhat bothersome." Harry was far more used to being the pursuer than the pursued. He pinned his friend with an accusing look. "You could have warned me."

"Where would be the fun in that?"

"I had no idea the mothers of unwed daughters could be quite so determined." Harry shuddered.

"This is just the beginning," Ben said, "and you may

consider *that* your warning. Heed it well. When you were merely the son of a scholar, those fearsome mothers looking for an excellent match paid you no attention whatsoever. Now that you have a title and fortune, you have become a highly sought after commodity."

"I'm not sure I like being a commodity, no matter how highly sought."

"None of us do."

"It's easier for you." Harry strode to the decanter of brandy the butler, Jeffries, had thoughtfully placed on a nearby table. "You have a mother and sisters to help guide you through the morass of society nonsense." Harry poured two glasses and handed one to Ben.

"You would think that would make it easier." Ben raised his glass to his friend. "But you would be wrong."

Ben was at least more used to the social requirements of the aristocracy than Harry. On those occasions when the two would return to London from Egypt, Ben was immediately pulled into the orbit of his formidable family and their endless social obligations whereas Harry usually spent those interludes in companionship with his father.

"On that score, you should be grateful. It's the females in my family who are the most determined to see me wed. Fortunately, I have three older brothers, including the next marquess, who have engaged their matchmaking tendencies to this point." He took a deep swallow of the brandy. "Unfortunately, my brothers have now all married and I am apparently fair game since I am now home for good."

It was not necessary for either man to mention the reason why Ben was home and yet it hung in the air between them. Unspoken and always present.

"All you have to do is find a suitable wife and you'll be off the market."

Harry sank down into the chair next to Ben's. "I can't say I'm interested in marriage. At least not now."

"Sorry, Harry. Your interests are of little concern." Ben shook his head in a mournful manner. "One of the prime responsibilities of any title holder is to marry, produce an heir and preferably a spare, so as to secure the title for the future."

"In my case it's a title I never sought, feel no particular loyalty to and don't especially want." Harry paused. "Except for the money, of course. The money is nice." He glanced around the elegant room with its paneled walls, shelves reaching to the distant ceiling and portraits of unknown ancestors glaring down at him. "And the house."

"Consider the house a bonus as you are stuck with the title, *Lord* Brenton."

"Yes." He blew a long breath. "I suppose I am."

Harry still wasn't used to the idea of being *Lord* anything. When he, Ben and Walter Pickering, had left their studies at Cambridge to seek ancient treasure in the deserts of Egypt, he had—they all had—assumed they would return having made their fortunes. Their friends were not as confident and many wagered the trio would come to a bad end and never be heard from again. There were moments when they came perilously close to fulfilling that expectation. What no one expected was that Harry and his companions would discover a passion and respect for Egypt and the mystery of its past that, combined with the influence of his father, would turn them from somewhat disreputable treasure hunters to relatively respectable archeologists. Why, Harry couldn't remember the last time they had blatantly smuggled or stolen a valuable piece of Egypt's past. Although admittedly, there might have been a piece or two, or several dozen, that they had obtained for the British Museum in recent years through questionable and possibly less than legitimate means. Not as much fun—or profitable—as their earlier days but fairly satisfying all in all.

But then Walter died of a fever that probably would have been a minor ailment in England. Logically and rationally, Harry knew it was no one's fault but knew as well that Ben blamed himself just as Harry did. Perhaps it was indeed Walter's death, or perhaps they had overstayed their welcome, or perhaps the passion they'd had for the excitement and adventure to be found in the land of the pharaohs had run its course. Or possibly they had at last grown up. No doubt the death of a close friend would do that to a man. Walter had been gone for more than a year when Harry received notice of his inheritance and decided to return to England permanently. Ben too was ready to turn toward home.

Harry wasn't quite sure what he had expected but his first few months in England had been filled with documents to be signed, legalities to be attended to and endless details regarding his new position in life. He'd had to hire a secretary to oversee his affairs and found himself not only with a country estate but an estate manager and tenants as well. He and his father had resided at Brenton Hall, a few hours by train from London, for several months while Jeffries was charged with moving Arthur's possessions and readying the London house.

Jeffries had been his father's butler for as long as Harry could remember and he was as much his father's best friend and a second father to Harry as he was servant. Theirs had always been a bachelor household. Harry had installed him, as well as the rest of their modest staff, in the new residence. The Mayfair house itself was apparently little used as the previous earl was somewhat reclusive and had preferred to reside at the country estate. It had then sat vacant for over a year due to the complexities of inheritance as well as identification and location of the new earl and the previous staff had moved on to other positions. Jeffries had been hard-pressed to hide his glee in overseeing setting the grand house to rights as well as hiring the additional staff the new abode required.

The frantic pace of the first few months did not prepare Harry for the tedium that followed. He had always been a man of action. His predecessor had retained competent employees—solicitors, estate managers and various other agents—who had been in their respective positions for years and from Harry's assessment no changes were necessary. His new secretary managed his correspondence, business and social obligations—invitations had virtually flooded the house since his arrival—and he had no particular interest in politics. All of which led him to wonder if perhaps he and Ben had made a mistake in deciding to return home permanently. Life now was rather dull and he feared he'd become somewhat dull as well. But upon further reflection—and God knew he had plenty of time for reflection—he realized his heart was simply no longer in the life of adventure he'd once savored. The past was the past and it was time to forge ahead.

Still, why waste a lifetime of experience? He was intelligent and capable. Why not take his almost twenty years of exploits and share them with the world? Why not write of his adventures? And not his alone but his and Ben's and Walter's. If H. Rider Haggard—who hadn't nearly the background Harry and his friends had—could become successful at it, so could Harry. He no longer needed the money but the fame—or rather—the *acknowledgment* of their deeds, validation of their life's work and recognition of their efforts in furthering the field of Egyptology as well as a modicum of respect would be rather nice. And didn't Walter deserve at least that?

"I think Mrs. Gordon's stories are remarkably well done," Ben said, bringing the topic back to the object of Harry's ire. "I find the *Tales of a Lady Adventurer in Egypt* most entertaining."

"You have no taste."

"And you have no tolerance." Ben picked up the latest copy of the *Daily Messenger* with Mrs. Gordon's newest offering from the table between the chairs. "The lady's stories are great fun, Harry. They have adventure, a touch of romance, even a bit of mystery. I quite enjoy them."

"They're inaccurate."

"Certainly she has left off some of the more unpleasant aspects of life in Egypt—"

"Some?" Harry scoffed. "You won't find so much as a mention of sand fleas or vermin in any of her stories."

"Perhaps because people don't really want to read about sand fleas and vermin. I know I don't."

"Details," Harry said firmly, "are important. You cannot go about leaving out particulars simply because they're disagreeable."

Still, upon the kind of deliberation one can only have in hindsight, too much accuracy might well have been Harry's problem. He had written several stories, and indeed had nearly an entire book completed, before submitting anything for publication. Each and every submission was met with polite but firm rejection and nicely phrased, yet still unflattering, comments about his ability to re-

late a story in an interesting manner. It made no sense to
him whatsoever. Even worse, he was tactfully told that
as long as Mrs. Gordon was writing stories about Egypt
that were adored by the public, there was no place for his
less-than-entertaining work. But he wasn't merely writing stories—his were true. Harry could only surmise that
those who never stepped foot outside of London could not
possibly be expected to appreciate the gritty realism of
his work, ignoring the fact that his readership was likely
to be made up of those very same people. He then asked
his father—a man as well-read as ever there was—and
Ben—who had lived Harry's adventures by his side—
to read his work.

Their reactions were less enthusiastic than Harry had
hoped. Father was evasive over the quality of Harry's
writing while swearing he wouldn't have had a peaceful
night's rest if he had known all that Harry was engaged
in during his years in Egypt, while Ben had simply muttered how it was all rather duller than he remembered.

Apparently, Harry Armstrong, who had never lacked
in confidence about anything and had mastered very
nearly everything he had ever attempted could write a
grammatically accurate sentence that was of no interest
whatsoever. He intended to work on that.

"Regardless of what people want, or think they want,
if one purports to be detailing factual experiences one
cannot leave off the less than pleasant aspects. Details
are what brings a story to life and facts are indisputable,"
Harry said in a lofty manner.

Ben laughed.

"This isn't funny." Harry scowled. "This is how I intend to spend the rest of my days. I am of an age where
squandering my time and money in a futile pursuit of

pleasure seems absurd and, oddly enough, has no particular appeal—"

"Who would have thought?" Ben shook his head in a mournful manner.

"And I'm far too young to do nothing at all. But no one is interested in my writing, which is based on unvarnished truth and unsentimental reality, because this woman—" he grabbed the paper from Ben's hand and shook it at him "—has fed them frothy tales of gallant desert chieftains, bandits more dashing than deadly, virtuous treasure hunters interested only in uncovering the grandeur of the ancients—"

"I'd say that's a fairly accurate description of us." Ben grinned. "Although I would add handsome and daring as well."

"The stories she spins are of a land of illusion and fantasy with no more substance to them than fairy tales. They're full of *feelings* rather than facts."

"There's nothing wrong with feelings and she does say she has taken occasional liberty with facts in pursuit of a good story," Ben noted mildly.

"Occasional? Ha!" Harry glared. "Camels, as you well know, are not noble beasts gliding over the sands like ships at full sail but unpleasant, rude, disgusting creatures whose only redeeming quality is their suitability for the desert climate. It's utter rubbish for God's sake. And people have accepted it all as fact."

"People, all in all, aren't very bright."

"Did you know they call her the Queen of the Desert?"

"Yes, I believe you have mentioned that." Ben pressed his lips together to keep from laughing. "More than once."

"More like the queen of deception, ill-conceived fables and outright fraud." Harry dropped the paper on to the table and then tossed back his brandy. It did not help.

"And you did not hesitate to say exactly that in your letters to *The Times*."

"Of course I did. I could do nothing less. People deserve to know when they're being hoodwinked," Harry said staunchly, ignoring what might have been the tiniest stab of regret.

He had always been rather gallant where women were concerned and women had always liked him. He did now wonder if boredom with his new life coupled with frustration at his inability to sell his work might have had something to do with initiating his letters to *The Times*. Not that he was wrong in calling attention to Mrs. Gordon's misrepresentations of fact in her *Tales*. Nor was he wrong in threatening her membership in the Antiquities Society, but he had opened the proverbial Pandora's box.

"And Egypt deserves better. She is grand and glorious, timeless and dangerous. And worthy of respect. The place is already overrun with tourists. Stories like Mrs. Gordon's, that depict the country as little more than a fanciful winter resort in the shadow of the pyramids, only encourage more visitors who refuse to relish in the very land they've come to experience but rather insist on bringing their own ways with them. This woman, with her inaccuracies and rose-colored portrayal, is assisting in the ruination of an ancient land."

"I can't say I entirely disagree with you there."

"Even worse, those who believe her nonsense, who think seeking the treasure of the ancients can be accomplished as easily as writing a few paragraphs, and with as little risk, flock to Egypt only to be rudely awakened."

"Isn't that what we did?"

"We were young and stupid and it was a different time. And, ultimately, we paid a price for being seduced by Egypt."

Ben was silent for a long moment. "Regardless, you could have been a bit more diplomatic in your censure."

"Yes, I suppose I could have." Harry blew a frustrated breath. "And I probably should have. I realize now that it might have been wiser, and certainly more courteous, to have been less strident in my condemnation."

"You did stir up something of a hornet's nest."

"I am well aware of that."

While the wisdom of his first letter to *The Times* was debatable, he could see now that it had not been a good idea to continue to engage the woman via additional letters. It had only served to escalate their dispute to the point where he had challenged her to travel to Egypt and prove that she knew what she was writing about. Apparently justifiable indignation negated any possibility of intelligent thought, but then prudence and discretion had never been Harry Armstrong's strongest qualities. Lord Brenton would have to do better.

"Given your attitude toward your new title—" Ben nodded at the newspaper "—I was rather surprised that you signed your letters as Lord Brenton rather than Harry Armstrong."

"At first, it didn't seem quite fair to identify myself as an earl and not at all sporting. She is a woman, after all, and a widow. I didn't want to intimidate her." Although, judging by her responses, a little intimidation might have served him well. "But the more I read of her work—" and the more rejection Harry Armstrong's writing received "—the more I realized writing to *The Times* as Lord Brenton would give added weight to my charges."

Ben picked up the paper and paged to the latest installment of *Tales of a Lady Adventurer in Egypt.* "Have you
read the stories in the *Messenger* and those in her book
closely or has your outrage prevented that?"

"Close enough."

"I doubt it," Ben said under his breath. "Have you noticed that her depiction of Egypt is somewhat, oh, dated
if you will?"

"Somewhat?" Harry snorted. "She might as well be
writing in the time of the pharaohs themselves. Obviously, she has based her *Tales* on old, poorly researched,
fictitious accounts."

"She never mentions the throngs of tourists that have
increased in the last twenty years, thanks to the railroads
and the Suez Canal, or the government regulations that
only serve to complicate excavations and any number
of other details."

"We've already established she is not overly fond of
accurate details." He paused. "Aside from vermin."

Ben studied the story for a moment. "It strikes me
that these might well be the accounts of someone who
has not been to Egypt for some time. Perhaps even de-
cades." Ben looked up from the paper and grinned. "I'd
wager you've been exchanging letters with an old lady."

"Surely not." Harry scoffed. "You've seen her responses to my letters. They're confrontational, unsuit-
ably forward and verge perilously close to rude although
she never engages in blatant discourtesy. She was quite
civil when she called me arrogant."

"Yes, I noticed that."

"Admittedly, I would expect any woman who writes
about lady adventurers in Egypt—whether those stories
are true or not—to defend her position although I do

think her polite implication that I am somehow resentful of her success because she's female is going a bit far."

"I noticed that too."

Harry narrowed his eyes. "She is always polite."

"Indeed she is. It must be most annoying."

"You have no idea." He shook his head. "But an elderly woman? Absolutely not. Those letters could not possibly be the work of a fragile, old lady. They're entirely too assertive and forceful."

Ben stared. "You don't know any old ladies, do you?"

Harry frowned. "No, but—"

"You, my friend, have been engaged in a battle with a dear, sweet old lady." Ben chuckled. "And even then you couldn't win."

Harry drew his brows together. "Are you sure?"

"You should meet my grandmother." Ben glanced at the paper. "These are exactly the kind of letters she'd write, this is the very tone she'd take and she'd do so with a great deal of satisfaction."

Harry stared at his friend. The idea that Mrs. Gordon was an older woman hadn't so much as crossed his mind. If Ben was right... "Bloody hell."

"I say leave her alone. End this nonsense right now." Ben sipped his drink. "Let this be, Harry. I don't think this is a war you can win."

Regardless, he did feel compelled to defend himself. "Her reckless disregard of fact destroys any shred of credibility she may have. Her work reflects badly on those of us who know what we are writing about. In many ways, she is my direct competition. Indeed, I've been told as much. Discrediting her—"

"Would probably expose her publicly. She obviously wants to be circumspect. You never see a photograph of her or hear of any kind of public appearance. I can't believe you want to do that to a dear, sweet old lady—"

"I would question your use of *sweet*," Harry muttered.

"Nonetheless, once the public gets a look at her, all that white hair and wrinkles, leaning on a cane—"

"You don't know that."

"No, but I daresay she'll look something like that. And people will be entirely on her side. Poor, little old lady pitted against the arrogant Earl of Brenton." Ben shook his head in apparent sympathy. "You will not only look like a fool, but like a mean, unpleasant sort as well."

"I would prefer to avoid that." Ben might well be right about Mrs. Gordon's age as well as the repercussions to Harry's reputation should this go any further. "I do see your point about dropping this whole matter. Unfortunately..."

Ben's brow rose. "Unfortunately?"

"You do know I challenged her to go to Egypt and prove her knowledge."

"Good God." Ben groaned. "She's accepted hasn't she?"

"The *Daily Messenger* did on her behalf." Harry winced. "I was notified this morning. They're sending a reporter as well." It had sounded like such a good idea when he had first thought of demanding Mrs. Gordon prove her legitimacy. Now it seemed rather stupid. "We leave for Egypt as soon as arrangements can be made."

"Can you get out of it?"

"Not without looking like an even greater idiot."

"One of those damned-if-you-do sort of things."

"So it would appear." Harry considered his options. There didn't seem to be any. "Say, why don't you come along? I could certainly use a friend by my side. It would be like old times."

"Absolutely not," Ben said firmly. "As much as I would

love to witness this debacle, my father has decided to put me to work in one of the family interests. Shipping I think although it's still rather vague." He sipped his drink. "He and my brothers are trying to decide where I'll do the least harm."

"Nonsense. More likely they're trying to ascertain where you'll be of greatest benefit."

Ben's family had never been especially pleased with his choices in life—wandering the desert seeking ancient treasure, no matter how legitimate he had become, was not what had been envisioned for the youngest son of a marquess. But Ben was far more competent and capable than his family might suspect and had saved Harry's neck on more than one occasion.

"I've decided not to use my title on this venture," Harry said. "In fact, the earl has already informed the *Daily Messenger* that he was sending a representative in his stead to accompany Mrs. Gordon to Egypt. One Harry Armstrong." He winced. "The earl's nephew."

"Nephew?" Ben snorted back a laugh.

"It has to be someone the earl trusts."

"Of course." Ben shook his head in disbelief. "Why not just use your title? It does open a lot of doors you know."

"You rarely used your title in Egypt."

"Mine is honorary."

"For one thing, I don't intend to write as Lord Brenton. It's Harry Armstrong's exploits I'll be writing about. Lord Brenton has never been to the desert."

"You do realize you're one in the same?"

"It doesn't feel like it. It doesn't feel, well, right. It feels as if I'm wearing a suit of clothes that doesn't fit. As if I'm trying to be someone I'm not. I was simply the only male on the right branch of the family tree. This title isn't something I wanted although I suppose I'm resigned to it." He paused. "Also, I wish to avoid undue attention and the possibility of unpleasant publicity and, well, scandal."

"Do you?" Ben snorted. "You have changed."

"Pity isn't it?" Harry got to his feet, strode across the room, grabbed the brandy decanter and returned. "Harry Armstrong's exploits need to be as far removed from the Earl of Brenton as possible. I am now the titular head of a family which evidently carries with it certain obligations, as was made very clear to me by a representative of said family. Not that they are interested in having much to do with me. Which does suit me, by the way."

"To be expected really." Ben nodded and held out his now empty glass. "You're the interloper who claimed their family heritage."

"Not by choice." Harry refilled Ben's glass, then his own, and settled back in his chair. "There are apparently a fair number of unattached female relations that I am now, at least in a hereditary sense, responsible for. My involvement in anything untoward, past or present, would reflect poorly on them, thus hindering their chances for a good marriage. Which would then be laid firmly at my feet." He grimaced. "Do you realize I now have a rather large family?"

"Again—the house in town, the estate in the country and, of course, the fortune make up for it."

"We shall see." Although it was an excellent estate, a very nice house and an even nicer fortune. "There are all sorts of responsibilities I never considered." He glanced at Ben. "It's not actually a requirement but I am expected to take a seat in the House of Lords now." Harry blew a long breath. "I know nothing about running a country."

"I wouldn't worry about it." Ben chuckled. "In that, at least, you'll fit right in."

There is nothing as delightful and exhilarating as the day one steps foot on board a ship bound for the shores of Egypt. As one turns one's face toward the rising sun and the land of the pharaohs, one's heart is filled with the heady anticipation of what is to come and the thrill of the adventures that lie ahead.

—*Tales of a Lady Adventurer in Egypt*

Steamship is now the most efficient way to travel between London and Alexandria. Before setting foot on any vessel it is always wise to investigate a ship's history to avoid unwelcome surprises of incompetence among captain and crew.

—*My Adventures in Egypt,*
The True Writings of Harold Armstrong

CHAPTER THREE

Three weeks later

THERE WAS MUCH to be said for having a lot of money.

The moment Harry had arrived at the Royal Albert docks, his luggage had been whisked away to be unpacked in his first class stateroom for the nearly two-week voyage to Alexandria. First class on the Peninsular and Oriental ship the *Ancona*. Harry couldn't resist a satisfied grin. He was not used to traveling in anything other than the most modest of circumstances. Having substantial resources would not be at all hard to adjust to.

He glanced around the bustling docks and ignored a

trickle of impatience. Harry had received a note from
James Cadwallender a few days ago saying the publisher
of *Cadwallender's Daily Messenger* would be on hand
today to make introductions and see their party off. According to Cadwallender, that party included not only
Mrs. Gordon and the *Messenger*'s reporter but companions of Mrs. Gordon's as well. And weren't additional elderly ladies exactly what this venture needed? The very
idea made Harry's teeth clench. He had considered pro-
testing to Cadwallender but, for once, held his immediate
impulse in check. He had resolved to follow the advice
of Ben and his father and be as charming and agreeable
as possible. Put his best foot forward as it were.

He had also decided, again on the advice of his father and his friend as well as the urgings of his own
conscience, to let the matter of Mrs. Gordon's accuracy
rest when it came to public exposure and not subject her
to ridicule and censure. Once he had undeniable proof
of her incompetence in all matters relating to Egypt, he
intended to have a firm talk with her, point out the error
of her ways in misleading her readers and strongly suggest she change the title of her stories to the *Fictitious
Tales of a Lady Adventurer in Egypt*. As he intended to
title his stories *My Adventures in Egypt, The True Writings of Harold Armstrong* when they were eventually
published, it did seem this was a solution that would at
least provide some separation of public appeal between
his work and hers, thereby avoiding direct competition. It
was not a perfect solution—and people might well prefer
her stories to his anyway—but he'd been feeling badly
ever since Ben had brought up the likelihood of Mrs.
Gordon being an old lady. Harry had reread all of her
stories and had come to the inescapable conclusion that

Ben was right. Even though in many ways Egypt was as unchanging as the sands of the desert itself, no one who had stepped foot in the country in the last twenty years or so would write about it in the same manner she had. Although admittedly, if one could overlook the flowery language and massive inaccuracies, they were somewhat entertaining.

It was the right thing to do. After all, she was an elderly widow, probably with a minimal income and no doubt needed the money from her writing to make ends meet. He may be trying to carve a new path for his life but he could certainly afford to be generous. With every passing year, Harry had become more and more cognizant of doing the right thing even when it was difficult. It provided a measure of moral satisfaction and made him a better man. He quite liked that.

Still, impatience was beginning to win over resolve and Harry resisted the urge to tap his foot. He did wish the others would arrive. He wanted to get this business of introductions over with and retire to his stateroom. But what could one expect from a group of females? He may not have much experience with older women, but he certainly had a great deal with younger members of their gender. Regardless of nationality, they were universally chatty, prone to excessive giggling and nearly always late. Although admittedly, they were frequently enchanting and could be a great deal of fun as well. He blew a resigned breath. He did not expect anything about this venture to be fun.

Harry had taken up a position near the *Ancona*'s gangplank, as Cadwallender had instructed, and now surveyed the docks, busy with provisions and goods being loaded onto ships as well as crowds of excited passengers headed for parts unknown.

"Mr. Armstrong?" A man a few years older than Harry stepped up to him with a smile. Three elderly ladies and a somewhat nondescript younger woman—probably a granddaughter seeing them off—trailed behind.

"Yes?" Harry adopted a pleasant smile of his own.

"Excellent. I'm James Cadwallender." Cadwallender thrust out his hand to shake Harry's. "Good day to start a voyage, don't you think?"

"Better than expected," Harry said. It was in fact quite cold but the inevitable January rain had held off today and the sun was making a weak effort to shine. Sun and warmth were two things he missed about Egypt. "I must say, I appreciate you taking the time to see us off."

"Oh, I wouldn't miss it." A wicked gleam of amusement shone in the man's eyes. "Allow me to introduce your traveling companions." Cadwallender turned toward the ladies.

"No need, Mr. Cadwallender." Harry braced himself, adopted his most charming smile and stepped toward the closest woman, the shortest of the three elderly ladies. She was exactly as he had pictured Mrs. Gordon right down to the fair, nearly white hair escaping from an absurd feathered hat and fur-trimmed wrap. He took her hand and bowed slightly. "I would know you anywhere, Mrs. Gordon."

"Would you?" Her blue eyes shone with amusement. "How very clever of you." She leaned closer and lowered her voice. "And how very wrong."

"My apologies." He dropped her hand and stepped back. Damnation. She was the closest to Cadwallender and he'd thought surely—

"We, however, would certainly know you anywhere."
The next elderly lady, with graying dark hair, a hat just as
ridiculous as the first woman's and the overbearing manner of a dragon about to belch flames, eyed him with obvious disgust. "Simply by the air of arrogance as well as
impatience about you. No doubt exactly like your uncle."

"I am working on that," he said and continued to maintain his smile. "Then you must be Mrs. Gordon."

She sniffed. "Wrong again, Mr. Armstrong. But then I
suspect you and your uncle must be used to being wrong."

He drew his brows together. "Now, see here, I—"

"Mr. Cadwallender," the third older lady, who was
surely Mrs. Gordon, said in a no-nonsense tone. "Are
you going to set the poor man straight or are you enjoying this entirely too much?"

Cadwallender chuckled. "I am enjoying it. However—" he turned to Harry "—I do apologize but it was
rather fun to watch someone else be maneuvered by these
three. Allow me to introduce Lady Blodgett."

"You are a scamp, Mr. Cadwallender. Fortunately,
you are smarter than you look," Lady Blodgett said and
held out her hand to Harry. "Delighted to meet you, Mr.
Armstrong."

He took her hand and nodded a bow. "Lady Blodgett."

"This is Mrs. Higginbotham," Cadwallender said.

"Mr. Armstrong." The dragon nodded and did not remove her hands from her fur muff to shake his.

Cadwallender indicated the remaining older lady.
"And Mrs. Fitzhew-Wellmore."

"Mr. Armstrong." Mrs. Fitzhew-Wellmore beamed.
"I can't tell you how pleased we are to be accompanying you and our dear Miss—Mrs. Gordon on this exciting venture."

Harry stared in confusion.

"And this," Cadwallender said, gesturing at the younger woman, "is Mrs. Gordon."

Ben was wrong.

The genuine Mrs. Gordon considered him with ill-concealed amusement. "Good day, Mr. Armstrong."

"You're not old," he said without thinking. She couldn't possibly be much older than thirty.

"Not yet." The corners of her lips quirked upward and she held out her hand. "I am sorry if you're disappointed."

"Not at all," he murmured and took her hand, gazing down into the loveliest eyes he had ever seen. Blue and fair and clear, the color of the sky on a perfect desert day. She was considerably shorter than he but then most people were. Wisps of pale blond hair escaped from a fashionable hat to dance around a heart-shaped face. Her cheeks were pinked by the chill of the day, her lips reddened by the wind and most inviting. How had he thought she was nondescript? "I am delighted to at last meet you in person."

"Delighted? Are you indeed, Mr. Armstrong?" She pulled her hand from his. "I must say I am surprised as I would think you would not be the least bit delighted to make the acquaintance of someone who, oh, let me think. How did your uncle phrase it?"

"He said your inaccuracy was stunning and you had as little regard for truth and facts as a fish does for a carriage," the dragon said with a distinctly murderous look in her eye.

"And he called your prose flowery, debilitating and enough to make any rational human being choke with the sweetness of it." Mrs. Fitzhew-Wellmore shook her head in a chastising manner. "Your uncle should be ashamed of himself, Mr. Armstrong."

Harry swallowed hard. It was one thing to write a letter to *The Times* criticizing a work and quite something else to be confronted by the author of that work and her band of elderly termagants. "Yes, well, he might have used words to that effect."

"He used those words exactly," Lady Blodgett said. "They were overly harsh and rather rude. I do think an apology is called for."

"Of course." He nodded. "And I do..." What was he doing? Blast it all. Three minutes with these women and they had him entirely turned around. He drew a steadying breath. "You're right, Lady Blodgett, and I do apologize for my uncle if his wording was less than tactful." He turned to Mrs. Gordon and met her gaze directly. "Which in no way means he was not correct in his assessment of your work."

"You agree with him, then?

He nodded. "I do."

"Have you read my work?"

"I have."

Her lovely eyes narrowed. "He said I was too inept to ever be allowed a pen in my hand. Do you agree with that?"

"You called him an arrogant ass, Mrs. Gordon," he said sharply.

"Mr. Armstrong," Lady Blodgett murmured. "Your language."

"In *The Times*?" The dragon gasped. "She would never call anyone an ass—"

"Effie!" Lady Blodgett snapped.

"—in *The Times*. Unlike the *Daily Messenger*, *The*

Times would never allow that kind of language. No matter how appropriate the term might be." She glanced at Lady Blodgett. "There are moments, Gwen, when nothing else will do."

"On the contrary, Mr. Armstrong, I believed she called your uncle an arrogant, ill-tempered buffoon," Mrs. Fitzhew-Wellmore said pleasantly. "If you choose to substitute another term, well, you would certainly know better than we."

"Lady Blodgett was right. An apology is in order and I shall gladly offer that apology." Mrs. Gordon smiled but her eyes blazed. "I am dreadfully sorry for having ignored the sensibilities of buffoons everywhere and unjustly insulting them by adding your uncle, and you as well, to their company."

"Now, see here," Harry began.

"Good day, Mr. Cadwallender." A man nearly as tall as Harry, and several years younger, strode up to their group. "I hope I'm not late, sir."

"Not at all, Corbin." Cadwallender was clearly trying not to grin. "Mr. Armstrong and the ladies were just becoming acquainted. Ladies, this is one of my finest reporters, Mr. Daniel Corbin. He will be on hand to record Mrs. Gordon's triumph."

"Or defeat," Harry said under his breath.

"And will be sending dispatches along the way as to Mrs. Gordon's new adventures in Egypt." The publisher paused. "That is a catchy title. I shall have to remember that." He turned to the ladies. "Corbin, allow me to introduce Lady Blodgett."

"Lady Blodgett." Corbin took her hand and raised it to his lips. "It's an honor and a privilege to meet you, my lady. I was a great admirer of your husband."

"Lady Blodgett's late husband, Sir Charles Blodgett, was quite a well-known explorer," Cadwallender said in an aside to Harry.

"Of course," Harry murmured.

Lady Blodgett tilted her head slightly and considered the reporter. "How very kind of you to say, Mr. Corbin."

"And this is Mrs. Fitzhew-Wellmore," Cadwallender said.

Corbin turned to Mrs. Fitzhew-Wellmore and took her hand. "Mr. Cadwallender did not tell me I would be in such august company. I am delighted to meet you, Mrs. Fitzhew-Wellmore. Your husband's reputation among his fellow explorers was legendary."

It was all Harry could do to keep from snorting in derision. He would wager significant money that Corbin did indeed know exactly who made up Mrs. Gordon's party and had made inquiries into their backgrounds in advance of this meeting.

"Thank you, Mr. Corbin." Mrs. Fitzhew-Wellmore dimpled. "Malcolm would be most pleased to know he has not been forgotten."

"I daresay he never will be," Corbin said firmly.

"And Mrs. Higginbotham." Cadwallender indicated the dragon.

"No doubt you have something nice to say about my husband as well." The dragon eyed the reporter suspiciously but offered her hand.

"Mrs. Higginbotham." Corbin took her hand and gazed into her eyes. "My favorite uncle served with your husband in the Crimea. He often said there was no finer officer to serve under than Colonel Higginbotham and credits your husband with his survival of that conflict. Allow me to offer my thanks from my entire family."

"Oh." The dragon looked a bit taken aback. Harry wouldn't have thought it possible. Then she smiled and for a moment, he could see she must have been quite lovely in her youth. "I was right. That was very nice, Mr. Corbin."

Corbin laughed and turned to Mrs. Gordon. "Which means you must be Mrs. Gordon."

"Well, if I must." Mrs. Gordon extended her hand.

"I can't tell you what a pleasure it is to meet you at last. I am an ardent follower of your *Tales*." Corbin raised her gloved hand to his lips in an absurd and well-practiced display of inappropriate gallantry, his gaze never wavering from hers. "But I had no idea the writer of such exciting adventures would be quite so lovely."

"What did you expect, Mr. Corbin?" Mrs. Gordon smiled, a distinctly flirtatious sort of smile in Harry's opinion.

"I'm not sure exactly." Corbin continued to gaze into her eyes. Did the man have no sense of restraint? "But I did not expect someone as lovely as she is brilliant. May I tell you how much I admire your work? I find your writing fascinating and completely absorbing. You, Mrs. Gordon, have the rare ability to take your readers on a journey of adventure and excitement."

Harry snorted.

"Unfortunately, Mr. Corbin, not everyone agrees with you." Mrs. Gordon nodded in Harry's direction.

"Ah yes." Corbin released Mrs. Gordon's hand reluctantly and turned his attention to Harry. "Mr. Armstrong, I presume?"

"Mr. Corbin." Harry nodded and accepted the man's offered hand. Corbin's handshake was even firmer than his employer's. Too firm really, as if he was trying to prove a point. Harry tightened his grip in response. Two could play at whatever game this reporter was playing.

Corbin released his hand and Harry ignored the need to flex his fingers. "You're rather well-known yourself among archeologists and Egyptologists, Mr. Armstrong."

Apparently the ladies weren't the only ones Corbin researched, although obviously not well as he made no reference to Harry's newfound title. Good. "I have spent a number of years in Egypt."

"Mr. Armstrong considers himself quite an expert on all things Egyptian," Mrs. Gordon said coolly.

Harry narrowed his eyes. "As do you."

Mrs. Gordon shrugged in an offhand manner as if her knowledge was not in question and turned to Cadwallender. "It was quite thoughtful of you to see us off, Mr. Cadwallender. And most appreciated."

"Here's to an excellent voyage and a successful journey." Cadwallender took her hand and smiled. "I have every confidence in you, Mrs. Gordon."

"Thank you, Mr. Cadwallender." She slanted a quick glance at Harry then smiled up at the publisher. "I assure you, you will not be disappointed." She stepped back and looked at the other women. "Ladies, shall we board?"

"Will we see you at dinner tonight?" Corbin asked, the most annoying note of eagerness in his voice.

"I doubt it. I prefer to spend the first night on a ship in my rooms. But tomorrow—" she cast the reporter a brilliant smile "—I will certainly see you tomorrow." She nodded at the publisher. "Farewell, Mr. Cadwallender."

Cadwallender tipped his hat. "Bon voyage, Mrs. Gordon."

"Mr. Armstrong," she said curtly, turned and moved toward the ship.

The other ladies bid Cadwallender farewell and then followed Mrs. Gordon in a flutter of feminine excitement. She started up the gangplank, her entourage trailing behind.

"Splendid job, Sidney." Lady Blodgett's voice drifted back to him. One thing he had already noticed about traveling with this particular group, whether it was intentional or simply the result of aging, but all three older ladies spoke a bit louder than perhaps necessary.

Mrs. Gordon's chin raised just a notch. He would have thought she couldn't hold herself any straighter but apparently he was wrong.

Cadwallender chuckled. "This should be an interesting trip. I'm almost sorry I'm not coming along." He grinned at Harry. "Bon voyage, Mr. Armstrong. I have no doubt Mrs. Gordon will prove his lordship's charges completely false. I would wish you good luck but I'm certain you understand why I don't." He glanced at the ladies, now stepping onto the ship. "Although I suspect you will need it. Corbin, a word please before you board." He turned and stepped away.

"Yes, sir." Corbin cast an admiring glance toward the ship. "A truly fine specimen of the very best England has to offer."

Harry wasn't sure he would completely agree. "She does appear to be a seaworthy enough vessel."

"Actually, Armstrong." Corbin tore his gaze from the ship. "I wasn't referring to the ship." He grinned in a self-assured manner and hurried after his employer.

The reporter was obviously an outrageous flirt. The kind of man who couldn't believe that any woman wouldn't swoon at the chance to be on his arm or in his bed. Arrogant, self-centered, charming, a man like

Corbin took conquest and seduction as his due. Harry knew that kind of man. For much of his life, Harry had been that kind of man. Perhaps he still was. Opportunities for female companions that were not seeking marriage had simply been limited since his return to England.

His gaze strayed up to Mrs. Gordon, stepping onto the ship to be greeted by the captain. Not that he had any inclination toward seduction but his intentions had certainly changed in the last few minutes. Now that he knew she wasn't a dear, sweet old lady his reasons for not exposing her fraudulent writings were no longer valid. She was not a fragile elderly flower but an outspoken, argumentative female who was apparently prepared to do battle. Or rather continue to do battle. The combat between them had begun when he'd sent his first letter to *The Times* and she'd responded. Now, it was a full-fledged war to be waged in the streets of Cairo and the sands of the Valley of the Kings. Even if she had a small army of elderly ladies by her side, he would not allow her to win.

It wasn't merely the future of his writing or the acknowledgment of his accomplishments in Egypt or even Walter's legacy at stake. Why, Truth itself was in the balance. He could not, he would not, permit a writer of frivolous fiction to stand in the way of truth.

No matter how lovely her eyes were.

CHAPTER FOUR

IT WAS ALL Sidney could do to keep her hand from shaking when welcomed on board the *Ancona* by the captain. She wasn't sure if it was from the cold or the excitement of boarding a ship for the very first time or finally taking the first step toward her dreams. More likely it was coming face-to-face with Mr. Harold Armstrong, the man who could destroy her future. She was heartened by the fact that she had held her ground even when he had glowered down at her although it had taken all the fortitude she could muster. But there was something about standing up to a man that was most invigorating and filled her with confidence. Aside from a few professors and merchants, she really had no experience dealing with men at all. Now, for good or ill, two dashing gentlemen would be part of the grand adventure that lay ahead. Perhaps Mr. Cadwallender was right. Perhaps she did have the courage to carry off this deception. Millicent certainly did. And she *was* Millicent.

The captain introduced the first-class steward, Mr. Gilmore, who escorted them on a tour of the ship. He showed them the ladies lounge, the saloon where evening entertainment would be provided, the library and dining room, and then ushered them to their accommodations, explaining there were ninety-one first-class staterooms and thirty-two second-class. Passenger rooms were along surprisingly narrow corridors. If one could not abide tight spaces, Sidney suspected it would be wise to avoid sea travel.

"Isn't this exciting?" Poppy said, a step behind Sidney. "I've never been on a real ship before."

"None of us has, dear," Lady Blodgett murmured.

Indeed, no one in their group—with the exception of Poppy who had spent time in Paris as a girl—had ever stepped foot off England's shores. Which was, for the most part, a little known fact although the ladies insisted it was not particularly a secret, simply that no one had ever asked. Regardless, its revelation would be at best embarrassing and at worst devastating to their positions as founding members of the Lady Travelers Society.

The three widows had started the society some three years ago as a service to other ladies who wished to plan future travel. Unfortunately, while they were really quite good at giving lectures, writing all manner of pamphlets and offering sage advice—based on the experiences of their husbands—they weren't quite as skilled at planning actual travel for their members. In fact, the only member they sent off on a grand tour of Europe managed to disappear—through no fault of the ladies as it turned out. Still, it was awkward, possibility fraudulent and there were questions of legality, so when an American entrepreneur offered to buy the Lady Travelers Society and keep Gwen, Effie and Poppy on as figureheads, lecturers and consultants, it was the perfect solution. The ever efficient Miss Charlotte Granville, another American, who now managed the society, had planned this trip to Egypt and there was no doubt in anyone's mind that it would go smoothly. At least when it came to the travel arrangements.

"I must say, I'm quite surprised at how very dashing he was," Poppy said as much to herself as to the others.

"Which one?" Gwen asked. "Mr. Armstrong or Mr. Corbin."

"Both, really, although I was speaking of Mr. Armstrong." Poppy sighed. "I have always had a fondness for men with fair hair the tiniest bit past due for a trim and just a little unruly. Why, it makes you want to run your fingers through it and muss it up even more."

"One surmises those shoulders are not due to the efforts of his tailor," Gwen said under her breath. "The man really is quite attractive."

"For an arrogant buffoon." Effie paused. "But admittedly a handsome buffoon."

Sidney stopped short and turned on her heel. "With all due respect, ladies, could you possibly wait until we are in a more private location to discuss Mr. Armstrong's and Mr. Corbin's appearance?"

"Yes, of course. We should have restrained ourselves but I'm afraid we're all too excited." Gwen's eyes sparkled. "This is our first adventure too, you know. And we have waited a very long time."

Poppy nodded. "And we never expected we would share it with not one but two handsome gentlemen. My goodness, it's most exhilarating."

"Even if one is an ass," Effie added. "Although, one does have to admit he is an extremely attractive—"

Gwen coughed.

"Aunt Effie!" Sidney cast a pointed glance at the steward in front of them, standing a few discreet feet away and obviously trying very hard not to listen as well as not to laugh.

Effie winced. "Oh dear. I didn't realize… Well." She

squared her shoulders. "I daresay it isn't anything he hasn't heard before." She peered around Sidney. "Am I right, Mr. Gilmore?"

"You are, madam," Mr. Gilmore said in a serious manner that belied the amusement in his eyes. "Indeed, I have heard far worse."

"Far worse?" Effie studied him curiously. "Really?"

He nodded. "But rest assured there is nothing more discreet than a first-class steward. It is my duty to respect the privacy of my passengers. Nothing that I see or hear during a voyage goes any further."

"Of course." A distinct look of disappointment passed over Effie's face. "As it should be." She glanced at Sidney. "I do see your point, Sidney dear."

"As I assume you all do." Goodness, they were all acting like schoolgirls. Sidney's firm gaze settled on one lady after another. Each had the good grace to look appropriately chagrined. Perhaps a little too chagrined. Sidney sighed, turned back to the steward and they continued down the corridor.

She really couldn't fault the ladies. Even in his fashionable clothing, Mr. Armstrong looked like he could have stepped right out of one of her stories. He wasn't at all as she'd pictured him. For some reason she thought he'd be an older man, brandishing a walking stick with a silver head in the shape of a cobra or something equally forbidding, with an air of superiority, whose only joy was reliving his past exploits. What she never expected was a dashing sort who towered above her with hair the color of the desert sand and stormy, gray eyes, intense and perceptive. Mr. Armstrong did indeed look like a hero come to life. Not her hero, of course. In her own story he was more of a villain.

The steward escorted them to their respective state-rooms, conveniently all in a row along the same side of the corridor.

"Your luggage has been unpacked and your baggage stowed for the voyage," Mr. Gilmore said when they reached Sidney's quarters. He opened the door and she stepped into the room. "Should you need anything at all, Mrs. Gordon, I am at your service." He nodded and closed the door behind him.

While not especially spacious, her first-class state-room was larger than she had expected with an iron bed, small sofa, writing desk, clothes cupboard and wash-stand. One did wonder if Mr. Corbin's accommodations were as nice. Mr. Armstrong's journey, of course, was funded by his uncle. In spite of his concern for finances, Mr. Cadwallender had spared no expense but then Effie, Gwen and Poppy had met several times with him alleg-edly about the Lady Travelers Society's plans for their trip. Or at least that's what Sidney was told. She really had no idea exactly what had transpired in those meet-ings. The ladies were unusually quiet about them which was suspicious in and of itself. Perhaps the publisher hadn't been at the dock to see them off out of courtesy but to make certain the elderly trio was indeed leaving the country and out of his hair.

Sidney pulled off her hat and gloves and tossed them on the bed. As eager as she was to further explore the ship as well as meet her fellow passengers, she was re-signed to taking her first dinner in her room tonight on the recommendation of the Lady Travelers Society. The pamphlet on sea voyages advised that one should always spend one's first night on board any vessel privately in one's own room, especially if one had never been on a ship before. The pamphlet delicately endorsed the wisdom of such advice as one never knew how one might respond to sea travel. Of course they wouldn't actually be at sea for the first sixty miles of the voyage and Sidney wondered if regardless of whether one was on the Thames or an ocean, one would feel substantially the same.

She glanced around her quarters and smiled. This would do nicely but then she would be quite happy with nearly anything. She was off to see the world. On a grand adventure and even if—thanks to Mr. Armstrong—it ended badly, it would still be an adventure. And there was no reason it couldn't start this minute with a walk on the deck. She would very much like to see London and the countryside pass by on their way to the sea. She grabbed her hat and gloves and pulled open her door.

"Sidney dear," Effie said brightly, her hand raised to knock. "May we come in?"

"Of course." Sidney pushed aside a momentary stab of disappointment. But the voyage to Alexandria would take nearly two weeks and there was plenty of time to enjoy everything the ship had to offer.

"We still have a great deal to discuss, you know," Effie said, stepping past her into the room, Gwen and Poppy right behind.

"My goodness." Poppy looked around. "This is identical to my room."

"I suspect they're all very much the same." Gwen settled on the sofa.

"Did you notice nearly everything is bolted to the floor?" Poppy sat down next to Gwen. "How very odd."

Effie rolled her gaze at the ceiling and took the last spot on the sofa. "Unlike a hotel, this room will tend to roll about with the waves."

"I knew that." Indignation sounded in Poppy's voice. "I simply thought it was curious."

"It is curious," Gwen said diplomatically, "as well as to be expected."

"Was there something in particular you wished to discuss?" Sidney closed the door, took off her coat, and placed it along with her hat and gloves in the cupboard, then perched on the edge of the bed. "I thought we had been quite thorough about our plans."

"One can never be too prepared for deception," Effie said firmly.

It did seem they had had endless discussions about how to make Sidney appear as if she was completely familiar with Egypt although none of them was certain exactly how to dampen Sidney's expected enthusiasm. If they had decided anything at all it was to take their venture one day—one step—at a time.

"I don't know why, but this feels rather delicate." Effie glanced at the others then drew a deep breath. "It's about your husband."

Sidney stared. "My what?"

"Your *husband*," Poppy said. "Your *dead* husband."

Sidney laughed. "I don't have a dead husband.

"We know that, dear. We wouldn't be having this discussion if you did." Gwen sighed. "We realized this morning that we had not discussed your husband—dear, dear whatever his name is."

"He should at least have a name beyond Mr. Gordon," Effie said. "Someone—Mr. Corbin or the buffoon or someone else entirely—might ask about him."

"You are supposed to be a widow," Gwen pointed out. "And widows generally have dead husbands."

"Not you, of course," Poppy added, "but most widows. We all do."

"I had forgotten about the dead husband," Sidney murmured. This was becoming more and more complicated but, as she wrote as Mrs. Gordon, it probably couldn't be helped. Not for the first time did she regret the decision to write under an assumed name. It had been at Mr. Cadwallender's insistence although he had initially proposed she write not as Miss Sidney Honeywell but as *Mr.* Sidney Gordon, which had struck her as being a traitor to her gender. However, she did agree to become Mrs. Gordon and while she'd never said she was a widow, the world assumed she was.

"You must never forget about the dead husband," Effie warned. "And he needs a name you can remember."

Sidney frowned. "I'm certain I'll be able to remember his name."

"You're not very good at remembering names, dear. You do tend to be a bit scattered," Poppy said gently. "What was your father's name? You should be able to remember that."

"My father's name was Charles."

Effie glanced at Gwen. "Unless you have any objections."

"Because my husband's name was Charles?" Gwen asked. "Don't be absurd. The world is simply littered with Charleses, a fair number of them dead. Why, if I was bothered by every dead Charles I encountered, I would spend most of my time being out of sorts." She cast Sidney an affectionate smile. "I daresay my husband would be honored to lend his name to your imaginary husband." She grinned. "As long as he was handsome and dashing, of course."

"Of course." Effie turned to Sidney. "He was, wasn't he?"

"Goodness, she wouldn't have married him if he wasn't. Not that a man's appearance is as important as his character," Poppy added quickly, "but, as we are inventing him, we might as well make him as attractive as we want. Or rather as Sidney wants."

"I don't see why not." Effie nodded. "What did he look like, Sidney?"

"I don't know." Sidney crossed her arms over her chest. "And I don't see why this is necessary."

"Because someone might ask and you need to be prepared. It's the details in a project like this that make all the difference between acceptance and being found out," Gwen said firmly. "Now, tell us. What did he look like?"

"Very well." Sidney sighed. This did seem absurd but the ladies probably had a point. "I suppose he was tall." She had always thought tall men to be particularly attractive. "With nicely broad shoulders."

"The result of a passion for out of door activities, no doubt." Effie nodded. "Go on. What color hair and eyes did he have?"

Sidney thought for a moment. "Blue eyes, I think. No, better yet—gray. Which might seem nondescript but are really quite warm. Yes, that's good. And they lit up when he smiled. He had a wonderful smile. And his hair…" One wouldn't think making up a fraudulent husband would be quite this difficult. "Brown perhaps? A light brown." No, not brown. What goes well with gray eyes? "Or… I know, a dark blond. The color of sand. Oh yes, that's better. I like that. What do you think?"

All three ladies stared at her with the oddest expression on their faces.

"What is it?" Sidney drew her brows together. "Is he not handsome enough?"

"No, he's fine," Poppy said with a weak smile. What on earth was the matter with her?

Gwen cleared her throat. "Now tell us about your life together."

"I thought we had discussed this as well. My story should be much like the one I created for Millicent." Sidney sighed. "There really wasn't much of a life together. I married Mr. Gordon—Charles—when I was eighteen—"

Poppy nodded. "He swept you off your feet."

"And we immediately set off for Egypt as he was a promising, young archeologist—"

"An excellent place for a honeymoon." Approval sounded in Effie's voice.

"And I was determined to be by his side."

"Most courageous of you," Gwen said. "Go on."

"We barely had a few months together before he died tragically." Sidney paused. "Should I know how he died?"

"Well, you would wouldn't you? As his wife." Poppy glanced at the other ladies. "How shall we do away with him?"

"Perhaps a camel sat on him?" Gwen suggested.

"Or he could have drowned in the Nile." Poppy brightened. "Yes, that's good." She fluttered her fingers. "Drowned and washed away never to be seen again."

"Better yet." Effie cast a triumphant smile at the others. "Egypt is full of vile creatures." She glanced at Sidney. "Isn't it?"

"Oh my, yes." Sidney nodded. "There are several varieties of venomous snakes as well as scorpions and crocodiles—"

"That's it!" Excitement rang in Effie's voice. "Poor, dear, dashing Mr. Gordon was eaten by a crocodile!"

Poppy frowned. "That doesn't sound very pleasant."

"It doesn't have to be pleasant." Effie huffed. "It simply has to be fatal."

"I know that," Poppy said. "I just think it would be extremely difficult to move past the death of a husband if he were eaten by a crocodile." She shook her head. "It's not at all the kind of thing a woman could put behind her." She shuddered.

"Which is precisely why," Effie said slowly, "Sidney prefers not to discuss it. She has never truly recovered from his loss, you see."

Gwen's brow rose. "After almost fifteen years? They were hardly married any time at all."

"Which makes it even more tragic," Poppy said firmly. "He was, after all, her true love and in spite of the passage of time, she is still mourning—like Her Majesty."

Sidney frowned. "Then shouldn't I be wearing black?"

"Very well." Effie cast Poppy an exasperated look. "Not exactly like the queen."

"Still mourning the loss of Mr. Gordon," Sidney said under her breath and nodded. "That sounds perfectly reasonable to me. However, in spite of my dreadful loss, I decided to stay on in Egypt because I couldn't bear to return to London without poor Mr. Gordon and I felt it important to carry on with his work. Besides, I fell madly, deeply in love with the country and its history and its people." That much was at least partially true. "Thus was the beginning of my adventures."

"Excellent." Poppy beamed.

"Well, fine, anyway." Gwen cast her an encouraging smile.

"It will do," Effie added then paused. "I think it might be best, all things considered, if we tried never to leave you alone with either the buffoon or Mr. Corbin."

Sidney stared. "You don't think I can do this?"

"Of course we do, dear," Poppy said quickly. "It's just that it's been our observation that while you're very good at writing, you're not overly skilled at deception or—"

"Prevarication." Gwen winced. "Or dishonesty or—"

"Lying," Effie said bluntly. "You do not lie well, Sidney. Which is an admirable quality really, under most circumstances. However—" Effie grimaced "—these are not most circumstances."

"I am well aware of that," Sidney said. "I have given all of this a great deal of thought. Indeed, I've thought of little else since I agreed to be part of this farce. And yes, I have always prided myself on my sense of honesty." She thought for a moment. "I am most grateful for your help and I daresay, I couldn't manage this on my own but do not for a moment think I do not understand the importance of this venture. My reputation and my future are at stake. And in many ways, this is no one's fault but my own."

"Well, we were the ones who responded to Lord Brenton's letters," Poppy said faintly.

"Regardless, that's not where this began." Sidney drew a deep breath. "If I had paid more attention, I would have realized the world was taking my stories as fact and I could have taken steps to correct that impression. I should have taken a stand then, regardless of the consequences."

Effie frowned. "But Mr. Cadwallender—"

"It's my life and they're my stories, Aunt Effie, and I should have stood up for both." Sidney shook her head. "I allowed myself to be convinced by Mr. Cadwallender that my revealing the truth would be disastrous. As he was my publisher and a man, I assumed he knew best. In that, I believe now that I was wrong."

Effie grinned.

"What I should have done scarcely matters now. Now I have a reputation to protect and a wrong to set right." Sidney raised her chin. "In the eyes of my readers, I am Millicent Forester. I am the Queen of the Desert. I shall not let them down."

"Excellent." Gwen beamed.

"I absolutely will not allow an arrogant ass—"

"Or buffoon." Poppy shrugged. "Both do seem accurate."

"—to ruin my life, my future and my livelihood." Determination washed through her. "This is a game I intend to win. I have a role to play, ladies. Mr. Armstrong is determined to prove I'm not what the world has been led to believe I am. All I have to do—" she squared her shoulders "—is prove him wrong."

CHAPTER FIVE

"I SEE I'M not the only one who enjoys watching the sun rise over the ocean," Harry said in his most cordial manner. It wasn't easy. This was the first dawn of their voyage and cordial was the last thing he felt this morning toward this interloper.

"Good day, Mr. Armstrong." Mrs. Gordon's gaze remained on the horizon.

"I wouldn't have taken you for such an early riser." Perhaps she would scurry back to her cabin once she had fully absorbed the sunrise.

"What a remarkable coincidence, Mr. Armstrong," she said coolly. "I would not have thought to encounter you at this time of day either." She glanced at him. "Especially not with a bottle of champagne in your hand."

"If I had known you were going to be here, I would have brought two glasses."

"I never indulge in spirits before breakfast, Mr. Armstrong."

"Perhaps you should, Mrs. Gordon." He paused. He'd been trying for nearly a year now to be the kind of man he was expected to be—the kind of man an *earl* was supposed to be—and, even though she didn't know of his title, he had decided not to reveal too much of his questionable past. Still, this was a fairly innocuous revelation. "When my friends and I first set off for Egypt, nearly twenty years ago, we marked the first sunrise of the first day with a bottle of the best champagne our collective resources could afford. Every voyage to Egypt after that, regardless of whether one or all three of us were traveling, we always greeted the first dawn with champagne. This bottle was delivered to my quarters before we left port from one of those friends."

"That's really quite charming." She considered him thoughtfully. "I would not have thought you so sentimental."

Rubbish. "I don't think *sentimental* is the right word—"

"Habit, then."

"I tend to think of it more in the manner of tradition."

"Regardless, I do not wish to interfere." She smiled. "I shall leave you to your tradition." She turned to go.

"Join me," he said without thinking.

She turned back to him, her eyes narrowed. "Why?"

"Why?" He grinned. "Are you always so suspicious?"

"No. In fact, I am quite trusting of most people. Trusting you, however—"

He winced. Not that he didn't deserve her distrust.

"—does not strike me as especially wise. I would be remiss if I did not question your motives. We are here after all because you are determined to prove me a fraud and I am determined to prove you wrong." She shrugged. "Under these circumstances, suspicion does seem the wiser course."

"I'll grant you that. However, just for the span of the sunrise, let us forget we are at odds. Do me the honor of joining me in the tradition of myself and my friends in a salute to what lies ahead. There is nothing as inspiring as watching the sun rise up out of the sea."

"Very well." Her eyes twinkled. "But you have only one glass."

"Which I shall gladly sacrifice for the pleasure of your company."

"How very gallant of you."

"I can be very gallant. You should make note of that." He opened the bottle, filled the glass and handed it to her, then raised the bottle toward the sun. "To the new day and the adventures it will bring." *And to those who are no longer with us*, he added silently. He took a long drink from the bottle and sent a prayer of thanks to Ben. It was an excellent vintage, even straight from the bottle.

"To the adventures that lie ahead." She raised her glass and took a sip, then wrinkled her nose.

"Is it not to your liking?"

"Oh no, it's quite lovely really but the bubbles tickle my nose." She fluttered her fingers in front of her nose. "Which is perhaps part of the enjoyment. I will confess I rarely have champagne and never in the morning. But it is delightful."

"There is no better way to start a trip than with a glass of France's finest."

"And there is something both optimistic and invigorating about watching the sun make its first appearance of the day over the ocean. I agree with you, Mr. Armstrong." She sipped her wine and turned her attention back to the sunrise. "The champagne makes it even better. I shall have to remember that. This is indeed an excellent way to start a grand adventure."

"I must say I'm impressed. From reading your stories one would assume that the first dawn of a new journey toward Egypt would be rather commonplace for you. And yet you seem quite enthusiastic."

"Would you prefer I be jaded and cynical as you appear to be?"

"I believe older and wiser a more accurate description," he said coolly. "And I certainly didn't mean to imply that you—"

"I daresay, Mr. Armstrong, you know nothing about me except for those details I have put in my stories." She glanced at him. "And I try not to focus on my personal habits."

"Why?" Curiosity sounded in his voice. "You are writing about your own adventures after all."

"It's very simple." She turned toward him. "Regardless of whose adventures they are, my purpose isn't to make readers admire the author but rather to become the hero or the heroine. Precisely why I chose to give the heroine of my stories a name different from my own. People cannot lose themselves in the story if they are too busy contemplating the author. Whether she is an early riser or prefers lemon to milk in her tea, it's of no importance. All that matters is that people who read my stories forget the tedium of everyday life and lose themselves for an hour or an afternoon in another world."

He stared at her for a long, disbelieving moment. "Rubbish, Mrs. Gordon. You can't possibly be serious."

"I most certainly am."

"People don't want to be swept away." He scoffed. "People want to be informed and educated and enlightened."

"Good Lord." She laughed. "What utter nonsense. While indeed many people read newspapers, as well as books, to be informed and educated and enlightened, the vast majority of readers want nothing more than enjoyment." She turned back to the sunrise.

"People want facts, Mrs. Gordon," he said firmly. "Indisputable facts."

"Do you really think people want to know that the

Great Pyramid at Giza stands four hundred and eighty feet, nine inches high with a base very nearly square of 764 feet per side?"

"I find that extremely interesting."

She ignored him. "Or would they prefer to read how the Great Pyramid rises into the heavens, dwarfing its companions as if they were insignificant interlopers and casting an ever growing shadow in the late afternoon sun, the hands of long-ago pharaohs, even in death, refusing to release their grip on their land and people and the Nile itself?"

"I will admit your way is certainly more inventive. It is not however, especially accurate."

"No?" She heaved a resigned sigh, cast a longing look at the sunrise then faced him again. "Tell me, Mr. Armstrong." She held out her glass. "Do the pyramids not cast a shadow in the setting sun that grows as sunset approaches and stretches toward the Nile?"

"One could say that, I suppose," he said and filled her glass.

She raised a brow.

"I admit, the Nile is to the east of the pyramids." He took another pull from the bottle. "And the setting sun does cast a significant shadow."

"And does the Great Pyramid not tower over the others?"

"Yes, of course."

"So what exactly was inaccurate?"

"Admittedly, *inaccurate* might have been the wrong word." His jaw tightened. This was exactly the kind of problem he had with her writing. "*Fanciful* is perhaps a better word. The pyramids are tombs, not the fingers of the hands of the pharaohs reaching out from death."

"My, you are stuffy."

He stared at her. She was right—he did sound stuffy. He laughed.

"You find that amusing?"

He grinned. "No one has ever called me stuffy before."

She shrugged. "Perhaps no one had the courage."

"Entirely possible." He chuckled. He never used to be stuffy. But then he'd never been an earl with property and wealth and responsibility before either.

"In spite of the imposing rhetoric in your uncle's letters to *The Times*, and the threatening manner he used, you do not scare me, Mr. Armstrong."

"Does my uncle?"

She met his gaze firmly. "No."

"I don't believe he intended to scare you, nor do I." Although he certainly had expected her to retreat or even ignore his letters rather than respond to what he could now see might well have been construed as intimidating.

Mrs. Gordon cast him a knowing smile—although he wasn't at all sure what she thought she knew and it was rather annoying—then returned to her perusal of the sunrise. As much as he had expected and wanted to be alone, he had to admit he was enjoying this bit of sparring with the lovely widow. He took another sip from the bottle. All things considered, this was probably a better way to begin this journey than drinking alone on deck accompanied only by the memories of friends who were gone or had moved on with their lives. The past was the past and both good times and bad were best left behind where they belonged.

"You must be pleased to be returning to Egypt," he said in an offhand manner.

"Must I?"

"As much as I disagree with your manner of writing

as well as dispute your depiction of, well, very nearly everything, I will not deny you do appear to have a certain passion for Egypt. So, I simply assume you are happy to be returning."

"Indeed I am. It has been some time since I was last there."

"How long?"

"Quite some time. Years, in fact."

"How many?"

"A number of years."

"Specifically?"

"Specifically? Come now, Mr. Armstrong." She shook her head in annoyance. "It's obvious that you are trying to solicit information from me although I must say you are not especially good at it."

His brow furrowed. "Was I that obvious?"

She cast him a disbelieving look. "Yes."

"Not subtle, then?"

"Not even a bit. Subtlety, Mr. Armstrong, is an art."

"One I apparently need to work on." He paused. "Although soliciting information was really not my intention. I intended nothing more than idle conversation, the same as one would have with any fellow passenger. The kind of thing people do when they're sharing a sunrise and becoming better acquainted."

"I have no desire to become better acquainted and we are not sharing a sunrise."

"Oh, but I believe we are." He nodded toward the east.

"Regardless, as your declared purpose is to prove me disreputable, I am not inclined to share even the most innocuous detail with you. Furthermore, you did say that for the length of the sunrise, we would ignore the dispute between us."

He grinned, he couldn't seem to help himself. "I believe the sun is now fully up."

"Then there is no need for me to remain and be plied with champagne," she said in a lofty manner.

He nodded and reached over to top off her glass. "No need at all."

"It is, however, excellent champagne."

"I can afford excellent champagne."

"Do you have a great deal of money?"

"Enough."

"But you haven't always had money." She studied him curiously. "You said on your first trip you had the best champagne you could afford."

"True."

"But you are now a wealthy man. Did you make your fortune in Egypt?"

"Now you too are trying to solicit information."

"What a shocking coincidence." She smiled pleasantly. "But it does seem only fair."

"Very well." He thought for a moment. Her queries were fairly harmless. "The response to your first comment is yes and the answer to the second is no."

"Oh." She considered him thoughtfully. "Mr. Corbin said you were well-known among Egyptologists and yet I have never heard of you."

He bristled. "Have you heard of every Egyptologist?"

"Yes."

"Surely not.

She raised a shoulder in an offhand shrug.

He stared. "You're extremely outspoken, Mrs. Gordon."

"Am I?" Surprise widened her eyes.

"Indeed you are."

"Oh." Her brows drew together, then her expression cleared and she cast him a brilliant smile. "Thank you."

He shook his head in confusion. "For what?"

"For your assessment of my nature. I've never considered myself to be outspoken. I'm really quite flattered. You did mean it as a compliment, did you not?"

Why not? "Of course."

"You do not lie well, Mr. Armstrong. It's good to know." She nodded. "But you do have my thanks for the champagne." She leaned closer in a confidential manner and the merest hint of a scent at once exotic and welcoming wafted around him. "Did I tell you that I am not at all used to champagne?"

"Not directly but I suspected as much." He bit back a grin. "Although I do find it difficult to believe that the celebrated Mrs. Gordon is not used to champagne."

"Nonsense, I'm not the least bit celebrated. A bit well-known perhaps."

"You are the Queen of the Desert after all."

"Well yes, there is that." She sipped her wine. "I do try to be circumspect."

"But you are a member of the Antiquities Society."

"I have not yet had the opportunity to attend any of the society's gatherings. And if your uncle has his way, I never will."

"Why not? The society is most prestigious." So prestigious, it had never offered him membership.

"And membership is a great honor but I am far too wrapped up in my work to frequent social gatherings."

"What? No literary society fetes? No grand balls in your honor?" He shook his head in a mournful manner. "I daresay I expected more from the Queen of the Desert."

"I am sorry to disappoint." She frowned. "And you needn't keep calling me that."

"Why? Don't you like it?"

"Not especially."

And wasn't that interesting? "If you're not indulging in London society, how do you spend your time?"

"I write, Mr. Armstrong. I have no time for anything else." She pinned him with a firm look. "And what do you do? Other than play errand boy for your uncle. Which does seem to me to be the mark of a man with nothing else to do."

"I have a great deal to do," he said staunchly.

"For example?"

"I have not been back in England for very long. I have any number of ideas as to how to spend my time. I am simply trying to decide my next course."

"Come now, Mr. Armstrong," she said skeptically. "You're the wealthy nephew of an even wealthier earl. You have no need to do anything productive at all."

"A life of boredom is no life at all."

"I wouldn't know." She tilted her head and studied him. "How long since your last trip to Egypt?"

"It's been some time." He grinned. "Quite some time."

"Why did you leave Egypt?"

"Why did you?"

"I believe you're hiding something, Mr. Armstrong."

"Yet another coincidence, Mrs. Gordon. I *know* you're hiding a great deal."

"Do you?" She considered him for a long moment. A slow, decidedly wicked smile curved her lips. Her exceptionally fetching lips. "This should be fun, Mr. Armstrong."

"Fun?" His gaze slipped to her mouth. He suspected her definition of *fun* at the moment and his were decidedly different. He cleared his throat. "Do you really think so?"

"Oh my, yes." A definite glint of challenge shone in her eyes. "There is nothing more fun than putting an arrogant man in his place."

"Then the game is afoot, Mrs. Gordon. And you're right." He leaned in, trying to ignore her scent, the long length of her lashes, the distracting *nearness* of her. "It will be fun. Although I have no doubt as to the ultimate winner."

"Nor do I, Mr. Armstrong."

His gaze meshed with hers and for a moment something one could only call awareness sparked between them. Not what he expected. Or wanted. But then Harry Armstrong had always been willing to adapt to new circumstances.

"There you are," a female voice sounded behind him. Before he could turn, someone short and determined nudged him out of the way as efficiently as a collie cutting a sheep from the herd, and Mrs. Gordon's band of determined elderly watchdogs surrounded her.

"Good day, Sidney," Mrs. Fitzhew-Wellmore said brightly. "And Mr. Armstrong as well. What a lovely surprise."

"And greeting the new day with champagne." Lady Blodgett cast an assessing eye at the bottle in his hand. "I never would have thought of such a thing but it is a charming idea."

"And how very thoughtful of you." The dragon plucked the bottle from his grip and smiled innocently. "Only one glass?"

"I'm afraid so," Sidney said with a shrug.

"Then there's nothing to be done about it." The dragon shook her head reluctantly. "We shall simply have to adjourn to Mrs. Gordon's stateroom and request additional glasses from the charming Mr. Gilmore."

Mrs. Gordon bit back a grin. Why shouldn't she smile? She had invaded his solitude—he ignored the fact that she had already been on deck when he arrived—commandeered his tradition and was now absconding with his champagne.

"Thank you, again, Mr. Armstrong," she said pleasantly. "Do enjoy the rest of your morning." She took the dragon's arm and they strolled down the deck.

"We would ask you to join us, Mr. Armstrong, but Sidney's room simply isn't big enough for everyone. Why, the four of us can scarcely squeeze in together. Although it is an exceptionally nice room." Lady Blodgett smiled. "Besides, it did look to me as if there was barely enough champagne left for a handful of glasses at the most and I am certain you would wish for us to have it."

What could he say? "With my sincerest compliments."

"I thought you would agree. This really is quite delightful. I might have to put the idea of starting the first day of any new journey with champagne at sunrise in a Lady Travelers pamphlet." Lady Blodgett turned to go then turned back. "Oh, and as it seems to me, to all of us really, as your purpose in this trip is the complete opposite of Sidney's, it might be wiser for all concerned if you avoided those occasions when it was just you and Mrs. Gordon alone. Besides, people being what they are, appearances are important. I'm certain you understand."

"Are you afraid I might attempt to ply Mrs. Gordon with spirits in an effort to wring a confession from her?" he said lightly. "Or do you think my intentions might be even more dishonorable? Seduction perhaps?" At once, the image of her delightfully inviting lips came to mind.

Lady Blodgett glanced at Mrs. Fitzhew-Wellmore, and then leaned closer to him. "Mr. Armstrong, my husband and his friends were explorers and adventurers. I have spent the better part of my life around such men as have Poppy and Effie. Men very much like you. I assure you, we are quite good at recognizing those who are honorable gentlemen and those who are not."

"And where do I fall in your assessment?" he said slowly.

"I haven't decided yet." She smiled sweetly but there was no misunderstanding the look in her eye. Regardless of whether she decided he was indeed an honorable gentleman or a despicable cad, the opportunities to be alone with Mrs. Gordon again, particularly with champagne, would be nonexistent. Were the ladies trying to keep her secrets or simply protect her? He could certainly understand the former if indeed he was right about her but the latter made no sense. A widow had no need of constant supervision and from his brief conversation with her it was apparent Mrs. Gordon—Sidney—could certainly hold her own.

"Good day, Mr. Armstrong." Lady Blodgett started after the others. Mrs. Fitzhew-Wellmore nodded, and then trailed after her friend.

"Do you always travel in packs, Mrs. Fitzhew-Wellmore?" he said mildly.

She turned back to him. "Goodness no, Mr. Armstrong. Not always." She smiled in a friendly manner. He wasn't sure he believed it. "Only when necessary." The older lady's eyes twinkled and she headed toward the others.

The game was indeed afoot. Harry thought he'd be playing with Sidney alone. Now, it appeared he was facing an entire team.

The fame of Mrs. Gordon's *Tales of a Lady Adventurer in Egypt* has spread well beyond England. Even on board ship any number of passengers had read her work and confessed it was a great influence on their decisions to turn their hopes for holiday adventures toward the ancient shores of Egypt.

—"The Return of the Queen of the Desert,"
Daniel Corbin, foreign correspondent

CHAPTER SIX

"WHY, MR. ARMSTRONG, what are you doing?" Sidney said behind the mask that had been passed out to all the passengers for masquerade night. A night that was every bit as bothersome as it sounded although it did seem to be the sort of thing first-class passengers required. It was their first dance of the evening, much to Harry's annoyance.

"I believe we are dancing," he said smoothly, steering her out of the saloon door and into the corridor. He cast a quick glance over his shoulder but no one seemed to note their exit. This was the first chance he'd had to be alone with her since their shared sunrise and it had taken a bit of creative manipulation on his part to manage it.

"I believe we *were* dancing and now you have somehow guided me out of the saloon and—"

He opened the door to the deck. "And onto the deck."

"Dare I ask why?" She stepped out onto the deck, a note of amusement in her voice. Obviously, she was not annoyed by this clever maneuver of his.

He smiled down at her. "It's a beautiful night, Mrs.

Gordon." He pulled off his mask with a sense of relief. He hated having the blasted thing pressed against his face. "I thought it a shame not to share it."

"It is a lovely night, Mr. Armstrong." She untied her mask and removed it. "But I assume we are not here simply to gaze at the stars."

"Oh, but they are magnificent stars."

"They are at that." She glanced out at the darkness, the brilliant stars reflecting on an endless sea. "There are any number of ways I can think of to describe this but you would not appreciate them."

He chuckled. "Probably not."

"I've never seen the stars so brilliant or a sky so black." She gazed at the sky for a long moment and it struck Harry that there were indeed any number of ways he could describe her face silhouetted against the stars. Most of them extremely sentimental and even, possibly, given the circumstances, romantic.

He ignored the absurd idea. "Except, of course, when you've been on a ship at sea."

"Yes, of course." She paused then heaved a slightly dramatic sigh. "It's been so long I had nearly forgotten…"

He didn't believe her but thought it best to ignore yet another example of her deception. "I simply thought you would look lovely under the stars. And I was right."

She arched a skeptical brow and then snorted in a most unladylike manner. "Good Lord, Harry. Did you expect that to work?"

"Yes." He grinned.

"There's that arrogance of yours again."

"I prefer to think of it as confidence."

"You may think of it as you wish. You will anyway, I

suspect." She rested her hands on the railing and gazed out at the night. "Why are we really here?"

"Aside from the stars and the balmy night?"

She laughed and it caught at something deep inside him. It was not the first time. "Yes, Harry, aside from all the accoutrements of a blatantly romantic interlude, why are we here?"

"I simply wished to talk to you." He paused. "Alone."

"That explains it, then."

He'd been right from the beginning. Try as he might, in the week and a half they'd been on board ship there had been no opportunity to be alone with Sidney. Her trio of guardians made certain of that. They weren't the least bit subtle about it either. There was at least one of them by Sidney's side or within sight every minute. It would have been most annoying except that it also served to prevent Corbin from being alone with her. Harry's initial impression of Corbin's untrustworthiness when it came to women was proving correct. Why, the reporter practically fawned over Sidney, showering her with compliments about her writing and her ability to tell a story at every opportunity. One did wonder what else the man was saying when he leaned in close to her and spoke low into her ear. Although the blush that washed up her face at such moments was certainly a clue as to the sorts of things Corbin whispered. Corbin was the one the ladies should keep their eyes on—not Harry. It was obvious that the man was interested in more than a mere newspaper story. Of course, the reporter was nearly as attentive to the chaperones as he was to Sidney, no doubt in an effort to earn their trust and thereby convince them to look kindly upon him.

Two could play at Corbin's game. Certainly it had been

some time but Harry used to play it quite well. When he inherited his title, he had made a concerted effort to behave more in the manner expected of a gentleman in his position. It hadn't been especially difficult. Harry attributed that both to the demands of his new circumstances as well as age. There was nothing that emphasized a man's passing years and the reality of mortality so much as the death of a friend. It now struck him that he had been somewhat melancholy in nature in the two years since Walter died as well. Certainly the most interesting thing he'd done since his return to England was dare Mrs. Gordon to prove her legitimacy.

She'd called him stuffy. *Stuffy?* Hardly. Admittedly, the Earl of Brenton might be stuffy and even perhaps—God help him—dull. But Harry Armstrong was daring and adventurous and far from dead. And hadn't he felt a bit more like his old self since he'd started this endeavor? There was nothing Harry Armstrong couldn't do if he set his mind to it. And earning the friendship—if not the affections—of Sidney and her band of vigilant widows was just the sort of challenge he had always relished. The ladies were pleasant enough and he had become rather fond of them with the exception of Mrs. Higginbotham, who continued to treat him with utter disdain which only made him try harder. After all, with friendship came confidences and, hopefully, the truth about the Queen of the Desert.

From that moment forward, Harry made it his business to be by Sidney's side every possible minute. He never missed an opportunity to sit next to her at dinner. Certainly there were moments when he had to outmaneuver Corbin—as well as the captain who quite liked having the Queen of the Desert on board his ship. As it happened, the blasted man had read her silly book. But then apparently—who hadn't?

Harry was doing all he could to follow his father's and Ben's advice. Really, could he be more charming? Every evening he joined Sidney and the other ladies in the saloon for whatever entertainment was scheduled and there was something scheduled every night. He had never been much for organized activities but it seemed they were an essential part of a passenger ship and could not be avoided. Amusements ranged from dancing to absurd games that struck him as little better than children's pastimes, to musical evenings employing the questionable talents of the other passengers, to hours of enthusiastic and distinctly cutthroat card playing. Such evenings were admittedly rather fun.

Harry had always enjoyed cards and considered himself quite accomplished. On board ship, they played for pennies, and higher wagers were frowned upon even though he suspected the older ladies would have agreed to increased stakes. All three of them played with a wicked intensity that was as surprising as it was successful. The only interesting wager to be found was the daily sweepstakes wherein passengers placed a miniscule amount—because it was all in the spirit of fun, although he would dispute that—on their guess of the distance the ship had traveled the day before. They were halfway to Alexandria before Harry discovered most of the gentlemen on board had substantial, private wagers of their own as well as serious card games in the gentlemen's lounge. One of the true satisfactions of the endless voyage was liberating Corbin from a tidy sum.

Still, while he scarcely had any opportunity to speak with Sidney alone, he did have the chance to observe her.

She was an enigma, a puzzle with flashing blue eyes, unbridled enthusiasm for nearly everything and a challenging attitude. The more he studied her, the more confusing she became. She was well versed on ancient Egypt, as well as current archeological endeavors and was practically a walking, talking guidebook. Try as he might, he'd been unable to catch her in a single mistake. It was absurd. Even he made mistakes on occasion. She was either the best liar in history—and he had met more than one woman who was skilled in the art of deception—or she was completely legitimate—and his opinion on that had not changed—or she was fighting for her life. He was fairly certain the last option was the correct one. It was the only answer that made sense. Harry had long prided himself on being an excellent judge of character and, in spite of the deception she had pulled on her readers, Mrs. Sidney Gordon struck him as a genuinely good person.

Which made his objective all the more awkward. Thanks to an innate sense of fairness and an inconvenient conscience, Harry found himself feeling rather bad about his determination to prove her a fraud. Through no fault of his own, he had everything a man could want: a father who loved him, wealth, property and even a place in society should he want it. And, as far as he could ascertain, all Sidney had was a makeshift family comprised of three elderly ladies and her work. What kind of selfish, arrogant man would take that away from her?

"I am prepared to offer you a bargain of sorts," Harry said in what he intended to be a pleasant, friendly manner. "A compromise, if you will."

"A compromise? How very intriguing. What kind of compromise?"

"Before we met in person I was convinced by a well-meaning friend that Mrs. Gordon was an elderly widow."

"Which is why you immediately assumed Mrs. Fitzhew-Wellmore was Mrs. Gordon and then, even worse, made the same assumption with Mrs. Higginbotham." She bit back a grin.

He shuddered. "She does not like me."

"That's not entirely accurate." Sidney slanted him an amused glance. "She detests you." She shrugged. "It's a matter of degree really. Although I must say, you have made every effort to win her friendship as well as that of Lady Blodgett's and Mrs. Fitzhew-Wellmore's. Successfully, I might add. They merely dislike you."

"We still have three days until we reach Alexandria. They could become quite fond of me in that time."

"I wouldn't wager even a penny on that." She scoffed. "So tell me, Harry, what is this bargain of yours?"

"As I said, I was led to believe that Mrs. Gordon was an older lady which led me to reexamine my, oh, conscience if you will. I discussed this with my uncle and neither of us had any desire to destroy the livelihood of an old woman who had no other means of making a living."

"Decent of you."

"We decided then that if she would simply change the name of her stories in the *Messenger* and any subsequent books to include the word *fictitious*…" He paused.

Her eyes narrowed slightly. "Go on."

"Then there would be no need to expose her publicly as a fraud," he said with a flourish. "She could continue to write her stories and make her living."

"And?"

"And that is the very same bargain I am now prepared to offer you." It really was a brilliant idea.

"Are you?"

Sidney didn't look nearly as pleased as he would have expected. In fact, she didn't look at all pleased. Still, that could be due to the minimal light on the deck. "I am indeed."

She studied him thoughtfully.

"Aren't you going to say anything?"

"I'm trying to find the right words," she said slowly.

"To be expected, of course." He smirked. "It's an excellent offer."

"Do tell me, Mr. Armstrong—"

Odd, he was Harry a minute ago.

"Why are you willing to agree to such an offer? I am not, as you had previously assumed, an old woman."

"You most certainly are not." He chuckled.

"Then why?"

"To save you from ultimate embarrassment and humiliation and scandal of course." There was a distinctly pompous note in his voice. He ignored it.

Her brows drew together. "I don't understand. We have not yet set foot in Egypt. Why now?"

"It's quite simple. In our time on board ship, I've had the opportunity to study you."

"Oh?"

"Come now, Sidney—"

"Mrs. Gordon."

"Mrs. Gordon, then. It's obvious that you are not an experienced traveler. I wouldn't be at all surprised if this was your first sea voyage. Which means you have never been to Egypt." He smiled in what might have been an altogether too smug manner.

"On what do you base this conclusion?"

"Why, I've never seen anyone so delighted with even

the most mundane aspects of the voyage. It's apparent, at least to me, that it's all new for you." Without thinking, he took her hand. "Your enthusiasm about very nearly everything is not only engaging but almost contagious."

"And that leads you to believe this is my first voyage?" She jerked her hand from his and the oddest sense of loss shot through him.

"It's hard to feign that sort of excitement," he said in a chastising tone.

"What utter nonsense." Disdain rang in her voice. "You pride yourself on being a man of facts, Mr. Armstrong, but thus far, you have made an assessment based on nothing more than impression and speculation. Surely you have facts to go along with your assumption."

He stared in disbelief. She should be thanking him at this point for an offer that would save her reputation and her livelihood. And would put an end to this farce. Instead, the blasted woman was asking for proof that he had determined without question that she was indeed a fake.

"Very well." His tone hardened. "Every aspect of this voyage delights you. You spend endless hours in obvious enjoyment of the coast passing by, be it Spain or Africa or Italy."

"Should I sit in my room and tap my fingers impatiently waiting for the voyage to end?"

He ignored her. "When we stopped at Gibraltar, you were enthralled when you used field glasses and spotted one of the apes on the rock. Furthermore, you were not at all knowledgeable as to the working of the glasses."

"The apes on the Rock of Gibraltar are a thrilling sight, regardless of how many times one sees it. And they were not my glasses so unfamiliarity is to be expected." She shrugged. "What else?"

"When we docked in Brindisi, and we took the opportunity for a brief stroll, you and your friends were fascinated but it is one of the more unpleasant and disreputable places I have ever been."

"Which makes it no less interesting regardless of how many times one has seen it." She paused. "Usually, one changes steamers in Brindisi. I found it most interesting that we did not."

"That's because we are headed to Alexandria and not Port Said. And anyone with a decent guidebook would know that," he added. She was filled with all sorts of minor details which proved absolutely nothing except that she was well-read about travel to Egypt. "You are awed by everything from the view of Tunis and the harbor of ancient Carthage—"

"Edmund Burke said those who do not know history are doomed to repeat it," she said primly.

"—to the workings of the ship and the schools of dolphins who trail in our wake."

"And you don't find those remarkable creatures fascinating?" She shook her head in a sympathetic manner. "How very sad."

"It's not the least bit sad." Indignation sounded in his voice. *She* pitied *him*? "I was just as fascinated as you the first time I saw any of this. Now however—"

"Now it has all become terribly familiar." She sighed. "I do find it sad and I am sorry for you."

"I do not need your pity," he said sharply. The blasted woman had turned the entire conversation on its head. He drew a calming breath. "Somehow, you have appropriated the discussion at hand and turned it in an entirely different direction altogether."

"Have I?" She smiled pleasantly. "How very clever of me."

"Clever or not you cannot continue this ruse throughout this entire trip."

"Unless, of course, it's not a ruse." She paused. "Is there more?"

"Your enthusiasm is boundless and very nearly contagious."

"You already said that."

"It bears repeating as obviously you did not take it to heart the first time!" Was the woman even listening to what he said?

"Very well. I suppose I should confess at this point."

Finally!

She leaned closer and lowered her voice. "My friends are not the seasoned travelers one might imagine and I have felt it important to share my observations—as boundlessly enthusiastic as they may be—with them as they have uprooted their lives to accompany us."

"Observations are one thing. Excitement is something else entirely." It was an explanation even if he did not consider it a good one. "I could go on and on but everything I've seen points to a naiveté and distinct lack of experience on your part."

"Does it, Mr. Armstrong? It seems to me your most gracious offer of this bargain to save my reputation and my livelihood is nothing more than a ploy on your part to save yourself."

"Save myself?" He fairly sputtered with indignation. He never sputtered and certainly not with indignation. What had this woman done to him? "From what?"

"From the absolute certainty that once in Egypt I will indeed be able to prove that I do know what I write about and you and your uncle will be forced to admit that you were wrong."

"Never!"

She leaned close. "*Absolute* certainty. Mr. Armstrong."

He stared down at her. God she was stubborn. And lovely in the starlight. And annoying. And shockingly appealing. And a fraud. And…

"I have the most absurd desire to kiss you, Mrs. Gordon," he said without thinking.

"And I have the not-at-all-absurd desire to smack you, Mr. Armstrong. Hard."

"Do I take that to mean you would not welcome my kiss."

"How very perceptive of you."

"Might I say that's a great pity?"

She stared at him for a long moment. "Yes, I believe you may." She nodded and turned to leave.

"Was that overly forward of me?" he called after her.

"Yes," she said over her shoulder.

"And yet I do not regret it."

She paused at the door. "Good."

"What do you mean *good*?" he called after her but the door was already closing behind her.

What on earth had come over him? He turned back to the railing, braced his hands on the cool metal and stared out into the night. He asked to kiss her! He'd never *asked* a woman if he could kiss her before. It had never been necessary to ask permission. And Sidney Gordon was not at all the type of woman that usually attracted him. Perhaps this was the kind of thing that happened when one spent all one's time in the company of a woman who was intelligent and amusing and far more attractive than she realized. It might be attributable to all that boundless enthusiasm. There was something about her that was appealing. Most appealing. But still—

"How did you manage to get her alone?" Corbin joined him at the railing. "I've been trying for days."

"Have you?" Harry had no desire to discuss Sidney with the reporter.

"Indeed I have." Corbin chuckled. "She's quite fetching, don't you think?"

Harry shrugged. "I hadn't noticed."

"Come now. I daresay every man on this ship has noticed," Corbin said. "The woman is a breath of fresh spring air. And a talented writer as well. I don't think I've ever met anyone quite like her."

"Yes, well, she is unique."

"As are her companions." Corbin shuddered. "How did you manage to evade them?"

Obviously Corbin was not going to leave without an answer. "They're on the committee for tonight's masked ball. They were called away to deal with an unexpected problem. Something to do with a box of missing masks."

"They were talking about that earlier," Corbin said thoughtfully. "Lady Blodgett and the other ladies agreed they could not recall signing up for the committee."

"They are getting on in years. A certain amount of forgetfulness is to be expected."

Corbin stared. "This is your doing, isn't it? You signed them up and misplaced the masks."

Harry was not about to admit to anything but he couldn't hide a small, satisfied smile.

Corbin laughed. "Excellent, Armstrong. I wish I'd thought of it myself." He adopted a casual note. "So was your conversation successful? Did Mrs. Gordon make a complete confession?"

"Why do you ask?" He straightened and glanced at the reporter. "I thought your purpose was to write about the return of the Queen of the Desert to Egypt."

"It is and I disagree with your theory about her legitimacy entirely. I find her work most credible."

Harry snorted.

"But, I admit, I could be wrong. If I am, I want to know."

"I can't imagine your editor would be pleased with your attitude."

"The truth, Armstrong, is not always what we want to hear." Corbin paused. "If you're right about her, well, that's what I shall report. It's a far more interesting story, really. One that could well change a career."

"Oh?"

"Proving your assertion that Mrs. Gordon is a fraud is the kind of story that would be wasted on the *Messenger*. The kind of story that might get an enterprising reporter a position at a more impressive publication. *The Times* perhaps."

"But it would ruin her."

"As I said—the truth is often unpleasant but it is the truth nonetheless." Corbin shrugged. "I must admit I'm surprised by your concern. After all, you and your uncle started this."

"Yes, I suppose we did." And regretting it more and more.

"Are you reconsidering your position?"

"Not at all," he said curtly. "We shall be in Egypt in three days. Then we will know the validity of Mrs. Gordon's writing and you shall have your story. One way or the other."

"I have to admit—I do hope she's legitimate." Corbin gazed out at the star-filled sky. "She's witty and amusing and quite attractive in a subtle sort of way. Frankly, I find her enchanting. A successful writer would be an excellent match for a man like me."

"An ambitious man like you, you mean."

"I have always been fond of widows." Corbin grinned. "Her disproving your suspicions wouldn't be the best story—as stories go—but it wouldn't be a bad start toward working my way into her affections."

"You would use your story to curry favor with her?"

"I don't see why not, especially if it was the truth."

Harry stared at him for a long moment. He wasn't sure what to say or rather what he wanted to say. But the distinct need to protect Sidney from this man washed through him.

"I believe I shall return to the saloon now," he said and started toward the door.

"Excellent suggestion, Armstrong." Corbin followed behind. "Perhaps I can have another dance with the delightful Mrs. Gordon."

"Perhaps," Harry muttered. *Not if I reach her first.* Regardless of how they had left things, Harry was damned if he'd leave Sidney in Corbin's grasp. But the reporter was right—Sidney was delightful. Bloody hell, he'd grown to like her. Although his request for a kiss had shocked him nearly as much as it had her. What had she done to him?

The oddest battle waged within him. On one hand, Harry knew he was right about Sidney's stories and he was determined to prove it. On the other—his success would destroy her life. He'd be proved right but...

The real question now was whether or not it was worth it.

CHAPTER SEVEN

"WHAT PRECISELY ARE we looking for?" Gwen peered into the distance.

"Egypt," Effie said in a crisp manner. "Although I suspect all the flat, dull, brownish shoreline we've seen thus far is Egypt."

"It's rather underwhelming, isn't it?" Poppy said under her breath.

"You can't see anything yet." Sidney resisted the urge to bounce on her feet in eagerness. Harry was right. She was blatantly enthusiastic but she couldn't seem to help herself. Especially now that Egypt was within reach. "The coast of Egypt is flat, at least this part of it. We're watching for the first glimpse of the lighthouse."

They were not alone. Most of the passengers had gathered on this side of the steamer for the first sighting of the ancient city. They'd been told Alexandria would be in sight momentarily although Mr. Gilmore had warned the ladies there would not be much to see.

"But it's not the original lighthouse," Sidney added. "Not the one that was considered one of the seven wonders of the world. The Pharos of Alexandria collapsed centuries ago and some of it was then used in local building projects. It's a pity it didn't survive."

"What's a pity is that there isn't anything of interest to look at. I did expect travel to be a bit more exciting. Thus far, it's been rather tedious." Effie peered around. "One does wonder where Mr. Corbin is. He's always amusing."

For the most part—Sidney agreed. Daniel was indeed always amusing and quite charming. He had scarcely left their side throughout much of the voyage. His absence now was not at all bothersome but rather something of a relief. His attentions, while flattering, were also a shade unnerving. She had the oddest feeling that there was more to Daniel's attentiveness than might at first appear. It was probably no more than the nature of a reporter, a man used to ferreting out secrets. Sidney wasn't sure where Daniel was but Harry was standing farther down the railing. Either the crowd was such that he couldn't find a space near them or he was choosing to keep his distance. Wise of him really.

Sidney had told the ladies about Harry's absurd offer, but not about the kiss that didn't happen, and they agreed while his reasoning might be sound and they all needed to make a better effort to keep up Sidney's subterfuge, it was certainly not too late. Effie, Poppy and Gwen agreed as well that since none of them were used to this kind of deception, they would surely get better with practice.

She glanced in his direction and caught him staring back. He grinned in that smug way he had and tipped his hat. She nodded politely and pointedly turned her attention back to the passing shore. She'd made it clear since the night on deck that she preferred anyone's company to his.

Dear Lord, Sidney never imagined she'd spend days actively avoiding the man who could very nearly be the hero in her stories. Harry Armstrong certainly looked the part with all that golden, slightly unkempt hair, that perpetually shadowed firm jaw and those perceptive gray

eyes of his. Add to that the man was tall with exceptionally broad shoulders and he was exactly the man of her,
well, her writing at least if not her dreams. The embodi-
ment of Richard Weatherly, the hero in all her stories.
Millicent's occasional partner in her adventures and the
man who was trying to work his way into her heart even
if his numerous flaws tended to keep them apart. And
wasn't Sidney trying to be the heroine of her own story?

Pity that, unlike Richard, Harry was so often stuffy
and horribly arrogant. While he certainly did have any
number of flaws, it was obvious that stuffy at least was
not natural to him although she would not say the same
for arrogant. When a man absolutely refused to leave
your side for days on end, when he ate his meals with you
and vied for you to be his partner when you played silly
games, one could certainly get a good sense of his nature. She'd had glimpses of someone not quite so proper
now and again. A hint of something wildly wicked. It
was most exciting.

Sidney really didn't know men at all but she assumed
she was an excellent judge of human nature. After all,
she wrote about characters readers believed were real.
There was something about Harry—in spite of the fact
that he and his uncle were trying to ruin her life—that
made her think he was a good man. And amusing and adventurous and almost irresistible. Thank God she had her
friends to protect her. Or possibly it was a great shame.

The man had wanted to kiss her. Her. Sidney Honeywell, imagine that. Rather average, ordinary, passable
Sidney Honeywell. Who was neither beautiful nor plain
but somewhere in between. Perhaps a shade more toward
the pretty side which was probably no more than wish-
ful thinking. Although her mother had said her blue eyes

sparkled and her hair was the color of ripe lemons but that was the sort of thing a mother was supposed to say.

And apparently, Harry wasn't alone. She was garnering a pleasant bit of male attention from some of the unattached officers and passengers as well as Harry. It certainly did boost one's confidence and was enough to swell one's head if one was not sensible and cautious and reasonably intelligent. Although Harry's motives were obvious. Even so, there had been moments when he would laugh or go out of his way to be charming, or whisper some delightfully wry observation in her ear when one did wonder if there was more on his mind than proving he was right. And he had asked to kiss her.

He obviously didn't like the attention Daniel paid her. There was the most interesting look in his eyes when Daniel was doing something—kissing her hand or gazing into her eyes or giving her the most absurd sort of compliment—that had no doubt tempted any number of ladies. With his walnut-colored hair and brown eyes the man was exceptionally handsome. But his charm struck her as vaguely rehearsed or overly practiced and she had a niggling feeling that he was not to be completely trusted. Not that he had done anything at all to confirm what was no more than the vaguest of suspicions. Regardless, the ladies seemed to like him and they were certainly more experienced with the nature of men than she.

"Is that it?" Poppy fairly squealed with excitement.

The coast was no different than it had been a few moments ago—flat and unbroken by a hill or a rise, the surf breaking on an endless expanse of sand. Low buildings had appeared, their grayish-brown color blending with their surroundings, as if they were part of the land itself. And there, rising out of the dust, was the lighthouse. It was remarkably unremarkable and Sidney tried to ignore a momentary twinge of disappointment.

"It's extremely ordinary, isn't it?" Harry said beside her.

"It always is," she said coolly. "One cannot help but compare it to the legendary structure that once looked over the harbor." No sooner had the words left her mouth but the first sight she had long awaited came into view as no more than a faint point on the horizon but recognizable nonetheless. She caught her breath and struggled to remain collected. "But then of course, the commonplace appearance of the lighthouse is forgiven the moment one again sees Pompey's Pillar rising into the heavens." While not Egyptian but Roman in origin and therefore rather young as Egyptian antiquities went, the granite pillar was the iconic symbol of Alexandria—at least to Sidney. More than anything it said she was at long last in Egypt.

"You do realize it's not Egyptian?"

"I was just going to ask you the same thing." She set her shoulders and stared up at him. "What are you doing here?"

"I thought I would be remiss if I did not join my party to disembark." He paused. "And I wanted to apologize."

"And which of your many rude comments do you wish to apologize for?"

He chuckled. "There haven't been that many."

She raised a skeptical brow.

"I've been trying very hard to be a congenial traveling companion."

"You shall have to try harder."

"Believe me, I will." He hesitated then drew a breath. "I've been wanting to speak to you alone."

"We're not alone now."

"No, but a crowd is often as private as a closed room."

"What did you wish to say?"

He looked as if he had no idea what to say or perhaps how to say it. It was rather endearing. "I wanted to apologize."

"You said that." She studied him closely. He did appear reasonably contrite. "Very well, then. Given that we are indeed traveling companions, I accept your apology and suggest we say nothing further about it."

"Excellent." He breathed a sigh of relief. "I'm not sure what came over me. I can assure you, I have never asked a woman if I might kiss her before."

Behind her one of the ladies choked.

"Frankly, I've never had to." He grimaced. "It was an impulse on my part. I have no idea where it came from. I should not have presumed. And, well, I do apologize."

"For asking to kiss me?" she said slowly.

"Yes."

"And not for your condescending and insulting proposal?"

He stared. "My what?"

"Your offer to drop this challenge of your uncle's in return for my declaration that my stories are fictitious." She narrowed her eyes. "That's what I assumed you were apologizing for."

"Don't be absurd. That was an excellent idea and I think it foolish of you to disregard it."

"Then we have nothing further to talk about." She turned her attention to the harbor, the ship now approaching the dock. For this moment at least, she was entirely too annoyed with the man by her side to need to hide her excitement. Apparently, an annoying arrogant beast of a man did blunt one's enthusiasm. Even for a country one had always yearned to see.

For a lengthy moment he said nothing and then sighed in a long-suffering manner. "Do you wish for me to arrange our transport to the railway station for the trip to Cairo?"

"Because I have never done it before?" she said sharply.

"No." His jaw tightened. "Because it's the sort of thing a gentleman does. It will be much more efficient if one of us handles this rather than everyone going in different directions at once."

"And leaves us free to enjoy our first moments in Egypt." Gwen stepped in front of her. "My, that is efficient, Mr. Armstrong, and what a generous offer." She thrust a packet at him. "Here are our landing papers and railway tickets."

"And you'll see to the luggage as well?" Sidney asked. Her trunk and her wardrobe were new and she preferred not to have her luggage misplaced. She'd also brought her writing materials, the story she was currently working on and her grandmother's final journal as both a talisman and a comfort.

"Yes, of course." Harry looked as if he wished to say something else but thought better of it.

"And don't forget to include Mr. Corbin in the arrangements. He is a member of our party after all," Effie said firmly. Sidney was not the only one who had noticed Harry's aversion to the reporter.

"I would never forget Corbin." A cool note sounded in Harry's voice. "Although it would be helpful if he made an appearance."

"Right behind you, Armstrong." Daniel's cordial tone rang over the crowd. "Good day, ladies. Sorry for the delay. I was querying some of the other passengers as to their plans. Background information you know. More details for my stories."

"It appears nearly everyone on board is a tourist." A faint note of derision sounded in Harry's voice.

"As is Mrs. Higginbotham, Mrs. Fitzhew-Wellmore and myself." Gwen slanted Harry a chastising glance.

"Indeed." Harry had the decency to look a bit chagrined.

"Mr. Armstrong has kindly offered to see to all the docking and transportation arrangements." Poppy beamed. "Wasn't that gracious of him?"

"Gracious and appreciated." Daniel grinned. "Never having been to Egypt before I've no doubt I would be completely lost. Even better, that allows me to escort the four loveliest passengers on board off the ship." He held out his arm. "Mrs. Gordon, would you do me the honor?"

Sidney glanced at Harry. While his expression was pleasant enough, his eyes were icy and his jaw tight. Good. "I would be delighted."

As much as she had no desire to cling to Daniel's arm, a few moments later she did just that. After a cursory official inspection, hordes of porters swarmed onto the ship in their voluminous trousers and turbans or red fez hats with black tassels, chattering in assorted languages and gesturing in an alarming manner, apparently in an attempt to earn employment. Harry handled them with an ease and competence she should have anticipated but came as a pleasant surprise nonetheless.

Sidney wasn't sure what she expected the moment she stepped off the ship and onto the ancient soil of Egypt. It was not substantially different from any of the previous stops. But this was Egypt. This was the world she'd read about and studied and lost herself in. She was hard-pressed not to grin with delight at nearly everything.

Everywhere she looked was a new scene straight from a book or a painting or a photograph. Here were travelers and merchants and seamen in exotic dress and assorted skin colors all speaking in languages both vaguely familiar and completely unknown. Stacked mountains of cotton bales waited to be loaded onto ships. Roped lines of camels and donkeys led by robed handlers wound their way through the composed chaos. This was the first time she'd seen camels outside of a zoological garden and it was hard not to squeal with excitement.

And there was something in the very air, not a scent exactly—the air smelled little different from any port they'd visited—but a knowledge perhaps. Subtle and ancient and elusive and yet there nonetheless. A knowledge that reached deep inside her and wrapped around her very soul like an unanticipated gift or an unexpected compliment or a lover's touch. She ignored the odd thought. She'd certainly never had a lover and why the idea came to mind made no sense at all. Although it was indeed an intriguing notion.

This was Egypt. This was where man had walked and prospered and built a great civilization thousands of years ago. And left grand treasures and remarkable monuments to be buried by the unrelenting sand for people like her grandparents to rediscover and celebrate and bring the ancients back to life.

They made their way through the examination at the customhouse—which involved little more than providing their names and a slight charge for the baggage. Harry was impressively efficient there too and in no time at all they were divided into two cabs and on their way to the train station. Sidney pointedly avoided his carriage, choosing to ride with Effie and Gwen instead.

"He asked to kiss you?" Effie said the moment the cab rolled off. "What nerve of the man."

"Well, he did ask, Effie," Gwen noted. "Most men would have kissed first and asked later or apologized later, depending on the circumstances."

"And what was your answer?" Effie asked.

"I said no, of course." Sidney huffed. "Imagine the audacity of the man, thinking I would kiss him simply because he asked."

Her refusal at the time was automatic. Only afterward did she consider what it might have been like to be kissed by Harry Armstrong. Or any man for that matter as she'd never had the opportunity to be kissed before. But to be kissed by Harry…it was a surprisingly exciting idea. One she couldn't quite get out of her head.

"But he did apologize," Gwen said thoughtfully. "And quite nicely too I thought. I don't believe I have yet to see Mr. Armstrong the least bit disconcerted—"

Effie sniffed. "As he is not used to admitting when he's wrong."

"—and I thought it rather sweet."

"He did appear somewhat less arrogant than usual," Sidney conceded.

Gwen considered her for a moment. "I thought he sounded most sincere."

"Regardless of how he sounded, I did accept his apology and we needn't discuss it further," Sidney said in an unusually firm tone and turned her attention to the passing scene.

Alexandria was unexpected in its European appearance. They could have been anywhere really. At each cross street, she strained for a glimpse of anything of note. Sidney ignored a distinct sense of disappointment and turned her expectations toward Cairo.

The rail trip itself offered tantalizing peeks of the Egypt she anticipated. They traveled past Lake Mareotis, with flocks of waterfowl and waters rising up the embankment and lapping nearly to the rails themselves. They passed villages with mud brick houses broken by occasional minarets and domed cupolas. Modern iron bridges crossed the Rosetta and Damietta branches of the Nile. The graceful curved sails of feluccas floated on the river and the canals in the distance.

A few hours south of Alexandria they entered the vast, flat plains of the delta with fields of cotton and other crops broken by canals and dykes. Sidney caught glimpses of palaces and ruins of Egyptian or Greek or Roman origins. And shortly before they reached Cairo, the great pyramids of Giza rose in the distance, a vision of an empire long lost to the ages and the unrelenting desert sands. It was enough to bring tears of appreciation to one's eyes.

Nearly six hours after they'd disembarked from the steamer, Sidney stood at long last before Shepheard's Hotel. The others went up the broad steps into the imposing structure but Sidney couldn't help but pause to stare up at the legendary inn with its raised terrace and gleaming stone facade. Her grandmother had written fondly of Shepheard's saying if one sat on the elevated terrace long enough, one would see the entire world pass by. Sidney had included the hotel in her stories but, while it was indeed grand, aside from the ancient stone sphinxes flanking the entrance doors, it was also somewhat plain and not quite the dazzling travelers' palace Sidney had envisioned.

"It's different than I expected," she murmured.

"Than you remembered, you mean," Harry's voice sounded beside her.

"Yes." Even when she thought she was alone, the blasted man was right there, recording every mistake to support whatever decision he ultimately reached. Why, he probably had a notebook in which he wrote any error she might make. "Memory is not always as accurate as one might hope. And it has been some time since I was last there."

"*Quite* some time."

She cast him a sharp glance but he did appear sincere. "One expects things to be as one remembers them. Pity they aren't."

He paused. "It's not your memory at fault. The entire hotel was torn down and rebuilt shortly after I left Egypt."

"That explains it." She resisted the urge to thank him even though offering that information was rather nice of him.

"Shall we go in?" He offered his arm.

"That's not necessary, you know. I am more than capable of walking into the hotel by myself."

"I have no doubt of that."

"Thank you, Harry." She took his arm and wondered if he realized she was grateful for more than his escort.

They climbed the steps and doormen flanking the imposing entry bowed and opened the doors in unison a second before they reached it. They stepped into the grand entrance hall and lobby although *grand* truly was an understatement. Now, this was the Shepheard's she'd imagined.

Harry chuckled. "They've certainly changed a lot."

"Indeed they have," she said softly.

Massive stone columns topped with capitals carved to look like palm fronds soared to a ceiling a good two stories overhead. A grand stairway swept upward to the next level guarded by bronze, life-size statues of dancing girls. With potted palms in ornate urns, patterned carpets and intricately tiled floors, it was the epitome of the Egypt she had long seen in her mind's eye. A pharaoh would have been right at home. If he didn't mind sharing his home with a sizable crowd of foreigners, most of them English or American, with German, French and other nationalities represented as well.

"Mrs. Gordon." A distinguished, elegant gentleman hurried toward her, Gwen and the others a scant step behind him. He reached Sidney and immediately took her hand. "I cannot tell you how delighted I was when Lady Blodgett informed me you were a member of her party. It has been a very long time."

"Entirely too long," Sidney said with a weak smile.

"You remember, Mr. Chalmers, of course," Gwen said. "The manager of the hotel."

"Goodness, I would never forget Mr. Chalmers." She beamed at the manager, wondering how on earth Gwen managed this. "It's wonderful to be back."

"I do hope you find the newly rebuilt hotel to your liking. We've made a number of improvements in our efforts to make your stay memorable." Pride shone in the man's eyes. "We are the only hotel in Egypt—indeed, in all of Africa—to be lit entirely by electricity, at great expense I might add. There is as well a telephone on every floor."

"Most impressive, Mr. Chalmers," Sidney said, glancing around.

"You'll find the food vastly improved as well. The kitchens are now under the direction of a French chef."

He leaned toward her and lowered his voice. "I will admit that the quality of the food here has in the past been the subject of some complaint."

Harry snorted and then tried to disguise it with a cough.

Mr. Chalmers's gaze shot to him. "Mr. Armstrong?" Surprise colored his voice. "You're back?"

Harry chuckled. "Good to see you, Chalmers."

The manager's eyes narrowed. "I was not aware you were a member of Mrs. Gordon's party."

"And now you are." Harry smiled pleasantly.

"Nor did I expect to see you again so soon." The manager's obvious training in hospitality kept his voice level but something that might well have been dislike shone in his eyes.

"Come now, Chalmers," Harry said smoothly. "It's only been a year after all. I've never been away from Egypt that long before."

"And we feared you had gone for good." While the manager's tone was pleasant enough, his jaw clenched.

Sidney glanced at Daniel who watched the exchange closely. Obviously, she was not the only one curious about the hotel manager's reaction to Harry's presence.

"How could I possibly stay away?" Harry grinned.

Chalmers pointedly turned his attention back to Sidney. "I regret that I cannot personally see you to your rooms but I have other matters to attend to." He raised his hand in an imperious wave. At once, another gentleman appeared by his side. "I shall leave you in the capable hands of Mr. Durning. He will show you to your rooms and your luggage will follow immediately."

"Thank you, Mr. Chalmers." Without warning, the sheer excitement of being at Shepheard's in Cairo bubbled up inside her. "And might I say how truly pleased I am to be here again."

"It's I who is pleased, Mrs. Gordon," Mr. Chalmers said. "I can't tell you the number of guests who have mentioned your book and its favorable depiction of Shepheard's. We will be forever grateful."

"Mrs. Gordon? Ladies? Sirs?" Mr. Durning stepped forward. "If you would be so good as to follow me."

"Before you go, Mr. Armstrong," Chalmers said, "if I might have a word. In my office if you please."

"I thought you might." Harry glanced at the others. "There is no better way to be introduced to Egypt than by having tea on the terrace at Shepheard's. Not for Mrs. Gordon, of course," he added. "She is well acquainted with Cairo but for the rest of you it should be quite entertaining. Ladies, Corbin, I shall join you then." Harry nodded and accompanied Chalmers across the grand hall.

"Isn't that interesting?" Daniel said quietly.

"Do you think so?" As much as Sidney agreed with Daniel, she thought it best not to feed his curiosity. "It struck me as being nothing more than casual acquaintances meeting one another again."

"You're probably right." Daniel cast a last speculative look at Harry and the manager and then favored her with his most brilliant smile. Goodness, didn't the man get tired of smiling like that all the time? She certainly would. He took her arm and followed Durning and the ladies. "While I'm looking forward to sleeping on dry land again, I'm fairly confident my room will not be quite as nice as yours. Mr. Cadwallender does not provide first-class accommodations for mere reporters."

"Oh, I'm certain someday you'll be more than a mere reporter," she said lightly.

"I intend to be, Sidney." He chuckled. "Have no doubt of that."

Her rooms were everything Sidney could have asked for—at once European and yet distinctly Egyptian in style with elaborately carved furnishings, ornate canopied bed, comfortable chairs, luxurious brightly colored fabrics, and located conveniently close to the toilets and lavatories. Her suite consisted of a large drawing room with deep oriental fringed carpets woven in intricate, native designs adjoining a bed chamber just large enough to hold the bed with an arched entry bounded by curtains to close it off should privacy be needed.

Sidney hurried to freshen up and then joined the other ladies at the wicker tables on the front terrace overlooking the street. Harry was right—this was an excellent spot to see much of what Cairo had to offer. Donkeys and their handlers stood waiting to be hired. Monkeys capered about their owners' feet hoping to charm visitors out of a few coins. Street performers of every kind vied with passing merchants eager to offer an amulet from the time of the pharaohs or glass beads from the tombs of ancient princes or painting on papyrus claimed to be ancient.

"Dare I ask why Mr. Chalmers greeted me as if I were a long-lost friend?" Sidney asked as soon as they had been served.

"Because I took the opportunity to mention to him that you had once been a frequent guest and surely he remembered you. And if he didn't…" Gwen smiled in an overly sweet manner. "Well, it might be in the best interests of the hotel if he acted as if he did."

"It helped that the request came from Lady Blodgett."

Effie grinned. "Apparently, hotel managers are just as awed by titles as everyone else who doesn't have one."

"And we mentioned your writing as well," Poppy added. "How terribly popular it was. And what a shame it would be if Shepheard's was not depicted with the same kindness you've shone it in the past."

Sidney stared. "You're enjoying this deception, aren't you?"

Effie snorted. "Good Lord, yes."

"The three of you are really quite astonishing." Sidney shook her head. "It had only been a vague suspicion before we left England, prompted by the willingness with which you were all prepared to carry out this charade, but I'd always thought that there was a touch of something not completely forthright about you."

"Thank you, dear." Gwen sipped her tea.

"Being unquestionably honest and unbearably upright is not nearly as enjoyable as one might think." Poppy smiled in an overly mischievous manner. "Oh, there's a certain virtuous satisfaction I suppose but even then it does become dreadfully dull."

"Besides if one is loosening one's moral corset strings in the furtherance of a good cause, well…" Effie shrugged. "I have absolutely no difficulty doing what must be done. Nor do I have any difficulty relishing it."

"I am glad my dilemma has some redeeming benefits," Sidney said wryly.

"Some?" Gwen raised a brow. "I daresay it's more than some."

"You—we—are in Egypt, Sidney," Effie said. "Egypt, the place you've always wanted to visit. The fabled land you have studied and written of and dreamed about."

"Why, we've already seen camels, and monkeys and

all of this." Poppy gestured in a wide wave at the street encompassing the passing show and a man with a stuffed crocodile on his head. "You never see anything like this in Bloomsbury."

"It's already most exciting and we haven't even truly started yet," Gwen said. "According to the schedule the ever efficient Miss Granville prepared for us, tomorrow you lead us on a tour of Cairo and the day after we head to the pyramids."

"Oh my, that will be exciting. I recall…"

The pyramids. A shiver of excitement raced through Sidney. She'd seen them from the train and caught glimpses of the ancient structures as they'd driven through Cairo but they were distant and indistinct and more an illusion than anything real. Harry had surely seen the pyramids. Why, he had commented on them on board ship. Still, anyone could make an observation without actually having seen the object in question. She certainly had.

"Sidney?"

One did have to wonder exactly how familiar Harry was with Egypt anyway. Other than Mr. Cadwallender saying Harry had spent time in his youth in Egypt, which apparently was not accurate as he had stated quite clearly to Mr. Chalmers he had been gone a year, and Daniel's reference to him as being well-known among Egyptologists—whatever that meant—she really knew nothing about him at all. She and the ladies had been so busy guarding against him learning too much about her, they had failed to learn anything of importance about him.

"Sidney!" Effie said sharply and Sidney's gaze jumped

to the older woman. "You're anywhere but here. What are you thinking?"

"Does it strike you, any of you, that we don't know anything about Mr. Armstrong?"

"Of course we do," Gwen said. "We know he's the earl's nephew."

"And?"

"And…" Gwen's brow furrowed. "I hadn't really noticed but…"

"Now that you mention it," Effie said, "I believe you're right."

"I can only think of one thing he's said about himself." And that was regarding his tradition of champagne at sunrise on board ship. "The man doesn't talk about himself at all."

"Rather refreshing really," Poppy said. "Daniel talks of very little other than himself."

"Aren't we doing much the same thing?" Gwen winced. "Haven't we all avoided saying anything about Sidney's life in an effort to minimize any sort of mistake. We can hardly fault him for following suit."

"Yes, but we're doing it for a noble purpose." Effie's eyes narrowed. "One does have to wonder what Mr. Armstrong's purpose is. What the man is hiding."

"Don't any of you want to know why the manager wished to see Mr. Armstrong alone?" Sidney's gaze circled the table.

"That was curious." Gwen nodded.

"I daresay it's probably not the least bit significant." Poppy shrugged. "No doubt a question about passports or luggage or something of that nature."

Sidney shook her head. "Did you see the look on the

manager's face? I've written that look. It does not say welcome but rather 'oh no, not you.'"

Gwen frowned. "Do you think Mr. Armstrong is in some kind of trouble?"

"I suspect Mr. Armstrong *is* trouble," Poppy said thoughtfully. "And not simply because he's trying to prove his uncle's charges about Sidney. Every now and then, on board ship, there was a hint, a vague suggestion..."

"Regardless, I daresay Mr. Armstrong can take care of himself." Effie met Sidney's gaze. "I suggest we ask Daniel what he knows—or can discover—about Mr. Armstrong's background."

"Yes, but do be discreet." Sidney hesitated but her friends should be aware of her concerns. "I realize he works for Mr. Cadwallender and one could say we are therefore on the same side but I'm not sure I completely trust him."

"Thank goodness." Poppy sighed with relief. "We don't trust him either. He's entirely too—"

"Charming," Gwen said.

"Amusing," Effie added. "As if he's trying too hard."

"I could also casually, mind you, see what I might be able to find out from Mr. Chalmers." Gwen smiled in a distinctly wicked manner. "He was quite helpful earlier and if indeed he is not Mr. Armstrong's friend, might be more than willing to divulge all sorts of interesting secrets. As for Mr. Armstrong—"

"I will handle Mr. Armstrong myself," Sidney said firmly. The man was hiding something. She didn't doubt it for a moment. Her deception was inadvertent—she hadn't intended for any of this to happen. His, however, was deliberate.

Who exactly was Harry Armstrong and what was he hiding?

CHAPTER EIGHT

"HARRY." CHALMERS SAT behind a solid desk in an office somewhat more ornate than one would have expected from a hotel manager, his eyes narrowed in an intimidating manner.

"Leo." Harry settled in the chair in front of the desk—a hard-backed, uncomfortable seat no doubt calculated to create the most unease in anyone who had to sit in it and face the displeasure of the manager of Shepheard's Hotel.

"Actually, I prefer Leonard now."

"A new name to go along with the refined accent?"

"You noticed that, did you?"

"It's hard to miss." Harry snorted. "You sound more properly British than the queen."

"Thank you. I've been working on it. One must keep up appearances when one is the manager of the finest hotel in Egypt."

"You've come up in the world, *Leonard*." Harry studied him curiously. "And rather quickly I'd say. When I left you were nothing more than a night desk clerk dealing in phony antiquities and anything else anyone might want."

"A thing of the past, old man." Leo waved off the comment. "I have discovered the benefits of a reputable life. I am a reformed man."

"And you're now the manager?"

"I can hear the skepticism in your voice, Harry, but

advancements come rapidly when one is clever and determined and makes oneself indispensable." Leo smiled in an overly satisfied manner. "The previous manager knew potential when he saw it and when he retired, he recommended me for his position."

"Retired?" Harry raised a brow.

"No need to look at me like that." Leo huffed. "Nothing untoward happened to him. I quite liked him, by the way. The man simply retired to a small village near Bristol. I heard he became reacquainted with a childhood sweetheart and is now exceptionally happy. It has all worked out nicely for him."

"And for you as well."

Leo grinned. "Definitely for me."

"And this is all…" Harry searched for the right word. "Legitimate?"

"I know you find it hard to believe." Leo chuckled. "I find it hard to believe myself but I quite like running an establishment like this. It's, oh, challenging."

"And lucrative."

Leo grinned. "Extremely."

"I can imagine."

"It appears you've come up in the world as well." Leo nodded toward the door. "You're traveling in interesting company. Old ladies and famous authors and even a reporter. What are you up to, Harry?"

"Not that it's any of your concern but nothing that isn't entirely legitimate. You could call it a wager of sorts." Harry's dealings had been more or less legitimate for quite some time but some reputations never truly faded—often as much a benefit as a curse. "I'm here as nothing more than a tourist."

Leo laughed. "Forgive me if I find that hard to believe."

"Believe what you want." Harry paused. "So you've met Mrs. Gordon here before?"

"Mrs. Gordon has long been a valued patron of Shepheard's."

"When was she last here?"

"Harry, my boy." Leo shook his head. "Privacy and discretion are a hotel's stock in trade. I cannot reveal the comings and goings of my guests, many of whom are willing to be most generous to ensure their secrets remain secret."

Harry frowned. "Did those old ladies pay you?"

Genuine shock widened the manager's eyes. "Of course not." Indignation rang in his voice. "My standards may be low but they are not nonexistent. I would never take money from elderly ladies, especially those who don't look as if they can afford it."

There was a time, not so long ago, when Leo Chalmers would do exactly that. Still, Harry could scarcely hold the man's past against him given his own circumstances.

"I'm not the same man I used to be. I am completely respectable now." Leo grinned. "For the most part."

"Congratulations. As much as I have enjoyed catching up—" Harry rose to his feet "—I should like to be seen to my room now."

"I'm afraid you missed the point." Leo shook his head regretfully. "This was not a strictly social meeting."

"Oh?"

"Perhaps you recall a little gathering here on the night before you left Egypt."

"Vaguely." Harry sat back down. "In the bar, wasn't it?"

"It was quite a party."

From what little he did recall—it was a great deal of fun. "It was at that."

"Unfortunately, there was a considerable amount of damage as well."

"Was there?" Upon reflection, perhaps there was although his memory of that night—his and Ben's last in Egypt—was unsurprisingly indistinct.

Leo opened a drawer in his desk, pulled out a document and slid it across the desk toward Harry.

"What is that?" Silly to ask really as he did have a fairly good idea.

"Your bill."

"You keep it in your desk?" Harry said lightly and picked up the invoice. It was impressive and probably padded more than a little.

"I am an eternal optimist." Leo leaned back in his chair and considered Harry. "Frankly, I had thought Deane, or should I say Lord Benjamin Deane—"

Harry adopted a noncommittal expression but his stomach twisted. Ben's family connections had never been a particular secret and had in fact come in handy now and again, but he hadn't used his courtesy title as a rule. And the last person Ben would have wanted to know that he was the son of a marquess was Leo Chalmers.

"—would reappear in Cairo sooner or later." Leo studied him curiously. "I wasn't sure about you."

"And yet, here I am." Harry waved the bill at him. "What do you expect me to do about this?"

"I expect you to pay it."

"Why would I do that?" Harry asked mildly. "The damage was not entirely my doing." Although, it was not out of the realm of possibility that a significant amount of it was indeed his doing. He had the faintest memory of a chandelier and a large statue... He and Ben were saying goodbye to Egypt and in many ways to their youth.

Walter was gone, Cairo was filling more and more with tourists, Ben's family was becoming increasingly insistent that he return to England, and Harry had inherited an unexpected title. It was time, past time really, to accept the responsibilities they had long avoided. That night in the bar at Shepheard's both men said goodbye to the past even if the details of exactly how those farewells were given were decidedly sketchy.

"Besides." Harry dropped the invoice back on the desk and slid it toward Leo. "The entire hotel was torn down shortly after I left. One could say, I gave you an excellent start on the demolition. Why, you should probably pay me."

"Excellent point, Harry." Leo smirked. "But I want that money. And as much as I would hate to bother those sweet old ladies, I would have no such hesitation when it comes to the charming Mrs. Gordon. I suspect, given your eminently proper appearance, she has no idea of your past. I daresay there are stories of your years in Egypt that would not paint you in the best light. It could be quite scandalous for her to be in the company of a man like yourself, regardless of how many elderly ladies she's surrounded by. I imagine it might hinder whatever your plans are as well."

"I wonder what she would do?" It was an interesting thought.

"We can find out."

Bloody hell. The old Harry wouldn't have cared and would never have allowed himself to be susceptible to Leo's blackmail. The new Earl of Brenton apparently was neither as daring or as impulsive. It was damnably hard to try to be a new man when the old one was so much more enjoyable. "That won't be necessary." He pulled out his letter of credit and accompanying documents from his waistcoat pocket and handed them to Leo.

"And a passport as well, if you please."

Harry tightened his jaw and handed over the passport.

Leo's gaze shifted from the documents to the passport and back. He glanced up at Harry. "Apparently, it's my turn to ask you—is this legitimate?"

"I'm afraid so."

"How in the name of all that's holy did this happen?"

"Blame the complexities of inheritance." Harry shrugged. "Believe me, it was as much a surprise to me as it is to you."

"Isn't this interesting." Leo studied him curiously. "If I recall correctly, you've never been particularly fond of men with titles. I believe I once heard you say something about men who did nothing to earn their positions being no better than—"

"Yes, yes." Harry cut him off sharply. "I might have said something like that."

"Deane agreed with you. Imagine my astonishment, when my efforts to track you down revealed that he was the son of a marquess. The youngest son but a son nonetheless. Pity, I didn't learn that sooner. It might have been quite useful."

"Deane didn't use his title while in Egypt, nor do I."

"Why not?" Leo asked. "I would."

"Yet another example of the differences between us."

Leo laughed. "Good God, Harry. You're still as noble as ever."

"Are we done?"

Leo nodded. "I'll withdraw the appropriate amount and return these to you." He paused. "My lord."

"With a receipt, of course."

"Of course."

Harry stood. "I assume they'll be a bill as well for your silence. I prefer no one here know of my title."

"Not this time." Leo chuckled. "I rather like the idea of an earl being in my debt."

"I knew you would."

Leo skirted around him and opened the door. "Do have a pleasant afternoon, sir. And should you need anything, there is a bell in your room. You merely have to ring for service."

"You really are enjoying this, aren't you?"

"Actually, I have never enjoyed anything more." He shook his head. "There comes a point in every man's life where he realizes looking over his shoulder every minute is not as much fun as it once was. I still have my amusements and one can always use extra funds but yes, I am content with my life."

"I suppose one can't ask for anything more than that," Harry said and took his leave, but Leo's words lingered in his mind. What would it take for Harry Armstrong to be content with his life?

HARRY SAT WITH a glass of excellent Scottish whisky in the newly built Long Bar, which was considerably nicer than the old bar. Better yet—in this bar too, women were not allowed. Joining the ladies on the terrace could wait and he had a lot to think about.

If he had needed further evidence of the truth about Sidney—and he didn't—it had been quite neatly supplied to him. If Sidney hadn't been to Egypt in years, she couldn't possibly know Leo. Their meeting in the lobby was no doubt orchestrated by one of her friends. Probably Lady Blodgett or possibly the dragon. Neither of whom had the slightest hesitation about invoking the names of their dead husbands to get what they wanted and, from what they'd said, Sir Charles and Colonel Higginbotham as well as Mr. Fitzhew-Wellmore had all spent time in Egypt. It was a rather significant mistake on the part of the ladies.

Still, Leo hadn't confirmed anything. And Sidney would have a plausible explanation why she had greeted the hotel manager as if she knew him. She was excellent at that sort of prevarication. No, he needed solid, indisputable evidence.

And then what?

Harry really hadn't considered what would happen once he had his proof. He had a vague idea in the back of his mind, which went no further than pointing an accusing finger at her and saying in his best triumphant tone, "Aha! I knew it all along!" Oh, his book would be published, Walter's memory would be preserved, Sidney's membership in the Antiquities Society would be rescinded, she'd be humiliated and her livelihood would be destroyed. None of which brought the tiniest bit of satisfaction at the moment. He was, in fact, somewhat ashamed of himself. He'd let some odd sense of pride and jealousy dictate his actions and had leaped into this debacle without thinking it through. In many ways, he was almost as despicable as the villains from Sidney's stories. He was better than that. Or at least he used to be. In spite of a past filled with less than completely legitimate exploits, overindulgence in drink and more women than he could remember, he'd always considered himself an honorable sort. He was beginning to think there was little honorable about the challenge he was engaged in now.

If he unmasked Sidney's deception before they returned to London, Corbin would be thrilled, which was enough of a reason not to do it. He had no desire to assist the reporter's career. Nor did he have any desire to destroy Sidney's. Not anymore. And any exposé by Corbin's revealing Sidney's lack of experience in Egypt would do exactly that. Interesting how when one became better acquainted with an adversary, one's perspective changed. Did Harry really want to start his own writing career on the ashes of Sidney's? Walter would think him an ass. Harry never should have started this. Apparently rejection did strange things to a man. Until he had submitted his writing, he couldn't remember ever being rejected before. But he'd taken her writing as a personal affront. To all that he and Ben had experienced. To Walter's memory. Absurd, of course, but a fact nonetheless.

Perhaps the best thing to do was nothing, at least not yet. There was the slimmest possibility that he was wrong about her. He wouldn't wager on it and there had been rare occasions in his life when he'd been wrong. Why not allow Sidney to continue her efforts to prove her credibility? See just how far this farce would go. As she seemed to know everything there was to know about Egypt she was no doubt delighted to be here in person. Besides— continuing this game with her might be rather fun. Sidney was clever and quick and verbal sparring with her was more enjoyable than anything he'd done in years. In spite of her ruse, she was, well, *genuine* was the only word he could think of. It made no sense given the circumstances but there it was. Sidney was a challenge and he'd never backed down from a challenge. This would be the perfect chance to get to know her better and perhaps, the more she knew of him, the better she would like him.

Not that that was important although, now that he

thought about it, he did want her to like him. He liked her. Quite a lot really. He couldn't remember ever having *liked* a woman before. Oh, he enjoyed women, he appreciated women, he considered women one of the more delightful things in life. But this *liking* a woman—this was something new. It would be foolish of him not to see where this might lead.

Harry had never been the sort of man to sit back and let events unfold as they may. He wasn't entirely sure that he could. But then he wasn't entirely sure about much regarding his life at the moment. He never thought he'd envy Leo Chalmers but perhaps he did. After a life of schemes and illegalities Leo seemed to have found a place for himself. Harry had a place—he was merely unclear as to what it was. His old life didn't fit him anymore. His new position as earl was not entirely comfortable. He was wagering that writing about his life was where his future truly lay. He just needed something—or someone—to occupy his time and his mind. To give his life purpose.

What if that someone was Sidney Gordon?

It was an intriguing idea. Of all his many adventures, she might well be the most enjoyable. Or the most dangerous. He'd never risked his heart before. He wasn't sure he was risking it now but there was something elusive and enticing and altogether irresistible here. He suspected if he didn't play this out—he would regret it. Harry Armstrong was not fond of regrets.

Sidney Gordon could well be the woman he could live with for the rest of his life. It was a sobering thought. He'd never so much as considered one woman for the rest of his life. But life had changed and he was trying to change with it. That too was a sobering thought. One that even fine Scottish whisky couldn't banish.

CHAPTER NINE

"I THINK IT looks quite…enjoyable." Poppy squared her shoulders. "And doing something you've never done before is the very definition of the adventure to be found in travel."

"I'm not sure I expected adventure to have four legs and glare at me." Effie stared with cautious horror at the donkeys lined up on the street in front of Shepheard's. The diminutive animals really were rather enchanting with bridles and reins bedecked with colorful cords and dangling bells. Although perhaps not to Effie. "There do seem to be an abundance of cabs. Perhaps we should take one of those?"

"I've never been on a donkey before." Gwen glanced at Sidney. "Wouldn't a carriage be more appropriate?"

"Not in Cairo," Sidney said firmly. "This is the only way to see the Arabian quarters of the city. It's next on the list of sights Miss Granville prepared for us and one of my own personal favorite parts of Cairo."

"Mine as well," Harry added.

Sidney continued. "There's no better way to get a true feel for Egypt than the Arabian quarters and we must manage to see as much as possible in a limited amount of time as Mr. Cadwallender has only given us two weeks in Egypt."

Effie cast an annoyed look at Harry. "Will that be long

enough for you to give up your foolish charge about Mrs.
Gordon's veracity?"

"I should think that will be more than sufficient,"
Harry said pleasantly. The man was becoming oblivi-
ous to Effie's continued disregard and today had been as
amiable a companion as anyone could want. "Although, I
must confess, I regret having a mere two weeks to spend
in such delightful company." He cast Effie a winning
smile. For a moment, Sidney could have sworn his teeth
flashed in the sun in the manner of any good fictional
hero.

"Humph." Effie turned her attention back to the donkey but it was obvious that she was not completely im-
mune to Harry's efforts.

Harry hadn't once complained about the nature of their
schedule which did seem to Sidney to be relentless. Still,
she had studied guidebooks, including one provided by
Shepheard's, and was prepared to lead her growing band
of elderly ladies and donkey boys wherever they wished
to go, as long as where they wished to go was on Miss
Granville's schedule of sights. Sidney would hate to have
to negotiate Cairo without Miss Granville's sterling rec-
ommendations in hand.

They had begun the day at the Citadel high on a hill
in the center of the city, the minarets and domes of the
mosques within its confines towering over Cairo, as if
aspiring to the heavens themselves. The fortress was built
some seven hundred years ago to defend the city from
the onslaught of Christian crusaders and was said to have
been constructed in part with stones from the small pyramids at Giza, which Sidney did think was something of
a shame. Still, one did have to credit the Egyptians for
making use of what was at hand.

Within the confines of the Citadel, they visited the Mosque of Muhammad Ali Pasha with its multiple domes, fountains and courtyards. The ladies stared in admiration at the endless hanging lamps and magnificent carpets while also privately speculating if similar items might be found at the markets and wouldn't something like that look glorious in London? The mosque's minarets were considered a landmark of Cairo that could be seen from the pyramids and beyond.

The view alone was well worth the visit. One could see all of Cairo, minarets from the more than four hundred mosques in the city rising above the rooftops. In the distance, beyond the confines of modern civilization, the pyramids shimmered in the sunlight, an eternal reminder of the past glories of Egypt and ancient man.

They had then strolled through the lush plantings, ponds and grottos of the Ezbekieh Gardens. It was a lovely way to pause for a moment in their determined pace. The weather was nearly perfect and cooler than Sidney had expected but then it was early February. Everything she'd read recommended winter as the best time of year to visit. She couldn't imagine how unpleasant it would be to travel Egypt in the height of the summer. They returned to the hotel briefly for a quick lunch. In spite of their age, the older ladies were eager to continue. After all, they were now headed toward the Arabian quarters and the souk, the bazaars of the city. Effie, Gwen and Poppy could scarcely wait to explore the offerings in the quarter and the bargains to be found. Sidney and Harry had both warned them to purchase with caution, especially anything deemed antiquated or historical, as there were often wares of a fraudulent nature, probably made in Europe, and passed off as genuine Egyptian antiquities.

Harry had insisted on hiring a dragoman to guide them through the quarters although Sidney asserted she was more than capable of finding her way around Cairo.

"Surely you don't object, Mr. Armstrong," Gwen had said. "Why, what better way for our dear Mrs. Gordon to prove her knowledge of Egypt than by showing us those places she knows and loves?"

Still, Sidney's protest was halfhearted at best and no one was more relieved than Sidney when she and the ladies graciously agreed to the services of the guide—Hamad, a man even shorter than Sidney, of indeterminate age with coffee-colored skin and a relentless grin who spoke passable English and was overwhelmingly eager to please. He had as well been highly recommended by the hotel. And Harry pointed out, since none of the ladies spoke Arabic, Hamad's assistance would be necessary as haggling was not merely expected but something of an art.

"Ladies, if you're ready," Harry said, gesturing at the waiting donkeys.

Every donkey had its own boy and Harry assisted the young men in maneuvering Sidney's companions properly into their sidesaddles. Assistance that was sorely needed. The boys were far more patient than was probably warranted as the older ladies were not quite as nimble as they once were and there was much muttering as to "indignity" and "absurdity." Still, the youths each maintained a determined smile, no doubt with an eye toward the coins they'd receive at the end of the day. By the time Harry finished with the other ladies, Sidney had been assisted into her own saddle. While the thought of him putting his hands around her waist to help her onto the beast was decidedly exciting, it was best to mount the animal before he had a chance to help and notice her inexperience. She'd never even ridden a horse before—she was born and raised in London—but Harry would certainly take her lack of skill as yet another piece of evidence against her. It was only their first full day in Cairo and already she was growing tired of being constantly on guard against mistakes.

"Well, that was certainly fun," Harry said under his breath, pausing by her donkey, apparently to make certain she was seated correctly.

"Sarcasm, Harry?"

"Not at all." He smiled. "I find nothing so delightful as assisting old ladies onto the backs of donkeys. Especially as neither the ladies nor the donkeys seemed especially enamored by the idea."

She laughed.

"It's not amusing. Did you see the looks on their faces?"

Sidney glanced behind her at the ladies on their respective beasts. Each one wore an expression of trepidation mixed with determination. "They do look a bit concerned. None of them have done this before, you know."

"You seem to be doing well." He shrugged. "But then this is not new to you although you've said it has been some time."

"Quite some time," she said without thinking.

"I must say, the fairer sex is hardier than they are given credit for." He shook his head. "I could never ride a sidesaddle."

"One does what one must for the sake of propriety," Sidney said with a lighthearted tone. "But I agree. A regular saddle is much easier and far more comfortable. Frankly, I prefer it."

"You've ridden astride, then?"

"It's not always easy to find an appropriate saddle when one is exploring the less traveled parts of Egypt." She waved off the comment in a blithe manner.

"No, of course not." He glanced around. "I gather Mr. Corbin is not joining us for this expedition?"

"I'm afraid not." Daniel had accompanied them to the Citadel but aside from remarking on the view, had not seemed especially interested in the history or the architecture. Nor had he enjoyed the mosques or the gardens. "He received a telegram from Mr. Cadwallender about a notable American staying at the hotel. Daniel is to find the man and interview him. It will take him most of today if not tomorrow as well."

"Pity he'll miss today's excursion." The satisfied look on Harry's face said better than words that he didn't think it was at all a pity but was rather glad Daniel would not be a member of their party. Sidney did tend to agree with him. "Let's get on with it, then." He nodded and started off, then turned back. "Oh, and when I mentioned the looks on their faces—" he leaned closer "—I wasn't talking about the ladies." He grinned and strode off to his waiting donkey.

Sidney returned his grin. Harry Armstrong was indeed becoming a great deal of fun. Something had happened to his, well, his demeanor since their arrival in Cairo. He was far nicer than he had been and more casual, more relaxed perhaps and while he'd never shown any particular lack of confidence, somehow, he did seem more sure of himself today. As if this was his natural element. Goodness, she did need to find out more about the man. Her smile faded. Misleading Harry was becoming increasingly difficult as well. The more she liked him, the more uneasy and even guilty she became. The result, no doubt, of a conscience that had rarely made itself known as it had rarely needed to. Still, it couldn't be helped.

They traveled in single file—Harry and Hamad at the head of their group followed by Sidney and the ladies. The boys trotted by the side of their animals or behind depending on the traffic. There were all sorts of interesting things to see on the streets of Cairo as they made their way to the Arabian quarters although Sidney spent most of her time simply trying to stay on her sidesaddle while maintaining an air of competence. It was dreadfully difficult. Especially since the donkey boys insisted on urging their charges to a faster pace whenever traffic allowed. Sidney didn't dare look back to see how the ladies were faring. It was all she could do to hold on herself. Although Harry might have had it a bit tougher, in spite of his saddle, as his height meant his legs dangled no more than half a foot above the street. It was a most amusing sight.

In no time at all—or perhaps an eternity—they passed through an ancient stone gate and into the Arabian quarters. The streets here narrowed considerably and there was barely enough room for their mounts amidst the crowds swelling around them. Here, they slowed to a walk. Even so it was difficult to take in the details of their surroundings as there was so very much to see: men in turbans of varying colors and long robes, merchants hawking their wares, women in veils and gowns, most in shades of blue, revealing nothing of their faces but their eyes rimmed in dark kohl, bracelets and bangles on their arms. The passageways were covered high overhead with awnings against the afternoon sun. Lattice-enclosed balconies jutted over their heads, narrowing the streets, concealing family residences or perhaps harems.

Scents assailed her, intriguing and mysterious—of man and beast, leather and tobacco and coffee, enticing perfumes and unknown spices.

They made their way through the markets for a brief time before Sidney's donkey boy halted her mount.

"I've had quite enough." Effie's voice rang out behind her.

Sidney turned to see Effie awkwardly sliding off her donkey. Poppy and Gwen followed her lead and the three made their way to Sidney's side.

"It seems to me we can make much better progress on foot," Effie said firmly. "As apparently every resident of Cairo has chosen today to frequent the markets."

"There are all sorts of interesting shops we would like to stop in and we can't do it from the back of a donkey," Poppy added.

"We've seen countless Europeans on foot here," Gwen said. "There's no reason for us not to do the same."

There were probably any number of reasons why this was not a good idea but Sidney couldn't think of any at the moment. And she too would prefer to dispense with the donkeys. "Very well."

Sidney slid off her donkey, delighted to have her feet back on solid ground but surprisingly stiff after the short ride.

"Ladies." Harry joined them. "Imagine my surprise when I looked back to discover you have all abandoned your rides."

"Nor do we intend to remount them." Gwen's jaw set in a stubborn manner.

Poppy nodded. "And, unless memory fails, Sidney has written several scenes in the souk. With her guidance and Hamad's and of course yours, what can possibly go wrong?"

"What indeed," Sidney said weakly. Although any number of things did go wrong in those pages Poppy had mentioned, including abductions and being chased by thieves or other villains.

"Do be a good sort, Harry, and send the boys and their beasts on their way. And pay them handsomely for their troubles." Effie waved at the line of waiting donkeys and their eager handlers. "Hamad," Effie called and headed toward the dragoman, Gwen and Poppy right behind her.

Harry stared after them. "She called me Harry."

"She does seem to be softening toward you."

"Lucky me."

Sidney smiled. "I call you Harry."

"Not always but I treasure those moments when you do."

There was something quite nice about his admission. "Then I shall call you by your given name from now on. But only if you call me Sidney."

"I've called you Sidney on occasion."

"But not with my permission," she said loftily. "Now you have it."

"Excellent." He grinned, then his expression sobered and he glanced at the ladies. "Is this a good idea?"

"I don't know." Sidney shook her head. "But I daresay I can't stop them. As long as we all stay together, we should be fine."

"Probably." The dubious note in Harry's voice belied his words. "I'll see to paying the boys. Don't wander off without me."

"I wouldn't dream of it."

Harry stepped away, apparently planning to start at

the far end of their line of donkeys. But once the boys
realized he intended to pay them, they clustered around
him chattering without pause, hands held out for pay-
ment. Which did seem to attract others, beggars or simply opportunists who saw an Englishman handing out
money and suspected he wouldn't notice one more out-
stretched hand.

Sidney looked around for her friends. The ladies were
already farther down the narrow street than Sidney would
have liked. She would soon lose them in the crowd if she
hesitated. Harry had told her to wait for him but there
really was no choice. She hurried after the others. Good
God, they were unexpectedly quick for their age. Obviously the lure of unusual wares for purchase and bargains to be found was not to be denied. Fortunately, the
shops were not shops so much as they were stalls, so it
was difficult for anyone to completely disappear from
sight. The merchants themselves sat on their counters or
on cushions low to the ground, their merchandise piled
on either side and behind them.

Led by Hamad, the ladies pushed their way through
the turbulent crowds, skirting around donkeys, occasional
water carriers, auctioneers holding their offerings high
overhead, beggars and other determined shoppers. Apparently, they had given Hamad a definite destination as
there was no hesitation in their relentless forward progress. Sidney looked back but couldn't spot Harry in the
crowd and did hope he would be able to locate them. Regardless, it was up to her to make certain everyone stayed
within sight. Without warning, the ladies turned into another street. Sidney managed to reach the corner no more
than a few seconds later. She knew specific goods were
available on specific streets and this was apparently the

street of leather workers. The rich earthy scent of freshly tanned leather hung in the air. The stalls were filled with saddles of any type one could imagine and others completely unique—saddles for military cavalry or for the grandest of princes, embossed with gold or silver and sidesaddles for ladies. Here were saddles obviously intended for donkeys next to the wood and leather saddles designed for camels. She'd never considered how many colors leather could be but here were hides of the palest golden tan and deep, rich reds and browns of every conceivable shade. It was nearly impossible not to stare at the finely wrought creations but Sidney was certain if she took her eyes off her friends for so much as an instant they would no doubt vanish in the crowd. They were already farther in front of her than she would have preferred. And where on earth was Harry? She couldn't keep track of everyone by herself. It was like trying to herd creatures who absolutely refused to be herded.

Far too far ahead, she spotted the feather of Effie's hat bobbing over the crowd, and then turning into the next street. Sidney picked up her pace but the crowded passageway made it impossible to progress with any significant speed. She turned into the street where she'd seen Effie head and paused but couldn't spot the old dear.

Still, there was no need to panic. Millicent Forester would never panic under these or any circumstances. Surely the ladies still had Hamad with them and surely he could be trusted to make certain no harm came to them. Unless, of course, he wasn't the decent sort he had appeared. Unless his sole purpose was to gain the trust of unsuspecting Englishwomen and then spirit them away to God knows where. Why, anything could happen to them. They could be kidnapped and carried off to a harem. Now she was being silly. They were too old to be desired for a harem. Still, they could be abducted and held for ransom. That too was absurd. The ladies did not look shabby but they certainly didn't look wealthy either. They looked like exactly what they were—elderly, English tourists. If Sidney stayed calm and rational, she would certainly find them. Yesterday, on the terrace, they had talked about purchases they wished to make. What precisely had they said? Sidney did wish she had paid more attention. Carpets had been mentioned as well as silks and tapestries. Someone had said something about copper teapots. Someone else had mentioned a desire for silver earbobs. There was talk of assorted souvenirs—antiquities and the like. Good heavens, they could be anywhere.

She drew a deep breath and continued forward, jostled constantly by the flowing crowed. She peered into one stall after another, ignoring the temptations of foreign and fascinating goods as well as the appeals of the merchants—frequently in broken English—offering madam an excellent bargain.

If anything happened to them—her heart clenched at the thought—she would never forgive herself. This was her fault. Those sweet old friends were only here because of her. She should have followed her instincts right at the beginning. In spite of what Mr. Cadwallender said she should have insisted on clearing up the public misunderstanding about her work being fictional. She should have faced the consequences then, regardless of how devastating they might have been. If she had, Harry's uncle wouldn't have challenged her. They wouldn't be in Egypt. And Effie, Gwen and Poppy would be safe at home, where they belonged.

She darted down one street and then another. Past

stalls of ornate slippers of velvets and silks, brightly colored with curved toes and beading and tassels. She turned into a street of carpet sellers, with rugs and carpets rolled or hanging, the designs intricate and glorious. She rushed through streets of tobacco and cigar merchants, others with coffees and sweetmeats and finally realized she was retracing her steps. And there was every possibility she was just as lost as her friends.

Sidney had no idea how much time had passed. Surely no more than an hour or two. Time had lost all meaning. Her world was an endless blur of stalls and uncommon merchandise and captivating people, of bright colors and foreign languages, of odd and enticing smells. This was not getting her anywhere. She'd been roaming the endless streets of the souk for what seemed like all eternity. She had no idea where she was. What she needed was a plan. Perhaps she should return to the hotel, if she could make her way out of the markets. If she could find the Muski, the main street that ran through the markets, she would be able to get her bearings and then find the hotel. Surely someone there could help her.

"Where have you been?" Harry's outraged voice behind her jerked her attention.

She whirled to face him, her relief at seeing him again dashed away by the tone in his voice and the look on his face. "Where have I been? Where have you been?"

"For the last two and a half hours I've been trying to find you." His jaw clenched. "I thought you understood you were to wait for me."

"I did. They—" she gestured wildly "—did not."

"They?" He looked around. "The old ladies?"

"Yes!"

"They're not with you?"

"Obviously not."

"Where are they?"

"I don't know!"

Harry stared. "You lost them?"

"I don't know if I lost them or they lost me. I was turned around, confused if you will. This is a most confusing place." This could very well be blamed on Harry. If he hadn't taken so long dealing with the donkey boys, they might all still be together now. A voice in the back of her head noted she wasn't being entirely fair. She didn't care. "The point is that they, *we*, are lost."

"How could you let this happen?"

"How could *I* let this happen?" She glared at him. Any thoughts about his newfound agreeable nature vanished in a wave of anger. "How could you?"

"I told you—"

"What was I supposed to do? They are grown women. It's not as if I could put a little bell around their necks like a donkey!"

"You could have tried!"

"I tried to keep my eye on them but they were too—"

"Fast?" His brow shot upward. "They're old ladies!"

"They're spry. And determined." For the first time she noticed the crowd had thinned as those passing by skirted around them, trying to put as much distance as possible between themselves and the squabbling foreigners. She crossed her arms over her chest. "And there's no need to yell."

"There's every need to yell!" He drew a deep breath and it was obvious he was trying to muster some semblance of calm.

"They are not your responsibility."

"Of course they are." He shook his head in disbelief.

"If we return without them, who do you think will be held accountable?"

"Me!"

"Hardly." He scoffed. "You're the bloody Queen of the Desert! You're practically beloved. No one will blame you for anything. I'll be the one at fault. The man is always the one held accountable."

"Well, perhaps if the *man* had been more conscientious—"

His jaw tightened. "I told you—"

"Mr. Armstrong?" A disembodied hand tapped him on the shoulder. "Mrs. Gordon." Hamad peered around Harry and smiled. "I am so pleased to have found you."

"Hamad!" Sidney held her breath. "Do you know where the other ladies are?"

"Of course." The Egyptian's smile widened. "And I have been sent to find you."

"Good man, Hamad." Relief echoing her own sounded in Harry's voice. "Are they all right?"

"They are very good, sir."

"Thank God," Sidney murmured. "How long have you been looking for me? For us?"

"Only a very few minutes, madam."

"*He* knows his way around the markets," Harry said pointedly.

She clenched her teeth. "Things change over the years!"

"Not in Egypt!"

Hamad cleared his throat. "If you would be so good as to follow me. The ladies are waiting."

"Excellent." She raised her chin and started after Hamad, Harry a step behind.

The man was a beast, that's what he was. How had she ever thought, even for a moment, that he was anything like Richard Weatherly. Certainly they bore a certain physical similarity, nothing more than coincidence really, but Richard was a figment of her imagination. Harry was entirely too real. Richard was heroic and daring and dashing. Harry had misplaced a group of helpless women in a market and now acted as if she was somehow to blame. Once again, that annoying voice in her head murmured this wasn't entirely his fault. Once again, she ignored it.

They walked no more than ten minutes before reaching a coffee merchant's stall. Hamad nodded to the man sitting serenely on the counter and led the way to the back of the stall, pulling aside a heavy curtain and allowing Sidney to precede him. The interior was dim and heavily shadowed. Sidney had the impression of lush fabrics hanging on the walls. The scents of cardamom and coriander and cinnamon wafted through the air.

"Oh good, Hamad found you," Poppy said brightly. She and the others were seated on cushions on the floor around a low brass-topped table accompanied by an Egyptian in European dress. "You're just in time for tea."

CHAPTER TEN

"TEA?" SIDNEY SAID in a strangled voice.

Obviously the ladies were fine and apparently enjoying themselves. The same could not be said for Sidney.

"Tea?" she said again.

"Be a dear, Harry, and help Sidney to a seat." Mrs. Higginbotham looked around the confined space. "Although *seat* isn't entirely accurate is it?"

"Pillow, then," Lady Blodgett said. "Or cushion if you prefer. Regardless, she will need assistance."

"We certainly did. Egyptian seating is not designed for appropriate English clothing." Mrs. Fitzhew-Wellmore beamed at the gentleman beside them. "But Mr. Nazzal was of great help."

Mustafa Nazzal rose effortlessly to his feet. "Mr. Armstrong." He nodded a bow. "It's a small world, is it not?"

"And growing smaller every day." Harry shouldn't be at all surprised to see the Egyptian although he never expected to find him in the company of Sidney's elderly friends.

Sidney leaned close, her gaze fixed on Nazzal, her voice barely above a whisper. "You know him?"

"I do."

"And he's…"

"An accomplished gentleman of many and varied pursuits," Harry said, managing to keep the sarcasm from his voice.

"Oh?" Sidney stared.

"I do try," Nazzal said in a modest manner.

Sidney eyed him suspiciously. "Then there is nothing to be concerned about?"

"Not at all," Harry lied. There was always something to be concerned about when Mustafa Nazzal appeared. Nazzal was a minor Egyptian official—although his precise position had always been somewhat vague—with connections to the Egyptian Museum of Antiquities and his finger in anything that might be profitable, regardless of whether it was unsavory or completely aboveboard. Nazzal was fiercely loyal to his country and was the kind of man who knew everything about everything and everyone. The kind of man one didn't want as an enemy. His services and assistance were often invaluable.

"And you must be the incomparable Mrs. Gordon," Nazzal said in a charming manner obviously designed to melt even the wariest heart.

Sidney smiled cautiously. "I'm not sure about incomparable…"

"Allow me to present Mrs. Gordon," Harry said. "Sidney, this is Mr. Mustafa Nazzal."

"An old friend of Mr. Armstrong's," Nazzal said smoothly. He took Sidney's hand and raised it to his lips. "I am enchanted to meet a woman of such accomplishment."

Sidney stared. "Thank you."

"We've been telling him all about you." Pride rang in Gwen's voice. "About your books and your adventures."

"My apologies, Mrs. Gordon." Nazzal gazed into her eyes. "I do not recall having heard your name before. But surely it has just slipped my mind?"

"Happens to the best of us, old man," Harry said

quickly. Excellent. Now he had to guard against Nazzal uncovering the truth about Sidney as well as Corbin. A question flashed through his mind. When had his purpose changed from exposing Sidney to protecting her? He ignored it. Besides, running into the Egyptian was nothing more than a momentary distraction. They probably wouldn't see him again during their stay. "Tell me, how did you come to meet my friends?"

"Ah yes." Nazzal chuckled. "They were concerned that they had somehow misplaced Mrs. Gordon and you as well. Hamad thought it more expeditious to search for the two of you without the ladies so he brought them here. Hamad is a cousin of my uncle's wife and this is my uncle's shop. I happened to stop by on a matter of business."

"Mr. Nazzal knew my husband," Mrs. Higginbotham said brightly. "What a remarkable coincidence, don't you think?"

"Remarkable." Harry met the other man's gaze.

"Even before our more formal arrangement with Britain, there has long been a sizable presence of British officers in Egypt. I daresay, Colonel Higginbotham isn't the only mutual acquaintance between us." Nazzal turned back to the older lady. "I'm not sure our chance meeting was as remarkable as it was delightful."

"Goodness, Mr. Nazzal." Mrs. Higginbotham uttered something that might well have been a giggle.

Harry stared.

Sidney nudged him with her elbow. "Stop that."

"Sorry," he murmured.

"Mr. Nazzal," Sidney said pleasantly. "You have my undying gratitude for extending your hospitality to my friends and, as much as I would like to join you, I'm afraid it is growing late and we must be going."

"To my eternal regret," Nazzal said.

Good. The sooner they were out of here the better. If Sidney had indeed spent any time at all in Egypt, Nazzal would know. Fortunately, Corbin wasn't with them at the moment and Harry had no doubt the older ladies were complicit in Sidney's deception.

"But perhaps you would join us for dinner tonight," Sidney continued. "At Shepheard's Hotel."

"That would be lovely, Mr. Nazzal." An eager note sounded in Mrs. Fitzhew-Wellmore's voice, the other ladies chiming in. It appeared they were all taken with the charismatic Egyptian.

"I'm afraid I have other plans tonight," Nazzal said with a reluctant shake of his head.

Harry released a breath he didn't know he'd held.

"However, I believe there is dancing at the hotel tomorrow night," Nazzal continued. "Perhaps I could join you then."

"Wonderful, Mr. Nazzal." Lady Blodgett smiled a distinctly flirtatious sort of smile. "It's been a very long time since I've had the pleasure of a dance and I quite look forward to it."

Nazzal cast Sidney an amused glance, as if they now shared some sort of private joke or connection about the older ladies' obvious liking of him. A connection he would use to his advantage if necessary. Harry knew exactly what the man was thinking and he didn't find it at all amusing.

"If we're agreed, then." Sidney glanced around the circle of older ladies. "We should be on our way."

"I suppose." Mrs. Higginbotham sighed. "But we are going to need a bit of assistance." Her gaze shifted between Nazzal and Harry, and then she extended a hand to Harry. He had the oddest sense of triumph. "If you would help me to my feet."

"Yes, of course." Harry stepped closer and took the lady's hand, carefully helping her stand. Sidney, Hamad and Nazzal assisted the other ladies.

"Goodness, Harry," Mrs. Higginbotham said under her breath. "You needn't treat me like a piece of fragile porcelain. I am much studier than I look."

He grinned. "I assure you, Mrs. Higginbotham, I never suspected otherwise."

"Humph." Her lips pressed together in a skeptical line. "I don't believe you for a moment. Oh, and after due consideration, I have an offer for you. I shall refrain from referring to you as 'the buffoon' if you cease to refer to me as 'the dragon.'"

"Oh, I never—"

"It's pointless to protest, Harry. You know it and I know it. And while I do like the idea of thinking of myself as a dragon—majestic beasts don't you think?"

"Um." He had no idea how to respond.

"Excellent answer, Harry." Mrs. Higginbotham rolled her eyes toward the low ceiling. "I would much prefer other people not refer to me that way. You understand."

He nodded.

"You are proving to be more acceptable than expected." Mrs. Higginbotham nodded approvingly. "Believe me, no one is more surprised than I."

The group said their goodbyes and Hamad arranged for a few boys to carry their considerable number of packages. The guide then easily led them out of the bazaar to the Muski where Hamad arranged for two cabs—one for Harry and the ladies, the other for Hamad and their parcels, all of varying sizes, some quite large. What in

the hell had they bought? Harry had no idea how poor
Hamad had managed to carry it all. The ladies settled on
one side of the carriage, Sidney sat beside him.

Once they were headed back to the hotel, Harry leaned
forward on his seat and addressed the elderly women in
his best no-nonsense tone. "Ladies, wandering off on
your own here is ill-advised. I would request that you
refrain from doing so. Furthermore, should we be separated again, we need a plan as to where we are to meet.
I cannot impress upon you strongly enough what sorts
of things could have happened to you. The markets of
Cairo are not akin to Bond Street or Harrods. Mrs. Gordon was extremely worried."

"There was no need." Lady Blodgett smiled at the
younger woman. "We were with Hamad after all."

"And what of Mrs. Gordon?" Harry nodded toward
Sidney. "She was alone."

Mrs. Higginbotham frowned. "We thought she was
with you."

"Mr. Armstrong and I were separated as well," Sidney said.

"I want your word that if we misplace one another
again you will return immediately to the hotel," he said
sternly.

"You needn't be so adamant about it, Harry." Mrs.
Fitzhew-Wellmore sniffed.

"We're not children and we prefer not to be treated as
such," Lady Blodgett added.

"He's right though," Mrs. Higginbotham said in a resigned manner. "We do need to stay together and we certainly should agree on procedures should we be separated
again. Not that we intend to be, but one never knows what
might happen while one is traveling." She glanced at the

others. "Don't we have a Lady Travelers pamphlet on what to do when one is lost in a foreign land?"

"I'm not sure." Mrs. Fitzhew-Wellmore's brow furrowed. "But I do believe we have recommended finding the British consulate in such circumstances."

"Perhaps we should write a pamphlet about being lost in something like the markets of Cairo." Lady Blodgett cast Harry an approving smile. "Excellent idea, Harry. We shall do so the moment we return to London. Do you have any other good advice?"

All three ladies stared expectantly.

"Not at the moment." There was apparently nothing like old ladies looking at you as if you had some sort of rare wisdom to impart to take the wind out of your sails. Especially if you didn't. He struggled to keep a firm note in his voice. "But should something come to mind I will be sure to mention it."

"See that you do, Harry." Mrs. Higginbotham nodded and waved him away, apparently the discussion was at an end. He settled back in his seat and she turned her attention to her friends. "I cannot tell you how pleased I am with my purchases. I never imagined I would find such remarkable goods."

"Oh my yes." Mrs. Fitzhew-Wellmore's eyes sparkled with the kind of excitement Harry had only ever seen in a man's eyes when he had unearthed a rare treasure or done something of great accomplishment. "Why the colors of the..."

Harry inclined his head toward Sidney and spoke quietly. "Why did you invite Nazzal to join us tomorrow?

"He did us a great favor, Mr. Armstrong," she said coolly. "I thought the very least we could do was invite him to dinner. I regret he couldn't join us tonight."

"The very least we could do was thank him and hope never to see him again." He blew an annoyed breath. "We're back to Mr. Armstrong are we?"

"For the moment." She paused. "You don't like Mr. Nazzal?"

"I don't trust Mr. Nazzal."

Her eyes widened with something that might well have been delight. Damnation. What was wrong with the woman? "Is he untrustworthy?"

"Let us just say he has his own agenda." He thought for a moment. "I'm not sure I would call him untrustworthy, at least not completely, but his loyalty lies first with himself and then his country."

"When were you last in Egypt, Harry?" she asked abruptly.

Given their encounter with Nazzal, anything but the truth seemed pointless. "About a year ago."

"You really haven't said much about your experiences here." Her eyes narrowed slightly. "Or about yourself at all for that matter."

"I don't believe this endeavor is about my experience but about yours." The carriage pulled to a stop in front of the hotel.

Sidney didn't seem to notice. "Even so, I would think—"

"Sidney," Mrs. Higginbotham interrupted. "It's nearly five o'clock, will you be joining us for tea on the terrace?"

"Haven't you already had enough tea?" Harry asked, helping the ladies out of the carriage.

"One can never have enough tea, young man." Lady Blodgett looked at him as if he were a small and exceptionally stupid child.

"Why, we said yesterday that we couldn't imagine anything more fascinating than the parade that passes by

Shepheard's terrace and I should hate to miss even one afternoon. We do need to make good use of our limited time." Mrs. Fitzhew-Wellmore cast him a sharp look as obviously this was his fault.

He smiled weakly.

The older lady glanced cautiously from side to side as if to make certain no one was listening. "Oh, I do hope to see a funeral today. Processions apparently pass by frequently and are said to be fascinating."

"People do tend to die on a regular basis, Poppy, so no doubt your wish will be fulfilled sooner rather than later." Mrs. Higginbotham started up the stairs toward the hotel door.

"I'm certainly not wishing anyone dead," Mrs. Fitzhew-Wellmore followed her friend. "But if they are going to die, I should like to see the spectacle. It would be quite…educational."

"And we are always interested in learning new things." Lady Blodgett started after the other ladies then paused and directed her words to Harry. "Although Daniel said he heard that Shepheard's actually pays funerals to march by the terrace. Can you imagine such a thing?"

"I wouldn't think the recently deceased would mind," Harry said. "Even here, funerals can be costly and defraying a little of the expense sounds like an excellent idea."

Sidney choked back a laugh.

"It does at that, doesn't it?" Lady Blodgett frowned thoughtfully. "And something to keep in mind for the future."

Harry restrained himself from pointing out such a scheme would not work well in London. In spite of everything, he had grown rather fond of the trio. He was beginning to think of them as something akin to family. It was not an unpleasant idea.

Sidney started after the others then paused. "Will you be joining us for tea?"

"I believe I will forgo tea today."

"Then will we see you at dinner?"

"Absolutely."

She studied him curiously. "Do you like being mysterious?"

"I didn't realize I was. But if I am…" He grinned. "Then yes I suppose I do."

"I wouldn't become accustomed to it if I were you." She nodded and continued up the stairs.

Harry had the distinct impression a gauntlet had just been thrown down. He chuckled. He'd always rather liked gauntlets.

...and so it was with great courage and unflinching determination as well as intimate knowledge of the twists and turns in the deepest recesses of the exotic bazaar, fraught with unknown perils and unexpected hazards, that Mrs. Gordon succeeded in locating the missing ladies and leading them back at long last to the safety and security of Cairo's grandest hotel.

—"The Return of the Queen of the Desert,"
Daniel Corbin, foreign correspondent

CHAPTER ELEVEN

"WE SAID WE intended to leave at half-past eight." Effie tapped her foot impatiently on the walk in front of the hotel.

"We don't have all day." Poppy frowned. "And it's some distance to the pyramids isn't it?"

Sidney nodded. "About an hour and a half I believe."

"Daniel isn't here yet either." Gwen huffed. "We do have a schedule to maintain and we really should make every effort to adhere to it."

"At dinner last night Daniel said he had to send his latest dispatch this morning," Poppy said. "Perhaps that's why he's not here yet."

"I would hate for him to miss the pyramids. Although he did say he was setting aside his interview for now to report about our little adventure yesterday. Not that he had any part in it," Effie added.

"But we did tell him all about it," Poppy added.

Sidney grimaced. "I'm not sure I wish to read that."

"Oh, I believe he intended to make it quite clear that you had saved us from being lost forever in the—how did he phrase it? Oh yes, 'the twists and turns in the deepest recesses of the exotic bazaar.'" Gwen arched a brow. "I don't think Daniel is a strict believer in the unvarnished truth."

"Good morning, ladies." Harry stepped confidently down the front stairs, and then stopped short and stared. "What is all this?"

"I do hope you do not intend to make disparaging remarks, Harry." Gwen's eyes narrowed. "Do you?"

For a moment, Harry appeared to be considering exactly that, then thought better of it and shook his head. "Not in the least. I have absolutely nothing to say."

"Excellent, Mr. Armstrong." Sidney shot him a warning look over her new glasses. "And quite wise of you to admit it."

"Ladies." Daniel bounded down the steps. "Sorry to be late. I had a few problems sending my report." He stopped and grinned. "I say, all four of you look splendid and ready for today's adventure."

Sidney had thought they did indeed look ready for adventure in the pith helmets and smoked eyeglasses that were among the ladies' purchases yesterday. They already had their parasols. While she'd had a momentary qualm at Harry's less than flattering reaction, this was exactly the kind of desert apparel recommended by her guidebooks. The kind Millicent Forester routinely wore. While the weather was quite pleasant, even in February the sun was far stronger here than it was in England and precautions were always a good idea. Besides, there was something rather dashing about a pith helmet and smoked glasses.

"Thank you, Daniel." Poppy beamed.

Sidney resisted the urge to cast a smug look at Harry. Effie, Poppy and Gwen had no such hesitation.

"I shall have to purchase a helmet myself," Daniel proclaimed, thus endearing himself yet again to the ladies. He wore a straw Panama hat while Harry had a wide-brimmed felt fedora that looked very much as if it had seen better days. It cast the most intriguing air of adventure and danger around him.

"Now, then," Sidney said, "we should be off."

Harry and Daniel helped the older ladies into the carriage. Their transportation was arranged through the hotel but they were to hire guides once they arrived at the pyramids. Sidney wasn't sure how Harry had maneuvered it but somehow he had managed to take the seat on her left. Gwen sat on her right. Effie and Poppy flanked Daniel on the other side of the carriage and engaged him immediately in lighthearted conversation.

Sidney had noted the crowd at the hotel and the number of travelers at the Citadel and in the markets but it wasn't until they were on the road to Giza that she realized just how many tourists there were here. This was not her grandmother's Egypt and not at all what she had expected. How on earth could she continue her pretense if things were not as they should be? She sighed in frustration.

"Is something wrong?" Harry said quietly.

"Not really. I was just noticing how the crowds do seem much larger than when last I was here."

"And that was?"

In spite of the twinkle in his eyes she glared at him. "Quite some time ago."

He nodded. "Years."

"Yes," she said in a sharper tone than was perhaps warranted. Honestly, one could never tell if the man was attempting to wring information from her or was teasing. Not that it mattered. One was just as irritating as the other. But this really was no way to start the day. She breathed deeply then smiled. "Although I daresay I can't think of a more fascinating place to travel to than Egypt."

"I agree."

"Do you?"

He laughed. "You needn't sound so suspicious. We don't have to be at odds over everything, you know."

"I didn't think we were," she said in a lofty manner. "Yesterday, I thought we had forged a sort of friendship. Of course that was before you were so vile and beastly."

"My apologies if I was vile and beastly although I would dispute both terms."

"I could understand your distress if you liked Effie and Poppy and Gwen but—"

"I do like them." His eyes widened in surprise. "They're a little overbearing and have no reluctance to speak their minds. They don't hesitate to chastise even people they barely know. They want to be treated as if they were forty years younger and yet will fall back on their age when convenient. They are the most interesting and annoying and delightful women I think I've ever met. I don't know why you think I don't like them." He chuckled. "Although they haven't made it easy."

"Understandable really. They don't trust you."

"Do you?" he asked without warning, his gaze locking with hers.

"I certainly shouldn't." Sidney stared into his eyes, deep and unfathomable and full of all sorts of wicked promises. "I can't imagine anything more foolish than trusting you, Harry Armstrong."

"You are a woman of adventure, Mrs. Gordon, according to your writing." His eyes darkened, if possible, smoldered although it might have been a trick of the light. "The first step in any adventure is leaping into the unknown."

Good Lord! Surely he wasn't trying to seduce her with his low, sensual tone and his penetrating gaze? Here? Under the Egyptian sun? In an open carriage in front of everyone? What utter nerve of the man. She should stop this—whatever this was—right now.

"Is it?" Unless, of course, she wasn't sure she wished to stop this—whatever this was. Unless she gazed into Harry's gray eyes and suspected wicked things might well be nothing less than quite wonderful. Unless she did indeed wish to leap into the unknown.

"Sidney," Effie said, and Sidney jerked her gaze from Harry. "Why don't you tell us about the pyramids so that we can fully appreciate what we are about to see?"

"Excellent idea." Gwen leaned forward and peered around Sidney to cast a pointed look at Harry, who smiled innocently in return. Sidney groaned to herself. How much of that had Gwen heard?

"Very well." Sidney glanced at Harry. The annoying man's unruffled expression belied the gleam of triumph in his eyes. She cleared her throat. "There are nine pyramids of note on the Giza plateau. The largest are the ones..." Sidney could certainly talk about the pyramids, the history of ancient Egypt, the current state of excavations, the latest discoveries and nearly anything else about Egypt without any real effort. Fortunate, as it was difficult to talk about anything with Harry's leg pressed next to hers.

"The largest, the Great Pyramid, was built by..."

She had tried to inch away but the carriage seat was simply not wide enough to allow any extra space. The man certainly did produce a lot of heat. Even if one discounted the feel of his leg against hers, or tried not to meet his gaze, there was no avoiding how very aware she was of him. His quick wit, the way he laughed and the intriguing spicy scent of him—faint and masculine and hinting of adventures as yet unknown and leaps not yet taken—simply refused to be ignored. There was a *presence* about the man that could not be denied. She wondered if she was the only one who noticed.

Midway through the drive, they stopped to stretch their legs and when Sidney returned to the carriage she found Effie had taken her seat. She was both grateful and the tiniest bit disappointed.

They passed Giza, once a prominent ancient city, now little more than ruins, and reached a point where the road was bordered by a wall on either side to prevent it being covered by the constantly shifting sand. The Mena House hotel was to their right and one of the ladies mentioned how wonderfully convenient it was if one intended to spend a great deal of time at the pyramids. The road then ascended upward to the rocky plateau some forty feet above the plains and upon reaching the top, found themselves a scant hundred or so yards away from the marvel of engineering and man's determination to defy death that was the Great Pyramid.

The ancient monument, and its smaller companions, had been in sight throughout the drive and had grown larger as they approached. Still, when they at last arrived, Sidney's breath caught at the immensity of it. Until the construction of the Eiffel Tower in Paris a few years ago, the Great Pyramid had been the tallest man-made structure in the world. She knew it covered an area as large as Lincoln's Inn Fields—the largest square in London—and was some sixty feet taller than the cross atop St. Paul's Cathedral but knowing facts and figures did not truly prepare one for the sheer immensity of it. It towered over the two smaller pyramids and they in turn dwarfed the remaining six on the plateau although some were barely recognizable as pyramids. It had once been covered with smooth polished limestone and the sun's reflection would have been blinding. The outer casing had been torn away eons ago giving the structure the appearance of a staircase of giants.

The moment the carriage stopped they were surrounded by Bedouins demanding attention and offering their services as guides. Harry and the driver managed to disperse them, at least momentarily. The ladies were assisted out of the carriage and Sidney nearly stumbled in the attempt. It was difficult to keep her mind on mundane matters when the most glorious symbol of ancient Egypt demanded her attention. She could hardly tear her gaze away.

"It's remarkable, isn't it?" Harry said quietly to her alone.

"Remarkable." She nodded then caught herself. "Each time one sees it, is very much like the first time. It takes one's breath away and touches one's soul."

"Yes, I suppose it does," he said thoughtfully.

"I assume you've been here before."

"One always visits the pyramids when one first arrives in Egypt."

"And when was that?"

"Some time ago." He grinned. "*Quite* some time ago."

She ignored him. "You never mentioned you spoke Arabic."

"You never asked. I'm not very good at it. In fact, I know little more than what one needs to get by. I did expect that you were familiar with the language," he added casually.

"I'm dreadful at languages. I always have been." That, at least, was true. Even her instructors at Miss Bicklesham's Academy for Accomplished Young Ladies had recognized that there were some people destined only to speak the language they were born to and continuing to attempt to teach her anything beyond *bonjour* and *merci* did nothing but produce needless frustration on both sides. "I long ago learned it was in my best interest, and that of anyone I wished to communicate with, to hire an interpreter."

"Very wise of you." He chuckled then turned to the others. "Ladies, Corbin, which do you prefer? Shall we go up first or shall we go down?"

Effie's eyes narrowed behind her glasses. "What do you mean?"

"Well, we can go down into the Great Pyramid itself but the passageways are extremely close and it is a fairly steep descent." He paused. "And an equally awkward ascent as well. I would not recommend it to anyone uncomfortable in enclosed spaces."

Daniel paled. "I'm afraid I'm not very good in tight spaces."

"And what was up, Harry?" Hope rang in Mrs. Fitzhew-Wellmore's voice.

"Climbing to the top of course." Harry waved in the

direction of the Great Pyramid. The ladies studied it thoughtfully.

"It doesn't look too difficult," Gwen said.

Poppy shrugged. "It's nothing more than a giant staircase really."

"Pity we're not giants," Effie said sharply. "What is wrong with the two of you?" She aimed her parasol at the pyramid. "Are you watching this?"

It really was an interesting sight. The Great Pyramid was dotted with intrepid souls attempting the daunting climb to the top. The blocks of stone did indeed look like stair steps but each riser was three to four feet high. Bedouins above the climbers pulled them up by their hands and those below pushed them up from behind. Some of the male climbers—particularly younger men—did not need as much assistance as the lady tourists. It was rather amusing if one wasn't considering attempting the climb oneself.

"I think it looks most invigorating." Gwen's brow furrowed as if she didn't quite believe her own words.

"It is frightfully high though isn't it?" Poppy shaded her eyes with her hand and stared upward.

"It's a challenge, ladies." Confidence rang in Daniel's voice. "One we are surely up to."

"Are you mad?" Effie shot an annoyed look at Daniel. "What on earth are you thinking, young man? For you it might be a challenge, for us it's out of the question." She turned to Gwen. "You have been known to use a cane recently, although I noticed you did not bring it along."

"I didn't think I needed it," Gwen said staunchly.

"And you—" Effie said to Poppy "—complain frequently about the ache in your knees."

"Only when it rains." Poppy frowned. "I do wish you wouldn't discuss such things around the others."

"I'm certain the others are aware that we are not as young as we once were." Effie huffed. "Climbing the Great Pyramid is certainly something we could have done at their age. No doubt we could have done it thirty years ago but it's ridiculous to think we can do so now. Besides, I am at an age where the very idea of an Egyptian hoisting me up by my hands while another attempts to boost my behind is not the least bit appealing." She crossed her arms over her chest. "Nor do I intend to crawl into the bowels of a stone tomb."

"Of course not, Aunt Effie," Sidney said quickly. "No one expects you to."

"You should certainly climb to the top as well as go into the interior as you have always want—" Effie cast a quick glance at Harry "—have always said how very much you would like to do both again. As for us—" she squared her shoulders "—I suggest we hire camels and visit the Sphinx as per Miss Granville's itinerary. It's a mere quarter mile from here and I rather fancy the idea of riding a camel."

Poppy's expression brightened. "Oh, that does sound like fun."

"Doesn't it though? Very well, then." Gwen nodded. "As much as I do hate admitting to the limitations of age, I think it's an excellent suggestion."

"I agree, Mrs. Higginbotham. Well done," Harry said. "I'll arrange the camels and guides for you. Then Mrs. Gordon and I will first descend into the pyramid—I'm sure she would hate to miss seeing the Great Hall and the King's Chamber again. Unless of course, as it's been so long, the idea of crawling through a king's tomb is worrisome and you would prefer not to."

"Goodness, not in the least," Sidney said with a confidence she didn't entirely feel. "I quite look forward to it. It has been a very long time and who knows when I'll return to Egypt." She smiled. "And then shall we climb to the summit?"

Harry grinned.

"Daniel, dear, would you be so good as to accompany us?" Gwen said in her best I-expect-agreement tone. "We certainly can't go off in the company of Bedouins without an appropriate escort."

"I'd be delighted, Lady Blodgett." Daniel glanced at Sidney. "But I had hoped to climb to the top. And perhaps share the view with Mrs. Gordon."

"Come now, Daniel, you saw the view from the Citadel," Effie pointed out. "And you did not seem overly impressed. This is simply the same view in reverse."

"Oh, but I was impressed." Daniel nodded vehemently. "Besides, I do need to report on Mrs. Gordon's activities."

"Very well, Daniel." Poppy thought for a moment then cleared her throat. "The intrepid Mrs. Gordon revisited those places she had first seen so long ago venturing into the dark and ethereal hidden funerary rooms of the Great Pyramid. The lady adventurer took a few minutes to reflect upon the...the..."

"Ancient past," Effie murmured.

"Ah yes, the ancient past and those great and small who had left their mark on this land thousands of years ago. Upon her return to the surface, she proceeded to climb to the top of the Great Pyramid where she could revel in the vistas that in many ways were no different than those seen by the pharaohs themselves." Poppy cast the reporter a satisfied smile. "There you are, Daniel. The essence of your next story all done for you. Now you have no excuse."

"Apparently not." He smiled halfheartedly. "Mrs. Gordon, do you think we might have a bit of a chat later today?"

"Oh, I think we can manage that," Sidney said pleasantly.

Harry spoke to their driver and a few minutes later, the party was introduced to their camels. No one on either side looked particularly enthusiastic but Gwen, Effie and Poppy were nothing if not determined. Daniel was little more than resigned. Even though Sidney had seen camels since their arrival, they did seem much taller here in the desert, under the endless Egyptian sky. There were a few moments of trepidation but once the ladies were all properly seated and the beasts had risen from kneeling positions all three, with their pith helmets, smoked glasses and parasols, looked as nonchalant as if they rode camels every day. Daniel had a bit more difficulty, sliding out of his saddle twice before finally finding his seating. With jaunty waves from the ladies and a weak smile from Daniel, they started off.

"I believe they're beginning to trust me," Harry said, watching the small caravan move away.

"Why on earth would you think that?"

"They left me alone with you."

"We were alone together yesterday."

"It was inadvertent yesterday. You were all lost."

"Perhaps they simply trust you more than they trust Daniel."

"Wise of them," he said wryly. "Shall we proceed?"

Sidney nodded. "I have to admit, I'm rather excited.

I can barely remember visiting the interior of the Great Pyramid."

"I'm somewhat excited myself." He chuckled.

A few minutes later, Harry had hired guides recommended by their driver and they climbed the pyramid assisted by their Bedouins to the entrance on the thirteenth tier of stones. A guide bearing a candle led the way. Harry followed next and she was most grateful to know he was in front of her. Another guide followed behind her. The passageway into the pyramid was narrower than she had expected. It was apparently one thing to read that the confined space was only three and a half to four feet in height and quite another to try to make one's way through it, primarily on hands and knees, especially as it sloped downward at an alarming angle. They crawled some twenty or so yards then found the way filled by massive granite blocks and veered into another passageway. Had Sidney not read numerous accounts of venturing into the pyramid and hadn't known the blocks were placed there for the express purpose of protecting the pharaoh's remains from robbers, she might have been most concerned. In spite of her excitement at this new adventure, she was acutely aware of the tons of stone directly over her head. The air here was musty and thick and the floor of the passageway slippery. She refused to consider why. After what seemed like an eternity, they entered the Great Hall. Their guides lit magnesium wires to provide better illumination than mere candles.

"Take my hand." Harry extended his hand to help her to her feet.

"Thank you," Sidney murmured. She was surprisingly stiff, to be expected of course. She wasn't used to crawling long distances. She released his hand, took a shaky step and at once lost her footing on the slippery floor. Harry caught her in his arms and for a long moment they stared at once another.

"Sidney," he said softly.

Dear Lord. He wasn't about to kiss her, was he? Here in the Great Hall of the Pyramid of Khufu? How terribly improper. How wonderfully romantic.

"Harry." She raised her chin and closed her eyes.

"Do try to be careful."

Her eyes snapped open.

"I would hate to have to haul you bodily out of here. The floor is extremely slippery." He released her and directed her attention to irregularly hewn hollows in the floor. "Those will help with traction."

"Thank you," she said curtly, stepped carefully away and perused the hall. The masonry here was so perfectly chiseled not even a hair could fit between the joints. She was determined to appreciate the skill of those long-ago craftsmen and not dwell on how terribly embarrassing it was to think a man was about to kiss you when he wasn't.

From the Great Hall they made their way to an antechamber and then the King's Chamber. Everything of value had vanished centuries ago. All that marked this final resting place of a pharaoh was a massive and sadly mutilated granite sarcophagus.

They retraced their steps and finally sunlight shone ahead of them in the passageway leading to the way out. Harry again offered his hand to help her.

"Now." He grinned. "To the top."

"Yes, indeed," she said brightly. She would have much preferred to sit on the stones right here for a time before attempting the climb to the top but she was not going to let Harry think for so much as an instant that she was the least bit weary. "To the top."

They were joined by additional Bedouins—apparently three were required to get the typical tourist up the pyramid. It was every bit as awkward as it had looked although Sidney managed it with only the two Bedouins above, each grabbing one of her hands, hoisting her up and no more than the occasional boost from the one below. Even Harry needed a hand up. Their progress was rather quicker than she would have suspected or, for that matter, desired but she was nothing if not determined. In no more than a quarter of an hour they stood on the summit, a relatively flat platform some thirty feet square. The Bedouins perched on the outcroppings below the summit and a handful of tourists on the top were just beginning the descent. They were alone at the top of the world and she could barely breathe.

"What do you think, Sidney?" Harry drew a deep breath and gazed out over Egypt. "Isn't this remarkable?"

"Remarkable," she muttered and sank down on a stone. All she needed was a minute or a day to catch her breath. "Aren't you even the least bit tired?"

"Not at all." He glanced at her. "I can't believe you are."

"You're wearing trousers, Mr. Armstrong." She sniffed in disdain. "You'd feel entirely different if you had made this climb in a skirt."

"I can imagine." He paused then laughed. "No, actually, I can't. Come on."

Before she could protest he grabbed her hand, pulled her to her feet, stepped behind her and turned her toward the vista, keeping his hands lightly on her shoulders. No doubt in the event that she lost her balance but it was rather nice regardless. He leaned close and spoke softly into her ear. "Welcome back to Egypt, Sidney."

The view was as extraordinary as she had expected. To the west, the desert glistened in the sunlight, barren and shaded in reds and golds and browns, broken only by occasional cliffs. A land stark and unforgiving and relentless. To the east, the Nile wound its way through verdant fields, crisscrossed by canals, its banks bordered with majestic palms. Cairo rose in the distance, glistening in the late morning light, its towers and minarets reaching toward the sun. And above it all, the Citadel perched like a crown on the city's highest point. From here, one looked down on the majestic Sphinx—part man, part beast, part god—half-buried in the sand, symbol of intellect and power. A mystery for the ages, already old when the Great Pyramid was built more than four thousand years ago. And in the distance to the south the pyramids of Abusir and Dahshur and Saqqara rose above the sands.

Here on top of one of the greatest wonders of the world, one could almost see the past unfolding at one's feet. The pharaohs, with their mighty armies, ruled for eons and vanished. Cities rose, shining in the Egyptian sun, and fell, buried and forgotten. Palaces and temples, monuments to the glory of gods or men created over a lifetime, lost now hundreds of lifetimes ago.

"What are you thinking?"

"Life and death, eternity and forever," she said quietly. "Here spread at our feet."

"I'm sorry I asked."

She turned around and crossed her arms over her chest. "Have you no soul, Harry? Have you no sense of the magnificence of all this? Of what man built thousands of years ago that still takes one's breath away? Can't you feel the past here as if it were a living, breathing thing?"

"Yes, I feel the past and yes, I do have a soul." He huffed. "I just don't express it the way you do. With all those *feelings* and flowery words. Actually, I was just thinking about the shadow of the pyramid being the hands of long-ago pharaohs who even in death—"

"Stop it!"

"—refuse to release their grip on their land and their people and so on and so forth."

"Perhaps if you had a bit of *feeling* in your writing you wouldn't have to resort to blackmail to get it published."

"Blackmail?"

"If you prove your uncle's point about my work your book will be published. What would you call it?"

"Well, I wouldn't call it blackmail. I would put it more in the category of a wager really." He glared. "And it doesn't need *feelings* to be accurate. And interesting."

"Hah."

"You can't make judgments about what you know nothing about. My judgments about your work are based on my reading of it. You've never read my writing."

"Do you have it with you?"

"Not here." He paused. "I do have something I've written in my room. I would be happy to show it to you."

"And I would be delighted to read it!" she said sharply, turned and stepped toward the edge then swiveled back. "And one more thing. The next time you indicate you intend to kiss a woman you should either do so or you should avoid the situation altogether."

He stared for a moment then realization dawned in his eyes. "Oh, I see. You mean in the Great Hall."

"Yes, in the Great Hall."

"I didn't think you'd appreciate me kissing you there. I thought you'd smack me. It would have been rather awkward and humiliating. I could practically hear the ancients snickering about it."

"Well, let me tell you something, Harry Armstrong." She poked a finger at his chest. "I would have and I would have thoroughly enjoyed it."

He grinned. "I would have enjoyed it too."

"Not kissing you, you annoying arrogant beast of a man." She rolled her gaze toward the heavens and whatever Egyptian god might smite an arrogant, annoying beast of a man. "And you know it."

She whirled around and signaled to the Bedouins that she was ready to climb down.

Behind her Harry chuckled. "That might have been fun too."

The climb down the pyramid was no less taxing than the climb up but Sidney barely noticed.

The offhand comments he'd made, yesterday and today, lingered in her head. Had Harry already confirmed his suspicions about her? Surely not. If he had, why on earth would he continue this farce? Oh, he could be enjoying his return to Egypt she supposed. Or he could be avoiding other responsibilities although she suspected the wealthy nephews of earls rarely had any responsibilities. Or he could be intending to seduce her as a means to get to the truth. Hadn't he been overly charming since nearly their first day on board ship? It was an absurd idea—surely the man had more honor than that—but it made as much sense as anything else. Seduce her first and then expose her as a fraud.

And wasn't he clever about it? Asking permission to kiss her. Casting her long meaningful looks. Dancing the tiniest bit too close. Murmuring quiet observations in her ear as if they shared private jokes. Appearing as if he had every intention of kissing her. Goodness, the man could have taken his efforts directly from a romantic novel.

Any qualms or doubts she'd had about continuing to pretend to be someone she wasn't vanished in the Egyptian sun. There was no need to try to be like Millicent Forester. Millicent was a product of Sidney's imagination fueled by her grandmother's exploits and was as much a part of Sidney as her arms or her legs. They were one in the same, at least in spirit. But Millicent was who Sidney wanted to be. No—*could* be. The only real difference was that Millicent had had her adventures. Sidney's were just beginning.

She could be courageous and adventurous. And didn't she owe that to the people who read her stories, who believed in her? Didn't she owe that to herself? She was a thirty-two-year-old spinster who needed to step away from the world she'd created on paper and take a leap into a real life. She could be bold and dashing and daring. She wasn't entirely sure how but she was confident she would recognize the opportunity when it presented itself.

Carpe Diem.

And then, perhaps, she would be the one to seduce him.

If he was very, very lucky.

CHAPTER TWELVE

IT WAS NOT DIFFICULT to tell when Sidney Gordon was annoyed with someone. She wasn't the least bit subtle about it.

One—she returned to calling him *Mr. Armstrong*.

Two—she spoke to him only when necessary.

Three—she stalked the entire way to the Sphynx with her chin held high and resolve in her step. And she was far quicker than he had expected as well.

Four—she sat beside Corbin when they lunched, chatting entirely too much with him. Harry didn't like it. The man was a threat in more ways than one.

No, when Sidney Gordon was annoyed with you—you knew it. Although it scarcely mattered. He wasn't especially happy with her either.

Blackmail? It wasn't blackmail. Once again she was playing fast and loose with the truth. She was wrong and he was right. It really didn't come any more straightforward than that. He wasn't at all sure he should show her his writing but it did seem yet another gauntlet had been thrown down. He didn't care for this one.

In hindsight he wasn't certain what their dispute was about or how it had started. Regardless, he was certain he was somehow to blame. Nor did he know if Sidney had said anything to the others about their disagreement although the ladies did seem to have some sort of sixth sense about it. Harry went to great efforts to be pleasant and charming but at any given moment, one or all three of them would be eyeing him closely with considerable speculation. And he did not like the look in their eyes.

He was out of the carriage the moment they reached Shepheard's to assist the ladies. Sidney pointedly turned to Corbin for help. Which was fine with Harry.

Lady Blodgett took his arm and walked up the front steps beside him. "I do expect you to join us for tea today."

"I shall certainly try."

"That's all one can ever ask, Harry," she said and patted his arm.

Sidney and the ladies proceeded to their respective rooms to freshen up, agreeing to meet on the terrace for tea shortly. Harry fully intended to join them. Regardless of his admonition, he would not put it past any of them—including Sidney—to take off on a whim should something prove interesting. He did not intend to lose them again.

He took longer than he had expected but the moment he stepped off the lift into the lobby, the desk clerk gestured at him. Harry stepped to the counter and was handed a note from Nazzal requesting a meeting in the bar. Harry glanced out at the terrace to find his party already seated and obviously settled for the time being, then headed for the bar. Only a handful of tables were occupied and it seemed there were more servers than customers. Nazzal waited for him at a table at the far end of the room.

"So, what is this about?" Harry said the moment the waiter delivered his gin and tonic.

"You wound me deeply, Harry." Nazzal shook his

head in a mournful manner. "Can't one old friend share a pleasant drink with another without being accused of ulterior motives?"

"Not you." Harry chuckled. "Out with it, Nazzal, what do you want?"

"If I recall correctly, you do owe me a favor."

Harry probably owed him any number of favors, but then he had done the Egyptian any number of favors in return. "It seems to me we were fairly even when I left Egypt."

"Who keeps track of such things?" Nazzal waved off Harry's words. "I help you. You help me. It's how we have always done business in the past."

"You have a unique view of the past."

"Which makes it no less accurate."

Harry took a sip of his drink. You could say whatever you wanted about the domination of the British Empire but it did guarantee acceptable gin was to be had wherever its shadow fell. "I am not the same man I was a year ago."

"You are better dressed." Nazzal's assessing gaze flicked over Harry. "I had heard you had come into money."

Harry shrugged. He was certainly not going to admit anything to this man.

"And your traveling companions are, shall we say, unexpected?"

Harry snorted. "Yes, you could say that."

"I must say this is rather more respectable than I would have predicted for you."

"Life is frequently unpredictable."

"Indeed it is. You were the last person I expected to

see in Cairo. It was my understanding when you left, you would not be coming back."

"No one is more surprised than I to be here."

"However, you are the answer to a bit of a dilemma I have encountered." Nazzal chose his words with care. "You and I have known one another for a very long time. Most Englishmen, as well as most Europeans, who come to Egypt do so only to steal the ancient heritage that is Egypt."

"There was a time when no one in Egypt minded," Harry said mildly.

Nazzal's expression darkened. "Such foolishness is no longer acceptable."

Harry was well aware of the governmental stipulations that had been developed in the last half century designed to keep ancient Egypt's most significant relics in Egypt where they rightfully belonged. Nearly everything of significance he had uncovered had gone to the country's main museum and the rest to the British Museum. Thanks to his father's influence, Harry agreed with that principle. Not all who sought Egypt's treasures did. Smuggling was one of the country's biggest industries.

Nazzal leaned across the table and lowered his voice. "There is an American—a Mr. Wallace, a collector of antiquities—staying here at Shepheard's. He has in his possession a medallion, an artifact that was among a number of now-missing antiquities. Part of a shipment destined for inspection by the Egyptian Museum."

"You can hardly take a step in Egypt without stumbling over an artifact. What's so special about this one?"

"For one thing, it's gold. Not pure, of course, but still impressive. For another, one side is carved with engravings that need further study but we believe might reveal the name of the queen consort of Amenemhat II."

"A queen's medallion from the Middle Kingdom?" Egypt's Middle Kingdom, some four thousand years ago, was still shrouded by the mists of time although Harry's father and other scholars considered it Egypt's classical period.

"You can well understand its importance." Determination underlaid Nazzal's words. "It must be recovered and returned to where it belongs. The American denies it's in his possession but my information is never wrong. It should be a simple matter for you to slip into his room, retrieve the item and slip out."

Harry chose his words carefully although he suspected the answer. "Why not just turn this over to the proper authorities?"

"Alas, the proper authorities are not as efficient as one would wish." Nazzal shook his head forlornly. "Mr. Wallace has friends and influence and money. He would no doubt know of any intention to seize the object before action could be taken and it would not be seen in Egypt again."

It was a common enough story. Egypt was not a wealthy country and even the most stalwart of local officials were susceptible to the lure of bribery. "If this is so simple, why don't you do it?"

"You are a guest of the hotel. Even if you're caught in the wrong room you can always claim besotted ignorance. You thought it was your room."

"So I am to be drunk?"

"Only if you're caught."

"I should think this is more suited to your skills than mine."

"Possibly, but my wandering the halls might be re-marked upon. The American has met me and would be immediately suspicious of my presence. Besides—" Nazzal smiled knowingly "—you were always excellent at this sort of thing."

"This sort of thing?" Harry raised a brow. "You mean theft?"

"I mean recovering relics."

Harry shook his head. "I don't recall doing this particular *sort of thing*."

"Perhaps my memory is faulty but I clearly remember you doing this sort of thing. Spiriting objects out of encampments or warehouses or barges." Nazzal shrugged. "I would think a hotel room would be no challenge at all."

"Probably but—" he shook his head "—as much as I hate to disappoint you, I no longer engage in matters of a questionable nature."

"Come now, Harry." Nazzal scoffed. "I don't believe that for a moment."

"Regardless, as I said, I am not the same man I once was."

"No?" Nazzal raised a skeptical brow. "I had a most interesting discussion with your charming traveling companions as to why you are here."

"Did you?" Harry said slowly, a knot forming in the pit of his stomach.

"Delightful ladies, simply delightful." Nazzal chuckled. "They remind me of my dear, departed grandmother. She too had a tendency to chat in what always appeared to be an aimless manner but was in fact quite deliberate."

"Go on."

"When we realized we shared a mutual acquaintance—

you—they seemed rather determined, in a subtle sort of
way to learn more about you."

"Did they?"

"You needn't be concerned. I did not reveal any of
your secrets."

"There is nothing to reveal."

"No? I am mistaken, then." Nazzal paused. "I did,
however, take the liberty of making a few inquiries after
our meeting."

Harry's jaw tightened. "And?"

"Again I was mistaken. I had heard of Mrs. Gordon, or
rather, I had heard of her book. It is not unknown here."

"Do you have a point?"

"Perhaps one you have already reached." Nazzal studied him curiously. "By my calculations, Mrs. Gordon's
alleged adventures in Egypt would have taken place some
dozen years ago. Odd that I, or you for that matter, had
never heard of her presence here." He shook his head.
"A lovely young widow carrying on the work of her husband is not something that would have gone unnoticed."

"Even you are not aware of every foreigner in Egypt,"
Harry said in a mild tone.

Nazzal laughed. "I was right. You do know the truth
about her." He paused. "Are you going to expose her?"

Harry blew a long breath. "My plans are uncertain at
the moment."

"You like her." Nazzal grinned. "A woman, no, four
women getting the best of Harry Armstrong? I never
thought I'd live to see that happen."

"Congratulations on a long life." Harry raised his glass
to the Egyptian. "But they have not gotten the best of
me."

"Not yet." He chuckled. "You know her secret but apparently she does not know yours. And it is indeed a secret, is it not?" He leaned across the table, his voice low. "Or does she know that it was you who challenged her to prove her veracity, *my lord*."

Harry narrowed his eyes. He wasn't the least bit surprised. While he'd tried to be circumspect as possible, Nazzal could have learned about his title from Leo, who could never be completely trusted, or any one of several officials who had seen his passport since his arrival. "I would prefer that you keep that to yourself."

"I would never dream of telling her anything you don't wish her to know. Unless of course…" He spread his hands out palm up and shrugged. "I had no other choice."

First Leo, now Nazzal. "Is blackmail the currency of Egypt these days?"

"Come now, Harry." Nazzal smiled. "It always has been."

Harry tossed back his drink and got to his feet. "I'll consider your proposal."

"Tonight would be the perfect opportunity for this venture of ours. Time is of the essence. Wallace is expected to leave Egypt tomorrow."

What choice did he have really? "Very well. Tonight it is."

"Excellent." Nazzal stood. "I'll give you further details then."

"Dare I ask what you get out of this?"

"Aside from the knowledge that a priceless piece of my country's ancient heritage stays where it belongs?" Nazzal shrugged. "Nothing of significance. A finder's fee. No more. A pittance really."

"Good to see you have not changed."

"Few things truly do in life." Nazzal paused for a moment. "We cannot deny our past any more than we can deny the color of our skin, Harry. The past is always with us."

"The wisdom of the ancients?" Harry said wryly. How he'd thought for so much as a moment that he could return to Egypt without his own past catching up to him was just as ill-advised as anything else he'd done lately.

"They too are part of the past and always with us. It is our duty to honor their teachings and that which they left for us." Nazzal glanced around then leaned close and lowered his voice. "You should know there are people who are aware you are here. Just a warning, my friend."

"And most appreciated." He raised a shoulder in a careless shrug. "But I have nothing to be concerned about." He cast the other man a confident smile and took his leave.

Still, his conscience wasn't entirely clear. While he had made no particular enemies he had also departed Egypt abruptly. There were no doubt any number of things he had left undone, loose ends left untied.

It might be best if he did not join the ladies for tea after all. Nazzal was probably right—this should be simple enough. Even so, if he was going to steal an already stolen relic from a wealthy American, his time might be better spent determining exactly how to do that.

And how not to get caught.

CHAPTER THIRTEEN

"You dance as if your feet were guided by the wings of the gods themselves." Mr. Nazzal smiled down at Sidney in his arms.

"What a lovely thing to say, Mr. Nazzal." Sidney adopted what she hoped was a flirtatious smile. "But I would credit any skill I have to my excellent partner."

"Then we are of one mind, Mrs. Gordon." His dark eyes twinkled in a wicked manner, disconcerting and yet distinctly exciting. "I was thinking precisely the same thing."

"Are all Egyptians so charming?"

He grinned. "Yes."

She laughed. A few weeks ago, the look in this man's eyes might have been cause for alarm. But Millicent Forester would never be alarmed by the flirtation of a handsome, engaging Egyptian and neither would Sidney. In spite of the minor problem of losing the ladies in the market, the trip so far had been filled with new experiences and had filled Sidney with confidence as well. Even though she couldn't take full credit for resolving yesterday's difficulties, everything had worked out quite nicely. Millicent couldn't have done a better job herself.

This was a scene straight from one of her stories. The grand, ornate ballroom was decorated in the style of a French king, with doors thrown open to the terraces over-

looking the gardens. The stars twinkled in the night sky
and a breeze gently wafted through the crowded room.
The perfect setting. The dashing, handsome, mysterious
gentleman who expertly guided her around the ballroom
floor—the perfect minor character. And the heroine had
never before in her life felt so, well, perfect.

Her new gown was the latest fashion, the color of sunlight with a daringly low bodice and quite the loveliest
thing she had ever worn. A maid provided by the hotel
had cleverly fashioned Sidney's blond hair into a riot of
curls at the top of her head and drifting down her back. It
was most effective. The mirror in her room said she was,
at least tonight, not merely adequate but indeed rather
pretty. There was something about not looking average
or ordinary and far more than passable that made her feel
poised and self-assured, as if anything was possible. As
if she could do anything. As if she truly was the heroine
of her own story.

Mr. Nazzal guided her through a turn and she followed his lead without difficulty, sending a silent prayer
of gratitude to Miss Bicklesham's for the dancing lessons
that she'd never had the opportunity to use until she'd
set sail for Egypt. Tonight she had danced nearly every
dance. Not yet with Harry but with any number of other
interesting gentlemen and once with Daniel—who was
in rather a mood tonight and muttered something about
camels being the devils of the desert. Whatever he had
wanted to talk about earlier was apparently overshadowed
by his encounter with camels. It might have been the adventures of the day, or the admiration in her partners'
eyes, or the fact that she was in the ballroom at Shepheard's and this was exactly as she had envisioned such

an evening, but the steps she had mastered a lifetime ago came back to her as if she danced every night of her life.

"I must thank you again for your assistance the other day." She smiled up at him. "And what luck for Mr. Armstrong, running into an old friend in the process."

"Not nearly as fortunate as meeting his lovely companions," Mr. Nazzal said smoothly.

"Tell me, Mr. Nazzal, have you known Mr. Armstrong long?"

"You are in my arms and yet you wish to speak of another man?" He shook his head in a mournful manner. "You wound me deeply, Mrs. Gordon."

"I doubt that." She laughed.

"Dare I ask why you wish to know?"

"It's quite simple really. I know very little about Mr. Armstrong. We only met when we left England." She heaved a resigned sigh. "One does like to know something about one's traveling companions. For safety and security, don't you agree?"

"Excellent point, Mrs. Gordon. In the interest of safety and security, then, I see no harm in telling you what you wish to know. It's common enough knowledge." He smiled. "I have known Mr. Armstrong since he first came to Egypt nearly twenty years ago I believe."

"I see." So much for the earl's nephew having visited Egypt only in his youth. And hadn't Harry admitted he was in Egypt as recently as a year ago? "And did he spend a great deal of time here?"

"Indeed, he was nearly always in Egypt, searching for the relics of the ancients, although he did return to England on occasion through the years."

"Is he an archeologist or perhaps an Egyptologist?"

"As your Shakespeare said, 'what's in a name?' Anyone who searches for the lost riches of the pharaohs will claim to be an Egyptologist. It sounds so delightfully legitimate." He thought for a moment. "But in the case of Mr. Armstrong, he has earned that title—both titles—as well as the respect that accompanies it. I don't believe he's been accorded that."

"Oh?"

"Like most men who come to Egypt in their youth, Mr. Armstrong and his friends were lured by the excitement of the hunt, the adventures to be found in the ruins and deserts and tombs, and the possibility of great fortune. But Egypt is a seductive mistress and the spells she weaves are most alluring and nearly irresistible."

She drew her brows together. "I'm afraid I don't understand."

"In the beginning, Mr. Armstrong was little more than a treasure hunter, interested only in the money his finds could bring. But for the last decade, no, longer if I recall, whatever artifacts he has unearthed have gone to museums—mostly here in Egypt—for nominal finder's fees. His years in Egypt, and his father as well, I believe, changed him."

"His father?"

"A highly respected scholar of ancient civilizations and an acknowledged expert on Egypt."

"I see," she said weakly. Unease twisted her stomach. If she had known what an expert Harry really was right from the beginning she would have… Would have what? Not come to Egypt? Admitted he was right? She'd had no choice if she wanted to continue her writing. And while Harry's suspicions had obviously not abated, he had apparently not found any real proof as to her deception. Good. If she could pull this whole thing off, perhaps she and Harry could… Where on earth did that come from? Surely she wasn't starting to care for the man. That would be the height of stupidity. Still, there was something about him… Regardless, this was not the time or the place to think about such nonsense.

"You mentioned his friends. Are they still in Egypt?"

"Mr. Deane returned to London at the same time as Mr. Armstrong." Mr. Nazzal hesitated. "Mr. Pickering was not so lucky."

"What do you mean?"

"He was struck by a fever when he and Mr. Armstrong and Mr. Deane were in the Western Desert two years ago. Unfortunately he perished."

"Oh dear," Sidney murmured. Harry had said it had been a year since he was last in Egypt. Did Harry leave because of his friend's death?

"Is there anything else you wish to know?" Amusement curved the Egyptian's lips.

"Yes." She braced herself. "It sounds to me as if Mr. Armstrong was rather disreputable in his younger days."

He chuckled. "No more or less than most men of my acquaintance."

"What a clever answer, Mr. Nazzal," she said lightly. "And no answer at all."

He smiled in a knowing manner.

"Answer me this, then." Sidney met his gaze directly. "Is he an honest and honorable man?"

"Honesty, my dear Mrs. Gordon—" he led her through a quick turn. "—is as much in the eye of the beholder as is beauty. If one does something that is not by definition honest but does it for a greater good, is he then dishonest? Or is he indeed honorable?"

"An interesting question, Mr. Nazzal." She thought for

a moment. The man just nicely cleared away any minor doubts she might have had about her plans for tonight. "I believe I agree with you."

"Excellent." He grinned. The music drew to a close and they slowed to a stop. "I don't think you and your friends could be in safer hands than Mr. Armstrong's. If necessary, I would trust him with my very life."

"Thank you, Mr. Nazzal. What a sterling recommendation." She smiled. "I shall keep it in mind."

"And while I regret losing the opportunity to claim another dance later in the evening, I'm afraid I must take my leave." He took her hand and raised it to his lips, his gaze never leaving hers.

"I believe this is our dance, Mrs. Gordon." Harry stepped up behind Mr. Nazzal. He cast the other man a pointed look. "You can let her go now."

"To my eternal regret." Mr. Nazzal reluctantly released her hand. "My apologies, Mr. Armstrong. I am putty in the hands of a woman as lovely as she is clever."

"Why, Mr. Nazzal, you do say the nicest things." Sidney favored him with her brightest smile.

The Egyptian grinned. "I do hope to see you and the rest of your party again before you leave Egypt." He turned to Harry. "I have a matter of some importance to attend to. If I might speak to you alone for a moment. With your permission, Mrs. Gordon?"

"Please go on." She waved him off and pretended to gaze absently around the ballroom, as any insipid, dutiful creature would. Really, men were absurd.

Mr. Nazzal leaned close to Harry and spoke low into his ear. Harry nodded. Mr. Nazzal turned back to her. "My apologies, but I must be off."

"If you must," Harry said cordially.

"Perhaps I shall see you tomorrow, Mr. Armstrong."

Harry chuckled. "I have no doubt of it, Mr. Nazzal."

Mr. Nazzal nodded and took his leave. The music began and Sidney stepped into Harry's arms.

"Secrets, Harry?"

"This is a land of secrets, Sidney, ancient and new."

"What a cunning yet completely useless answer." And the second one she'd received tonight. Still, she hadn't expected anything more.

"Have you forgiven me yet?"

"Do you deserve forgiveness?" she said in an off-hand manner.

"Absolutely not."

She laughed. "There is something quite agreeable about a man who admits when he's wrong."

"I wasn't—" he began, then grimaced. "My apologies, then."

"Accepted." It wouldn't serve either of them for her to continue to be annoyed with him. The man had decided not to kiss her for a perfectly logical reason and that was that. Still, one would think logic would be discarded when it came to a kiss.

"I've been waiting all night to dance with you," he said in a disgruntled manner.

"Nonsense. The evening is still young." She smiled up at him. "And you did not appear to be lacking in partners."

Harry had quite properly danced with Effie, Gwen and Poppy, who were obviously having a wonderful evening. It had been some time since any of them had shared a dance with a handsome, dashing partner.

"Your friend is quite charming," she said lightly.

"Nazzal considers it an art. Charm, Sidney," he added in a scolding manner, "is not always as it seems."

"Why, Harry." Delight widened her eyes. "Are you jealous?"

"Yes."

She grinned. "Good."

"You look…radiant tonight, Sidney." Harry stared down at her as if seeing her for the first time, his voice low, almost a caress. Her heart thudded in her chest.

"Goodness, Harry, you'll quite turn my head with such compliments." A heretofore unknown breathless note sounded in her voice. No doubt to go along with her rapidly beating heart.

"You seem to be having a fine time." He gazed into her eyes.

"Aren't you?" There was that breathlessness again.

"I am now." He pulled her the tiniest bit closer, admiration or something perhaps even better shone in his eyes. The oddest frisson of anticipation skated up her spine. Why, with very little effort, he could lean in and brush his lips across hers. Right here on the dance floor. Terribly improper and dreadfully scandalous but really quite perfect. Would he?

It was shocking to realize how much she wanted Harry to kiss her here and now but more—she wanted him to see her as something other than a cordial opponent. She'd almost entirely dismissed the idea that he hoped to seduce the truth out of her. He really didn't strike her as that sort of man. Which meant his flirtation and everything that went along with it was sincere. It was entirely possible the man truly had feelings her.

Not that any affection he might have for her or she might have for him made any difference, of course. If she disproved his charges she would spend the rest of her life living a lie. If he proved his point, she'd be ruined. How could she ever forgive him for that? Still, there was the vaguest idea in the back of her mind about a way to escape the mire she found herself in and perhaps, possibly, a way to an unforeseen future.

"I must confess, I have been waiting to dance with you as well."

"Have you?" He grinned down at her. "Excellent."

"We have a great deal to discuss," she said in an overly prim manner, trying to ignore how truly wonderful—how very perfect—it felt to be in his arms. Pity it would not last.

"Do we?" Amusement sounded in his voice. "And what do we need to discuss?"

"I think you should do it." She held her breath.

"Do what?"

"Help Mr. Nazzal retrieve the artifact from the American."

"What?" He stumbled on the next step. "What did you say?"

"Come now, Harry, you heard what I said."

"Bloody hell." He quickly steered her to the open doors and out on to the terrace, fairly dragging her past a handful of other people enjoying the refreshing night air, to the shadows at the far end overlooking the gardens. "What did Nazzal say to you?"

"Nothing." She shook free of his grasp. "Well, nothing of any real significance. He certainly didn't mention what he had asked of you."

Harry's eyes narrowed and he looked as dangerous as he was handsome. She shivered with, well, excitement. "Explain yourself, Sidney. How do you know about this?"

"Oh, you know how these things are."

"No, I don't."

"Very well." This was exactly the reaction she'd expected, the man really was endearingly predictable. "When I came down to meet the ladies for tea, I stopped at the front desk. I was curious as to whether I had any mail from Mr. Cadwallender. I didn't by the way."

"Go on."

"But the desk clerk said he had a note for you and I said—as we did intend to meet for tea—that I would be happy to deliver it." She shrugged. "Naturally, I read it."

"Naturally."

"You needn't take that tone. It was simply a folded piece of paper and opened without any effort on my part. I assure you it was quite inadvertent. You really should tell Mr. Nazzal if he wishes communication to be private, he should use an envelope."

Harry's jaw tightened. "I shall keep that in mind."

"See that you do." She nodded. "I thought it might be important and I know you had warned me not to trust him although really, Harry, I find him quite agreeable."

Harry opened his mouth but it did seem best to continue as she wasn't sure she wanted to hear what he was going to say.

"So I paid a server to linger about your table and attempt to overhear your conversation."

"You did what?" His voice rose.

"Do be quiet, Harry. I don't think you want anyone to hear us."

"Anyone else you mean," he said but lowered his voice nonetheless.

"Again, you did warn me not to trust him. And I thought perhaps he was up to something nefarious and you might possibly be in some sort of trouble." She squared her shoulders. "So, I thought it best to find out what Mr. Nazzal wanted should you disappear into the night and were in need of rescue."

"From you?"

She ignored the skeptical note in his voice. "At any rate, the server really wasn't very good. His English was questionable, he didn't hear everything and he failed to get the American's name. However." She grinned in triumph. "I did."

He stared. "What? How?"

"Well, while there are a number of Americans staying here, most are traveling in groups. Only one fit what we thought a wealthy collector would look like."

"We?" Harry barely choked out the word.

"Yes, we." She cast him a pitying look. "Goodness, Harry, I couldn't possibly sort all this out by myself. I am not nearly that devious. Anyway, we made a few casual inquiries and discovered his name." She grabbed his hand and led him close to the nearest door. "He's sitting at the third table from the wall on the right side of the ballroom. His name is Mr. Edgar Wallace."

Poor Harry looked rather stunned but he obediently peered around the doorway then jerked back as if scalded. "He's not alone!"

"Exactly according to plan."

"The old ladies are with him!"

Sidney frowned. "They prefer not to be called *old ladies*. They're somewhat sensitive about their age."

"But—"

"Yes, I know they're with Mr. Wallace. We made his acquaintance on the terrace at tea." She shook her head in a chastising manner. "You really should have come to tea, Harry."

"Apparently."

"They'll keep him occupied while we slip into his room—"

"We?" His eyes widened in horror. "All of you?"

"Don't be absurd. I just said the ladies would keep Mr. Wallace occupied. You do need to pay attention if this is going to work."

"My apologies," he snapped. "I'm not used to having plans of this nature dictated to me by a group of old ladies."

"Not necessary but appreciated." She waved off his apology. "Understandable really. I can see how you might be somewhat unnerved by all this."

"Do you think so?"

"Sarcasm, Harry, is not appropriate at the moment. Now, as I was saying, the ladies will keep an eye on Mr. Wallace, and you and I—"

"Absolutely not." He shook his head. Apparently, the shock of the brilliant plan they had devised had worn off. "You are not going with me."

"Oh, but I am. This is exactly the sort of thing Mill— that *I* would have done in my days in Egypt. After all, an important remnant of ancient Egypt is at stake. And my life has been rather dull in recent years. Frankly, I'm running out of adventures to write about."

"This is not an adventure!"

"Don't be silly. Of course it is." She paused. "Do you want to hear the rest of the plan?"

"By all means, continue."

"There's really little more to it. We slip into Mr. Wallace's room—his room is just a few doors down from mine, which I thought most convenient. Oh, and I have a passkey." She reached into her bodice then hesitated. Harry's gaze fixed firmly on her hand. "Perhaps you should turn around."

"Sorry." He cleared his throat and turned. "How did you get a passkey?"

"There's a closet on each floor with cleaning equipment, fresh linens, that sort of thing. Poppy borrowed the key from the closet." Sidney pulled the key from the top of her corset. Poppy had advised her it was the perfect place to hide small objects should it be necessary to do so. "I find it amazing that a hotel of this quality doesn't have better security, although in fairness the closet door was locked."

Harry groaned. "Do I want to know how Mrs. Fitzhew-Wellmore opened the door?"

"Probably not." Sidney paused. "Although she didn't open the door, Effie did. It's remarkable the skills one picks up over a lifetime. And with nothing more than a hairpin and a buttonhook. Oh, you may turn around now."

He turned and pinned her with a hard look. "I don't want you further involved in this."

"How very gallant of you, Harry, but I am already involved."

"There is no way in hell I'm going to allow you to accompany me."

"Really, Harry, your language." She crossed her arms over her chest and again his gaze flicked to her décolletage. It was remarkably satisfying. "There's no way in hell I'm going to let you go without me."

"This is not open for debate."

"No, it's not." She smiled pleasantly. "First of all, I still have the key in my hand and if you attempt to force it from me, which would be most ungentlemanly, I shall scream as loud as possible, which would draw unwanted attention. Second, I know which room is Mr. Wallace's and you do not."

He shrugged. "I daresay I can discover that in a matter of minutes."

"Without question. However, getting into that room, with me standing outside my door and, I don't know, singing perhaps might rouse people from their beds to check on the noise." She grimaced. "You should be aware that my singing is not especially musical. I'm afraid I can't carry a tune."

His jaw tightened and he studied her for a long moment. It was all she could do to hold her ground and not give in to the temptation to thrust the key at him and flee. But this was indeed an adventure in the service of a noble cause. Millicent Forester wouldn't back down. Nor would Sidney Honeywell.

"You have given me no choice."

"Yes, I know." She grinned. "Rather brilliant of me, don't you think?"

"No," he snapped then heaved a sigh of surrender. "Perhaps."

"I knew you'd see it my way," she said with a satisfied nod. "We should get to it, then. I suspect our time is limited."

"There is more than a touch of larceny in you isn't there, Mrs. Gordon?" He shook his head. "Apparently, we have more in common than I thought."

Mrs. Gordon? He must be annoyed. She bit back a grin. No need to rub salt in the wound. "I simply think if one can recover a piece of history, to save it for the future, one should do so."

"You do realize we are skirting on the edge of illegality?"

"Come now, Harry. I think we're well beyond skirting. And isn't that part of the fun?"

"Fun?" He nearly choked on the word.

"Retrieving something that has already been stolen, to return it to where it rightfully belongs, strikes me as nothing less than morally right."

"You've never been in an Egyptian jail, have you Mrs. Gordon?

"Of course not." She paused. "Well, not yet."

He started to respond then apparently thought better of it.

"Shall we?" She smiled pleasantly.

He studied her for a moment longer then sighed. "After you."

They slipped back into the ballroom and casually made their way around the room. Sidney's gaze met Gwen's and the older woman gave her a slight nod. They had learned, when they'd met Mr. Wallace at tea, that he was fascinated by stories of exploration in Egypt and other lands. Between Effie, Poppy and Gwen, they had more than enough stories of their husbands' exploits to regale the American for hours. And he did appear to be completely engrossed in their tales. It struck Sidney that the ladies were engaged in a version of *The Book of the Thousand Nights and a Night*, even if Scheherazade was considerably younger than the three lady travelers and Mr. Wallace not at all a handsome king. Still, the stakes, while not as dire as Scheherazade's, were significant.

They took the lift to the first floor and started toward her room, until the lift and its efficient operator had descended from sight. Her heart thudded with excitement although she did wish Harry hadn't mentioned Egyptian jails.

"This is his room." Sidney stopped in front of a suite three doors down from her own. She handed Harry the key.

He frowned. "Are you certain about this? There's no need for you to go in. You can stay in the hall and warn me if anyone comes."

"What kind of an adventure would that be?" she said with far more confidence than she felt. It was extremely thoughtful of him to consider that she might be having second thoughts. Regardless, what kind of heroine allowed the hero to venture into the unknown by himself? "Go on, open the door."

"Very well." Resignation sounded in his voice and he unlocked the door, allowing her to enter first as he cast another cautious look up and down the corridor. He then closed the door, locked it behind him and flicked on the light. Electricity was certainly convenient. The room had a similar layout to hers although the furniture was not exactly the same. "Any idea where it might be?"

"It's in the chest of drawers." She gestured at the large piece of furniture flanking one side of a washstand. "In the drawer with his undergarments and his socks."

He stared at her. "How the devil do you know that?"

"At tea, one of the ladies said she was concerned about keeping her jewelry in her room and thought perhaps she should leave it in the keeping of the hotel. Mr. Wallace said he always put his valuables in the drawer under his unmentionables as no one ever thought to look there."

"You are a clever little group, aren't you?" Harry strode across the room to the chest and opened the top drawer. "Remind me never to cross a determined author and her band of aged miscreants."

"Do hurry, Harry." She twisted her hands together. This was more unnerving than she had anticipated. Perhaps she should have waited in the hall after all.

"One minute." Harry rummaged through the top drawer, quite thoroughly and entirely too slowly.

"Have you found it?"

"You'll know when I do," he murmured. Odd, the more confident he sounded, the more nervous she grew. He moved to the second drawer and a moment later he paused. "I think I have it."

At once her trepidation vanished and she hurried across the room to join him.

He drew out a black sock, weighted down by something in the toe. He slid his hand in, pulled it out and presented the stolen artifact with a flourish and a smile. "The missing medallion of Amenemhat II's queen consort. Well, possibly, anyway."

"May I?" She held out her hand.

"Certainly." He handed it to her then returned the sock to the drawer.

It was heavier than she would have thought but then it was gold and warmed in her hand. The medallion was grayish yellow in color which was to be expected. Ancient gold usually had some silver in it. It was about an inch and a half in diameter and both sides were engraved, with one side's design looking more complete than the other. How very intriguing.

"Isn't this interesting." She tilted it toward the light.

"You read hieroglyphics?" Surprise sounded in his voice.

"Don't you?" she said absently.

"More or less." He closed the drawer. "I would say our work here is done."

"Shouldn't we look around to see if there are any more of the missing items? I understood this was part of a shipment of antiquities."

"I do hope you paid that server well," he said with a huff. "And no. We need to leave."

"It would only take a minute."

"If Wallace was in possession of more than the medallion, Nazzal would have told me and ask me to retrieve those as well. Now—" he waved toward the door "—let's go, shall we?"

"If you're—"

A knock sounded at the door and they froze.

Her heart skipped a beat and her gaze met Harry's. He put his finger to his lips.

The knock sounded again. At least it wasn't Mr. Wallace. He would never knock on his own door.

"It's the maid to turn down the bed," she whispered.

Harry nodded toward the wardrobe. "Hide. In there."

"It's not nearly big enough for both of us." She still had the medallion in her hand. Without thinking she slid it between her breasts, tight against her corset.

"Only one thing to do, then." He grabbed her hand, strode to the bed and yanked back the covers. "Get in."

"Are you mad?"

"Apparently."

The distinct sound of a key in the keyhole vanquished her hesitation. She swept the back of her skirt tighter around her and fairly leaped onto the bed, Harry immediately following suit. He pulled the covers up to hide any indication of their clothing, then wrapped his arms around her. In spite of the precarious nature of their situation, and the fear that gripped her, this was not at all unpleasant.

The doorknob turned.

"My apologies," he whispered, pulled her tighter to him and pressed his lips to hers.

And her world stopped.

Perhaps it was the element of surprise. Or the simple fact that she'd never been kissed before or the sheer terror of discovery. Or more likely it was him. Annoying, sanctimonious, heroic Harry Armstrong.

A squeal sounded from the doorway along with a stream of apologetic Arabic. Sidney barely noticed. Almost at once the door snapped shut.

And yet he didn't release her and she didn't push him away. She had never imagined the sheer intimacy of a man's mouth pressed to hers. The shimmering sense of longing that swept through her and made her insides quiver. Oh, she had considered the idea of being kissed but had long ago accepted if she hadn't been kissed by the age of thirty-two the chances were good she never would be. Certainly, Millicent Forester had shared the occasional kiss with Richard Weatherly but writing about a kiss was one thing. Experiencing it in real life something else entirely. Something quite remarkable that left the oddest flutter in the pit of her stomach and the strangest ache for something, well, more. At last he drew back and stared in a disconcerted sort of way.

"No apologies necessary, Harry." She mustered a shaky smile. "You did what needed to be done."

"Yes, well, we should—"

"Indeed we should." She forced a brisk note to her voice. "Perhaps if you would release me?"

"Of course." He shook his head as if to clear it then

threw off the covers, slid out of bed and helped her to her feet. They remade the bed as best they could, moving as quickly and silently as possible. There was the distinct possibility the maid might realize at any moment that the couple in bed did not belong in that room.

Sidney stepped to the cheval mirror, adjusted the off-the-shoulder cap-sleeves of her gown and tried to smooth away wrinkles in her skirt. She patted her hair back into place and decided it would do. Harry stepped up behind her and straightened his collar and tie. Her hands stilled and her gaze met his in the mirror. She had no idea what to say. What she should say. And, aside from "kiss me again, Harry," no idea what she wanted to say. Ridiculous, of course. He had kissed her out of necessity. A kiss he had apologized for in advance. It was nothing more than a ruse. Certainly he had asked to kiss her on board ship but he had not made such a request again. And aside, from that moment in the pyramid, he'd had other chances that he'd squandered as well. Surely a man who wanted to kiss a woman would seize on any opportunity.

Harry looked every bit as flustered as she. Was he also at a loss for words? Because he regretted his actions? Because he didn't want her to think it was more significant than it was? Or because he too wished for more?

"We should go," he said abruptly and moved to the door, opened it cautiously and peered into the hall. He opened it wider and waved her through.

"Thank you," she murmured and stepped past him.

They made their way back to the ballroom in near total silence, awkward and uncomfortable. She had no idea what the man was thinking although he did seem distracted and deep in thought. Sidney too had any number of thoughts crowding her head.

Not the least of which was wondering what it would be like to be kissed by Mr. Harry Armstrong when it wasn't spurred by necessity but by desire.

And what it might take to find out.

CHAPTER FOURTEEN

WHAT IN THE name of all that was holy had come over him?

It was a kiss. A fully clothed kiss at that and nothing more than the brilliant solution to an unexpected dilemma, even if perhaps it wasn't entirely necessary. Regardless, it was of no real significance whatsoever. Why, he had kissed any number of women. And most under circumstances far more intimate than tonight's. Even so, the feel of her in his arms, her body pressed against his, her lips responding first with demure hesitation then with rapt abandon, refused to leave his head. No, he might as well admit it. It was more than a kiss, more than a spur of the moment ploy to prevent discovery. He wasn't sure exactly what but definitely more. And hadn't he been wanting to kiss her for some time?

Harry accepted a glass of champagne from a passing waiter and lingered near the doorway, watching Sidney across the room. The moment they returned to the ballroom she joined the other ladies at Mr. Wallace's table. Judging from the look on the portly American's face when he stood and took her hand, he too had probably read her blasted book. Surely Wallace's attention had more to do with his admiration of her work than the fact that—in spite of her efforts—she looked the tiniest bit tousled and eminently desirable. The idea that Wallace might be interested in something other than her writing was extremely annoying. When she'd accused Harry of being jealous of Nazzal and he'd admitted it, he hadn't really meant it. Or perhaps he had. He had no idea what he was thinking anymore. This awkward business of *liking* a woman was proving to be most confusing.

"She's really quite remarkable, don't you think?" Lady Blodgett appeared at Harry's side.

He glanced at her in surprise. "I didn't realize you had left the others."

"You're not very observant, then, are you?"

He chuckled. "Apparently not."

She rolled her gaze toward the ceiling. "It's a wonder you're still alive."

"Luck, Lady Blodgett." He sipped his drink. "I will take luck over skill any day."

"Luck frequently runs out, young man."

"It hasn't yet." He paused. "At least not for me."

"You didn't answer my question."

"About Mrs. Gordon?" His gaze shifted back to Sidney. "Yes, I do think she's remarkable."

"Did you and she take care of your little errand?" she asked in an offhand manner, as if inquiring about nothing more important than fetching a forgotten item from her room. Apparently Sidney wasn't the only one with a touch of larceny in her soul.

"We did."

"And it was successful?"

"It was."

Bloody hell. He'd completely forgotten that Sidney still had the medallion. Although no one knew that but him. And even when Wallace discovered the artifact was missing, he would not sound an alarm. A man in possession of stolen goods rarely made a public outcry when they went missing. There was nothing to connect Sidney, or Harry either for that matter, to the relic. The maid had seen nothing but two entwined figures covered nearly to the tops of their heads. Even so, the longer Sidney and her friends were in Wallace's company, the greater the chances one of them would unintentionally say something. He was not overly confident in their ability to keep quiet. "Perhaps it would be prudent if you and the others bid Mr. Wallace a good evening."

"I was thinking exactly the same thing." She slanted him a curious look. "You can trust us, you know. We are far cleverer than we may appear."

"I have absolutely no doubt of that, my lady."

"It is, however, when engaged in any sort of subterfuge, wise to err on the side of caution."

"Exactly, Lady Blodgett." He doubted the ladies ever engaged in any sort of *subterfuge* whatsoever unless, of course, one included their assistance with Sidney's own deception. And, while they might not realize it, they hadn't been entirely successful with that. He stifled a smile.

"Age does not denote stupidity, Harry. Unless, of course, one was stupid in one's younger days. I assure you neither Effie nor Poppy nor I was stupid in our youth."

"I never—"

"Furthermore, we were all married to men who were hardly ever present. They were off exploring the unknown or, in Effie's case, serving the Crown. They had grand adventures and epic exploits and, we privately suspected, a great deal of fun." She pinned him with a firm look. "Do you know what happens to women who marry such men?"

"I've never thought about it," he said cautiously.

"Which indicates you never seriously entertained the

thought of marriage with any particular woman. Good to know." Before he could ask why she nodded and continued. "Women who marry men of adventure either become helpless, delicate flowers who can barely take care of themselves or they become independent and self-reliant." She paused. "There isn't one among the three of us who wouldn't have done very nearly anything if it had meant our husbands would be home to build a life with us. But, as that was not to be, we became the women we are now. Do you understand what I'm saying?"

He stared in confusion. "I'm afraid not."

She sighed. "We have always done what needed to be done. On our own or with our friends. In some cases, we did so to set things right. In others, because it was the right thing to do. Or because someone needed our assistance, even if they might not have realized it at the time. And now that we are in the inevitable final period of our lives, when we are no longer troubled by the bothersome rules of propriety or even laws, we still do what we believe is necessary. For the greater good, a noble cause if you will, of course, not merely for fun."

"I see," he lied.

"No you don't but it is sweet of you to say." Her gaze turned back to Sidney and the others. "I should gather my little flock and be off."

"Good evening, then. Sleep well."

"Oh, we have no intention of retiring." She scoffed. "It's not yet ten o'clock and we are on holiday. Although I daresay we will be in our rooms before midnight. But I met a lovely group of travelers this afternoon, here on a tour. Not, unfortunately, a Lady Travelers tour but a Thomas Cook excursion. Those people are everywhere you know."

"There are a lot of tourists in Egypt."

"I've even run into a few people from London right here in the hotel who know people I know. I must say I did not expect that." She shook her head. "Many of those from the Cook's tour have read either Sidney's book or her stories in the *Messenger* and are eager to meet her. They did not dine at the hotel tonight but we arranged to gather here in the small dining room shortly after ten. That charming Mr. Chalmers arranged it for us. Wasn't that thoughtful of him?"

"Mr. Chalmers is nothing if not thoughtful."

"It provides the perfect excuse for bidding good evening to Mr. Wallace." She smiled in a smug manner.

"Brilliant, Lady Blodgett." He grinned. "You and your friends never fail to amaze me."

"What a lovely thing to say, Harry." She took a step toward Sidney's table then paused. "But I much prefer *devious* to *brilliant*." She cast him a sly smile and took her leave.

Harry was still chuckling when she reached the others. Their ploy appeared to work perfectly and within a few minutes the older ladies and Sidney had excused themselves and left the ballroom. Perhaps *devious* was indeed the right word.

He toyed with the idea of retiring for the evening himself but knew he wouldn't get a moment's rest as long as the medallion was in Sidney's possession. Not that he was concerned that she might be in any kind of danger. Still, as Lady Blodgett pointed out, it was best to err on the side of caution. Besides, it did seem to him the successful conclusion of their *adventur*e called for a celebration. What better way to celebrate than with champagne? The woman did like champagne. Why not bring a bottle to her room? He could bring his writing for her to peruse later as well. Not that he wanted to but it would be cowardly to flee from her opinion.

And should a shared bottle lead to something more… She was a widow, after all, and had quite enthusiastically returned his kiss. He had no intention of seducing her but if one thing were to lead to another…

A few minutes after midnight, he knocked softly on her door, champagne and glasses in one hand, his writing tucked under his arm. He'd never been the least bit nervous about an assignation before but this was different. This was Sidney. The woman who had outraged him with her less-than-accurate writing, even if her actions tonight were very much like something the character in her stories might do. The woman who had brought him back to Egypt. The woman who might possibly be working her way into his heart. No woman had done that, ever. He had thought no woman ever could.

He knocked again, louder. No doubt she was already fast asleep. Even he was feeling the tiring effects of the long day. As much as he wanted to pound on her door, that would awaken any number of other guests. He had no desire to encounter Wallace in the hall or anyone else. There was as well the slim possibility that he had completely misunderstood Sidney's response to his kiss. Although he wouldn't wager on that. He had kissed enough women to know when one shared his desire.

Still he couldn't quite disregard the idea. Sidney was unlike any woman he'd ever known. He slipped the twenty-odd pages he'd brought with him under her door and started toward his room, his stomach twisting in what? Disappointment? This was certainly not the first time an anticipated liaison had not come to fruition although it had been rare. But what if he was indeed mistaken? What if what he was feeling was not mutual? What was he feeling?

Good God, she'd turned him into some kind of sniveling mass of indecision. A creature mired in confusion and overly concerned with *feelings* of all things. He'd never been like this with a woman before. No doubt all that effort to behave like a gentleman, like an *earl*, was to blame. Or possibly the blame could be placed on Sidney. Or even on Egypt. He had no idea. He had never liked unanswered questions. He much preferred knowing where he stood and what exactly was going on but apparently his head was now filled with endless questions and few answers. And *feelings*!

It was impossible to sleep. He tossed and turned all night when he wasn't pacing his room and stopped himself more than once from stalking to Sidney's room and breaking down the door. It was ridiculous, of course. What would he say then? *My apologies for shattering your door but I was curious as to your thoughts on whether the kiss we shared was nothing more significant than a pretense to fool the maid or was it perhaps something extremely important?* By morning he'd come to the realization that he could hardly demand to know what, if any, feelings she had before he came to terms with his own mind and perhaps his heart.

Sidney was not at breakfast and neither were the other ladies. There was however a note at the desk for him from Mrs. Higginbotham saying they were joining their new friends from the Thomas Cook group for a morning tour of the several of the city's mosques but they would resume their schedule in the afternoon. As the note did not list which of the hundreds of mosques in Cairo they would be visiting, Harry had no choice but to await their return. It was most annoying. Patience had never been his strongest quality. Regardless of whether or not he knew his own feelings, for good or ill, he wanted to sort this out with Sidney. He ran into Corbin in the lobby who was of no help whatsoever and was in fact rather pleased not to have to trail after the ladies. He intended to spend the morning writing a dispatch on Sidney's visit to the pyramids. The details of which he had apparently heard from Sidney at tea. Harry made a mental note never to miss tea again.

Harry tried to do a little of his own writing in the writing room off the main hall but his gaze kept straying to the door and he finally accepted that his efforts were futile. Besides, while he hadn't seemed to have any difficulty in London writing about the adventures he had shared with Ben and Walter, there were apparently too many memories here to write accurately. Blasted *feelings* kept getting in the way of telling a story properly. And when he wasn't trying to record the past, he found himself writing silly things about hair the color of spun gold and the caress of a cheek as soft as a rose petal. A *rose petal* for God's sake?

Harry finally moved to the terrace, taking a table near the front steps and attempting to read the English edition of the *Egyptian Gazette*. But his attention wavered with every new arrival. He did note the departure of Mr. Wallace. The man did not look happy. It was shortly after one when the ladies finally returned.

Sidney was not with them.

"Good afternoon, ladies." Harry met them in front of the entry between the sphinxes. "Where is she?"

The ladies traded confused glances.

"She?" Lady Blodgett asked. "Who?

Mrs. Fitzhew-Wellmore frowned in confusion. "Which she?"

"What are you talking about, Harry?" Mrs. Higginbotham's eyes narrowed. "And why do you look so annoyed?"

"Because I am annoyed." He ushered them to his table and waited until they were seated. "I see Mrs. Gordon is not with you. Did you lose her again?"

Again the ladies exchanged looks.

"You mean she isn't here? At the hotel?" A worried note sounded in Mrs. Fitzhew-Wellmore's voice.

"She isn't with you?" A trickle of unease ran up the back of his neck.

Lady Blodgett shook her head. "She didn't come with us." She thought for a moment. "We bid her good-night at the lifts, a bit before midnight I think." She glanced at the other ladies who nodded in agreement. "Then we all retired to our respective rooms."

"I realize it's past one but perhaps she overslept," Mrs. Higginbotham said. "She did seem quite tired last night, as we all were."

"Sidney is usually an early riser," Mrs. Fitzhew-Wellmore murmured what they were all thinking.

"Did you check her room, Harry?" Mrs. Higginbotham asked.

"No," he said sharply. "I assumed she was with you."

"Very well, then, I will." Mrs. Higginbotham stood and strode into the hotel, the very epitome of determination. Woe to anyone who might stand in her way.

"And I will check with the front desk." Lady Blodgett rose. "If Sidney is not here, perhaps she left a note." She turned and disappeared into the building.

"I'm certain there's nothing to worry about." Mrs. Fitzhew-Wellmore's words belied the look of concern in her eyes.

"Of course not." Still, there was a distinct sense of apprehension curling in his stomach. It had been some time since he'd had that horrid, queasy feeling. Unfortunately, it had never been wrong.

Lady Blodgett was the first to return. "There was indeed a note from Sidney saying she was meeting with another group of readers. She added that we shouldn't worry and she would see us later today." She paused. "The clerk said it was there this morning so it was probably left last night."

"Last night?" Harry met Lady Blodgett's gaze. "Was he sure?"

"Quite sure."

"Sidney said we shouldn't worry and I for one do not intend to." Mrs. Fitzhew-Wellmore nodded firmly as if trying to convince herself as much as the others. "If anyone can take care of herself it's Sidney."

"Because of all those adventures she's had in Egypt?" he said in a sharper manner than he had intended.

"Well, yes," Mrs. Fitzhew-Wellmore said weakly. "Among other things…"

Other than her vivid imagination, her skill at deception and her delight in larceny, Harry was afraid to ask what those *other things* were.

Mrs. Higginbotham returned and sat down heavily at the table. "She isn't in her room and it appears she did not sleep there."

"What?" Harry stared.

"How could you possibly know that?" Mrs. Fitzhew-Wellmore twisted her hands together.

"The gown she wore last night is missing." Mrs. Higginbotham heaved a deep sigh. "This is all my fault. If it wasn't for me, we wouldn't be here."

"What do you mean?" Harry asked.

"Don't be absurd." Mrs. Fitzhew-Wellmore ignored him and patted her friend's hand. "If anyone is to blame…" She turned an accusing eye on Harry.

"I suggest we dispense with pointing fingers for the moment," Lady Blodgett said calmly. "Sidney is an intelligent woman and we might be making more out of this than it is. There could well be nothing to be concerned about whatsoever. She could return at any moment with a perfectly logical explanation. Harry." She met Harry's gaze directly and in spite of her cool demeanor, unease shone in her eyes. "What do you think?"

He hesitated but it seemed pointless to try to hide anything as they probably already knew everything. "Are you aware she has the medallion?"

"We were not," Lady Blodgett said slowly.

"Oh dear," Mrs. Fitzhew-Wellmore murmured.

"However, Mr. Wallace was returning to America today." Mrs. Higginbotham nodded. "So I daresay he is not a concern."

But who knew how many others were aware of the stolen items. Harry ignored the disquieting thought.

"Harry." Mrs. Higginbotham's gaze pinned his. "What are we to do now?"

He drew a deep breath. "Nothing."

"Nothing?" Mrs. Fitzhew-Wellmore's voice rose. "What do you mean nothing? Surely there's something we can do."

"Absolutely not." His gaze settled on Mrs. Fitzhew-Wellmore. "The three of you are to stay here in the hotel.

I don't want to lose any of you in addition to Mrs. Gordon." His gaze shifted to Lady Blodgett. "None of you are familiar with Cairo, none of you speak Arabic and none of you are suited to this kind of search." He turned to Mrs. Higginbotham. "Mrs. Gordon's note said not to worry which indicates to me she is not in any sort of trouble and wherever she went she did so willingly. I understand you are not overly fond of me, but I ask you to trust me now. Will you?"

"We really don't have much choice, do we?" Mrs. Higginbotham huffed. "So yes, I suppose we will trust you."

"Not a rousing endorsement but I'll take it. I agree this is probably nothing of any consequence." From the looks on their faces, it was obvious they didn't believe him any more than he believed himself. "I assure you, I will locate Mrs. Gordon and we shall all laugh about this later."

"How?" Lady Blodgett asked. "If you expect us not to do anything, we must know what you intend to do."

"Fair enough." He nodded. "It seems to me—"

"Mr. Armstrong, ladies." Nazzal appeared beside the table and smiled a greeting. Excellent. While he'd told Harry last night he would return today to collect the medallion, Harry's first thought now was to contact him. If anyone could find a missing Englishwoman in Cairo, Nazzal could. "Might I say how lovely you all look today? Oh, but your numbers are not complete. Where is the delightful Mrs. Gordon?"

The ladies looked at each other. He did hope they were shrewd enough to stay quiet. Gaining Nazzal's help wasn't always a simple matter of requesting it. But possession of the artifact did give Harry some leverage at the moment.

"Missing," Mrs. Fitzhew-Wellmore blurted.

Lady Blodgett grimaced. "We don't know where she is."

"She's been gone since last night and we're quite concerned," Mrs. Higginbotham added. So much for keeping their mouths shut.

"Is she?" The Egyptian looked at Harry, a dozen questions in his eyes. "Are you sure?"

"Unfortunately, yes," Harry said. "I was hoping you could be of assistance."

"I shall do whatever I can." Nazzal paused. "But first Mr. Armstrong, a private word if you will? In the bar perhaps?"

Harry got to his feet.

"Oh, he doesn't have your medallion, if that's what you want," Mrs. Higginbotham said.

"What?" Nazzal stared.

"Mrs. Higginbotham!" Harry snapped.

"Oh dear." Mrs. Higginbotham winced. "I wasn't thinking." She leaned toward Nazzal and lowered her voice to something she might have intended as a stage whisper. "He doesn't have your *object*."

Harry groaned.

"Oh?" Nazzal's gaze shot to his. "What does she mean?"

"It's really a somewhat amusing story," Harry began.

"You were to notify me at once if you failed to retrieve the—" he glanced at the ladies "—*object*."

"Yes, well about that." Harry grimaced. "I did retrieve the *object*, I just don't have it at the moment."

"Mrs. Gordon has the—" Mrs. Fitzhew-Wellmore paused in a dramatic fashion "—*object*."

"How did she get the object." Nazzal's brow furrowed. The man looked decidedly confused, but then he was not accustomed to Sidney's elderly companions. Apparently his last encounter with them did not sufficiently prepare him. Harry suspected he frequently had that same look himself. "And how do any of you know about this?"

"You should sit down, Mr. Nazzal." Lady Blodgett waved at Harry's chair beside hers then signaled a waiter for another. "We'll be happy to explain everything."

Nazzal cast Harry a dubious glance and sat.

Once they were all settled Lady Blodgett explained how Sidney had learned about the *object*, Mrs. Fitzhew-Wellmore's contribution with her appropriation of the passkey to Wallace's room, Mrs. Higginbotham's skills at opening locked doors and their mutual effort to keep the American entertained.

"And while Sidney did tell us she and Harry had been successful, she did not elaborate as to the details," Lady Blodgett finished and directed an annoyed look at Harry. "And she never mentioned she had the object."

"How did she come to have the object, Harry?" Mrs. Higginbotham's eyes narrowed.

"Yes, Harry," Nazzal chimed in. At some point in Lady Blodgett's explanation—somewhere between Sidney's hiring of a server to eavesdrop on them and Wallace's admiration of her work, Nazzal's annoyance had turned to amusement. "How did Mrs. Gordon come into possession of the object?"

"We were nearly caught by a maid and Mrs. Gordon hid it in her dress," Harry said simply. He was not about to divulge all the details of their foray.

Mrs. Higginbotham's brow rose. "That dress was not conducive to the concealment of anything."

Mrs. Fitzhew-Wellmore cleared her throat and cast a quick pointed glance down at her bosom.

Mrs. Higginbotham stared, then her expression

cleared. "Oh, I see. Quite right." She nodded. "Excellent place to hide a small object. Always has been."

Nazzal choked back a laugh.

"What do you find so amusing, Mr. Nazzal?" Lady Blodgett said coolly. "The fact of where Mrs. Gordon hid the object or the fact that we are not embarrassed to mention it?"

"Lady Blodgett." Nazzal took the older lady's hand and lifted it to his lips. "I find you and your friends to be most enchanting."

"Do you?" Lady Blodgett stared for a moment then nodded. "Well, we do try."

Harry studied him curiously. "You're not at all worried about this are you?"

"Mrs. Gordon's absence is a matter of some concern although I doubt it has anything to do with the object. Nor do I think it possible that anyone would know it's in her possession. You're not a player in this particular game anymore and I don't think you would be connected to the object. Yet another reason why I asked *you* to retrieve it," Nazzal said. "Mr. Wallace was not unobserved during his stay here. He's made no contact with whomever sold it to him nor did he make any telephone calls. And, according to my information, he was on the train to Port Said a few hours ago."

Harry nodded. "I saw him leave."

All three ladies looked relieved if not entirely convinced. Harry agreed with them.

"You'll help us." Harry met Nazzal's gaze. It was as much a question as comment.

"Anything for a friend, Harry." Nazzal stood. "I shall make some inquiries and return as soon as I learn anything."

"As soon as possible, if you would, please, Mr. Nazzal," Mrs. Fitzhew-Wellmore said with a feeble smile.

"Yes, of course." He nodded in a gallant manner and took his leave.

"Ladies." Harry retook his seat. "Your plans for the rest of the day?"

"Do you really think it will take that long?" Worry creased Mrs. Higginbotham's brow.

"Mrs. Higginbotham. Effie." He stared into her eyes. "I know you have heard stories about western women being abducted and never seen again. But I assure you, a widow—a woman who has been married, a woman past her twentieth year—is not as tempting a target as one might think."

Her eyes widened with indignation. "Rubbish, Harry. Sidney is a lovely woman and I would think kidnappers would find her most desirable."

"Beyond that, she's brilliant," Mrs. Fitzhew-Wellmore added. "And one couldn't find a nicer, more generous person."

"It would be dreadful if we misplaced her." Lady Blodgett's eyes narrowed. "We would all miss her, wouldn't we, Harry?"

"Yes, of course." That awful feeling in his stomach was back.

"Even though you and she are at odds over her writing," Mrs. Higginbotham began, "it's our observation that you have become quite fond of each other. As traveling companions and perhaps friends?"

"Well, yes, I suppose."

"Or even something more?" Mrs. Fitzhew-Wellmore pressed.

"Something…" Harry paused. All three ladies wore

the same look of anticipation on their faces. As if they now expected him to declare his *feelings*, whatever they may be. Still, he couldn't bring himself to deny that there might indeed be *feelings*. "Now is neither the time nor the place to discuss a matter that is none of your concern."

Anticipation turned to disbelief and then indignation.

"Well." Lady Blodgett rose to her feet and the others followed. "I believe I shall go to my room. And then perhaps the writing room."

"I daresay we have any number of Lady Travelers pamphlets we should write based on our recent experiences," Mrs. Higginbotham said.

"One alone on the necessity of leaving notes that are perfectly clear as to whether or not one is being abducted." Mrs. Fitzhew-Wellmore glanced at her friends who nodded in agreement.

"Do let us know if there's any word." Mrs. Higginbotham's gaze bored into his. "At once, Harry. Do you understand?"

"Perfectly. And as we are making ourselves clear—" a hard note sounded in his voice "—you will not, either individually or as a group, under any circumstances, leave the hotel." He wouldn't put it past them to try to find Sidney themselves.

"Goodness, Harry." Lady Blodgett huffed. "I told you last night we were not stupid. I assure you, our intelligence has not lessened since then." She and the others cast him nearly identical disparaging looks then marched into the hotel. As long as they didn't take it upon themselves to find Sidney, he didn't care how they looked at him. But the last thing he needed was to lose them all.

A message from Nazzal finally arrived shortly before tea. Harry spotted the messenger and met him at the front desk. The moment he opened the note, he was surrounded by Sidney's friends who must have been watching the desk as closely as he had.

Mustafa's note was straight to the point.

Mrs. Gordon has been located in a harem.

CHAPTER FIFTEEN

THE PROBLEM WITH being in a country when one didn't speak the native language was that there was likely to be all sorts of misunderstandings.

When Sidney returned to her room, she found a formally phrased note on royal stationery had been slipped under her door inviting her to call on the Princess Naile—an aunt of the khedive, the viceroy of Egypt. Apparently the princess had quite enjoyed her book and would like to meet her. Sidney was, of course, both flattered and delighted. And really, how could anyone turn down a royal request? The note also said she would be provided an escort to one of the royal residences and was to accompany the bearer of the note. Sidney hadn't been back to her rooms for hours. Who knew when the invitation had been delivered. Surely, her escort was no longer waiting for her. Still, it would be rude not to at least make certain.

The night clerk directed her to an impatient-looking Egyptian gentleman in the lobby, dressed in long flowing robes, and more than a little irate. His English was passable although he spoke so quickly it was not possible to understand everything he said. And while Sidney tried to explain she could not go anywhere at this hour—why, it was nearly midnight—he was adamant that his instructions had been to fetch her and fetch her he would. Before she knew it, he had whisked her out of the hotel and into a waiting carriage. It was most annoying and on the drive to the residence she did wonder why she was indeed irritated but not the least bit frightened. If anything, she was rather excited. How thrilling to meet a real Egyptian princess in the dead of night. Admittedly, she could be in the midst of an abduction but that seemed rather far-fetched. Her escort was determined but not the least bit threatening. He made no attempt to be circumspect or discreet and even in Cairo she imagined a kidnapper would try to be inconspicuous. Furthermore, she would wager kidnappers rarely sent formal invitations and were probably never acknowledged by desk clerks. Certainly Millicent Forester would not be frightened. She would see this as an adventure and so would Sidney.

In no time at all they arrived at one of the gates that separated one part of the city from another. Her escort—a Mr. Gamal she thought although she might have misheard his name—assisted her out of the carriage then accompanied her a short distance down the dark narrow street and around the corner to a nondescript door. It might have been somewhat distressing had not Mr. Gamal continued to mutter under his breath, obviously at the inconvenience she had caused him. He knocked sharply and the door opened almost at once. Sidney was led through endless corridors, twisting and turning and not all conducive to remembering the route, should she need to do so later. In spite of lit oil sconces, it was entirely too dim to see much of anything. Sidney had the impression of endless stone walls and patterned tiled floors and glimpsed the occasional high, lattice-covered window. And while she did try to stay unconcerned, even Millicent might be a bit apprehensive at this point.

At last they reached another door, this one ornate with

carvings and brass ornamentation. Mr. Gamal knocked sharply and a few minutes later the door opened. A lovely woman, a bit younger than Sidney, clad in the filmiest of silken robes with wide flowing trousers, looked from Sidney to Mr. Gamal and frowned in confusion. Before she could utter a word, the man let forth a rapid-fire stream of Arabic complete with frenzied gestures—most directed at Sidney—and accompanied by obvious indignation. One didn't have to know the language to recognize that. The moment he paused for breath, the lady responded— her words coming just as fast and her indignation matching his own. At last they seemed to come to some sort of grudging agreement. Mr. Gamal bowed to Sidney then hurried away, obviously relieved to be rid of her.

"My fervent apologies, Mrs. Gordon. Please, come in," the lady said, her voice refined, her English almost perfect. She stepped back and waved Sidney ahead then closed the door. "This wing of the palace is reserved for the harem."

"The harem?" Sidney stepped forward cautiously.

The lady glanced at Sidney's feet. "Your shoes, Mrs. Gordon?"

"Of course," she murmured and removed her evening slippers.

A gallery bordered by columns opened up into a large court with high curved ceilings. Sconces cast a dim light in the expanse. A fountain splashed musically in the center of the room and low sofas and mattresses and cushions were scattered about, all covered with brilliantly colored fabrics in traditional Egyptian patterns.

"This is where the women and children of the household reside along with their servants. It is not quite the den of immorality and salacious behavior Europeans and the west have been led to believe." She tilted her head and studied Sidney. "But I assumed you would know that."

"I have heard any number of things about harems. But—" Sidney shook her head "—I've never had the opportunity to visit one." Nor had she ever been in a royal residence.

"I'm afraid it will be far more ordinary than you expect." She smiled. "I am Lady Hatice, a distant cousin of the royal family, and I'm afraid there has been a dreadful mistake."

"Has there?"

"Gamal left quite early in the evening to deliver our note and request your visit. My mistake was in telling him to wait and escort you here. I didn't intend for him to wait all night." She rolled her gaze toward the high ceiling. "Some men are scarcely more intelligent than the donkeys they ride. Indeed, I have known any number of donkeys far cleverer than any man."

"I was engaged for the evening so I did not get your note until a short while ago," Sidney said. "And then Mr. Gamal was quite adamant in his insistence that I was to come with him."

Lady Hatice shook her head in disbelief. "Again, my apologies, Mrs. Gordon. Nearly everyone is abed at this hour. But as it is now so late, we would be honored if you would agree to stay the night. Then you may visit with Princess Naile in the morning."

Sidney hesitated. "I really should get back."

"Ah, but you said you've never seen a harem before." She smiled. "I will reveal all our secrets to you and perhaps they will find their way into one of your stories."

Sidney laughed. "Very well, then, I'll stay." Besides, if she recalled correctly, she had read that it was considered rude not to accept hospitality when offered—especially when it came from a royal household. "But I do need to send a note to my friends at the hotel. I would hate for them to worry."

"Of course. I will have writing materials provided at once." Lady Hatice nodded. "Now, allow me to show you to your room." She led Sidney out of the court and into another corridor, stopped after a short distance and opened the nearest door. "I hope it is acceptable."

A gas lamp burned on a low table next to an equally low bed piled high with comforters and coverlets. Tempting and almost irresistible. Sidney bit back a yawn. "It's lovely, thank you."

Two young maids appeared at the doorway. "Asim and Fenuku will assist you with your gown and help you change. We have garments for sleeping for you."

It was fortunate Sidney had thought to hide the medallion in her room before coming down to meet Mr. Gamal. She had no idea how she would explain a gold object falling out of her corset.

"And I shall send someone with pen and paper. When you're done with your note, Asim will bring it to me and I'll see to it that it is delivered to the hotel immediately."

"Thank you."

"I can see you're weary so I will bid you good evening." Lady Hatice turned to leave.

"Might I ask you a question before you go?"

"Please do." She turned back to Sidney and smiled. "As many as you wish."

"I was curious about your English. It's very nearly perfect."

"How kind of you to say." Lady Hatice's eyes glowed with pride. "I had an English governess and spent three years at a school for girls in England. My father believed, given the British presence in Egypt, his children should learn the language as well as the nature of the people."

"And did you learn the nature of the people?"

Lady Hatice considered the question. "Like people everywhere they are concerned with status and rank, and place those they don't know in—what is the word? Ah yes—pigeonholes. We do the same. Those who are different from ourselves are always looked upon oddly." She shrugged. "I did enjoy my stay in England but I do not regret leaving."

"I see." Sidney wasn't sure what to say. She couldn't really dispute Lady Hatice's assessment as much as she wanted to. And wasn't Sidney in a pigeonhole of her own?

"Did you have another question?"

"Quite a few really."

Lady Hatice raised a brow. "About harems no doubt."

"I'm just wondering how one comes to live in a harem."

"It is not so different than any large family that shares a domicile. There is nothing more important to us than family. Like you, I am a widow. After my husband died, my children and I came here to live. When I marry again, and I do hope to marry again, I shall leave."

"You don't mind living here?"

"I am not a prisoner, Mrs. Gordon. Contrary to what you might have heard, we can come and go as we please." Her eyes twinkled with amusement. "I suspect you will have additional questions in the morning but is there anything else you wish answered now?"

"Not really." Sidney drew a deep breath. "Although I have never met a princess before and I'm not sure what is expected of me."

"You would greet her in very much the same way you would greet a princess in England—no more than a courteous bow is necessary. Respect, Mrs. Gordon, is truly all that is needed."

"Very well," Sidney said faintly.

"I can assure you, the princess and everyone else is going to be quite taken with you."

"Really?"

"Oh my yes." Lady Hatice's eyes widened in surprise. "I am sorry, I thought you understood. Princess Naile as well as all the other ladies here absolutely adore—" she grinned "—Millicent Forester, Richard Weatherly and all the *Tales of a Lady Adventurer in Egypt*."

…and with a cry of "Let us rescue Mrs. Gordon!" we were off to save the Queen of the Desert from an uncertain fate. From perhaps spending the rest of her days in a harem, no doubt at the mercy of…
—"The Return of the Queen of the Desert,"
Daniel Corbin, foreign correspondent

CHAPTER SIXTEEN

"SIDNEY IS IN a harem?" Mrs. Higginbotham peered over his shoulder. For an old lady, she certainly had extraordinary eyesight.

"Mrs. Gordon is in a harem?" Corbin's voice sounded behind them. Fine time for Corbin to finally make an appearance.

"What are you doing here?" Harry said sharply.

"I was coming to find out why you didn't inform me about Mrs. Gordon's kidnapping."

"I might have mentioned it to him," Mrs. Fitzhew-Wellmore said with a wince. "But I did think he already knew."

"There was no kidnapping," Harry said firmly and turned his attention back to Nazzal's missive.

"Well, what was there?" Lady Blodgett asked. "And why is Sidney in a harem? Did she go there of her own accord?"

"Where is this harem?" Mrs. Higginbotham squared her shoulders. "We shall have to fetch her ourselves."

"You have my assistance in any rescue of Mrs. Gordon," Corbin said staunchly. "It will make an excellent story," he added under his breath.

"Come now, Mr. Corbin." Mrs. Fitzhew-Wellmore glared at the reporter. "Our first priority is retrieving Sidney, not your story."

Corbin winced.

"Furthermore." Mrs. Fitzhew-Wellmore raised her chin. "I daresay we can rescue Sidney without you."

"And yet I do not intend to be left out," Corbin warned.

"I don't know that anyone needs to be rescued." Harry glared at the group. "If you would all restrain yourselves, and allow me a moment to read this, then we can decide what needs to be done."

"Yes, of course." Lady Blodgett waved at the note. "But quickly would be appreciated."

"Perhaps we should adjourn to somewhere more private." Mrs. Higginbotham glanced around the entrance hall. Tea at Shepheard's always attracted a crowd, especially on weekdays when a military band played.

"Your rooms perhaps, Harry?" Lady Blodgett asked.

"Excellent idea."

A few minutes later, they were in Harry's suite on the first floor, down the hall from Sidney's.

"According to Nazzal," Harry began, "Mrs. Gordon is in the harem in one of the lesser royal residences, not far from here."

"May I see that?" Lady Blodgett held out her hand for the note and Harry passed it to her.

"Is she being held against her will?" Corbin asked, a bit too eagerly.

"He doesn't say but I doubt it." Harry shot him an irritated look. "Do you know anything about Egypt at all?"

"Only what I've read in Mrs. Gordon's stories," the reporter snapped. "You tell me if they're accurate or not." A distinct challenge sounded in the man's voice.

"Oh, I don't believe Sidney has ever written about harems," Mrs. Fitzhew-Wellmore said in an aside to Lady Blodgett beside her.

"I would suggest we have far more important matters to discuss at the moment than the veracity of Sidney's stories." Mrs. Higginbotham aimed a pointed look at Corbin.

"You're right, of course." Corbin straightened his shoulders as if about to head off to conquer the unknown in the best manner of a fictional hero. "Far more important." What an idiot.

"Harems, Mr. Corbin, are not bastions of immorality. That's a false impression advanced by European fiction. They are simply the quarters of the female members of a household as well as their servants and children. The wives of the household, limited to no more than four, are free to come and go as they please. Servants and, well, slaves, have no such liberty."

Mrs. Fitzhew-Wellmore gasped. "Do you think they want Sidney for a slave?"

"No, I do not," Harry said firmly. "As I do not think she has been kidnapped. Frankly, if that was the case, even Nazzal would not have been able to find out where she is this quickly. She would be hidden and she's not. From what Nazzal has written—"

"Why isn't he here?" Mrs. Higginbotham crossed her arms over her chest. "We could certainly use his assistance."

Harry's jaw tightened. He had thought exactly the same thing himself. "Unfortunately, he was called away but expects to return within a day or so."

"Then this is in your hands." Lady Blodgett offered him an encouraging smile.

"You can manage this, Harry," Mrs. Higginbotham said as if there wasn't a doubt in her mind. It was most gratifying.

"And if you can't," Corbin added, "I can."

"No one needs to manage anything," Harry said sharply. "The fact that Sidney has not yet returned could be due to any number of as yet unknown reasons. I suggest we wait until this evening. If she has not returned by then, we should turn this over to the British consulate. Sidney is in a royal household and this could be better handled through diplomatic means."

The three ladies and Corbin stared in disbelief.

"That's it?" Mrs. Higginbotham glared. "That's your plan?"

Lady Blodgett shook her head. "We did expect more from you, Harry."

"Richard Weatherly would certainly do more," Mrs. Fitzhew-Wellmore muttered.

"Why wait?" Corbin said slowly, staring at Harry, a definite challenge in his eyes. "I think we need to go and fetch her. Rescue her as it were."

Mrs. Higginbotham huffed. "Isn't that what I just said?"

"It's an excellent idea, regardless of who said it first." Mrs. Fitzhew-Wellmore nodded.

"No." Harry shook his head. "It's not."

"If you're not willing to go—" Corbin smirked "—I can certainly do this without you."

"I doubt that, Corbin."

"At least I am willing to try."

"As are we," Mrs. Higginbotham said staunchly.

Determination showed on each lady's face and even Corbin adopted an expression of resolve.

Bloody hell. Why not?

There was the slimmest possibility he was wrong. That Sidney was indeed in trouble and being held against her will. He doubted it. It made no sense and Nazzal didn't seem to think that was the case. Even so, the nasty feeling in his stomach had never been wrong. Of course, he had never *liked* a woman before which had certainly mucked up everything else in his life.

The proper, appropriate thing to do was to contact the consulate. It was exactly what the Earl of Brenton would do.

Charging off to *rescue* Sidney was probably a dreadful mistake, a reckless and irrational course of action and there was every likelihood that it could go terribly wrong. It was exactly the kind of stupid, brash thing Harry Armstrong would do. The kind of thing that ridiculous character Richard Weatherly would do that would sweep Millicent Forester off her feet. Would it do the same to Sidney Gordon?

"Very well." He blew a resigned breath. "Let's go rescue Mrs. Gordon."

HARRY AND CORBIN stood in a narrow street before what he assumed was the west door of the palace. Fortunately, this particular royal residence was not far from the hotel. Even better it was now dark. Harry had sent out errand boys with inquiries to several Egyptian acquaintances who, like Nazzal, usually knew what was going on in the city. While he had gotten directions and some information as to the interior of the building, he had also received visits from two more creditors—apparently among

those Nazzal had warned knew he was in Egypt. As he
had no time to argue about charges and simply paid what
they claimed he owed, they offered whatever assistance
he may need in any future endeavors. As well as credit.
That, coupled with the purchases of a few essential items,
took longer than he had wanted which was more a matter of his own impatience than any sense of real urgency.
Still, it was for the best. The later they attempted this,
the darker it would be and the fewer people they would
encounter. Besides, the longer this escapade took—the
more likely it was Sidney would return on her own. He
did feel the need to keep Corbin busy as well. There was
no telling how much trouble the man would get into attempting to *rescue* Sidney by himself.

Harry had hired horses, much to Corbin's dismay. The
reporter insisted Sidney would prefer a carriage but had
given in when Harry had pointed out the narrowness of
the streets surrounding the royal residence. Once they
were out of sight of the hotel, they donned the robes and
turbans of a typical Cairo resident. They had hidden the
garments with Harry's other purchases in sacks each man
had slung over his shoulder. Harry would never pass for
an Egyptian in the hard light of day but at night, with his
dark blond hair hidden beneath a turban, he knew from
past experience no one would give him a second look.
They had left the horses around the corner at the quarter
gate under the alert eye of a young man who had agreed
to watch the animals for a price.

The street was poorly lit by no more than a handful
of lanterns. Infrequent pools of illumination were threatened by dark pockets of unnerving shadow. The door was
simple and traditional—wood with an iron knocker and a
wooden lock. Directly above it, a squared bow window—

what the Egyptians called a *mashrabiya*—jutted outward, supported by scalloped wooden brackets.

"It doesn't look much like a palace," Corbin said skeptically.

"It's not supposed to. That's precisely the idea."

Harry had done any number of stupid things in his life. Usually he realized they were stupid when there was no going back. Tonight, from the moment he agreed to this, he'd known it was stupid. And probably nothing more than a desire to put Corbin in his place. Also stupid.

"This is not the main entrance but a door used for function and discretion."

"I understand that but the building itself does not look like a royal residence."

"One never knows what's behind the walls on any street in Cairo. Especially the older ones. The stonework is all the same, the doors are similar and unadorned. It's really quite brilliant. But if you look down on the area from the rooftops you see something entirely different." Harry studied the building. "According to my information, if we climb to the roof, we'll be able to identify the west wing which houses the harem. There is a large covered courtyard within the harem which should be fairly easy to spot. There are usually latticework screens that allow for ventilation. That's probably the easiest way to get into the building."

"Are you mad?" Corbin stared at him. "I've read about this sort of thing. Do you know what they do to men who violate the sanctity of a harem?"

Perhaps this was something Corbin should have considered before insisting they do this. Harry met his gaze. "Yes."

"Are you at least going to tell me that too is a false impression?"

Harry was not about to relieve the man's concerns. He pulled a metal hook and a coil of rope from his bag. "No."

"You do realize, this is a three-story building."

"The roof will be flat."

Corbin looked at the rope in horror. "If we make it to the roof."

"It's not that difficult," Harry said coolly. "Do you have a better idea?"

"No." Corbin huffed then paused. "Yes."

Harry clenched his teeth. "Well, now would be a good time to mention it."

"Well…" Corbin studied the building. "If we just climb to the top of that projecting window—"

"It's called a *mashrabiya*."

"We can probably get in through there."

"Of course then we'll have to make our way to the women's quarters inside the building, thus increasing the likelihood of discovery." It was a bad idea. They could break the window but that would create a great deal of noise and attract attention. They would have to open the window as quietly as possible. Chances were good that it wasn't locked—given their height, *mashrabiyas* rarely were. But to do that, it would be necessary to dangle upside down from the top of the *mashrabiya*. An idea only made better by the thought of dangling Corbin by his heels. No doubt Corbin would come to his senses as soon as he realized that. Harry shrugged. "Why not."

Approaching voices sounded at the far end of the street. Harry tossed the rope and hook back in the bag and whispered to Corbin to follow his lead. The men huddled together as if engaged in a financial negotiation.

As soon as the passersby had vanished from sight, Harry pulled the rope out and knotted it about every three feet.

"What are you doing?" the reporter asked.

"Handholds," Harry said curtly.

Once he had enough knots, he tied the hook to one end then stepped away from the wall and assessed the height of the windows. This was not going to be easy. But with decent aim and a great deal of luck, the hook would wedge at the point where the *mashrabiya* attached to the wall. He drew a deep breath, hefted the hook in his hand and let it fly. It fell short by a few inches then clattered to the stone street.

"Quiet," Corbin snapped. "Do you want to wake everyone up?"

Harry resisted the urge to point out as it was barely past eight o'clock the chances were slim they would awaken anyone although attracting attention was a distinct possibility. "Do you want to do this?"

"Sorry," Corbin muttered.

Harry tried again. Again it fell short. Corbin wisely refrained from comment. Harry drew a steadying breath and threw the hook once more. This time it caught on the edge of the *mashrabiya*'s roof. He carefully inched it toward the wall until it wedged in the niche between *mashrabiya* and wall, exactly where he wanted it. He yanked hard to set the hook then glanced at Corbin. "Do you want to go first or should I?"

"By all means." Corbin gestured at the rope. "Go on."

Harry wrapped the rope around one hand, braced one foot on the stonework around the door and pulled himself up. The first few feet were always the hardest. Slowly he walked up the side of the building until he reached the window. He grabbed on to the ornate carved moldings that would provide excellent hand- and footholds. From there it was a simple matter to climb onto the top of the *mashrabiya*.

"Your turn," he called quietly to Corbin.

"I've never done anything like this." Unease edged the reporter's voice.

"Always a first time. Get up here." Harry resisted the urge to raise his voice. "Now."

Apparently Corbin, in spite of his apparent physical fitness, was not athletically inclined. It took him more than one attempt and far longer than it had taken Harry to finally reach the top of the window. Harry pulled up the rope after him.

"What are you doing?" Horror rang in Corbin's hushed voice. "How are we going to get down?"

"The same way we got up," Harry said sharply. "But if we leave the rope dangling and anyone wanders by or worse, comes out of the door, there will be questions."

"Of course. Yes. Sorry." He shook his head. "I'm not used to this sort of thing."

"Apparently."

Corbin studied him curiously. "You are though, aren't you?"

"Not anymore," Harry muttered. "Now, all we have to do—"

A creak sounded beneath them.

Corbin froze. "What is that?"

"It's the door. Quiet!" Harry flattened himself against the wall and—much to Harry's surprise—Corbin immediately followed suit.

Beneath the *mashrabiya* the door slowly creaked open. Thank God for ancient hinges and the lax nature of those responsible for their oiling. The distinct sound of female voices drifted up to them. A moment later four—no—five figures appeared below them. A short man, carrying a large bundle, accompanied a cloaked woman and three others dressed in European fashion but from this angle little could be seen. A nasty suspicion—because surely he was wrong—struck him and was confirmed not more than a moment later.

"That was certainly interesting." Lady Blodgett's distinct voice sounded below them.

"Quite the adventure I'd say," a voice that was definitely Mrs. Higginbotham's added.

"I have so much to tell you." What was surely Sidney's voice rang with excitement.

Relief washed through him. Sidney was fine. He had known it all along even if he now realized, somewhere inside him, he hadn't been completely confident. Without warning it struck him—this could have been truly perilous. Her life could have been at risk. He had refused to think it overly serious for fear that it really was. She could have been in grave danger.

He could have lost her. His heart clenched at the thought.

"I say, Armstrong," Corbin said in an urgent whisper. "Can we get down now? They're gone."

Good Lord! He was in love with the woman! How had something this absurd happened? How ironic. How inconvenient. How…right? Certainly he *liked* her but… God help him, how was he going to deal with this?

"Wait another minute," Harry said absently.

How had this happened? When did it happen? Certainly not the moment he first met her. No, while he had been surprised by her age and that she was really rather lovely, especially when she smiled, he certainly hadn't fallen for her then. When she denied her excitement for everything she saw? No, that was definitely annoying. When he'd realized he was indeed right about her? Not that it was difficult. From the beginning she was a bad liar. He liked that about her.

When he'd first wanted to kiss her?

"Armstrong?" Corbin waved his hand in front of Harry's face.

Harry's attention jerked to the other man. "What? Oh. Right." He'd have time later to think about Sidney and *feelings*. "I'll go first."

Harry threw the rope down and was on the street in no time. Corbin took a little longer but the man seemed to be catching on. They returned to their horses, and headed to the hotel, pausing to discard their robes. They rode back in near silence but it was a short ride and Harry's thoughts were on other matters. Upon their return, Harry was presented with a note at the front desk from the ladies, succinctly detailing Sidney's absence starting with an invitation from a princess to her return no more than an hour ahead of Corbin and Harry. There was no mention of the old ladies' role in this. They had assured him they would not leave the hotel and yet they had merrily done exactly what they wanted. This kind of nonsense would have to stop. Harry passed the note to Corbin.

Corbin scanned it and shook his head. "Blasted woman was in a harem telling stories for God's sake. Do you know the kind of stories I've been writing since my arrival?"

"No." Nor did he care.

"I might as well have been reporting on the last meeting of the Women's Co-operative Guild. Or the latest society outing. We're in Egypt! But there's been no dis-

covery of a new tomb, no uncovering of an ancient artifact, no locating of lost treasure."

"Is that what you expected?" Harry asked mildly.

"Didn't you?"

"I'm not sure what I expected."

"Frankly, I did expect more from the Queen of the
bloody Desert. The most interesting thing that's happened thus far was losing the old ladies and even that was
insignificant. Her stories are filled with adventure and
excitement but this has been no better than an organized
tour. I'm beginning to agree with you about her authen-
ticity. Mrs. Gordon's return to Egypt has been decidedly
ordinary. Unless of course…" He brightened. "You've
found proof that she's a fraud?"

"I'm afraid not," Harry lied. He wasn't about to tell
Corbin about the little discrepancies in Sidney's story
that added up to the truth. Besides he had no choice. Not
if he loved her.

"I didn't think so." Corbin shook his head. "According to this—" he waved the note at Harry "—she was
answering questions and reading from her book. She was
in a harem discussing books? That was it? Do you know
what kind of story that is?"

"Rather charming I'd say." Or terrifying depending on
whether one was cheerfully sipping tea with an Egyptian
princess or one was trying not to think what dire fate had
befallen someone whose whereabouts were unknown.

"Charming?" Corbin snorted in disdain. "Readers
don't want charming. Charming doesn't keep them turning the pages and wanting more. Charming, Armstrong,
does not sell newspapers or further careers." He blew a
frustrated breath. "I suppose I can make something out
of the harem angle."

"The truth is usually a good idea."

"The truth, Armstrong, is relative." Corbin glanced at the door to the Long Bar. "I believe I'll stop in the bar before going to my room. They don't allow women in there, do they?"

"A last bastion, Corbin. Someday they'll probably even be voting."

"God help us," Corbin muttered and strode across the entrance hall toward the bar.

As much as the bar was tempting, Harry had no desire to do anything except see Sidney. Ascertain for himself that she was all right.

And then what?

Proclaim his feelings? Announce his undying love? Sweep her off her feet?

Marry the woman?

Not a bad idea. She did apparently know everything there was to know about Egypt. And she did tell a fairly good story. Not to mention that she was clever and amusing with the most remarkable blue eyes and a kiss that did something unexpected to his senses.

And it was entirely possible he could no longer live without her.

By the time he headed for Sidney's room relief had been swept aside by anger at her irresponsible behavior as well as that of her friends. What were they thinking? Any of them? Whether he wanted to be or not, he did feel responsible for each gray- or white-haired head. He would never forgive himself if something happened to the old ladies. They wouldn't be here if not for him.

As for Sidney, apparently it was not enough to protect her from Corbin's ambition.

He had to save her from herself.

CHAPTER SEVENTEEN

"...AND WHILE THE princess herself did not speak English, the Lady Hatice had read my book to her and the other ladies of the harem—which is not nearly the kind of place one might have thought it was," Sidney added and took the opportunity to draw a deep breath. She'd been talking very nearly without pause since she and the ladies had left the residence but she had a great deal to tell them. It had been a delightful day and she did want to share every detail. It would make a splendid new story.

Effie waved off her comment. "Oh, we know all about harems, dear."

"Harry told us," Poppy added.

"Where is Harry?" Sidney held her breath. She wasn't entirely sure she was ready to see him. She hadn't spoken to him after they'd returned to the ballroom last night. She hadn't known what to say and what to say did seem exceptionally important. They had, after all, finally shared a kiss. Oh, it had been a kiss of necessity but a kiss all the same. A kiss that lingered in her mind and produced an odd fluttering in her stomach and made her heart sigh. Even though she had no previous experience it did seem this particular kiss was exceptional and extremely significant. Besides, she was fairly certain he wouldn't see her visit to a harem the same way she did.

The ladies looked at each other in a distinctly guilty manner.

"He went to rescue you," Gwen said somewhat reluctantly.

"Daniel insisted," Poppy added quickly. "We tried to tell him that you were perfectly capable of taking care of yourself but he refused to be dissuaded."

"Harry was confident in your abilities as well but he couldn't let Daniel go off on his own." Effie shrugged. "Who knows what trouble the poor man might have gotten into."

"I didn't need rescue," Sidney said with a sigh. She should have known something like this would happen when she decided to stay the day with the princess and Lady Hatice and the rest of the ladies. But it did seem an opportunity she could ill afford to pass up. And she had sent a note last night as well as another today and had assumed all was well.

"Which we would have known had we received today's note," Poppy said.

Apparently, there was some confusion over her last message, the desk clerk thinking it was *for* her rather than *from* her. The mistake was only discovered when Sidney returned to the hotel. Hoping to avoid any further confusion, they left a brief, but thorough, note for Harry.

"So Harry wasn't concerned?" Sidney asked in an offhand manner. Not that it mattered really. Although if a man was going to kiss a woman—even out of necessity—in a manner that could only be called passionate and not the least bit necessary, then he really should care about what happens to her.

"Oh no, dear. Harry was concerned," Gwen said firmly. "He tried to hide it but it was obvious to all of us that he was just saying what he thought he should to relieve our minds. Even though he did say, according to the information he had, he did not think a rescue was called for."

Sidney drew her brows together. "I must say this is rather confusing."

"Indeed it is." Effie huffed, Gwen and Poppy nodded in agreement.

"But what can you say about men?" Poppy shrugged and the other two mirrored her actions. "They frequently make no sense."

"In my experience they never have." Gwen shook her head, Poppy and Gwen following suit. "And I daresay they never will."

A sharp knock sounded at the door. Poppy, Gwen and Effie were all perched on the sofa but Poppy was the closest. She moved to the door and opened it then immediately slammed it shut and flattened her back against it. "It's Harry."

Sidney stared. "Then let him in."

Gwen wrinkled her nose. "He's probably not especially happy."

"He was rather adamant about our not leaving the hotel." Effie winced. "And he might have assumed we had promised as much."

"But we didn't," Poppy said quickly. "Although he might have thought we did."

"It's all a matter of inflection really." Gwen gestured aimlessly. "Or perhaps semantics."

"It's entirely possible he doesn't even know we left the hotel," Effie said thoughtfully.

Gwen nodded. "Then we should proceed as if he

doesn't. No need to tell him anything he'd probably prefer not to know."

"We are just thinking of him," Poppy murmured.

Harry knocked again. Wasn't it interesting how a man's knock said all sorts of things about his mood? Perhaps they shouldn't let him in after all.

"This is silly." Sidney gestured at Poppy to open the door.

Poppy hesitated, obviously trying to decide if this was indeed wise or not, then adopted her brightest smile and swung the door open. "Harry! It's you."

"It was me a moment ago when you shut the door in my face." He strode into the room.

"I'm afraid I didn't recognize you." Poppy heaved an overly dramatic sigh. "My eyesight is not what it once was."

"You, Mrs. Fitzhew-Wellmore—" he pinned Poppy with a hard look "—could probably read a newspaper from fifty paces."

Poppy beamed. "Thank you, Harry."

"We have things to discuss." Harry's gaze shifted from one lady to the next and finally settled on Sidney. "All of us."

"First, you really should listen to Sidney's recounting of her visit." Enthusiasm sounded in Gwen's voice. "It's quite fascinating."

"No doubt." Harry glared at the ladies. "Regardless—"

"Did you know they eat with their fingers?" Effie asked. "And Sidney says it's not at all messy but really rather refined."

"Yes, I am aware of that. However—"

"And she met a real princess who is apparently quite

fond of Sidney's stories." Gwen fairly glowed with pride. "An Egyptian princess—isn't that remarkable?"

"Indeed it is but—"

"Of course everyone does like Sidney's stories except for you," Gwen added under her breath.

"And they supplied Sidney with clothing, as she certainly couldn't continue to wear last night's gown, especially to return to the hotel." Poppy shook her head. "That would have been most awkward. But I think she looks wonderful in her foreign garb." Her eyes widened innocently. "Don't you?"

"Yes, of course." He glanced at Sidney, then his gaze snapped back as if he hadn't noticed her apparel on his arrival. He stared and she wasn't entirely sure if he was appalled or entranced. Regardless, either sentiment was most gratifying.

Sidney had never worn anything like this in her life and never imagined she would. In many ways, the Egyptian garments, in varying shades of green embroidered with gold threads, were every bit as complicated as her usual clothing but they were far more comfortable. Especially as a corset was not required. The full sheer trousers ballooned out from the waist then fell softly to a cuff around her ankles. Next came a sort of soft shirt that reached just above her knees. A sash wrapped around her waist. Over it all was a type of sheer coat or robe that buttoned from below her bosom to her hips, the sides slit all the way from the bottom of the garment, near her ankles, to the top of her legs. Lady Hatice had also presented her with a shimmering beaded and jeweled headpiece—a gift from the princess—that held a sheer muslin veil in place. All in all, Sidney thought she looked quite fetching. As did the ladies. It was difficult to determine exactly what Harry was thinking.

"Very nice," he murmured, still apparently unable to wrench his gaze away.

"Do you really think so?" she said in an overly innocent manner, inspecting the clothing. "It's extremely comfortable. We were just saying that we should all purchase several pairs of the trousers along with the robes and shirts to wear at home."

"In London?" Skepticism sounded in his voice.

"Goodness, Harry," Poppy teased. "It's not as if we would wear such things on the streets of Bloomsbury."

"Although we would make quite an impression at the next Lady Travelers meeting," Gwen said thoughtfully.

"Brilliant idea!" Poppy grinned.

"We saw several stalls in the souk that offered female garments," Effie said. "I daresay it will be a simple matter to return before we leave Cairo and make our purchases."

It was apparently the wrong thing to say as it brought Harry's attention firmly back to the matter at hand.

His eyes narrowed. "And will you be returning to the markets on your own?"

"Whatever you think best, Harry." Effie cast him a contrite smile.

He snorted in disbelief. "You three promised that you would not leave the hotel."

"Did we leave the hotel?" Poppy said to Effie who summoned a not at all convincing look of confusion.

"Don't try to deny it." Harry glared. "I saw you. And you gave me your word."

"On the contrary." Gwen squared her shoulders. "You told us we were not to leave the hotel under any circumstances—"

Poppy nodded. "You were quite firm about it."

"Which we thought was a bit, oh, arrogant on your part." Effie cast him a chastising look. "You have no right to tell us what to do. You're not a relation, you know."

"Regardless." Triumph rang in Gwen's voice. "We never agreed not to leave the hotel. We simply mentioned that we were not stupid."

"And proved it by leaving the hotel?" Frustration sounded in his voice. "Why?"

"Because you didn't think rescuing Sidney was necessary," Effie said as if it were obvious. "We considered all you had said and decided you were probably right. And how absurd it would be for you and Daniel to rescue someone who didn't need rescue. It would also be most embarrassing on an international level as well." The ladies shuddered in unison. "After all, we do represent England. Not officially, of course, but as subjects of Her Majesty's, our actions reflect on her."

"We should write a pamphlet about the responsibilities of travelers to queen and country," Poppy murmured.

"We trust you, Harry, and we trust your judgment. If you didn't think Sidney had been kidnapped, the chances were good that she hadn't." Gwen smiled.

"And yet we worried all the same," Poppy added.

"We simply thought it was an excellent idea if we went to the residence to see if Sidney was there. Thereby saving you—and Daniel too, of course—from a potentially difficult situation." Gwen leaned toward him and lowered her voice in a confidential manner. "You really should try harder to stick to your convictions, Harry."

"My convictions?" Harry said in a strangled voice. "My convictions?" A muscle twitched in his jaw. He closed his eyes and Sidney assumed he was counting to ten as the man was obviously fighting to hold himself in check. He opened his eyes and Sidney resisted the urge to take a step back.

"I must disagree with you, Lady Blodgett, on the question of stupidity. You claim you and your friends are not, and have never been, stupid yet tonight's escapade was the very definition of *stupid*." His voice rose. "Do you have any idea what might have happened to you on the streets of Cairo? Alone? At night?"

"Nonsense." Gwen sniffed. "It wasn't very far from here, you know. Why, we were scarcely gone any time at all."

"Mr. Chalmers assisted us and provided a carriage, a driver and a rather burly interpreter as an escort. Really a charming man," Effie added.

"We simply knocked on the door of the residence— which none of us thought looked anything like a dwelling for royalty really although it was extremely opulent inside. A few minutes later we were escorted to the women's quarters where Sidney was just about to leave." Poppy cast him a placating smile. "So you see there was nothing that need concern you at all."

"This was not calling on friends for tea!" Harry glared as much in frustration as anger.

"One never makes uninvited calls at teatime," Gwen said under her breath. "That would be most impolite."

Harry ignored her. "Do you understand even remotely what might have happened to you? None of you speaks the language nor are any of you familiar with the customs. And while I do pity anyone who might try to detain you, what if I had been wrong?"

"Nonsense, Harry," Poppy said brightly. "You're never wrong."

"Harry," Sidney began, "I really think— "

"I'll get to you later," he said in a rigid tone and turned his attention back to the ladies. "You could have gotten yourselves kidnapped. Or worse—killed. I will not allow that to happen."

"Goodness, Harry," Gwen said. "While we do appreciate your concern, you are not responsible for us. We are adversaries remember?"

"I don't care what we are, it's my duty to protect you." His voice rose. "All of you."

"Why?" Poppy shook her head. "We've never asked for your protection."

"Because it's my fault you're here in the first place."

"Although we have always wanted to travel to Egypt," Gwen said in an aside to Poppy, "or anywhere really."

His jaw tightened. "Because that's what a proper gentleman is expected to do."

"Come now, Harry." Sidney scoffed. "Even I know that's utter rubbish."

"Because." His gaze met hers. The man was a towering rock of barely suppressed ire. "In spite of my best intentions, I like them. Even Mrs. Higginbotham!"

"Why, Harry," Effie said wryly. "Such lovely sentiment will go straight to my head."

"I am doing my best to protect you—" he glanced at each of them in turn then shot Sidney a pointed glance "—all of you."

Sidney stared for a moment. She didn't expect that kind of heartfelt declaration from him. And he did have a legitimate point. "You're right. They shouldn't have left the hotel by themselves. Ladies, the next time Mr. Armstrong asks for your promise you should be forthright in extending it to him."

"And what about you?" Harry glared at her.

"What about me?"

"A man you have never met hands you a request allegedly from a princess asking for your presence and you blithely go off with him?"

"Oh, I wouldn't call it blithely."

"Are you mad?" His eyes widened and his voice rose. "There was absolutely no reason to believe this man was who he said he was."

"The invitation was on excellent stationery complete with a royal crest. It was engraved." Sidney shook her head. "Not the kind of thing you can easily forge."

"No but it is the kind of thing easily stolen." He shook his head in disbelief. "You simply trusted this stranger."

"I am an excellent judge of character," she said in a lofty manner.

"Not that I've noticed," he snapped.

"I like all your friends. Mr. Chalmers and Mr. Nazzal." She almost added that she'd probably like his friend Mr. Deane as well but that would bring to mind his late friend, Mr. Pickering and, at the moment, that didn't seem wise.

"I believe I just made my point!"

"We like them as well," Poppy murmured.

Harry shot a hard glance at her then returned his attention to Sidney. "You are an enigma. I don't know from one moment to the next if you're going to be rational or impulsive or determined. It's the most annoying thing I have ever encountered. *You* are the most annoying woman I have ever met! Did you know your eyes light up whenever anything of a questionable nature arises?"

"Do they really?" She grinned although she knew he did not intend it as a compliment and stepped closer to him. "And I would call things of a questionable nature *adventures*."

"Only in your stories!" He stared down at her. "And would it be possible for you to change your clothing? I find what you're wearing to be most distracting."

"What utter nonsense. This isn't the least bit revealing." Sidney crossed her arms over her chest. "Besides, you've seen women all over Egypt wearing precisely the same thing."

"Indeed I have but they were not you!"

"And they are allowed to wear clothing that I am not allowed to wear?"

"Exactly."

"That's irrational, Harry."

"I tend to be irrational when I worry and I don't like to worry, Mrs. Gordon."

"No one likes to worry, Mr. Armstrong." He'd been worried? For her? The far-more-than-she-had-expected Harry Armstrong? If he was afraid for her then it did stand to reason that he cared for her. Her heart leaped at the thought. "I'll try not to scare you again."

His gaze slid to the ladies on the sofa, not even bothering to pretend they weren't listening, then back to hers. "See that you don't."

She gazed up at him. "You're coming perilously close to talking about something like feelings."

He stared at her for a moment. "No, I'm not." He turned to leave then turned back. "Oh, and I'll take the object if you don't mind."

She frowned. "What object?"

"The medallion, dear," Effie said.

"Oh yes, the medallion." Sidney nodded. "Is Mr. Nazzal here to claim it?"

"No. I expect to see him tomorrow."

"Then you may have it tomorrow." She smiled pleasantly but held her breath. "I would like some time to study it."

"Why?"

"I simply would, that's all." There was something about the images on the back that seemed vaguely familiar.

"I'd prefer to keep it where I know it's safe."

"It's perfectly safe with me."

"Yes, but as long as it's in your possession there is the possibility you are not safe."

"Don't be absurd," she said calmly. "I understand Mr. Wallace has left Cairo so I'm perfectly safe. And the object is hidden so it too is perfectly safe."

Harry glanced at the chest of drawers.

"Did you really think I'd put it there?" She cast him a pitying look. "But do go on and look if you want." Heat washed up her face but she refused to back down. Apparently it was one thing to encourage a man to dig through the unmentionables of a collector in possession of stolen goods and quite another to encourage him to go through your own.

"Why do you want to study it?"

She hesitated. "I'd prefer not to say anything at the moment."

Harry leaned in and lowered his voice. "Do you trust me, Sidney?"

"Yes, Harry, I believe I do."

"Good. I however do not trust you." He stepped back and addressed the others. "Or any of the rest of you. We shall continue this discussion in the morning." He pointed at Sidney. "You might want to hide that head-dress as well."

Sidney reached up and adjusted the piece. "It is lovely isn't it?"

"Indeed it is. And unless I'm mistaken, those are real diamonds." He nodded curtly and took his leave.

Sidney pulled off the headpiece and stared at it. Diamonds? She'd never had anything quite so lovely or valuable. What a remarkable gift. She would treasure it always.

The ladies waited almost a full minute before saying anything.

"Well, that was not nearly as dreadful as I expected," Poppy said brightly.

"I do feel rather bad about misleading the man." Gwen sighed. "But I suppose it couldn't be helped."

"Am I the only one who sees what is clearly evident here?" Effie looked at them expectantly. "Aside from the fact that the man has grown fond of us, which I would have wagered against, he is obviously in love."

"Come now." Poppy's brow furrowed. "I don't think he's in love with us. He probably simply feels the sort of affection one would feel for any older female relation."

"She didn't mean he's in love with us, dear." Gwen patted the other woman's hand.

"Oh no, of course not." Poppy's gaze slid to Sidney. "Oh, I see."

"I don't think you do. And I don't think that's love," Sidney said quickly but she wasn't entirely sure she believed her own words. Or perhaps didn't want to believe. It was, after all, a wonderful idea. "The man thinks of all of us as his responsibility. Nothing more than that."

"And how do you feel about him?" Gwen asked.

"I'm not sure." For a moment she considered everything she liked about Harry. He was amusing and really very clever. He was incredibly dashing and adventurous. He'd crawled down shafts in the Great Pyramid and then climbed to the top with scarcely any effort. He was far nicer to her friends than they frequently deserved. When he looked into her eyes she felt like he was looking into her very soul and when he'd kissed her… And the thought of coming to the end of this trip and never seeing him again twisted her heart and tightened her throat. "I believe I might, possibly, care for him. Rather a lot."

"How lovely." Poppy beamed.

"Indeed, we couldn't be happier. However…" Gwen paused and the ladies traded glances. "We're not sure how to say this but we have discussed it and we do think something does need to be said."

"We do want to be as delicate as possible," Poppy added.

"Good Lord." Effie blew an annoyed breath. "This might not be the time for delicacy. The man has already kissed her." She glanced at Sidney. "Hasn't he?"

Heat flushed her face. "Well yes."

"I thought so." Effie nodded. "And he does think she is a widow."

"I'd forgotten about that." Poppy winced.

"What are the three of you talking about?" Sidney stared in confusion.

"While it is proper to wait until marriage, when one has passed a certain age, well, things are bound to happen. Human nature being what it is and all. Especially in tropical climes," Effie added.

Poppy nodded. "And one couldn't help but notice how he looks at you and how you look at him."

"How I look at him?" Sidney still wasn't sure what they were trying to say.

"Sidney, are you aware of what occurs between a man and a woman?" Gwen said in a casual manner.

Sidney widened her eyes. "What do you mean—what occurs between a man and a woman?"

"Intimately," Poppy said and waved at the bedroom. "You know, in there." She paused. "Or really all kinds of other places depending on one's mood and opportunity and adventur—"

"Poppy, that's enough," Gwen said sharply.

At once Sidney realized what they were talking about and she wasn't at all sure she wished to hear what they seemed compelled to say. "I do read a lot."

"We just want to make sure you're prepared," Effie said.

"Oh, I'm certain I'm prepared." Indeed, she'd read a few novels that were quite explicit, although she did doubt that every man wished to turn a woman over his knee and spank her. And she was not unaware of the sensations she could experience just by touching herself, as sinful as it was. The idea of a man doing something similar was at once exciting and a bit unnerving.

"Did your mother discuss this with you?" A hopeful note sounded in Gwen's voice.

"No, but—"

"Let's see if we can explain it," Effie began.

"Oh, please don't." Sidney twisted her hands together. Certainly Harry was the first man who'd ever kissed her and admittedly she had never actually been with a man but she did think she had a basic understanding of the process.

Effie continued. "The man has, oh, for our purposes we'll call it a sword. And the woman has a…a…"

"A scabbard?" Poppy suggested.

"Excellent." Approval rang in Effie's voice. "I was going to say a sheath but *scabbard* is much better."

"Is there a difference?" Sidney asked weakly.

"I have no idea." Gwen thought for a moment. "Probably not but either will serve for our purposes."

Effie nodded. "You should know that it's not always wonderful the very first time one tries to place the sword in the scabbard—"

"Or the sheath," Poppy added.

"Sometimes the scabbard is rather tight and not at all used to the sword—"

"Or any sword for that matter," Gwen said pointedly.

Effie grimaced. "And it could be awkward."

"Perhaps a bit unpleasant," Poppy said with a wince. "Even possibly painful."

"But not always and not for everyone," Effie said firmly. "After that, it really does become enjoyable."

Sidney had no idea how to respond. "Oh?"

"Quite enjoyable." Poppy nodded. "Why people would never do it so frequently if it wasn't."

"Really, I don't think—"

"A great deal of fun usually." Gwen smiled knowingly.

"Ladies!" Sidney snapped, a distinct note of desperation in her voice.

The older women quieted and waited with expectant expressions.

"That's really quite enough." She drew a deep breath. "I do appreciate the, um, instruction as well as the advice. And now if you don't mind—it's been a very long day."

"Yes, of course." Gwen cast her a sympathetic look. "Even the best of adventures take their toll."

"We are sorry, dear." Effie rose to her feet, Gwen

and Poppy joining her. "We should have realized you'd be tired. But we didn't want you to be, well, shocked, if something were to happen."

"Mind you, we don't expect something to happen and we're by no means encouraging immoral behavior," Poppy said firmly. "But we are realistic. His feelings for you and yours for him are obvious, at least to us. I'm not sure the two of you have realized it yet." She paused. "Life is shorter than you ever imagine, Sidney. And sometimes, on occasion—"

"The unexpected does indeed happen." Gwen nodded. "You are a delightful woman, past the point when most women marry, on your first adventure of any kind and Harry is roguishly charming although I never would have suspected it when we first met."

"Nor would any of us," Effie said. "But he's turned out far better than we anticipated. We like him."

"And even in the most civilized and ordinary surroundings, that is a potent combination. Now, however, you are in a romantic foreign land, with a handsome dashing man who wants to keep you safe. You really are right in the midst of one of your own stories. And just like in your writing—" Poppy smiled in a decidedly wicked manner "—one never knows what might happen."

CHAPTER EIGHTEEN

HARRY SWORE IF he were ever to meet a poet who waxed euphoric about the joys of love, he'd thrash him thoroughly. Love, thus far, was not birds singing under blue skies or joyous hearts all atwitter. No. It was annoying and frustrating and, yes, frightening. Especially when one was in love with a woman who absolutely refused to understand that the realities of life were a far cry from stories she made up. Beyond that—he had no idea if she shared his feelings.

Harry paced the floor in his room and considered his options. That, in itself, was irritating. He'd never been one to pace, at least not before his life had become entangled with Sidney Gordon. He'd always considered himself more a man of action than someone who simply *paced*. Of course, he'd never found himself in the mess he had to deal with now. How on earth was he supposed to keep Sidney and her friends from harm if they insisted on doing exactly what they wished?

Sidney had absolutely no sense whatsoever. Nor did her friends. The fact that their little adventures had not ended in disaster was due to nothing more than luck. None of them seemed to realize that. No doubt because they were not visiting Egypt—the real Egypt—with its dangers and secrets and intrigue. No, they were all vis-

iting the fairy-tale land Sidney had created in her ridiculous stories.

He could continue his efforts to protect Sidney from
exposure by Corbin but, as much as he disliked the man,
he recognized the reporter was not a complete idiot. If he
had been doing his job as an observer instead of trying
to charm every female in sight, and had watched Sidney
closely, he would have realized by now she had never
stepped foot in Egypt. It was only a matter of time until
he did. In addition, Corbin was obviously taken with
Sidney although not so much that he wouldn't sacrifice
her to get what he wanted. Harry didn't like that one bit.

He paused in midstep. There really was only one way
to shield Sidney from Corbin, one way to keep Sidney,
and the old ladies, safe from themselves. It would mean
a change in his plans but it couldn't be helped. He would
find some other way to do what he wanted to do.

Harry sat down at the desk and pulled a telegraph
form from the rack of stationery supplied by the hotel.
He hesitated for no more than a minute. No, this was
the right thing to do. He selected his words carefully
so there could be no mistaking his message. The moment he finished he sat back and blew a long breath.
For the first time in what seemed like a very long time,
Harry Armstrong had taken matters back into his own
hands. Satisfaction washed through him. He reread the
telegraph and decided to send it first thing in the morning even though the bellman had said the telegraph office was open all night. Past experience had taught him
sending a telegram—anonymously informing the authorities as to a misdeed or announcing a possible new
discovery—without thorough consideration did not always work out well.

He'd read it again tomorrow and then he'd send it. The only way to keep Sidney protected from exposure, as well as keep her and her friends safe from their own misguided escapades, was to get them out of Egypt. With luck, they would be heading back to England no later than the day after tomorrow. Not soon enough but it couldn't be helped. In the meantime, even though he didn't think Sidney's possession of the medallion put her in any real danger, he was not going to take any chances. Harry grabbed a pillow from his bed, left his room and strode down the corridor to Sidney's door then knocked sharply. A few moments later, he heard movement on the other side of the door.

"Who is it?" Sidney asked quietly.

"It's me."

"Harry?"

"Yes, were you expecting someone else?"

"No, but I wasn't expecting you either."

"May I come in?"

"What do you want?"

"Do you want to discuss this through the door or will you let me in?"

"I suppose." She pulled open the door and he stepped inside.

Sidney had on the most absurdly proper nightwear, an unseen gown covered by a heavy robe. There was barely an inch of her exposed. She reminded him of a well-wrapped present on Christmas morning. He'd always been fond of Christmas morning. "Why are you here? And why do you have a pillow?"

"Because I am going to sleep here." He stepped around her and tossed his pillow on the sofa.

"You most certainly are not."

"I most certainly am." He sat on the sofa, bounced twice and nodded. "This will do."

"If you don't leave at once, I'll ring for help."

He winced. "That would be awkward." He stretched out on the sofa, his feet dangling over the end, folded his hands behind his head and grinned. "I'd probably have to sing. And while I can carry a tune I have always been more lauded for my volume than my quality." He paused. "Of course, you could give me the object and I would gladly leave."

Her eyes narrowed. "I said I wanted a closer look."

"And I said I intended to protect you."

She frowned. "Do you really think there's any kind of danger? Mr. Wallace is gone after all."

"I don't know, which is precisely why I'm here. All we do know is that the object has been stolen at least twice and may well have come from the tomb of a queen."

"That's quite a bit though, don't you think?"

He studied her curiously. "Do you?"

"Perhaps," she said slowly.

"It has been entirely too long a day to play games, Sidney." He'd had no sleep last night and he wasn't sure tonight would be any better. "Either tell me what you're thinking or go to bed."

"What I'm thinking is that you're being ridiculous." She waved her hand at the sofa. "You can't sleep here."

"Oh, but I can." He closed his eyes.

"I assure you I don't need protection. I can take care of myself."

"Because you're the Queen of the Desert?"

"Well…yes." She paused. "That sofa is extremely un-comfortable."

"I've slept on worse."

"This is terribly improper." Irritation rang in her voice. Good. "How do I know your intentions are honorable?"

"You said you trusted me."

"I do. About most things. But this is different."

"I assure you, you are quite safe with me."

For a long moment she didn't say anything. "Are you sure you're safe with me?"

Harry opened his eyes and grinned.

"Good Lord, Harry. Apparently arguing with you about this is pointless." She heaved a frustrated sigh. "Very well, then." She turned and went through an arched, curtained opening to the bed beyond. "Sleep well. If you can," she added and jerked the curtains closed.

Harry chuckled. There was something truly enjoyable about annoying Sidney. He sat up, pulled off his coat and tie and slipped off his shoes. Then he turned off the lamp and tried to get comfortable. She was right—the sofa was hard, unforgiving and entirely too short. It had been nearly a year since he'd slept in anything other than utter comfort. Odd how quickly one gets used to something.

The curtains between the sitting area and the bed chamber were shockingly sheer with the light on and Sidney's figure was perfectly, teasingly, delightfully silhouetted. Harry knew the proper thing—the *gentlemanly* thing—to do would be not to look. Apparently, he was not that much of a gentleman.

How convenient that the woman he had fallen head over heels for had such an enticing form. The curve of her hips, the swell of her breasts... Good God. He'd have no sleep again tonight at this rate. He rolled over to face the back of the sofa and willed himself not to think of what was just behind the curtain.

The springs creaked when she got into bed and he assumed it was safe to turn over. The sofa was not exceptionally wide. Even as tired as he was, sleep evaded him. It didn't help that Sidney's bed creaked every time she moved and she moved endlessly. The creaking punctuated with frustrated sighs indicated she was getting no more sleep than he.

"Are you asleep?" Sidney asked softly.

He toyed with the idea of pretending to be asleep.

"Harry?" She was a bit louder now. "Are you asleep?"

He bit back a smile. "If I was I wouldn't be now."

"Oh. Sorry. Good night, then."

"Did you want something?"

"I can't sleep." She shifted on the bed. "I thought perhaps we could talk. Unless, of course, I did wake you up in which case I should probably   "

"I was awake. I can't sleep either. You were right about the sofa."

"I did warn you." She paused. "I'm afraid I wasn't very gracious about your insistence on staying in my room. I do understand that you think it's a matter of safety and I appreciate your concern."

"And?"

"And I shall try to consider my actions before taking them in the future."

"Good." It wasn't much of a promise but it was better than nothing. He propped his head up on his elbow and gazed at the archway to her room. Not that he could see anything. "That's a hard lesson to learn—giving due consideration to anything before leaping into it."

"I've never really been rash. I've always thought too much about anything I've ever done." She sighed. "But, then, I've never done much."

"What about the adventures you base your lady adventurer stories on?"

"Oh yes, of course. They were simply so long ago. I haven't done anything, except study and research, that wasn't a product of my own mind in longer than I can remember." Regret sounded in her voice. "Sometimes those adventures feel like they belong to someone else entirely."

Was she about to confess? Not that it mattered anymore. Although it was one of those things one couldn't quite move past. After all, if he was going to have a wife—and apparently he had made that decision— shouldn't she trust him with her secrets? He had known women who weren't particularly good in character and Sidney was not one of them. No doubt she had an excellent reason for deceiving the world.

And shouldn't he trust her with his secrets as well? Of course he should and really his secrets were so much more insignificant than hers. Yes, he was an earl and, yes, he was the one who had criticized her work and, no, he hadn't mentioned either of those points. But the latter could be forgiven and he was already taking steps toward that and the former surely wouldn't be a problem. After all—what woman didn't want a titled husband?

"Tell me about your husband."

"My husband?" Caution sounded in her voice. "Why?"

"I was just curious. You never mention him."

"I don't, do I?" She paused. "It sounds dreadful to admit but, to be honest, I can barely remember him. We weren't together very long. We were just married when we came to Egypt and then he died—drowned," she added quickly. "In the Nile."

"My condolences."

"He was not eaten by crocodiles."

"Well, that's something at any rate."

If Sidney had never been to Egypt, how could her husband have drowned in the Nile? Were some elements of her stories true? One did wonder if she even had a husband. Surely a woman wouldn't prevaricate about something like that. But one never knew. In his experience, women lied about far less.

Well, if she wasn't a widow but had had *unfortunate experiences*, he could overlook that. In truth, it meant she was no better than he. He'd had any number of *experiences* although he wouldn't recall any that had been unfortunate. But the world judged women differently than they did men. He'd never really thought about what he wanted in a wife—had really never considered a wife at all until he'd inherited his title—and it was too late now. Sidney was the only woman in the world for him, the only one he wanted now and for the rest of his life. He was more than willing to ignore anything in her past and hoped she would be willing to do the same. Nothing mattered before they met.

Still, he did want her to admit that he was right.

"As I said it was a long time ago." She paused. "I am sorry about your friend."

"My friend?"

"The one who died here? Mr. Pickering."

"Walter." He blew a resigned breath. "How did you hear about Walter?"

"Mr. Nazzal told me. I asked him about you."

"I see." If Nazzal had said anything about Harry's title, Sidney would have mentioned it by now. If she knew he wasn't the nephew of the man determined to destroy her career but the man himself, without question she would have confronted him. Even so, he held his breath. "And did you learn anything interesting?"

"Nothing, apparently, that isn't common knowledge. I learned your father is a scholar and an expert on Egypt. I discovered you were more familiar with Egypt than I had been led to believe and you and your friends spent nearly twenty years here."

"He was right." Harry chuckled. "All common knowledge."

"He said some very nice things as well."

"I wouldn't believe them if I were you."

"I would tell you but they'd go straight to your head." She chuckled softly.

Nothing else was said for some time. He thought she was asleep and was just on the verge of slumber himself. "I understand why you don't want to talk about your friend."

Yet another secret. He drew a deep breath. "Walter Pickering, Benjamin Deane and I left Cambridge to conquer Egypt and make our fortunes nearly twenty years ago now. And we were fairly successful although our purpose, oh, evolved I would say, through the years. Monetary reward became less important than saving the past. Preserving it, I suppose, from people very much like we were. It was how we intended to leave our mark.

"Two years ago, we were searching for a tomb reputed to be in the Western Desert. Walter contracted a fever. It came on quickly." Even now, he could clearly recall the details as if it were yesterday: the merciless heat, the relentless sand, the never-ending battle against biting insects. The flush of Walter's face and the look of resignation in the eyes of the locals they had hired, as if they knew efforts to save Walter would fail. "We were some distance from Cairo, from anywhere of significance really. Walter was delirious. We tried whatever we could to bring down his fever and thought we had succeeded. At last he had fallen asleep and it seemed the worst had passed. We were all exhausted." Aside from his father, Harry had never told this to anyone. He wasn't sure why he was talking about it now. He and Ben never really spoke of it. What was there to say? "When we woke up he was gone. Apparently in his delirium he wandered out into the desert."

A soft gasp sounded from Sidney's bed.

It was hard even now to forgive that failure. Harry knew Ben had never forgiven himself either. "We searched for months and never found his body. The nature of the desert really. But Egypt wasn't the same for us after losing Walter. We decided to return to England permanently not long after that. I didn't think I'd ever come back to Egypt."

"In spite of the circumstances, I'm glad you did."

"In spite of the circumstances, so am I." He hadn't realized it before now, but returning to Egypt was probably a good thing. It was time to put the past behind him. Time to lay Walter to rest.

"Why are you really here tonight, Harry?" Sidney asked quietly.

"Because I'm not sure I could forgive myself if anything happened to you." He held his breath. He'd never made such a declaration before.

She was silent for so long he wasn't sure what to think. Surely she hadn't fallen asleep. Or perhaps she didn't think a response was called for. Because he had overstepped? Or revealed too much?

"Good night, Harry," she said at last, a distinct smile in her voice.

"Good night, Sidney."

Something inside him warmed to hear Sidney's voice knowing it was the last thing he would hear at night. With any luck—it would soon be the last thing he heard every night for the rest of his life.

"HARRY," SIDNEY'S VOICE sounded softly beside his ear. "You need to get up now. We're to meet the others in less than an hour."

He reluctantly opened his eyes. She was already dressed for the day.

He wasn't sure when he'd had a worse night's sleep. He'd barely had any rest at all between the discomfort of the sofa, the creaking of her bed and endless dreams of her. Sidney as a Queen of the Desert, in a terribly proper robe she discarded to reveal something vaguely resembling traditional Egyptian garments, only far more erotic and tempting. There was another dream where she was attired as a dancing girl performing a native dance that he would be hard-pressed to forget and wasn't sure he wanted to. He dreamed he had awakened during the night to see her sitting at the writing desk, holding the medallion and reading from an old book. He'd immediately abandoned this dream for those far more interesting— Sidney on a chaise dressed as Cleopatra and beckoning him closer. It was a wonder he'd survived the night. He glanced at the desk. There was no evidence of any nocturnal activity. It was probably nothing more than her insistence on studying the medallion lingering in his head.

"You do need to leave now," Sidney said briskly. "I would prefer no one knew you spent the night here."

"Quite right," he muttered and slowly unfolded himself from the cramped position forced on him by the sofa. He'd slept in tents, on the floors of caves and the antechambers of tombs—all of which seemed mild compared to the instrument of torture that was her sofa.

"What's on the schedule for today?" he asked, hopping from one foot to the other in an attempt to put on his shoes.

"Today, we're taking a steamer for a daylong excursion up the Nile." She handed him his coat and he got to his feet.

"More sightseeing?" He pulled on his coat and tie.

"Well, we don't have time to sail to Luxor or the Valley of the Kings or Karnak. I do regret that I won't be able to visit once again all those places that are so dear to my heart." She shook her head in a mournful manner. "The ladies did so want to sail on the Nile and I'm afraid this will have to do. Surely you wouldn't deprive them of that?"

"No, of course not." This was absurd. Corbin was right—this was nothing more than a tourist excursion. It certainly did not prove the veracity of Sidney's writing. "Sidney." He took her hands and gazed into her eyes. "Don't you think it's time we ended this farce?"

"Why, Harry." Her eye widened in feigned innocence. "I have no idea what you mean."

He would wager every penny he had she knew exactly what he meant. Still, if she wanted to continue this charade, why not?

"Very well, then." He nodded and released her hands. "Today, we shall sail the Nile."

"Excellent." She cast him a satisfied smile. "Try not

to be late. I'm told the steamer always leaves promptly on time."

"Oh, and I would hate to miss it." He was still chuckling when he left her room. One thing he could say about the love of his life: she did not admit defeat easily. He rather liked that. And admittedly, he was enjoying this game of theirs even though he intended to end it.

He changed his clothes, stopped by the telegraph office and then joined the rest of their party in front of the hotel.

Daniel was assisting the ladies into a carriage and did not look especially happy.

Harry glanced around. "Where's Mrs. Gordon?"

"Poor dear girl." Mrs. Higginbotham shook her head. "She woke up with a blinding headache this morning and sent word that she would be staying in bed today."

"Did she?" Odd, she looked the picture of health less than an hour ago. What was Sidney up to now?

"Such a pity." Lady Blodgett sighed. "We know how much Sidney was looking forward to a sail on the Nile. It's been such a long time since she last did so."

"She has always spoken of those days so fondly." Mrs. Fitzhew-Wellmore smiled pleasantly.

"Well, if Mrs. Gordon isn't coming," Corbin began, "perhaps someone should stay here in case she needs anything."

"Nonsense, Daniel." Lady Blodgett waved him into the carriage and he climbed in with barely concealed reluctance. "Women, in general, do not want men around them when they are not feeling quite up to snuff."

"Are you sure she isn't feeling well?" Harry climbed into the carriage.

"Without question," Mrs. Higginbotham said firmly.

"Why she wasn't looking at all well when I stopped in her room before coming down."

"I thought you said she sent word that she wasn't feeling well?"

"She did," Mrs. Higginbotham said with a smug smile. "Through me." She met his gaze directly as if daring him to challenge her statement.

"Hopefully, she'll feel better by the time we return," Harry said slowly.

"I have no doubt of it." The tiniest gleam of something that might well have been triumph shone in Mrs. Higginbotham's eyes.

Whatever Sidney was planning, Mrs. Higginbotham—and the other ladies he assumed—was in on it. A familiar queasy feeling settled in the pit of his stomach. By the time they reached the landing at Boulak, where the Nile steamers departed, Harry had realized, while his vison of Sidney in suggestive harem dress had certainly been a dream, her studying the medallion had not. Whatever she was up to no doubt had to do with the artifact. He was not about to allow her to do whatever it was she had planned alone. Not if he had anything to say about it.

They boarded the steamer and he waited until the deckhands were just about to remove the gangplank.

"Damnation." He gasped and patted his waistcoat pockets. "I don't have my watch."

"You probably left it in your room." Mrs. Fitzhew-Wellmore smiled in sympathy. "I forget things all the time."

"You don't understand." He adopted a note of panic. "That watch is a talisman of sorts, a good luck charm if you will. I never go anywhere without it. I have to have it. You understand." He hurried toward the gangplank.

"You'll miss the boat, Harry," one of the ladies called after him.

The gangplank had just been pulled onto the deck. Damn! He had cut it entirely too close. Still there was nothing to be done about it. He had no choice. He took a running start and jumped for the dock across the rapidly widening water, not entirely confident as to the outcome. His feet thudded on the wooden planks with a good inch to spare and he grinned with relief. And a certain amount of pride. It had been some time after all.

On the steamer, the ladies stared in disbelief. He took off his hat and swept an exaggerated bow, in the best manner of any stage performer. The ladies waved back at him although he thought their efforts rather halfhearted. No doubt their mission for today was to keep him and Corbin out of Sidney's way. He grinned and headed for the cabs.

Sidney had underestimated him. He said he intended to protect her, and protect her he would.

Whether she wanted him to or not.

CHAPTER NINETEEN

SIDNEY WAS IN her room when Harry returned to the hotel, according to a helpful maid. He grabbed today's *Gazette* and took a seat in a shadowed corner of the grand lobby, with an excellent view of the lifts, the stairs and the exits. He didn't wait long.

Scarcely three-quarters of an hour later, Sidney came down in the lift carrying a large envelope. She stopped at the post office, reappeared without the envelope, then headed out the hotel door, as relaxed and serene as if she were going to a picnic at the khedive's palace. He doubted she'd received yet another royal invitation but then one never knew who might have read that blasted book of hers. She'd been given diamonds by a princess because of it for God's sake. In spite of the fact that her stories weren't true, one should perhaps give her credit for her success. Obviously people liked what she wrote. The moment she walked out the door, he was up and following her.

It was not at all hard to keep her in sight but then she had no reason to think anyone might be following her. She certainly took no precautions of any kind. His teeth clenched. The woman had no fear whatsoever. It was at once charming and exceptionally annoying. Women did not go wandering around Cairo on their own, even in the middle of the day. It was a bad idea and he did not like it.

At the very moment he decided he'd had enough of this and he needed to join her for her own good, she turned into the Hotel d'Angleterre. He was no more than a few yards behind her. He entered to see her disappearing into the dining room. Surely she wasn't here simply to eat? Unless they'd hired a new chef, the food here was no more than adequate. He slipped into the dining room and positioned himself behind a huge urn filled with palm fronds set in front of a column. The waiters ignored him. They'd probably seen far stranger behavior.

Harry scanned the room, more than half-full of diners. He spotted Sidney, her back to him—good God! She was meeting Nazzal? Wasn't this interesting. They talked for a few minutes then Sidney discreetly reached into her bag, palmed something and handed it to Nazzal. Nicely done. The Egyptian however was not as circumspect and Harry could see it was the medallion. Obviously, Sidney's study of the object was not as aimless as she had implied. At one point she passed him a piece of paper that they appeared to discuss for a few minutes before he folded it and put in a pocket. Nazzal then returned the relic, which made no sense at all.

Harry caught Nazzal's eye when Sidney got up to leave a half an hour or so later. Nazzal showed no more than a flicker of surprise but his smile grew slightly wider. Harry followed Sidney back to Shepheard's, waited until she was in her room and paid a bellboy to let him know if she so much as poked her head out the door. Then he headed for the bar.

Nazzal had chosen a different table today. This one in the corner, far more private and far less susceptible to eavesdropping.

"Sit down, my friend." Nazzal indicated the empty chair. "I took the liberty of ordering for you."

"Because you knew I'd need it?" Harry settled into the chair and took a deep swallow of the gin and tonic.

"Well, I knew when I spotted you you would want to talk as well." Nazzal chuckled. "I was right in the beginning. About a woman getting the best of you."

"Not yet. So what's this all about?"

"Regardless of the truth about her experiences as detailed in her writing, she is well versed in the study of Egypt. Did you know she reads hieroglyphics?"

"I read hieroglyphics."

"As do I but this is the land of my birth and you learned out of necessity. And slowly I might add."

Harry shrugged.

"She convinced me to let her keep the medallion for now."

"Why?"

"Because she thinks it fits into a larger piece. Possibly rectangular. There are four evenly spaced notches on the medallion. Mrs. Gordon thinks that's what holds it in position in the larger piece."

"Interesting assumption." Harry thought for a moment. "Does she have any other basis for this conjecture?"

"The images on one side are a complete design within the circle of the medallion. On the other side, the engravings appear to be only part of a larger design. She also thinks the perspective indicates a four-sided shape."

"Does she?" Harry studied Nazzal closely. "There's more isn't there? What is it?"

"She thinks when this medallion is reunited with the larger piece—possibly a pectoral—it will reveal something quite significant."

"For example."

"The location of Itjtawy." Nazzal's tone was matter-of-fact, as if it wasn't the least bit important.

"Itjtawy," Harry said slowly, the true significance of the Egyptian's statement gradually dawning on him. "Middle Kingdom? Capital of Egypt for hundreds of years? Lost for thousands more? That would be the find of the century."

"Wouldn't it be amusing if this woman you claim is a fraud leads us to find something quite remarkable."

"*Amusing* isn't the word I'd use." Was it even remotely possible that Harry had been wrong all along about Sidney's writing? No. There had to be another explanation.

"Perhaps not for you." Nazzal leaned forward and lowered his voice. "Mrs. Gordon asked me to help her find a man who used to work with her grandparents."

"Her grandparents?"

"Apparently they spent quite a lot of time in Egypt. Before my time, of course, but they had an excellent reputation and made a few significant discoveries."

Harry shook his head. "I had no idea."

Nazzal raised a brow. "You did not make inquiries about her before you started this venture?"

"Afraid not." He hadn't even thought of it and he certainly should have. But he'd been too busy being righteous and indignant.

"I see. Tell me, when one receives a title and money does one then become an idiot?"

"Apparently."

"There's more but I think it best if she tells you herself. I will say, I am quite impressed with your Mrs. Gordon." He paused. "You might find it interesting that she said she was not at all who people thought she was but she did intend to be."

"I don't know what to make of that." Yet another piece of the puzzle that was Sidney Gordon.

"She might not be the Queen of the Desert, Harry, but she might be something quite a bit more interesting."

"That, at least, my friend—" Harry raised his glass "—I do know."

"HARRY!" SIDNEY'S EYES lit with welcome. "You're back. And far earlier than I expected. I thought you wouldn't be back until evening."

"I missed the boat." He stepped into her room and she closed the door behind him.

"Did you?" Her eyes widened. "Then where have you been all day?"

"I think a more pertinent question is, where have you been?"

"Come now, Harry." She moved close and gazed up into his eyes in a decidedly flirtatious manner. "I think you know."

"What do you mean?" he asked cautiously.

"I mean—" her voice hardened and she stepped back "—I saw you."

"Saw me?"

"Yes, in the lobby. And on the street. And at the Hotel d'Angleterre." She huffed. "I don't like being followed and I don't like being spied upon and I don't need your protection. I am not some sort of feeble, insipid creature who swoons at the mere hint of trouble. I have taken care of myself for a very long time."

He started to protest but she held up her hand.

"However, I will confess there was something quite

heartening about knowing you were there should I need you. So you have my thanks."

"You're welcome," he said slowly. Of all the things he thought might happen, this was not one of them.

"Furthermore, it works out quite nicely that you are not cruising the Nile as I would appreciate your help."

"Finding lost cities?"

She raised a brow. "I see you've already spoken to Mr. Nazzal."

"I have."

"Excellent." Her eyes sparkled. "Then there's less for me to explain. Although we have some time." She frowned thoughtfully. "I do want to be here when the others return. The fewer people who know about this, the better I think. Erring on the side of caution and all."

"I've heard that."

"First—" she fetched the medallion from the desk and handed it to him "—you might want to look at this."

"Given you appropriated the thing the moment I found it, I certainly would."

"You needn't be so indignant about it." Amusement sounded in her voice. "Oh, but I forgot. You don't trust me."

"You shall have to work on that," he said under his breath. He turned the disk over in his hand, noting the engravings on both sides. It really was an exquisite piece. Hard to believe it was probably thousands of years old. Sidney was right. While the design on one side was perfectly centered, the engraving on the other definitely looked like it was only a small part of a larger design.

"And do sit down." She nodded toward the sofa. "This is rather complicated."

He cast a skeptical look at the sofa.

"I assure you, it's much more comfortable to sit on than to sleep on."

"It couldn't possibly be worse," he muttered but sat anyway.

"This is all very exciting but I don't want to repeat myself so why don't you tell me what Mr. Nazzal told you."

"Very well." He studied the medallion for a moment. "He said because of the notches, you thought this was part of a larger piece. And looking at this, I tend to agree. They serve no other purpose but to hold the medallion in place."

She nodded. "Good."

He turned it over. "He also said you think when this medallion is joined with the larger piece it could reveal the location of Itjtawy."

"Isn't it exciting?" She sat down beside him.

"Very, but you've made some assumptions here that may not be warranted."

"Have I?" She smiled in a distinctly superior manner. "Oh, I don't think so." She took the medallion and placed it on her palm. "On this side we have hieroglyphics that seem to indicate the name of the queen consort of Amenemhat II, or part of her name at least. Right here—" she pointed to a symbol on the medallion "—that says 'great royal wife.' Well, more or less. It's always difficult to be entirely precise with hieroglyphics. As you know, this particular king is rather obscure—"

He didn't but he let it pass.

"—and nothing yet discovered has given any name at all for any of his wives, as he would have had more than one."

"But if that's the name of a queen wouldn't it be in a cartouche?" As all royal names were contained in a cartouche. Anytime he'd run into hieroglyphics bound by an oblong border with a bar on one end indicating how it should be read, it had always signified royalty.

She shook her head. "That's true of kings' names, but queens' names weren't written in cartouches until at least a century or two after Amenemhat II."

"Go on."

"If indeed this side reveals the name of Amenemhat II's queen," she said, flipping the medallion over, "this side might well indicate where the city her husband ruled from can be found."

Her reasoning actually made sense but was rather far-fetched.

"Well? Aren't you going to say something?"

He chose his words with care. "I think you may be jumping to conclusions."

"You would be right. However..." She grinned with sheer satisfaction. "There's more." She thrust the medallion into his hand, fairly leaped off the sofa, crossed the room to the desk and returned with an old book. "This is my grandmother's journal. Her last journal actually." She resumed her seat and opened the book. "She and my grandfather spent most of their lives in Egypt searching for tombs and antiquities and, well, knowledge. It's my understanding that they were modestly successful and highly respected."

"Nazzal said something about your grandparents but he didn't mention a journal."

"I didn't know my grandparents, they died when I was very young. Lost at sea on their final voyage to Egypt."

"My condolences."

"Thank you, but as I said I never knew them. In fact, I didn't know anything about them at all until I met Aunt

Effie. She was a very dear friend of my grandmother's. When my grandparents would go off on another expedition to Egypt, my grandmother left her journals with Effie, in the event something happened." She grimaced. "And of course it did."

"Again, I am—"

"It's quite all right, really. You needn't continue to offer your sympathies although it's nice of you to do so." She patted his hand in a comforting manner, and continued. "In the last journal, she writes about a small cache of artifacts, no more than two dozen separate items, they stumbled onto near Dahshur."

He drew his brows together. "A tomb?"

"No, a cave. It appeared this collection of items had been hidden eons ago. Probably by tomb robbers who, oddly enough, never returned."

"So it remained for hundreds, possibly thousands of years," he said thoughtfully.

She nodded. "For whatever reason—and grandmother's journal is unfortunately vague about this—they put the cache back where they found it, intending of course to return on their next trip."

"But they never made it back."

"No and when I saw the medallion the other night, it struck me that it looked very much like one of the relics Grandmother wrote about. She listed all the objects in great detail and made drawings of some of them, those she considered most significant. She believed they were from the tomb of Amenemhat II's queen." She opened the journal and turned to one of the last entries. "This is a sketch of a rectangular piece, a pectoral I believe, a sort of necklace or breastplate—"

"I know what a pectoral is."

"Of course you do. Sorry," she said absently. "Now look right here…" She tapped a section of the drawing. "That circular area? It's not very detailed and it's a bit faded but it does look to me very much like the medallion we have."

Harry placed the medallion on the page next to the drawing. "It does seem to match."

"There's another drawing—" she turned the page "—here that matches the back although the ink is both faded and smudged and not distinct enough to provide any real information."

"Even so, there is a resemblance."

"Exactly." She turned another page. "And here is a drawing of the cave itself. This rocky outcropping looks somewhat like a sitting camel, don't you think?"

"No." He paused. "Perhaps."

"Now all we need to do is find the rest of the piece and that could lead us to the location of Itjtawy." She snapped the journal shut.

"Possibly." He held out his hand. "May I see that?"

"Certainly." She handed him the book.

He leafed through it. Was it possible that these journals of her grandmother's were the inspiration for Sidney's stories?

"It's one of the last entries." Impatience sounded in her voice. "Just think—we can follow in my grandmother's footsteps."

"Not your grandfather's?"

"Not really." Sidney waved off the question. "Aside from the occasional comment—the kinds of things one says about a husband I suppose—Grandmother rarely mentioned him. Her journals are her story not his. From what she wrote—and from what Effie has said—she was not the sort of woman to faint away at the first sign of danger." She paused. "Although she did have a fear of snakes."

"As do many of us. And there are far worse footsteps to follow in I suppose." He found the right page and studied the drawings, trying to ignore that distinct sense of mounting excitement he'd always had when he had been on the trail of an important find. Those days were behind him. "Or perhaps it would be better to turn this all over to Nazzal."

"Are you mad?" Disbelief blazed in her eyes. "This is the opportunity to uncover history." She jumped to her feet, snatched the book from his hands and waved it at him. "To ensure my family's legacy. To finish my grandmother's story." Sidney met his gaze directly. "Furthermore, I can think of no better way to prove to you that I am not a fraud than by finding a lost city."

Maybe he should tell her now that was no longer necessary. Would she still want to continue then? Admittedly, the idea of finding something this important was almost irresistible. The old Harry Armstrong wouldn't have hesitated. He got to his feet. "Sidney—"

"It seems to me you might have something to prove as well."

He narrowed his eyes. "I have nothing to prove."

"Don't you?" She crossed her arms over her chest. "Daniel said you were well known among Egyptologists— which is not the same thing as being an Egyptologist—"

"I've never cared much for titles."

"—and I am very well versed in every exhibit, every lecture, and very nearly everything else that involves the study and discoveries of Egypt both past and present. Yet I have never so much as heard your name."

"I'm not sure why that matters."

"Perhaps it doesn't. But you spent years here, you lost a dear friend, and, as far as I can tell, have received no recognition for your work whatsoever. Why, you've never even been invited to join the Egyptian Antiquities Society."

He stiffened. "You don't know that."

"Before we left London, I checked the membership list and neither your name nor your uncle's is on it. Which brings up another point. Until your uncle wrote his vile letters to *The Times* I had never heard of the Earl of Brenton. And while I don't know them personally, I am familiar with the names of most of those supporters of expeditions or enthusiasts of Egyptian history and archeology. Which leads me to believe his letters were at your urging and the only reason for trying to discredit my work is to lessen competition with your own."

He wasn't sure he wanted to hear more. "About my uncle—"

"It's obvious you feel responsible for your friend's death. Writing about your adventures in Egypt—and I did read those pages you left for me—would keep his memory alive and provide him, and you, with the recognition you've been denied but probably deserve."

"You've given this a great deal of thought."

"I would be a fool not to. You and your uncle are trying to ruin me."

"I don't want to ruin you," he said slowly. "Frankly, I really wasn't thinking about you when this whole mess started. And you're right. I do feel responsible for Walter's death. And yes, I was thinking about my own work and my own legacy but more than that—" he met her gaze firmly "—Walter and I and Ben made a contribution here and I wanted it acknowledged. Not really for myself although I will admit that was indeed part of it." It was difficult to put into words. He blew a long breath. "I didn't want Walter's life to have been for nothing. He had no family to speak of, there's no one left to remember him except me and Ben. I didn't want him to fade from the world as if he was never here."

She stared at him for a long moment. "That's rather noble of you."

"I can be noble."

"I've become quite fond of you, Harry Armstrong, in spite of your uncle." She shook her head. "Was that a mistake?"

He grinned. "Probably. But it's a mistake I've made as well as I've become more than merely fond of you." He stepped closer, took the journal from her hand and set it on the desk.

"Oh?" She stared up at him. "How much more?"

"A great deal more." He pulled her into his arms.

She gazed up at him and wrapped her arms around his neck. "Why, Harry Armstrong, are you finally going to kiss me when it isn't out of mere necessity?"

"My dear, Mrs. Gordon, I'm afraid you're mistaken." He pulled her closer against him. "It was never out of mere necessity." With that he pressed his lips to hers.

The oddest sense of inevitability and with it acceptance swept through him at the feel of her lips against his. The taste of her, the scent of her invaded his senses and wrapped around his soul. A kiss would not be enough. A day, a year, a lifetime would not be enough. He wanted this woman in his bed, in his life, by his side for the rest of his days. Her mouth opened to his and he savored the taste of her—warm unknown spices and adventures yet to come. Her body pressed against his and his blood pounded in his veins.

She gasped. "Harry."

"Sidney." He fairly sighed her name, wrenched his lips from hers and feathered kisses along the line of her jaw.

"Harry!" She pushed harder. "There's someone at the door."

"Ignore it." He kissed the side of her neck, just below her ear. She shivered in his arms and his muscles tightened.

"I would dearly love to, Harry." Her voice had the most delightful breathless quality. "But we can't."

He groaned. "Why not?"

"Because that might well be another piece to our puzzle."

He raised his head and looked down at her. "What? Now?"

"So it would seem." Her eyes sparkled.

"I'd be willing to forgo a lost city right now for time together if you are."

"Goodness, Harry." She reached up and nibbled the lobe of his ear. "We might be able to have both."

CHAPTER TWENTY

"GOOD DAY, MR. NAZZAL." Sidney ushered the Egyptian into her room. Her voice was steady, her demeanor serene and she was confident there was no outward sign of the kiss she and Harry had just shared. Nothing to indicate her insides were quivering with what was probably sheer, undeniable desire. Good Lord, if Nazzal hadn't arrived when he did Harry could have had her right there on the floor. Or she could have had him. For a woman who had not yet lost her virginity, she was more than eager to do so now. It seemed it just took the right man—and the right kiss—to turn a woman who had never given a great deal of thought to longings of the flesh into someone who could think of little else. Undeniable desire was apparently quite a powerful thing. Perhaps it would fade, was no more than a momentary peculiarity, although she doubted it. Pity, there were other pressing matters to attend to first. "I didn't expect you quite so soon."

"Good afternoon, Mrs. Gordon, Harry." Mr. Nazzal nodded a greeting to Harry then addressed Sidney. "I found our quarry much more quickly than I had expected and I knew you were eager to proceed."

"Wonderful! I don't know how to thank you." Sidney beamed.

"Oh, but you do," Mr. Nazzal said with a smile. "Are you ready?"

"I just need to get my hat and gloves."

"I beg your pardon," Harry said, obviously a bit disgruntled. Perhaps that's what happened when undeniable desire was indeed denied. She bit back a grin. "What does he mean—you know how to thank him? And where are you going? Don't think for a minute you're going anywhere without me."

"Goodness, Harry, we didn't expect you to be here, did we, Mr. Nazzal?"

"In truth, I suspected he'd be here," Mr. Nazzal said.

"That's right." Sidney's gaze slid from one man to the other. "The two of you had a little chat without me."

"I assure you, Mrs. Gordon—"

"Sidney, it really wasn't—"

"It's of no consequence." She waved them quiet. "Harry, I never intended to do this without you." She drew her brows together. "Well, actually I had intended to do this part without you until I saw you lurking in the streets rather than enjoying a day on the Nile."

Mr. Nazzal snorted in amusement and tried to hide it with a bad pretense of a cough.

"Yes, well, good. I am part of this now, you know, and I do not intend to be left behind," Harry said firmly then paused. "Where are we going?"

"Whenever my grandparents were in Egypt, they employed the same man—a Mr. Bishara—to serve as guide, interpreter and general superintendent." She picked up her hat and stepped to the wall mirror to adjust it. Aside from a slight flush in her cheeks—which was rather becoming—there was no evidence at all that a few minutes ago she was more than willing to throw herself into bed with Harry Armstrong. She pushed the thought aside. Now was not the time but later... "He managed all their trips, expeditions and digs, arranged transportation and hired workers. They trusted him implicitly. They had a long and beneficial relationship for nearly a quarter of a century." She turned toward them and pulled on her gloves. "According to Grandmother's journal, he was with them when they found the cache of artifacts in question. He was charged with drawing a map and marking directions, some way to locate the cave again. It was the sort of thing he did routinely."

Harry glanced at Mr. Nazzal. "Don't you see any problems here?"

Mr. Nazzal shrugged. "I am an eternal optimist."

"Then let me spell them out." Harry ticked the points off on his fingers. "First—this must have been a good thirty years ago. You don't even know if Bishara is still alive."

"He is," Mr. Nazzal said. "He is old but still breathing."

"And we are going to see him." Sidney nodded. "Now."

"Then let me rephrase—you don't know that he'll be able to remember any of this."

"We don't know that he won't. It's a chance well worth taking I'd say." Sidney sighed. "Really, Harry, is all this explanation necessary?"

"Yes," he snapped.

"Well, go on, then." She gestured impatiently. "I assume there's more?"

Harry nodded. "As I said, it's been thirty years. That cache may be long gone by now."

"It could have been long gone hundreds of years ago and yet no one ever found it." There was something wickedly enjoyable about countering Harry's overly rational points. "Now, are you finished?"

"No." Harry huffed. "Even if we manage to find this

cave, in the desert, after thirty years of sandstorms and who knows what else and the cache is still there, and we find the pectoral and put the medallion back in the larger piece, that doesn't mean it will indeed then give the location of a city that vanished more than three thousand years ago."

"Yes, but it might. Goodness, Harry. Isn't the unknown part of adventure? Isn't not knowing what makes it so much fun?"

Harry stared at her for a long moment. He had the distinct look of a man trying to come to terms with himself. Or perhaps with the past. Or possibly deciding to move forward.

"Well?" She was doing this whether he joined her or not. Without thinking she straightened her shoulders. Millicent would do it alone if she had to and so would Sidney. But the idea of doing it with Harry made it much less terrifying. Even Millicent would be a bit daunted by the task ahead.

"Very well." A slow grin spread across his face. "Let's go find your lost city."

Now there was the man she loved. Richard Weatherly couldn't have done it better. She knew all along Harry would—

The man she loved?

It was pointless to deny it. How long had she known she'd fallen madly, passionately in love with the annoying, arrogant, amusing, decent man? Did she realize it just now when he'd truly kissed her for no other reason than he wanted to? Or did she know the moment he mistook one of the ladies for her at the docks in London? Did she know it always?

Harry glanced at Mr. Nazzal. "And what do you get out of this?"

"Aside from being a witness to the solving of a centuries-old mystery?" Mr. Nazzal asked. "Any objects recovered will, of course, remain in Egypt—which was never up for discussion at any rate although Mrs. Gordon has graciously agreed to give up any claim based on her grandparents' original discovery. For which she has my thanks."

"You're quite welcome." Not that she would have made such a claim but it was nice to be thanked.

"If the pectoral does indeed reveal the location of Itjtawy, any excavation attempted will be under the supervision of *Egyptian archeologists*," Mr. Nazzal continued. "Mrs. Gordon will be part of it if she wishes and you as well if you'd like."

"Yes, that does sound like an adventure," Harry said wryly.

She beamed. "Then we should be off."

HAD HE ASKED—Sidney would have told Harry she had every confidence he could find the residence of the family of Ahmed Bishara without any assistance and it was not at all necessary for Mr. Nazzal to accompany them. Fortunately, he did not ask and Sidney was grateful for Mr. Nazzal's guidance. In no time at all, they had maneuvered their way through narrow, winding streets in one of the oldest areas of the city and were sitting with Mr. Bishara in his son's house.

She guessed Mr. Bishara was probably the same age as Effie, Gwen and Poppy, somewhere in his late seventies, but he might have been centuries older. *Wizened* was the only word Sidney could think of to describe him, as

if years spent in the desert had sucked all the moisture
from his body. He wore a patch over one eye and tended
to cackle more than laugh. She did wish she spoke some
Arabic beyond *yawm jayid*, "good day," and *shujraan*,
"thank you." It was beyond frustrating to listen to Mr.
Nazzal speak with Mr. Bishara and not know exactly
what was being said. Harry did seem to understand most
of it—at least he nodded and occasionally asked a question. Evidently he was more fluent in Arabic than he had
previously admitted. They had agreed it would be best
to let Mr. Nazzal handle the discussion as Mr. Bishara
might be more forthcoming with a fellow countryman.
Sidney could do little more than sip the bitter coffee she'd
grown to like during her stay in Egypt and try to appear
as if she could follow what was being discussed.

Finally, Mr. Nazzal turned to her. "My apologies, Mrs.
Gordon. Mr. Bishara has lived a long and interesting life
and seems to enjoy a new audience for his stories."

"Understandable." Sidney smiled at the old man.
"Does he remember my grandparents?"

"Quite fondly, it seems," Mr. Nazzal began. "On their
last exploration, the one where they found the hidden
cache in the cave, there was an unfortunate accident. One
of the workers was badly injured. Bishara did not say exactly how." He glanced at the older man who beamed a
toothless grin. "Regardless, that led to the rumor that the
objects had been cursed by the tomb robbers who had
originally hidden them. Nonsense, of course, but those
working for your grandparents refused to have anything
to do with the find."

"Which is probably why your grandparents left it, intending to return on their next trip," Harry added.

Sidney nodded.

Mr. Nazzal continued. "Mr. Bishara, however, being a sensible man, thought it was nonsense and after your grandparents left Egypt, returned to the cave and took the artifacts."

"Did he?" Sidney raised a brow.

"You must understand, Mrs. Gordon, he was very aware that if he did not collect the cache, others who had worked for your grandparents would. In addition, he had a family to support and he was getting older as were your grandparents." Mr. Nazzal shrugged. "He could not be certain they would return or that they would continue his employment."

"He then sold the items a piece at a time, so as not to arouse suspicion," Harry said, "He separated the medallion from the pectoral because he could sell two pieces and make twice as much."

"Of course," Sidney murmured.

"It was after he sold the medallion that he had a streak of misfortune. Among other things he broke his leg and lost his eye." Mr. Nazzal turned to Mr. Bishara and asked him something. The old man responded in an animated manner then flipped his eye patch up, apparently to show his missing eye and indeed there was nothing but an empty socket. Sidney tried not to wince but her stomach was not as cooperative. The Egyptian replaced his patch with a slight smirk. One couldn't help but wonder if he rather enjoyed the response to his missing eye and this was a parlor trick for him. "That led him to believe the pectoral was indeed cursed. He'd already sold everything else but he returned that piece to the cave."

"I can see why he might think that," Sidney said weakly and was glad they hadn't brought the medallion along.

Mr. Nazzal again spoke to the old man who shrugged and barked a command to one of the ladies lingering in the shadows of the room. She left at once but returned a moment later and handed him a yellowed scrap of paper. He passed it to Mr. Nazzal.

"Fortunately, Bashir is nothing if not practical. He kept directions to the cave." Mr. Nazzal handed the paper to Sidney, who glanced at it briefly, long enough to note it was indeed a map but crudely drawn and worn, then passed it to Harry.

Harry studied the fragile scrap for a moment then folded it and put it in his pocket. He exchanged a few words with Mr. Bishara, who occasionally gestured at Sidney, and directed some comments toward Mr. Nazzal, a distinct warning in his tone. One didn't need to speak the language to understand—the old man thought the medallion was cursed. Better not to let him know they had it although she was fairly certain Mr. Nazzal had already come to that conclusion. A few minutes later, they took their leave.

Harry suggested it might be best not to discuss any of this until they were safely back at the hotel as one never knew who might overhear. He cast her a pointed glance as he said it and she smiled innocently in return. It was a short enough ride but it did seem like forever. She could barely contain her excitement. This could lead them to the lost capital of Egypt. Sidney had always thought she was a patient sort but apparently, at the moment at least, she was wrong.

"Well?" she said as soon as she closed the door to her suite behind them. Her gaze shifted from Harry to Mr. Nazzal and back. "Will we be able to find this cave or not?"

"Possibly." Caution edged Harry's voice. He unfolded the map and spread it on the desk.

It didn't look like any map she had ever seen but was a disjointed collection of squiggles and lines and arrows and in the corner, the face of a clock. Even so, she refused to be discouraged. Fortunately, it seemed to make sense to Harry and Mr. Nazzal. And they did have her grandmother's drawing of the cave.

"There's enough on this map to give it a try," Harry said at last.

"Excellent." She resisted the urge to bounce up and down like an overexcited child. "When?"

"We do need to study this more carefully, along with the latest maps of the area. Give some consideration as to the best way to get there and back. Purchase a few supplies." Harry thought for a minute. "It's not that far from Cairo. Somewhere in the region between Dahshur and the ancient site of Memphis."

"When, Harry?"

"What do you think, Nazzal? Can we manage it by, I don't know—" Harry grinned "—tomorrow?"

"Tomorrow?" Sidney widened her eyes. "I think tomorrow sounds perfect."

"I can assist with whatever you need," Mr. Nazzal said. Sidney glanced at the Egyptian. "You're not coming?"

"It's not really the sort of thing I do." Mr. Nazzal shrugged and turned to Harry. "You should leave no later than dawn. Do you think you'll need to set up camp?"

"Best to be prepared for anything, I think," Harry said, and the men launched into a detailed discussion of what might be needed. Mr. Nazzal pulled out a notebook, made a quick copy of the map and jotted notes as they talked.

Sidney paid as much attention as possible given she

was bursting with excitement. Tomorrow, with a great deal of luck, she would recover at least part of her grandmother's last find. It seemed only fitting for Sidney's own grand adventure to be a legacy of sorts of the woman who had started her down this path.

"I think that's it, then." Harry folded the map, blew a long breath then cast her a wicked grin. "Tomorrow, Sidney, we might just find out if this is nothing more than a wild-goose chase or something quite significant."

"I'll make the arrangements," Mr. Nazzal said. "You might want to consider what to tell your friends. I assume you're not going to want them to accompany you."

Sidney shook her head. "I wouldn't think so."

"And we definitely don't want Corbin along," Harry added firmly.

Mr. Nazzal stepped to the door and pulled it open, then turned to her. "I nearly forgot. You might be interested in something else Bashir mentioned about your grandparents."

"Yes, of course."

"He said your grandfather, while quite competent and knowledgeable and recognized as the head of their excursions, was not the one behind any of their discoveries." He grinned. "It was your grandmother." With that he took his leave.

Harry smiled. "I can't say I'm surprised."

"Isn't that wonderful? Isn't it all wonderful?" Without thinking, Sidney threw herself into Harry's arms and laughed. "Quite, quite wonderful."

"Well, yes. I would say it's wonderful." He chuckled and his arms slid around her waist. Even finding a lost city paled in comparison to the feel of Harry Armstrong's arms around her. There was little better in life than Harry holding her close. "You do realize this is a long shot. Even with this map, there are a lot of caves. The chances we will find this cave are slim."

"Yes, but we might."

"And even if we do, the possibility that the pectoral is still there after thirty years is remote."

"But it could be."

"And should we be lucky enough to find the cave and the artifact, there's no guarantee that it will provide so much as vague clues about the location of Itjtawy."

"Good Lord, Harry." She drew her brows together. "Sometimes the quest alone is enough. The journey is more significant than the destination. The ends aren't nearly as important as the means."

"That's all very well and good but I want you to be prepared if this doesn't work out as you want it to."

"Oh, I'll be terribly disappointed if this is all for nothing. But isn't risk part of it?"

"I suppose it depends—" his tone was abruptly somber, the look in his eyes intense "—on what you're risking."

Her breath caught. "It certainly wouldn't be much of a risk if…" His gaze searched hers, his gray eyes the color of an oncoming storm. "If…what I mean…well…if what you're risking…"

"What are you risking?"

"Everything," she whispered and pulled his head to hers.

His lips met hers in a gentle exploration that melted her insides and weakened her knees. Her mouth opened to his eagerly and he responded in kind. She wanted to taste him. To touch him. And dear Lord, she wanted him to touch her.

Her arms tightened around him and she pressed herself closer to him. She could feel the hard heat of his body through his clothes and hers. He slanted his mouth over hers, hard and demanding and she demanded in return. All sense of restraint and caution shattered. This was what wanting a man meant—this overwhelming need for his lips and his touch and more. Need that claimed and swept her away.

The world—her world—distorted, shifted to a fog of sensation and desire. Of lips and hands, of tugging and pulling and the distinct sound of something tearing. Within moments, Sidney had nothing on but her corset and chemise, her clothes discarded, tossed on the floor or the chairs or who knew where. She wasn't sure how it happened and, aside from a twinge of trepidation when she realized his coat and shirt were gone as well, found she didn't care. Her back pressed against the wall and the moment her breasts flattened against his bare skin she shivered with the remarkable feeling of the solid muscles of his chest pressed against her. The hard length of him nudged between her thighs and there was yet another twinge of trepidation. She had no idea when he'd discarded his trousers. Claiming to be knowledgeable about what truly transpired between a man and a woman was a far cry from actually being engaged in such a thing.

He pulled his lips from hers to kiss the side of her neck, his mouth trailing ever lower. She moaned. A tiny still-rational voice somewhere in the back of her head whispered she could call a halt to all this if she wanted to. He sank down before her and cupped her breasts in his hands, caressing and teasing. He took her breast in his mouth and she was lost. Her fingers tightened on his shoulders. He teased and tormented first one tightened nipple then the next and she marveled that she hadn't slid down the wall to puddle in a molten mass of sensation at his feet. And oh dear Lord, she wanted more.

Time stretched, slowed, blurred. Nothing existed save the feel of his mouth, his hands, his flesh beneath her fingers. He trailed kisses down her stomach and slid his hand between her legs. She cried out when he touched her, the intensity beyond anything she'd ever felt. He stroked her until her breath came in short gasps and an awful joyous yearning threatened to tear her apart.

Harry rose to his feet, his body sliding against hers. She ran her hands over the hard ridges and valleys of his back and his neck and his arms and wondered at the heat of him. Searing her body and reaching into her soul.

Her leg entwined around his and his erection slid between her thighs. She could feel him slick against her and realized with an odd sense of satisfaction that was her doing. Any lingering doubt vanished.

He slid his hands behind her to cup her buttocks and lifted her. She wrapped her legs around him and pulled him closer. He slid into her slowly, the feeling odd yet not unpleasant, and she urged him on. Longing that was almost frantic gripped her. She needed him, wanted him joined with her, united with her, one with her. And she wanted him now. She dug her heels into his backside. He pushed deeper and then stopped and stared down at her.

"Sidney, is it at all possible that you've never—"

"Do you really want to discuss this now?" Her voice was breathless and she rocked against him. "Now?"

"Now seems the appropriate time."

"Not to me!" Oh Lord, this was so extraordinary.

"Sidney, if there's something—"

"Do shut up, Harry." She captured his mouth with hers

and pressed hard with her heels. She gasped against his mouth. The ladies were right—it did sting a bit. And her inner core throbbed with his invasion.

Harry paused and Sidney's heart swelled. The man knew without words that she needed a moment. Slowly he began to move within her. Her discomfort eased, mellowed, transformed. With every stroke, the sort of pleasure she'd never known, never suspected grew more and more intense, claiming her senses, narrowing her very existence to nothing more than spiraling need. Her fingers dug into his back and she urged him on. She vaguely noted odd whimpering sounds of sheer pleasure and realized they came from her. Somewhere, deep inside, a spring wound tighter and tighter and she feared its release. And ached for it. Craved it. Demanded it. He thrust into her faster and harder, and her body rocked against his in response, driven by unyielding desire and newfound passion. He groaned against her and his body shuddered and he thrust again and again. And when she thought surely she would die of the taut, increasing tension within her, release exploded through her. She shook with the power of it and cried out and clung to him. Unimagined pleasure, absolute and all-consuming, swept through her, claimed her body and marked her soul. And she marveled that she could survive such sheer, unadulterated joy. And more that she had found it in the arms of the man she had not been inclined to even like but instead grew to love. The annoying, arrogant, wonderful man.

And realized finding a lost city might not be the greatest adventure ahead.

CHAPTER TWENTY-ONE

"WE NEED TO TALK," Harry said the moment he had deposited her onto the bed. How thoughtful of him to pick her up and carry her to the bed. She would have been quite happy to remain a disheveled heap sagging against the wall. It wasn't as if she could walk on her own. Every bone in her body seemed to have dissolved into a quivering state of spent ecstasy.

"Do we really?" All she really wanted to do was curl up like a contented cat in the sunlight. Preferably, with Harry wrapped around her.

"Yes, we really do."

"Very well, then." She heaved a frustrated sigh, moved to the side of the bed and got to her feet.

"What are you doing?"

"From the tone of your voice I gather we are about to have a discussion of a stern nature. Unless I'm wrong?" she added hopefully.

"I would say that's fairly accurate."

"Well I'm not going to have such a discussion clad in my chemise and corset. It's...undignified."

The corners of his mouth quirked upward. "We would hate to be undignified."

She started to unhook the front of her corset then paused. "Turn around, if you will."

"That's ridiculous. There's little left that I haven't seen." He grinned. "And you do realize I'm naked."

"Indeed you are." Her gaze traveled over him. She might well be inexperienced in such matters but Harry Armstrong did strike her as a fine figure of a man.

He cleared his throat and her gaze jumped back to his. "Perhaps you could hand me my trousers."

"I suppose I could. But first—" she fluttered her fingers at him "—turn around."

"Very well." He huffed and turned his back to her. The man had the backside of a marble statue. Greek or Roman—she really couldn't decide. It was all she could do to keep from reaching out and running her hands over his bottom, but he would probably not take that well as he did have a discussion of a stern nature planned. "This is absurd."

"I don't care." She finished with her corset and pulled off her chemise, torn in more than one place. She bit back a grin. Sidney Honeywell's chemise torn in a fit of passion. Who would have imagined such a thing? She found her robe at the foot of the bed and shrugged it on. "Do you still want your trousers?"

"That would be nice."

"Very well." She glanced around the room. Clothes were scattered everywhere. Goodness, it looked like the setting of a French farce. She located his trousers under a table and fetched them for him.

"Now perhaps you would turn around."

"I don't think so, Harry. I'm rather enjoying the view."

"I was rather enjoying the view and you made me turn around." He stepped into his trousers. He really did have an excellent backside.

"I know. Dreadfully unfair of me," she said and sat on the edge of the bed.

He buttoned his trousers and turned toward her. "Tell me more about your dead husband."

"Now?" Oh dear, she did hope he didn't think he was being clever. Or subtle.

"Yes."

"It seems rather inappropriate."

"He's dead." Harry shrugged. "I daresay he won't mind."

"Still I scarcely think—" She rose to her feet. He stepped in front of her, his eyes narrowed and she reluctantly sat back down and sighed. "What would you like to know?"

"Where did you meet?"

"Oh, you know, out and about." She waved vaguely. Admitting the truth about her alleged widowhood was only a scant step away from admitting the truth about her stories. She wasn't quite ready for that yet. "One never remembers those sorts of silly details."

"Every woman I've ever known has remembered those sorts of silly details."

"Then I'm unique." She cast him her brightest smile. "How delightful."

"How long were you betrothed?"

"Hardly any time at all." Good Lord, he had a lot of questions and each one came faster than the last.

"Where were you married?"

"London." The man was engaged in his own version of the Inquisition.

"What was his name?"

"Charles," she said and sent a silent thanks to her friends as she surely couldn't remember any other name right now.

"Where did you live?"

"London." She was saying the first thing that came to mind but so far, the answers required no particular effort.

"When were you married?"

"I've never been good with dates." These questions were coming entirely too quickly. She barely had any time to come up with acceptable answers.

"How old was he?"

"Older than I."

"How did he die."

"Eaten by crocodiles," she said without thinking and winced.

"Last night you said he wasn't eaten by crocodiles."

"Did I?" she said innocently and shook her head. "It can be quite confusing and—"

"You said he drowned."

"Well, he did." She searched for something clever to say and could find nothing. "While he was being eaten."

"That must have been most distressing."

"You have no idea." She buried her face in her hands. "I try not to talk about it."

For a long moment he didn't say anything and she thought perhaps he might just let this subject drop.

"You've never been married at all, have you, *Mrs.* Gordon?"

"For you to question my marriage as if it never happened and to malign poor, dear dead Charles…" She forced a sob that sounded horribly like a hiccup.

"Sidney." A warning sounded in his voice and the bed on either side of her dipped. Even without looking, she knew he'd trapped her between his arms. Knew if she raised her head she'd be looking straight into his gray eyes. Knew it was past time to admit to what he had obviously determined. "Sidney?"

"Yes?"

"You've never done this before."

"I beg your pardon." Even so, there was no need to make it easy for him. She snapped her head up and met his gaze directly. "Never done what before?"

"A man does tend to notice that sort of thing, you know."

"What sort of thing?"

"Obviously you've never been with a man and I doubt you've ever been married. Is your name even Gordon?"

"Of course." She paused. "Well, one of them." She blew a resigned breath. "Sidney Althea Gordon Honeywell. Delighted to meet you."

"Miss Sidney Honeywell." He grinned. "I like it. Dare I ask why you're pretending to be a widow?"

"Mr. Cadwallender thought it was for the best."

"Imagine my surprise."

"Now that that's settled." She wrapped her arms around him and pulled him down onto the bed.

"Nothing is settled," he growled against her skin but didn't pull away.

"Really, Harry?" She nuzzled his neck. He moaned softly and she grinned. "Nothing?"

"There's more we need to discuss," he said in a ragged voice.

"Oh, I don't think so."

"Isn't there anything else you wish to confess?"

"Not really." She nibbled at his earlobe and his body tensed against hers. "I think there are other things we could do."

He rolled over until she was beneath him looking up into his eyes. "I think..." He stared down at her.

"Yes, Harry." She adopted what she hoped was a sultry tone. It wasn't difficult. She wanted him again as much as he wanted her. At least judging from the obvious evidence. And it would no doubt be great fun to try it lying down. She rubbed her leg against his. "What do you think?"

"Bloody hell, Miss Honeywell." It was fascinating to watch the look in a man's eyes change from determined to aroused. "You are damn near irresistible."

She giggled. "Thank you, Mr. Armstrong."

He hesitated. "About that."

"What? Isn't Harry Armstrong your real name?"

"Well yes, of course, but—"

"I told you mine. If you have another name I should very much like to hear it."

A knock sounded at the door.

"Sidney, are you in there?" Effie's voice sounded from the other side of the door.

"Good God!" she whispered, a distinct sense of panic fluttering in her stomach. "They're back. I didn't expect them so soon. What time is it?"

"I don't know." He glanced around. "My watch is here somewhere."

"They can't find you here!"

His brow furrowed. "There's no other way out except for the window."

"Well, then—" She waved at the window.

"Absolutely not." He stared at her. "I am not sneaking out a window."

"Very well." She pushed him aside and stood. "Then hide."

"Sidney?" Gwen called. "How are you feeling?"

Harry groaned. "It's all three of them, isn't it?"

"Yes, of course, they always travel in a pack." She raised her voice. "Sorry, one moment please." Sidney scrambled around the room collecting various items of clothing.

Harry just stood there looking rather stupidly helpless. "Where am I supposed to go?"

She thrust the bundle of clothes at him. "Under the bed."

He shook his head. "I'm not hiding under the bed."

"You do have a lot of objections for a man with no ideas!" She frantically scanned the room. "In the bedroom, then, and I'll close the curtains." She pushed him toward the bedroom, then yanked the curtains closed behind him. "Don't make a sound, don't even move. I'll try to keep their visit as brief as possible."

"Sidney?" Poppy said. "Are you all right?"

"Yes, quite all right." Sidney sprinted to the door, cast one last look around—it would have to do—drew a deep breath then pulled the door open. "How was the Nile?"

"Oh, you know. Endless, eternal, that sort of thing." Gwen and the other ladies filed into the room and immediately took positions on the sofa, apparently intending to stay.

Effie studied her closely. "Were you sleeping?"

"Oh, not really," she said weakly and sat on a nearby chair. "Just resting."

"She does look a bit flushed, don't you think?" Poppy said with a frown. "I do hope you haven't caught some sort of rare disease. One never knows what might start with a headache."

"What are you talking about?" Effie stared at her

friend. "She wasn't feeling the least bit poorly—remember? She simply wanted us to get Harry and Daniel out of her way."

"Oh, yes, I forgot." Poppy frowned. "Still, I do think she looks rather flushed."

"She does at that." Gwen cast her a thoughtful look then continued. "I am sorry but Harry managed to evade us. He can be quite clever when he puts his mind to it. Did you do what you needed to do?"

Sidney nodded. "I did."

"And?" Effie prompted.

"And…" Sidney said slowly. She wasn't entirely sure how much to say. She trusted all three ladies implicitly but they did have an appalling tendency to say things without thinking. "And I shall need your help again tomorrow."

Eagerness sparkled in Gwen's eyes. "What do you want us to do?"

"I won't know for certain until we hear from Mr. Nazzal but I imagine you will have to keep Daniel occupied."

"Oh good. That's always fun." Poppy grinned. "The man gets so delightfully inconvenienced."

"What are you and Harry up to, dear?" Effie asked pleasantly.

There was no point to protest Harry's involvement. The ladies knew he wasn't with them today. If it wasn't for these friends, Sidney wouldn't be in Egypt at all. She wouldn't be on the greatest adventure of her life. And she never would have met Harry. They deserved to know everything. She caught a faint flutter of the curtain out of the corner of her eye. Well, not everything.

"Very well, then. It goes without saying not a word of this leaves this room," she said firmly.

Effie and Gwen leveled the exact same warning look at Poppy.

"You needn't look at me like that." Indignation rang in Poppy's voice. "I'm not the only one who speaks out of turn. Why, I can name any number of times—"

"We're sure you can but now is perhaps not the best time." Gwen cast her friend a conciliatory smile. "Sidney has something to tell us." She paused then raised her voice. "Harry, did you want to join us or are you happy where you are?"

Sidney bit her lip. She wasn't sure if she wished to laugh or cry.

"I'm fine where I am, thank you," Harry said at last. "Just pretend I'm not here."

Effie leaned forward and lowered her voice. "Difficult to do with his bare feet sticking out from under the curtains and the light from the window silhouetting him rather perfectly."

"And there's a stocking hanging from the sconce," Poppy added.

"Now, then," Sidney said firmly, "do you want to hear this or not?"

The ladies nodded.

Sidney quickly explained about the medallion and the pectoral, about Mr. Bishara and her grandmother's journal. When she was done, all three ladies stared. For a moment, none of them said a word—obvious testament to their disbelief.

"Good heavens, Sidney." Gwen shook her head. "This is a venture worthy of Millicent Forester herself."

Poppy beamed. "And how brilliant of you to have figured it all out."

Effie reached forward and patted Sidney's hand. "Your grandmother would be quite proud of you, my dear girl."

Sidney wasn't certain but she could have sworn Effie's eyes misted with tears. Sidney's certainly did. She blinked hard and sniffed. "Thank you, Aunt Effie."

She drew a steadying breath. "You do realize, this is all highly speculative. We might not find the cave or the pectoral could be gone. Any number of things could go wrong."

"But you do intend to try?" Gwen asked.

"Of course."

"That's all one can ever ask, dear." Gwen nodded then she and the others rose to their feet. "Now, we need to freshen up and change for dinner."

"Yes, well, we shall see you at dinner, then," Sidney said with relief and ushered them toward the door.

Gwen paused at the door, glanced at the curtains and raised her voice. "You do understand this sort of indiscretion calls for marriage, don't you, Harry? Nothing else will do."

"I am aware of my obligations."

"While there is no official connection, do keep in mind we consider Sidney to be family just as much as we feel that way about each other," Effie said in a hard tone. "We will not look kindly upon anyone who does not do right by her."

Sidney bit back a groan. "Ladies, you really do need—"

"Do not think this a threat, Harry," Poppy called. "We would never threaten anyone. You may, however, consider it a promise."

"I understand that, ladies." Surely that was not amusement in Harry's voice. Surely he was smarter than that.

"See that you do, Harry." Effie smiled at Sidney and at last she and the others took their leave.

The door closed behind them and Harry called from behind the curtains. "Are they gone?"

"Yes."

He stepped out from his hiding place and grinned. "I thought they'd never leave."

"Neither did I," she said absently. Now that they were gone and she had a moment to think, she wasn't at all sure she liked what she was thinking. Or what she had heard. "You should go as well. I do need to dress for dinner."

Caution sounded in his voice. "Is something wrong?"

"What could possibly be wrong?"

"I have no idea."

She turned away from him, as much to give herself the opportunity to think without being distracted as to give him a measure of privacy to dress.

A few minutes later, he came up behind her and put his hands on her shoulders and kissed the side of her neck. "Until dinner, then."

She nodded.

Behind her he hesitated then apparently decided discretion was indeed the better part of valor and took his leave.

How could everything be so wonderful one moment and so dreadful the next? Sidney probably wasn't being the least bit fair but she didn't care. She didn't need Harry Armstrong's protection and she had no desire to be anyone's obligation.

"WHAT DO YOU think you're doing?" Sidney said as Harry locked the door to her room and proceeded to pull off his tie. The last thing she wanted in her room right now was Harry. She'd tried to avoid speaking unnecessarily to him at dinner although it was nearly impossible as they all sat at the same table. Immediately after dinner, Mr. Nazzal had arrived to discuss tomorrow's arrangements and they had adjourned to her rooms. The Egyptian left a few moments ago. "I thought you were leaving?"

"I don't know why you thought that. I am going to have another miserable night's sleep on the sofa of torture as I did last night. As I will do every night until that medallion is out of your hands." He glanced around. "Where did you hide it?"

She nodded at the chest of drawers.

He grinned. "You said it wasn't in the chest of drawers."

"It wasn't." She shrugged. "Now it is."

He took off his cuff links and set them on a table. "I was rather hoping I wouldn't have to sleep on the sofa tonight." He glanced pointedly at the bed.

"We have an important day tomorrow that's certain to be quite strenuous and I would like to sleep tonight." She nodded and moved to the bedroom, yanking the curtains closed behind her. She had no desire to talk to him at the moment. In truth she wasn't at all certain how she felt. Or rather what to do about how she felt. It was most confusing. She was certainly upset and somewhat hurt as well. And apparently angry.

"That's all you're going to say?"

"I really have nothing to say."

"You've been saying nothing all night." Frustration sounded in his voice. "I know you're angry with me, as does everyone else who was with us this evening, but I can't fix the problem until I know what it is. At least tell me what I've done!"

"Good night, Harry."

"I don't think this is the least bit amusing, Sidney."

"Then we have that in common."

Sidney struggled to get her evening gown off but she'd decided against calling for a maid with Harry in the room. Under other circumstances, she might ask him for help but then one thing would lead to another. She shivered at the mere thought of one thing leading to another. How on earth could she want the man this badly when her heart felt like a leaden weight in her chest? *An obligation?* Hadn't she taken care of her mother, managed their household, studied everything she could find about Egypt and then become a rousingly successful writer? That was not the kind of woman who was anyone's *obligation.* Damn the man—she was Queen of the blasted Desert! She threw on her night things, snapped off the light and fell into bed.

"It's no fun arguing by yourself, you know," Harry called after a few minutes of silence.

She refused to say anything. Hopefully he'd think she was asleep, not that she thought he would. Besides, she had no idea what to say. On one hand—it did seem rather unfair to fault the man for doing what was expected of him. Of being willing to do the right thing. On the other—an *obligation* was not how one wanted to be regarded by the man one loved.

"Can we at least talk in the morning?"

Not that he had done anything at all yet. He certainly hadn't offered to make an honest woman of her. Marriage had not been mentioned. Nor had she expected it. She really hadn't thought about it one way or the other. Still, when one has fallen head over heels for a man, one did tend to hope that he felt the same way about you.

One certainly did not want to hear that he considered you an obligation.

An obligation? That was even worse than kissing her out of necessity.

She tossed and turned for what seemed like an eternity but was probably no more than an hour or so. She wasn't going to get any sleep like this. It was pointless to even try. Nor did it seem right that the cause of her restlessness was probably having no problem sleeping at all. What nerve of the man! She threw off the covers, stalked to the curtains and flung them aside. "An *obligation*? You think of me as an *obligation*?"

"What?" His groggy voice sounded from the sofa.

"You're asleep?" How could he possibly sleep when she was so upset? How...inconsiderate!

"What?"

She flipped on the overhead light and took a measure of satisfaction in the way he cringed in the brightness. She at least was prepared.

"I don't want to be your obligation, Harry. I want—well, I'm not sure what I want but I don't want to be someone you're with out of duty or expectations." She raised her chin. "And I certainly don't need to be."

He rose stiffly from the sofa and a twinge of guilt stabbed her. She ignored it. "What are you talking about?"

"Right here in this very room, you told Effie and Gwen and Poppy you were aware of your obligations."

He blinked at her. "That's what you're angry about?"

"I don't want to be an obligation." She knew she was repeating herself but it did seem to be a pertinent point. "Not to anyone but especially not to you. I have made my own way in the world, for the most part, for years. Why, for the first time in my life, I haven't had to concern myself about money—money I earned on my own. Some of us don't have fortunes and wealthy uncles you know."

"You're mad, you do realize that." He stepped closer. She didn't like the look in his eye.

She stepped back. "What do you think you're doing?"

He ignored her. "Fortunately for you—" he scooped her into his arms and started toward the bed "—I like a touch of insanity."

"I assure you, I'm completely rational!"

"You are a lunatic, Sidney Honeywell." He dumped her on the bed and she scrambled under the covers. She had obviously pushed him too far. He stripped off his shirt and tossed it aside. "For future reference—not that I expect you to be in a situation even remotely comparable to this for the rest of your days—the things a man says to an old lady who is demanding he make an honest woman out of the woman he loves while he's hiding behind a curtain, half-dressed, should be taken not only with a grain of salt but the entire salt cellar!"

She stared.

"As for you being my obligation, yes, you're my obligation. You became my obligation the moment I realized I couldn't live without you." He shook his head in obvious disbelief then sat on the bed and removed his socks. "And I refuse to sleep on that blasted sofa again!"

"I see." This was certainly something to consider. Not that she really needed to do so. Her heart warmed, her ire vanished and she held her breath. "Would you say that again?"

"Which part?" He stood and unbuttoned his trousers.

"The good part."

"The part about my not being able to live without you?" Harry stepped out of his trousers, slipped into bed and pulled her into his arms. She toyed with the idea of resisting but it seemed pointless. And stupid.

"Yes, well, that was good," she murmured. "But not that part."

"Then perhaps you want to hear the part where I said a man should not be held accountable for comments made while he's hiding behind curtains."

"Also good but not exactly the part I was curious about."

"I can't think of anything else—"

"Good Lord, Harry." She twisted out of his grasp, sat up and glared at him. "You know exactly what part I'm talking about."

His brow furrowed and he shook his head. "I'm really not sure."

"Are you truly trying to drive me mad?"

"I told you I like a little insanity." He grinned and drew her back into his arms. "In the women I love." He paused. "Although that's not entirely true."

"It's not?" Her heart froze.

"No." He chose his words with care. "I used the word *women* which is not accurate. I have never said that word to any woman."

"Which word? *Women?*" she said innocently.

"No, not women." He studied her suspiciously. "You know what word I'm talking about.

"Say it, Harry."

"I said it once."

"Not to me."

"I said it about you."

She shook her head. "Not the same."

He stared at her for a long moment. "You're teasing me, Miss Honeywell."

"Indeed I am, Mr. Armstrong. It's a great deal of fun."

"I can think of something even more fun." He ran his hands along her side and tried to inch up her gown. "However, if you don't take this shroud with its endless yards of fabric off right now I shall have to rip it off."

"Harry!" She didn't know if she should be appalled or thrilled. Or a little of both. She grinned. "Would you?"

He laughed and between the two of them her nightgown was soon gone without so much as a lost stitch. But with a great deal of laughing and touching and all sorts of things they hadn't done earlier today that were quite, quite delightful.

And later, as she drifted off in the arms of the man she loved, she realized there was still one minor point she had yet to clear up. Although really she'd already settled it. He just didn't know it yet.

The man had lost and she wasn't sure if she wanted to be right there when he realized that or very, very far away.

CHAPTER TWENTY-TWO

"I swear to you, Sidney." Harry shook his head in disbelief, his gaze fixed on the scene in front of him. One could hardly blame him. "I have ventured into the desert any number of times through the years to seek discoveries that had been buried by endless sands or obscured by time with little more than a guide and a few handlers to manage things. It was not nearly as difficult as maneuvering three old ladies and a disgruntled reporter."

"Some things are more easily managed than others," Sidney said under her breath.

They had caught the earliest train to Bedrachin, the closest station to the remains of the ancient city of Memphis. Daniel had grumbled about taking the early train but the ladies insisted it would be so much easier to see everything they wished to see before crowds of tourists descended on the area. From Bedrachin, they would travel the scant half hour to the ruins of Memphis. Well, some of them would.

Their party was met by a representative of Mr. Nazzal's who had arranged for a guide and camels. Unfortunately, there were only enough camels for Daniel and the ladies. Precisely according to plan. Harry insisted the ladies go on ahead, accompanied by Daniel, of course, and arrangements for additional camels would then be made. He assured the others he and Sidney would catch up with them in no time. They intended to tour the necropolis to the west of Memphis, see the colossal statues of Ramses II then visit the pyramids of Sakkara and Dahshur. It would take all day. The ladies were a bit overly dramatic in their eagerness to begin their exploration of ruins and pyramids and tombs, but Daniel was too busy trying to hide his annoyance at once again having to accompany the older members of their party to notice.

Right now there was a dispute over which lady was to ride which camel as Effie insisted one of them had taken an instant dislike to her, judging by his disdainful expression. It did seem to Sidney they all had disdainful expressions.

"Harry." Sidney drew her brows together. "You do need to come up with another way to refer to them. *Old ladies* is not at all endearing. However, if you called them something else they might look upon you quite fondly."

"I can think of any number of things to call them," he said mildly.

She ignored him. "You could refer to them as, oh, I don't know, lady travelers perhaps? That sounds much better and I daresay they would like that."

"Regardless of what you call them, they're taking far longer than I would have thought possible."

"They are, aren't they?" Sidney was as impatient as Harry to be on their way. "Apparently, their experience at the pyramids taught them what they did and did not like in a camel."

It took another quarter of an hour but at last the ladies—in their pith helmets and smoked glasses—and the rest of the entourage was ready, and Sidney waved farewell to her friends. Their job was simply to keep Daniel occupied but Sidney wanted them out of the way as well. If she hadn't had a specific role for them to play, she was certain at least one of them would have insisted on accompanying Sidney and Harry to find the cave. As much as she loved them dearly, she had no desire to be accompanied into the desert by elderly travelers. It took another quarter of an hour after the ladies had safely disappeared from sight for Mr. Nazzal's man to return with horses, provisions, tools and sleeping bags all tied to their saddles. They did not intend to need the sleeping bags but one never knew.

"Harry, would you mind standing on the other side of the horses for a minute," Sidney said, glancing around the area. This looked like an opportune time. "And make sure they don't move."

"All right. Why?" Harry said but did as she asked nonetheless.

"I'm changing my clothes."

"Here?"

"It's as good a place as any." She unfastened her skirt and removed it, then unbuttoned her jacket and the top of her blouse, just enough to be comfortable. She never would have considered such a thing at home but here, well here everything was different, as was she. Besides, if one was going to get on a horse for the first time—especially one with a man's saddle instead of a sidesaddle—one shouldn't need to worry about one's clothes. She'd considered removing her corset as well but discarded the idea as both improper and impractical.

"I'm finished." Sidney folded her skirt, circled around the horses and held it out to Harry. "Can you secure this somewhere?"

Harry's eyes widened. "What in the name of all that's holy are you wearing?"

"These are riding trousers, Harry. I had them on under my skirt. They're quite progressive." Sidney looked down at the garment she'd bought before they left England. She'd never worn anything so daring and was rather proud of herself for having the courage to do so now. Besides, she liked them and they were certainly comfortable. "Do you like them?"

"They're a far cry from proper attire, aren't they?"

"Well, yes I suppose—"

"I do like them. I'm just not sure I like you wearing them. They're entirely too risqué."

And wasn't that delightful. "Why, thank you, Harry."

He shook his head and stuffed her skirt in one of the leather saddlebags. "We should be off. We have at least an hour's ride before we're even in the right area."

"Excellent." She forced a smile then turned and started up the mounting blocks, assisted by Nazzal's man. She'd never realized just how big horses really were. This was it, then. She swung her leg over the saddle and managed to find her seat, noting a slight twinge of soreness between her legs. A flush of heat washed up her face and she ignored it. There were far more important matters to worry about at the moment.

It was one thing to pretend one was entirely comfortable in the saddle when one was in the saddle on a donkey, only a few feet from the ground, and something else entirely to be in a saddle on a horse, miles above the earth.

Harry pulled his horse up beside hers. "We'll be traveling to the southwest. I'm ready if you are."

She adopted a confident smile. "More than ready."

He nodded and started off in the direction indicated. How difficult could this be anyway? She had mastered the donkey. Well, with the help of a donkey boy. Sidney nudged her horse with her knees and he started moving forward. Why, what an excellent beast. She patted his neck. A few steps later, he stopped. She nudged him again. Again he walked for a minute then stopped. She tried again. And again. And again.

"You realize you're going the wrong way."

Sidney started at the sound of Harry's voice, the unexpected jerk apparently telling her horse it was time to do a bit of a terrifying hopping step with her on his back. Harry caught her reins before she could shriek in terror. Not that she would, of course.

His eyes narrowed. "You don't know how to ride, do you?"

"It's simply been a long time since I've ridden and I daresay..." She caught the look in his eyes and thought it best not to say anything more.

"Sidney?" A firm note sounded in his voice. "Now is not the time for evasion or prevarication or any of those clever elusive answers you are so good at." His gaze pinned hers. "Do you or do you not know how to ride?"

"A horse?" She grimaced. "Not exactly."

His brow rose.

"Well, I've written about riding." She smiled weakly.

"I see." He thought for a moment. Wasn't he going to say this was yet more proof that she was a fraud? After all, Millicent Forester was frequently on a horse. Or a camel. Hopefully, when one had had intimate relations with someone who had more or less declared his love, that someone no longer wished to ruin the other person. And wasn't that a lovely thought. "We don't have time now to teach you even the most basic bits of instruction but I will try to advise you as we go along. For now, I'll hold your reins and lead your horse."

"What am I supposed to hold on to?" The slightest hint of panic sounded in her voice.

"Anything you can, I'd say." He grinned and urged his horse forward.

At the first tug of the reins her horse obediently followed. She leaned forward and hooked her fingers under the front edge of the Egyptian saddle. This was going to grow uncomfortable quickly. Obviously it was in her best interests to observe how Harry handled his horse and to learn as fast as possible.

An hour into their journey, they reached an area of caves marked on the map and Sidney was managing the reins on her own. There was still a dispute with her horse over who was in charge but they had come to a sort of truce which allowed Sidney to relax enough to study their surroundings. She'd never experienced any place so vast before. Endless and forever and nearly empty. Now and again they would see a horseman or camels in the far distance but for all intents and purposes they were completely alone. For a woman raised in the city, it was a bit disquieting but Millicent handled it and so would Sidney. Besides, she had Harry by her side. Harry, who was completely at ease as if this was nothing more than a ride in Hyde Park. Her heart fluttered. He really was something of a heroic figure.

Somehow, she had expected the relatively flat nature of the landscape near Bedrachin to continue. But now she found herself surrounded by hills and ridges, plateaus and limestone cliffs riddled with caves and rocky ledges. And sand everywhere. Fortunately, the day was pleasant enough and not overly hot. Still, she was glad for the slight shade afforded her by her pith helmet and the relief her smoked glasses offered her eyes. As much as Mr. Bishara's map had given her confidence she wondered if perhaps it was not entirely warranted. How on earth would they find one specific cave—even one that resembled a camel—in an endless world of rocks and caves and sand?

It was another three hours before they located a cave at the base of a cliff that she and Harry agreed best matched both the map and her grandmother's drawing. Mr. Bishara's map had proved surprisingly accurate. Her flagging spirits lifted. Not that she'd allow Harry to know she had ever been anything other than supremely confident. Unfortunately, the entrance was more than half buried in sand. Whether the cave itself was filled was the question.

"You do realize what this means?" Harry dismounted then circled around the horses to help her down.

"I'm afraid I do," she said briskly.

"I'm glad one of us is looking forward to it." Harry untied a rolled-up piece of canvas from the saddle then unrolled it to reveal coarse leather gloves, metal tubes and a shovel head. He handed her the gloves and in less than a minute, he had assembled the various parts into a shovel. He passed it to her. "Do you know what to do with a shovel or do you need instruction on that too?"

"Well, I don't know, Harry. Am I supposed to start digging the sand from the entrance or should I simply bash you over the head and be done with it?" She smiled pleasantly.

He chuckled and untied a second canvas roll. "Sarcasm, Sidney?"

"Not really." Of course she knew what to do with a shovel. It wasn't as if she had a gardener to do such things at her house in London. She did however have a small garden that she faithfully tended. When she remembered. She dug into the sand. "I meant every word."

He laughed, assembled his shovel and joined her.

She scooped out a shovelful of sand and the hole immediately filled back in. On her third try she finally made a small but noticeable dimple. It was not encouraging.

"There is an awful lot of sand," she said more to herself than to him.

"Odd how you tend to find that in a desert." He dug out another shovelful. "It was quite clever of you to purchase your riding trousers. I should think that would help protect against sand fleas. But then you know that."

"Of course." *Sand fleas?* "Nasty little beasts."

"Just one of the more unpleasant aspects of the desert." He dug in again. "Along with snakes—" he punctuated his words with every thrust of his shovel "—scorpions, lizards, rodents." He glanced at her. "I've noticed you have never included the more unpleasant aspects of exploration in Egypt in your writing."

"Because I don't particularly like fleas and snakes and lizards and rodents." She brushed back an annoying strand of hair that insisted on getting in her face.

"Yet it's those factual details that improve a story."

"Or get in the way," she said firmly and resumed digging with renewed determination.

"I hadn't thought of that," he murmured.

For some time, they worked in silence. She did not consider herself fragile by any means but this was far harder than she had imagined. If Harry was a gentleman, he'd insist on doing this himself. Not that she'd allow him to do so. She was trying to prove a point after all. Although in many ways he was indeed doing it himself.

Each scoop of sand he shoveled out was three times the size of hers. Apparently, occasionally spading a small garden in London did not truly prepare one for shoveling the sands of Egypt.

"You do realize that there are few, if any, crocodiles still left in the Nile in Egypt?" he asked casually.

"Well, there was one," she said sharply. "Probably why he was so hungry." And wasn't that just the stupidest thing she'd ever said?

He choked back a laugh. "That would explain it."

"Indeed it would," she muttered. Admittedly it was amusing and, as she had already confessed about her widowed state, her misstatement scarcely mattered now.

A few minutes later she straightened and rubbed her back. "Much more, do you think?"

"I don't know." He considered the opening. They had indeed enlarged the entry but there was no indication how far into the cave the sand had drifted. With luck it was only a few feet. If this was the right cave it was fairly big according to Grandmother's journal so once they broke through, it should be easy to clear away enough sand to enter. *If* this was the right cave. "But that's it for now." He planted his shovel in the sand and started toward the horses.

"What do you mean that's it?" She leaned her shovel against the rock and hurried after him.

"I mean, after all that talk of hungry crocodiles, I want something to eat myself." He untied one of the hanging saddlebags, pulled out an orange and tossed it to her. "We have oranges, figs, cheese, bread—"

"And water?"

He nodded. "And water."

They spread the cloth the cheese and bread was

wrapped in on a rock then perched beside it. Sidney wasn't certain she'd ever tasted anything quite so wonderful in her entire life. But then she'd never worked so hard in her entire life either.

"Why did you first come to Egypt?" she asked between bites of bread and cheese.

"It seemed the thing to do at the time." He shrugged. "You know how these things happen. One day you're trapped in a classroom and the next you've escaped and gone off to see the world."

"I see. Just an arbitrary sort of thing, then. Like throwing a dart at a map and going where it lands."

"I shall have to remember that should I ever decide to see the world again." He chuckled. "But it wasn't quite that random. Indeed, looking back on it, I'm surprised it wasn't entirely anticipated."

"Oh?"

"My father is a scholar of ancient civilizations. Egypt is his specialty. My mother died when I was very young so it was just the two of us. Other children grow up hearing fairy stories or tales of knights and dragons." He smiled. "I heard the legends of Osiris and Isis, Horus and Set, Anubis and Ra."

"So naturally you wanted to see where it all began."

"Yes, that and it seemed the perfect place for three arrogant young men to find their fortune." He gazed out at the desert as if he was looking back into the past.

"But you said you didn't make your fortune in Egypt."

"I didn't." He paused and his brow furrowed. "But I did find a respect for the past. For what man built and left behind for all of us. Not just those who can afford it."

"My, you are noble," she teased but she quite liked

that he was noble and good and decent. And decidedly, wonderfully wicked.

"I do have my moments." He grinned and took a long drink from the water bag. "We should get back to it. It's already midafternoon." He got to his feet and held out his hand to help her to hers. And then pulled her into his arms.

Harry smiled down at her and her breath caught at the look in his eye. She did hope he would always look at her that way.

"Goodness, Harry, what are you thinking?"

"I'm thinking about last night." A wicked gleam sparked in his eyes and something inside her quivered. "And about tonight."

"Or, oh, I don't know." She reached up and nibbled his lower lip. "Sooner?"

Surprise flashed across his face and he laughed. "Why, Miss Honeywell, I believe I have thoroughly corrupted you."

"As well as ruined me."

"You should know, it's only because of the sand that you and I are not now, well… It's the sand."

"Come now, Harry. A little sand can't hurt."

"On the contrary, Sidney, a little sand can hurt. A lot. I have a rule about sand. Now." He kissed her, a quick, totally possessive kiss that sent the loveliest shivers down her spine then released her and moved toward the cave. "Back to work."

"Oh yes, I'd much rather do that anyway," she muttered but a voice of questionable sanity in the back of her head did speculate on exactly how unpleasant sand might be.

Amazing how a short break, a bit of food and a little

flirtation made returning to her efforts much easier. Her spirits were certainly lighter. She stopped for a moment and let her gaze wander over the remarkable scenery of this ancient land. Even if this wasn't the right cave and they never found the pectoral, this would be a day she would never forget. Whether she spent the rest of her life with Harry or not. It really could go either way. She knew what she wanted and thought she might know what he wanted as well, but there were no assurances at the moment. If there was one thing she did know without question about the man—he liked to win. And, even if she had never realized it before this journey, apparently so did she. But at what cost?

"That's it!" Excitement rang in Harry's voice. "We're through!"

Her attention snapped back to the entrance. They had dug nearly four feet into the cave and the level of sand now tapered downward into the interior of the cavern.

"I had every confidence in us." She tried to tell herself there was no guarantee the pectoral would still be there nor was there any certainty this was indeed the right cave but it didn't matter. This was a definite victory. "You know, Harry, in spite of our difficulties, I think we make a most impressive team."

"You can't ride. Your digging is not unlike a small child on the seashore and you don't seem to have any real sense of direction. Even so—" he flashed her a quick grin "—I agree. Now, it's probably easier for just one of us to do this."

"Well, if you think it's best." She tried to sound sincere rather than delighted. "I would hate to get in your way."

Harry returned to shoveling with a vengeance and the work went quickly. Once enough of the packed sand was removed, the rest was easy. Well, it looked easy. Sidney fetched the candles and matches stored in the saddlebags as well as the water bag. In no time at all, the opening was wide enough to allow entry.

"Ready?" Sidney lit the candles and handed one to him.

"You realize if you take credit for this find, it will make the Queen of the Desert invincible." He smiled. "Your critics would be silenced."

"Even you?"

"Especially me."

"Regardless, a find like this would give you the acknowledgment you deserve." And really, she didn't need it anymore.

"That is a dilemma. One I suggest we wait to discuss until after we've found something." Harry held his candle out in front of him. "I'll go in first." Harry stepped into the cave, Sidney inches behind him. The floor was sand and leveled out after the first few feet. The cave was far larger than she expected, curved like the inside of a bowl, probably some twenty feet wide and perhaps twice that at its deepest point. There was no way to tell the height—the ceiling hidden in the shadows overhead. "According to your grandmother's journal, the pieces they found were in a niche close to the ground covered by rocks. There are a lot of rocks here, Sidney."

The answer struck her without warning. "That's what the clock was for, on the map. There was only one hand and it was pointing to ten."

"Very good." He shot her an admiring smile. "If we stand with our back to the entrance—"

"Then it's right—" she aimed her arm in a direction slightly to her left "—there."

She wasn't sure what she was expecting to see. Apparently in the years since her grandparents had been here, any number of rocks had fallen from the walls or the ceiling and the joint between the cave walls and the floor was piled with rocks, the largest no bigger than her head. She would guess the arrangement of the rocks was an act of nature but any grouping of stones could have been placed by human hands. It was impossible to say for certain where the niche in the rocks where the artifacts had originally been found might be located.

"I was rather hoping the right spot would be obvious," Sidney said with a disgruntled sigh.

"Nothing in Egypt is ever obvious." Harry considered the possibilities. "I'll get the shovels." He nodded and left the cave.

With only her candle for light, the shadows grew closer. For a moment, Sidney allowed the past to wash over her. She could clearly see her grandparents finding the ancient treasure trove. Their excitement at realizing the pieces might have come from the tomb of a forgotten queen, left here eons ago by those who had raided her final resting place. And more, she could see the men who had hidden here those objects meant to assist the queen in the afterlife. Men determined to ignore the superstitions and traditions of their world in their quest for fortune. And she could see the queen herself, perhaps personally selecting the pectoral and other pieces she would wear for all eternity. Never knowing her rest would be disturbed, her possessions stolen and scattered. With only one piece traveling the centuries to at last reveal her name and the whereabouts of the place she called home.

"What are you doing?" Harry came up behind her.

"Nothing really. Thinking about the queen and how

her name has been lost." She shook her head. "The ancient Egyptians believed if one's name was lost, so too was their path to immortality. They might as well have never existed." The oddest lump settled in her throat. "I think it's sad, that she's been lost. I hope she is resting in peace."

"You do know she's not here. This is not her tomb."

She huffed. "You have no soul, Harry Armstrong."

"You've said that before. At the moment, it doesn't concern me. Here." He handed her a shovel, then moved to the point they had agreed was the most likely spot indicated by the map. She trailed after him. "We can scoop the smaller rocks with the shovel but we'll have to move the larger ones by hand."

"I was hoping we would," she said under her breath.

"Hand me your candle." He studied the rock wall, found a ledge for the candles then started removing rocks.

Sidney drew a deep breath and bent to the task at hand. Good Lord, she was weary. Still, in spite of the work they had already undertaken thus far today, and the grueling nature of what they were now engaged in, with every rock moved from the wall a distinct sense of excitement grew. If they were very, very lucky they would find the pectoral. And if their luck held, it would reveal not only the name of the queen but the location of Itjtawy.

This was the end of her grandmother's story and just the beginning of hers. She did hope that story would include Harry. Sidney was rather certain her heart would shatter if it didn't but she would survive. She had her friends and she had her work—even if its direction in the future would be decidedly different. She wasn't the same woman who had started this journey. That woman wanted to be Millicent Forester. The woman she was now understood Millicent was simply a part of her and being Sidney Honeywell was much better.

"Sidney?" Caution sounded in Harry's voice. "Do you see that?"

"No, what?" Sidney set aside her shovel and grabbed a candle from the ledge.

Harry dropped to his knees and she knelt beside him, bringing the candle closer to the wall. He brushed aside a handful of pebbles to reveal a cloth-wrapped bundle. Anywhere else in the world, the fabric would have molded and decayed but in the dry desert air it was still intact.

Harry glanced at her. "What do you think?"

"I think if you don't open that right now, I really will bash you with the shovel."

He grinned and carefully unwrapped the packet. There, covering the palm of his hand, was the gold pectoral of a queen of Egypt. Rectangular in shape, falcons flanked each side of the piece and a scarab was positioned around the hole in the center where the medallion would sit. The relic was covered with intricately inlaid stones—lapis lazuli, turquoise and carnelian were among those Sidney recognized.

Harry blew a long breath. "Well, this was certainly worth the effort.

"Wait." Sidney reached into her blouse, between her breasts, pulled out the medallion and grinned. "Now we can fully appreciate it."

Harry stared in disbelief. "You brought that with you?"

"Of course I brought it with me. I wanted to see if it did indeed fit. And I wanted the pieces reunited."

"A bit irresponsible don't you think? You could have lost it."

"Yes, I suppose I could have but I didn't. Besides, I would have noticed. Believe me, it was most secure and I was aware of it every minute."

His gaze shifted to the valley between her breasts. "You certainly do hide a lot in there."

"It's remarkably convenient," Sidney murmured. "Now, let's see how this fits."

She lined up the notches on the medallion with the prongs in the empty space in the pectoral then tapped the disc firmly into place. She could have sworn it took on a sort of unearthly glow. Absurd, of course, it was simply a trick of the candlelight. Still…

"Isn't it amazing," Sidney said softly. "She would have believed one's name was connected to one's soul, you know. If we accomplish nothing else, we might at least be able to give her back her name."

"Next you're going to say you can almost hear the queen whispering her thanks, like a breeze skittering across the sands."

"Why, Harry, there may be hope for you yet." She smiled.

He shook his head. "I doubt it."

"And yes, I can indeed hear the whispers of the queen. Can't you?"

He cast her a wry look.

Sidney took the pectoral from him and turned it over. "I'm not sure if I want this to lead to Itjtawy or not."

"You are mad."

"I simply like the idea of a city lost forever."

"Well, Egypt's scholars will hopefully be able to decipher all of this. Until then…" He shrugged. "I never thought I'd return to Egypt but it was good to come. I've laid some ghosts to rest. To a certain extent anyway. But I would like to go home. For the immediate future at least. I've spent too many years away."

Sidney wasn't quite sure what to say. She wasn't sure if there was a place for her in his plans or not. It was past time to find out. And to tell him everything.

He met her gaze firmly. "You and I need to talk."

She nodded. "I was thinking much the same thing."

He got to his feet and pulled her up. "Then let's be on our way."

"Oh good." A silhouette loomed against the entrance— "I thought I'd missed you"—and stepped into the candlelight.

CHAPTER TWENTY-THREE

"DANIEL?" SHOCK SOUNDED in Sidney's voice.

"What are you doing here, Corbin?" Harry narrowed his eyes. "And how did you get here?"

"And more to the point," Sidney said slowly, "why do you have a gun?"

"I don't usually carry firearms but Mr. Cadwallender presented it to me when I left. He said a reporter in a foreign land should always carry a pistol." Daniel glanced at the weapon in his hand. "I did not anticipate using it. I've never been overly fond of guns as a rule but I can see where they might prove useful."

"What are you doing here, Daniel?" Sidney glared.

"You know I'm the one used to asking questions but let's see if I can answer yours. First—I'm here for that priceless piece of gold you have in your hand."

"Well you can't have it." She clasped the pectoral against her chest. "It does not belong to you."

"It doesn't belong to you either," he said mildly.

She ignored him. "You want to sell it, don't you? Smuggle it out of the country and then sell it to the highest bidder. How could you?" Sidney gasped. "You're in league with that dreadful Mr. Wallace, aren't you? No doubt he's the American you were to interview. You obviously saw a better way to get ahead than with a mere story."

Corbin shot a puzzled look at Harry. "Who?"

"An antiquities collector." Harry shrugged. He'd never been overly fond of anyone pointing a gun in his direction. At the moment, playing along with Corbin seemed the wisest move. At least until he could come up with a way to disarm the reporter. And as soon as possible. Who knew what Corbin might do if provoked.

"You really do have a splendid imagination." Corbin chuckled. "Sorry, I've never heard of this American. And I'm not an uncivilized lout, Sidney. I have no intention of selling this find." A smug note sounded in his voice. "I fully intend to turn it over to the proper authorities. I simply plan on taking the credit myself."

Her brow furrowed. "Why?

"For the story, of course. Come now. Surely you understand." He shook his head in disappointment. "Then allow me to explain. It's a good story if Mrs. Gordon recovers a significant artifact. It's a better story if I do. The headline practically writes itself—'Intrepid Reporter Solves Mystery of the Ages,' or something like that. Readers love it when a reporter is part of the story. This is the kind of story that makes careers." He smiled in a condescending manner. "And you of all people know how much the public loves anything to do with Egypt."

"I thought you were here to observe, to report." Indignation sounded in Sidney's voice.

"And I thought you were here to prove you knew what you were writing about."

"I do," she said in a lofty manner.

"You've proved nothing other than you're a passable tour guide." Daniel shook his head. "No better than my guidebook really."

She shrugged.

Corbin shifted his attention to Harry. "As for how I got here, once I traded that blasted camel for a horse—"

Sidney sucked in a hard breath. "What did you do with my friends? If you've hurt them—" She started forward. Harry grabbed her jacket and pulled her back. The woman really was frighteningly fearless.

"They are perfectly well." He paused. "If you want the truth, one might say they abandoned me. A few minutes after we left you, we met a large tour group all on camels and ready to go. It too consisted mostly of older English females and your friends thought it would be an excellent idea to join them." He rolled his gaze toward the heavens. "I assure you, I had no intention of being trapped all day with that group. You understand."

"More than most," Harry murmured.

"So amidst a moment of confusion—and let me tell you I could see there would be confusion all day—my camel and I slipped off, intending to join the two of you. Imagine my surprise when I saw you with horses. I promptly traded the camel for a horse and set off after you. I might not sit a camel well but I do know how to sit a horse. And I had a fairly good idea of what you were doing and what you were after."

"How?" Harry adopted a cold tone. It wasn't difficult.

"A bit too much conspiracy and entirely too many secrets in this group. Things were happening that I didn't know about. Reporters hate secrets. It's our mission in life to uncover secrets. So when your friends finally decided that perhaps they shouldn't reveal every secret to me, I found other methods."

"Maids? Bellmen?" There was a way out of this, Harry simply hadn't determined what it was yet.

"Exactly." Corbin shrugged. "It's amazing how much

listening at doors a few piastres will purchase. Although I admit I missed this little venture today. I really thought you had planned nothing more than another endless day viewing the remains of the ancient dead." He shuddered. "I also did a good bit of checking into all parties before we even set foot on board ship." Corbin eyed him curiously. "From what I was able to find out before we left England, you certainly have lived an interesting life."

"Goodness, Daniel, I don't know that any of that matters." Sidney waved off his words. "You're aiming a gun at us. Do you really think anything else is important?"

He gestured with the pistol. "That is."

She clutched the pectoral closer to her chest. "You really have no decent moral standards, do you, Daniel?"

Moral standards aside, Harry didn't think Corbin was truly dangerous. At least not yet. Still, they should watch their step.

"That's rather like the pot calling the kettle black isn't it, Sidney? You with your silly little stories and that Queen of the Desert nonsense. Although I will admit, you are a good writer. We would have made an excellent couple."

"You and I? A couple?" She snorted. "Not in this lifetime."

Harry cringed to himself. Not the worst thing to say but not good.

"I suppose you intend to kill us now." She squared her shoulders.

That was probably the worst. "I don't think he needs any suggestions."

"You wound me deeply, Sidney." Daniel heaved an overly dramatic sigh. "I have no intention of killing you. I am however, sending your horses off, returning to Cairo then heading back to England. Oh, I did notice you're well stocked and I will leave your supplies. When I am safely on my way, I'll send someone for you. It shouldn't be more than a day or two. You'll be perfectly fine. Probably."

"You can't get away with this," Harry said slowly. "If, as you say, you intend to send someone back for us, what's to prevent us from revealing everything you've done?"

"You can't possibly be serious about taking credit for the pectoral," Sidney added.

"And yet I intend to. You can read all about it when you return home."

Her eyes widened as if she couldn't believe such a thing. "But it's a lie."

"We all lie to a certain extent." Corbin looked at Harry. "Don't we, my lord?"

Confusion sounded in Sidney's voice. "My lord?"

"Later, Sidney."

"And you, the famous Mrs. Gordon." Daniel shook his head. "You have deceived your readers for a long time."

"Not deliberately," she snapped then winced, apparently realizing she had just confessed.

He grinned. "Thank you for confirming it. Yet another story for my readers. If I intended to write it but I don't. It all comes back to secrets. Mine but more importantly yours. You see, my dear Sidney, if you and his lordship—"

"Why does he keep calling you that?" Sidney frowned.

"I have no idea," Harry lied.

Corbin's eyes widened. "She doesn't know, does she?"

"Corbin." If the man was smart he'd understand the threat in Harry's voice.

"Oh, this is perfect." The reporter chuckled. "I would think after yesterday—"

Harry lunged forward but Sidney grabbed his arm.

"Now, now, Armstrong." Corbin shook his head. "I would hate to have to shoot you." He paused. "On second thought, I believe it would be remarkably satisfying to shoot you. But then I'd have to shoot Sidney as well and that would be regrettable." He glanced around. "Still, no one would ever find you here."

"I would prefer neither of us be shot," Sidney said quickly.

"I'm not a murderer, so unless one of you does something stupid we can conclude our business and I will be on my way. As I was saying, if the two of you keep your mouths shut about the discovery of the relic, I won't reveal what I know about the Queen of the Desert."

"Come now, Daniel, how can we possibly believe you?" Sidney glared. "You want my grandmother's find and even though you say you intend to hand it over to the proper authorities, we'd be fools to trust you. And that—" she nodded at his gun "—along with your intention to abandon us to an uncertain fate does not inspire trust."

"*You* don't trust *me*?" He snorted. "That's rather amusing all things considered, don't you think? You've been lying to your readers and he's been lying to you. I'm the only one with a clear conscience." He paused. "Well, until now."

"You do realize anything could happen to us out here," Harry said coolly.

"I do feel bad about that but it can't be helped." The reporter grinned. "Although, from what I've heard, Harry Armstrong can handle a few days in the desert. Has he told you about his colored past here in Egypt or is that yet another secret?"

"Yes," Sidney said staunchly. "I know a great deal about his days in Egypt."

"That's enough, Sidney," Harry said firmly.

She ignored him. "Admittedly, he hasn't told me every detail of his life but I know enough to know Harry Armstrong is a good man. Honest and honorable and decent."

"Really?" Corbin's skeptical gaze swept over Harry. "You know, the more I think about it, the more I think I might be chasing the wrong story. Perhaps the better story isn't my find of an ancient object but the story of the two of you."

The oddest sensation of what might well have been helplessness twisted Harry's stomach. He could see what was coming and had no idea how to stop it.

Corbin continued. "After all, everyone loves a good story of seduction—"

"I was not seduced," Sidney snapped.

"The beloved Mrs. Gordon swept off her feet by a man with a less-than-reputable past. The man whose sole purpose was to prove her a fraud."

"Corbin," Harry said in a hard tone. "I would consider my words carefully if I were you."

"Good advice, Armstrong, which I would most certainly heed, except—" he grinned "—oh yes, that's right. I have the gun."

"Actually, Daniel." Sidney raised her chin. "I quite agree. I think it's a wonderful story."

"Excellent. I wasn't sure you'd like it but I'd wager the public would. They do love this sort of thing. Deception, duplicity, scandal." He chuckled. "The Queen of the Desert falling into the—"

"Corbin." Harry clenched his fists.

"Into the—" Corbin cleared his throat "—*arms* of her nemesis. The man who publicly derided not only the substance of her stories but her writing ability as well. I have always thought real life was so much more inventive than fiction. Why, one would never have imagined the two of you together—the Queen of the Desert and the Earl of Brenton."

Sidney stared at Daniel then looked at Harry. "What is he talking about?"

"It doesn't matter, Sidney," Harry said quickly. "It's over. I ended it."

"It does matter. It matters very much." Her eyes widened. "You're the Earl of Brenton?"

"I can explain."

"Can you? I doubt that."

"I admit I should have told you who I was from the beginning. That was an error in judgement on my part."

"To say the least!"

"But I've fixed it."

She shook her head in confusion. "What?"

"Yesterday, I sent a telegram to Cadwallender saying that I was wrong. That I had all the proof I needed. That you had convinced me as to your familiarity with Egypt. I conceded defeat. You won."

Shock shone in her eyes. "But why?"

"Why indeed," Corbin murmured.

"I was concerned that the longer we stayed in Egypt, the more likely it was that you and the old ladies—"

Corbin sorted.

"—would find yourselves in serious trouble. You are all too bloody stubborn for your own good and there isn't one among you who realizes her own vulnerability. The more you tried to prove your legitimacy, the greater the possibility of trouble. Good God, Sidney, you don't even know how to ride a horse!"

"I do now." She shrugged in an offhanded manner. "It wasn't that difficult."

"I wouldn't call that riding, more clinging to a horse in desperate hope of staying in the saddle. No, I did what I thought was best." He met her gaze firmly. "I conceded defeat and hoped to have you all on a ship home as soon as possible."

"I don't know what to say about any of this." She shook her head. "How...how..."

"Thoughtful? Considerate? Unselfish?" Harry suggested.

"Hardly! More like arrogant, controlling and manipulative!"

"Not exactly what you were hoping for, Armstrong?" Corbin chuckled.

"Shut up, Daniel," Sidney snapped.

"I say." Corbin had the nerve to look offended. "Don't forget who has the gun."

"I don't care!" Sidney said and directed her ire back to Harry. "This is exactly the sort of thing an earl would do. You really are your uncle."

"Not exactly as I don't actually have an uncle."

"Brilliant point, Harry!"

"I don't know why you're so upset. I was only trying to save you from yourself."

"From myself?" Her voice rose. "From myself?

"I'm touched that you would allow me to witness all this," Corbin said, "but I would like to be on my way."

"You're being unreasonable, Sidney." Harry adopted a placating tone. "Which admittedly might be warranted to a certain extent but there's no need to be so angry. Perhaps in your feminine irrationality—"

"Feminine irrationality?" Her eyes flashed.

"Ouch." Corbin winced. "Poor choice, Armstrong."

"—you've overlooked the fact that you won."

"You let me win!"

Without thinking Harry grinned. It was a mistake and he knew it.

Sidney glared. "I don't know that I can forgive you for this."

"You should know this pistol is heavier than it looks," Corbin pointed out.

"Forgive me for what?" Now she was being absurd. "Wanting to keep you safe? Protecting your reputation by conceding defeat and looking like an idiot in the process by the way. For having money and a title?"

"Yes! For all of it. You told me your father was a scholar."

"He's actually my stepfather but I've known no other father."

"Well he should have taught you better! This whole thing only started because of your despicable letters."

"You didn't have to answer them!"

"I didn't!"

"Well, somebody did!" The answer struck him at once. Corbin chuckled. "Now, that's a twist."

"You lied to me!" Sidney's voice rose. "You lied to me from the beginning."

"You lied to everyone!"

"That was entirely different." She waved off the charge. "I never set out to lie to you. Or anyone. Besides you didn't believe me for a minute. I could tell, you know."

"That's quite enough," Corbin said sharply. "The two

of you will have plenty of time to determine fault and blame and argue about it. As entertaining as this is—and I do wish you luck, Armstrong—but frankly, I'm finding it rather tiring." He nodded at the pectoral still clasped in Sidney's arms. "I'll take that now and be on my way."

"No." She clutched the breastplate tighter. "Absolutely not. This was my grandmother's last find. She would have wanted it to go to a museum or the Antiquities Society…" Her gaze shot to Harry's, her eyes blazing. "You wanted my membership in the Antiquities Society rescinded! How could you?"

"I admit," Harry said, choosing his words with care, "that might not have been my finest moment."

"My grandparents were among the founders of that organization! My grandmother—" Sidney paused, her eyes widened. "My grandmother would have been most dismayed by this. All of it." A distinct note of panic sounded in her voice.

"There's no need for alarm." Harry stepped closer. Good God what was wrong with the woman? This was not like her. "Really, Sidney, everything will be fine."

"No, no it won't!" She covered her eyes with one hand and sobbed. Or hiccupped—it was impossible to tell.

"What is she doing?" Corbin frowned.

"She's obviously upset," Harry snapped. "Can you blame her? Bloody hell, man, you're pointing a gun at her."

"I'm terrified!" she wailed. "He's going to leave us here to die! With the lizards and the vermin and the snakes!"

"We won't die," Harry said confidently. Even if Corbin didn't send someone back for them, Nazzal had copied the map. They'd be fine for a few days. Still, he'd rather avoid that and get Sidney out of here now. What he needed was a distraction. Something that might allow him to grab Corbin's gun.

"Just the thought of snakes! Snakes, Harry, snakes!" Her gaze met his, the look in her eyes determinedly fearless. "My head is spinning... I..." She crossed both hands over the pectoral on her chest in a pose vaguely reminiscent of *Hamlet*'s Ophelia, her eyes fluttered shut and she sank gracefully to the ground in a dead faint. Or what looked like a faint. At once it struck him that this was deliberate on her part—in which case the woman really was mad or brilliant. Of course, if she had truly swooned he could either go to her assistance or tackle Corbin. One or the other.

Bloody hell, she'd be fine on the ground. This was about her life. It took no more than a handful of seconds or an eternity. At the same time he lunged at Corbin, Sidney snapped her wrist, flinging the spinning pectoral and a fair amount of sand toward the reporter. The artifact missed, but Corbin screamed and covered his eyes as Harry hit him around the knees and knocked them both to the ground, the gun flying out of his hand. Sidney scrambled after it. Corbin was too busy wailing about his eyes to struggle. Rather a shame really. Harry wouldn't at all mind planting one in the reporter's face. Harry got to his feet.

"That worked out nicely." Sidney aimed the gun at the reporter. "But I thought I'd hit him with the pectoral. I never expected the sand would do him in."

"It had a better chance than your throw." Harry grabbed Corbin and pulled him to his feet.

"Nonetheless, it worked." She waved at the cave opening with the pistol. It did not inspire confidence. "The water bag is by the entrance. You should probably get it for him." She paused. "You can let him go now, I don't think he's going anywhere."

"I'm blind!" Corbin cried.

Harry released him. "There can't be much in his eyes. Most of it went in my ear."

"There needn't be much." In her riding pants, with her blond hair escaping from her pith helmet, her cheeks flushed and holding a revolver, she looked damned near invincible. Now, that was what he wanted in a wife. The woman really was Millicent Forester. At this point, in one of Sidney's stories, that annoying Richard Weatherly would sweep her into his arms and kiss her thoroughly. Weatherly might have had a good point. Still, even Weatherly had never been faced with a furious Sidney Honeywell before. Caution was perhaps the best tact at the moment.

Harry fetched the water then helped Corbin slosh some in his eyes. "What? No thanks?"

"You have my undying gratitude," Corbin muttered and splashed more water in his eyes.

"That was quite clever, but I think I'll take that." Harry took the pistol from Sidney. "How did you think of it?"

She shrugged. "I did something similar in one of my stories."

"Once I realized what you were doing—"

"Yes, yes, we worked together nicely." She waved off his comment. "Don't think because we cooperated now, it was anything other than a matter of life and death."

"I would never think such a thing," he assured her even if he had hoped.

"I have neither forgiven nor forgotten anything. I am still extremely angry. *My lord!*"

He nodded. "I can understand that. But I did intend to tell you everything."

"When?"

"As soon as we returned to Cairo. I think I mentioned that earlier today."

"I don't recall." She picked up the pectoral where it had landed. "Regardless, I have a great deal of thinking to do and decisions to make. And I have no desire to talk to you about any of this at the moment."

"Also understandable." Harry nodded then paused. "You should know, as you're thinking, I've felt very bad about this whole thing almost since the beginning."

"Guilt will do that to you." She met his gaze firmly. "Quite frankly, Harry, I don't know how I feel. But I do know I want to go back now. I want the comfort of the hotel, I want a long bath and I don't want to see you." She turned and stalked out of the cave.

Corbin dabbed at his eyes with a handkerchief. "You're not very good with women, are you?"

"I wouldn't make any comments if I were you. I have the gun now."

Corbin shrugged. "It's not loaded."

Harry flipped open the revolver and spun the chamber. "You didn't load the gun?"

"It didn't strike me as a particularly good idea."

"But you fought me for it."

"*You* didn't know it wasn't loaded." Corbin smirked. "It served the same purpose whether it was loaded or not. I really had no desire to shoot you accidentally, even though I do find you most annoying. As it is, there's no harm done."

Harry narrowed his eyes. "Do you now intend to expose Sidney?"

"Oh, that, well…" Corbin considered him thoughtfully. "Perhaps there's another deal to be made here."

Sidney strode back into the cave and glared at Corbin. "What did you do?"

"What did *I* do?" Corbin waved the handkerchief at Harry. "He's the one you're angry with. And with good reason too I might add."

She had been livid when she left the cave. Now livid would have been an improvement. Harry took a step back.

Sidney ignored him, advancing on Corbin like an avenging goddess of death. "What did you do with the horses?"

"Nothing. I retied their reins so it would be faster to let them go when I was ready." Horrid realization crossed Corbin's face and he grimaced. "I might have tied them a little too loosely."

"They'll be halfway home by now." Harry stared at Corbin. "What were you thinking?"

"I had a plan." Corbin huffed then brightened. "We still have my horse."

Harry shook his head. "One horse won't do."

Sidney's jaw clenched. "Was he with the others?"

"He was," Corbin said slowly.

"He's gone now. They're all gone. Along with everything we brought with us."

Corbin winced. "This is awkward."

"Awkward?" Sidney's voice rose. "It's more than merely awkward." She nodded in Harry's direction. "Shoot him, Harry."

"As tempting as that is, I can't."

"I knew you couldn't." She sighed in resignation. "You really are horribly noble."

"And there are no bullets." Harry shook his head. "The gun wasn't loaded."

Corbin offered a weak smile.

Sidney leveled a disgusted look at the reporter. "You are an idiot. If you learned nothing else from reading my stories you certainly should have understood that if you were going to be a villain, be a good one. No bullets, indeed." She turned her attention to Harry. "As for you, *my lord*, I hope you have some sort of brilliant idea."

"Not yet. And you needn't keep saying *my lord*," Harry said in a hard tone. "I assure you, Sidney, I will think of something."

"None of this would have happened if you hadn't written those blasted letters. All because that arrogant male pride of yours was wounded."

"It wasn't pride." He paused. "Well, not entirely. Yes, I did find it annoying that work I thought was frivolous and inaccurate—"

"Good God, and she thinks I'm an idiot," Corbin muttered.

"—but enjoyable nonetheless, was so highly regarded and mine was—"

"Dreadful?"

"Yes, dreadful." He shook his head. "But it wasn't for me."

"Yes, yes, I know. It's that noble nature of yours. You didn't want your friend to be forgotten." She blew a long breath. "Well, since we're probably going to meet him in the afterlife soon, you might want to decide how you're going to explain to him the despicable lengths you went to in the guise of preserving his memory. I didn't know him, of course, but I imagine anyone worth remembering would point out what an arrogant, sanctimonious beast you've been and I daresay your Walter would have been no exception."

A shadowed figure at the cave entrance chuckled. "Don't blame me for this."

CHAPTER TWENTY-FOUR

THE STRANGER STEPPED into the light. Tall and dressed like a Bedouin, with robes and a traditional *kufiya* on his head. Even so the man's English was perfect and he was clearly not Egyptian.

Harry's face paled, as if he'd seen a ghost. Disbelief sounded in his voice. "Walter?"

Apparently he had seen a ghost.

"You said Walter was dead," Sidney said under her breath, her gaze firmly fixed on the newcomer. The man looked like he could have walked out of one of her stories—dashing and handsome and adventurous.

"I thought Walter was dead." Harry stared, frozen in place.

"Who is Walter?" Daniel asked.

The stranger pulled off his *kufiya*. His blue eyes were vibrant against his deeply tanned skin and his hair was lighter than Harry's.

"Not anymore." He grinned. "How are you, Harry old man?"

Harry continued to stare, a myriad of emotions crossing his face.

Sidney nudged him. "You might want to say something at this point."

Walter chuckled. "I think he's a bit too stunned to say anything."

"Well, I'm not." Sidney stepped forward and extended her hand. "I'm Miss Sidney Honeywell. It's a pleasure to see you alive and well, Mr. Pickering."

"Walter." He took her hand. "It's a pleasure to be alive and well. I must say, Harry's taste in women has certainly—"

"You're supposed to be dead!" Something suspiciously close to outrage rang in Harry's voice. "We searched for you. For *months*. And we mourned for you. We still do. What in the name of all that's holy happened to you?"

Walter studied his friend for an endless moment. "It's a long story."

"It better be a good one," Harry said sharply.

"I'll bet it is," Daniel murmured.

Walter glanced at Sidney. "I thought explanations could wait."

"They may have already waited too long." She shook her head. "I think now would be best."

"Very well." Walter thought for a moment. "There's a lot in the beginning that I have only vague memories of. All I really know is that a tribe found me, took me in and saved my life.

"It took a long time to recover. And even longer to get my strength back. It's only been a few months since I learned that you and Ben thought I was dead."

"Why didn't you let us know you were alive?"

"I intended to. I just haven't had the opportunity." He shook his head. "It's hard to explain but time moves differently here. The days slip away. It's easy to lose track of them. And I do like the life. For now anyway."

"Bloody hell, Walter." Harry had the distinct look of a man who wasn't sure if he wanted to punch his resurrected friend or hug him. Sidney held her breath. At last, Harry stepped closer, grasped Walter's shoulders and stared into the other man's eyes, his voice tight. "I have never been so glad to see anyone in my life. We had given up. I never thought, never imagined..." His voice caught and he paused.

"Neither did I," Walter said with an odd sort of smile.

Sidney's eyes fogged and she sniffed back a tear.

Harry grinned. "Damn it all, Walter, it's good to see you."

Sidney tried not to grin with satisfaction. She'd suspected all along he had feelings.

"Now." Walter looked at Sidney. "Can we leave?"

"Yes, I think so." She was still clutching the pectoral. She hadn't even noticed. "How did you find us?"

"You can thank Nazzal for that. I'll explain when we get back to camp." He looked at Harry. "It's getting late. You'll have to spend the night. You can't get back to Bedrachin before the last train and you can't get a steamer before morning."

"I say, if you don't mind," Daniel began, "I would much rather go back tonight. Surely some arrangement can be made."

"We're staying, Daniel," Sidney said pleasantly. "If you choose to go back, in the dark, on foot, you shall do so alone. You wanted to leave us out here and I am not inclined to forget such a thing. I'm certain Mr. Pickering agrees with me, don't you, Mr. Pickering?"

Walter raised an eyebrow at Harry then nodded. "Apparently, I do, Miss Honeywell."

"And is there any way to get a message to our friends?"

"Possibly," Walter said thoughtfully. "I'll see what can be done."

"Thank you." She cast him her brightest smile.

Harry blew a long breath. "We have a lot to talk about. A lot has changed."

Walter nodded. "For me as well."

For all that had transpired on this trip, that never would have happened had they not left England—the blame or the fault or the credit would go to Harry. For good or ill, he had started it all. The man had changed her life—all their lives—forever. It was a point worth remembering.

SIDNEY HADN'T REALIZED how late in the day it was. Walter's men had found their horses and the sun was sinking in the west by the time they reached the Bedouin encampment—a village of tanned skin tents with families, children, elders. And a lot of sand. Walter was greeted like one of them but, then, he was one of them.

Even in the grandest hotels, Sidney could not imagine such hospitality. They were welcomed, given coffee and a tasty stew of unidentifiable contents. Daniel was confined to a tent. She tried not to feel smug but he deserved it. Sidney wasn't quite sure what they would do with him yet but the punishment really did need to fit the crime.

"Did Nazzal know about your survival?" Harry asked as they sat around the fire talking late into the night.

"He had heard rumors but wasn't interested in verifying them until a few days ago." Walter studied Harry over the fire. "You know Nazzal. Until you came back to Egypt there was nothing in it for him."

Harry nodded.

"This morning I received a message from him suggesting I watch for you. He even sent directions as to where he thought you would be. When we found your horses, it wasn't hard to figure out it might be you. We tracked the horses back to the cave."

"We're most grateful you did," Sidney said with a smile.

Walter returned her smile then looked at his old friend. "Did you ever plan on coming back to Egypt?"

"It didn't seem there was any reason to return and, frankly, no desire. You were, well, dead and Ben and I were, I don't know, disillusioned I suppose." Harry thought for a long moment. "But I'm glad I did."

"If you gentlemen will excuse me." Sidney scrambled to her feet. It was obvious to her there were things Harry and Walter might wish to discuss privately. "I'm going to retire for the evening."

Harry got to his feet. "I'll walk you to your tent."

Sidney had been given a place to sleep with the other women. Their tent was not far away but Harry steered her out into the desert.

"What do you think you're doing?"

"There's something I want to show you." They climbed up a slight rise that sheltered the camp. "Take a look, Sidney. Have you ever seen stars so brilliant in a night so endless?"

"On board ship but this…" She gazed out at the night sky and her breath caught. Sidney had never been one for star-gazing and between overcast skies, fog and the city lights, the nights in London were not conducive to staring at the heavens. While she knew the position of celestial bodies as seen from Egypt would be different than in England, she did not expect to see the sky so filled with stars that one could almost read by the light. And feel the magic left by the ancients. "This is magnificent, Harry. Thank you," she said softly.

"I would gladly take credit but I did not arrange the stars." He paused. "Are you still angry with me?"

"I'm trying very hard to be. It would be much easier if you weren't being so contrite."

He grinned. "Then my plan is working."

She sighed in frustration. "I'm finding it difficult not to feel betrayed. Which might not be fair but there you have it."

He was silent for a long moment. "The Earl of Brenton wasn't the man who spent years in Egypt or lost a friend here—that was Harry Armstrong. It seemed only right that I leave the title behind. Besides." He chuckled. "I didn't want to intimidate you."

"That's...very thoughtful of you."

"Of course, that's when I thought you were an old lady."

"I rescind my thanks." She bit back a smile, took his arm and he escorted her to her tent.

Harry took her hands and raised them to his lips. "Sleep well, Sidney."

"Good night, Harry."

He turned away and started off. At once it struck her how devastated she would be if he walked out of her life forever. "Harry?"

He turned back and before he could say a word, before she could change her mind or consider the foolishness of her actions, she grabbed his jacket and kissed him hard and far longer than she had anticipated. Until his arms wrapped around her and he pulled her closer.

At last she drew away and breathed in a deep breath. "Don't think that means I have forgiven you anything. I have a great deal of thinking to do."

He grinned. "I can wait."

She pushed out of his arms. "Good night, Harry." She

turned, pulled aside the flap and went into the tent. His laughter drifted on the night air behind her.

Even if her thoughts had been entirely serene, Sidney doubted she could have slept a wink. She was not accustomed to sleeping on the ground. And, as she could not get her mind off sand fleas, whether they were present or not, she was beginning to itch.

This morning everything had been so clear. Well, certainly clearer than now. Harry had not directly declared his affections but he had spoken of love. That was before she had learned he was the one who had started all of this. One could argue trying to destroy her livelihood was unforgivable.

Or one could point out that she wouldn't be here at all—on the kind of grand adventure she'd never truly in her heart expected. She would not have recovered her grandmother's last find. She would not have fallen in love.

A restless sleep finally claimed her shortly before dawn. She had managed to summarize her dilemma in two questions: Did she want to live the rest of her life without Harry Armstrong?

And what would Millicent do?

By morning, she knew what should be done with Daniel. Harry was still in question.

Sidney made herself as presentable as possible before joining the others—including Daniel—for breakfast. "Good morning, gentlemen. I have an idea I think will serve us all well."

She shifted her gaze to the reporter. "The way I see it, Daniel, you could certainly write about my deception, thus destroying my career, and it would be an excellent story. For you. Or we could tell the authorities that you planned to leave us to die in the desert—"

"I wouldn't put it that way," Daniel protested.

She ignored him. "And you attempted to steal an ancient artifact. While I suspect the Egyptian authorities won't be overly upset at your leaving us behind they will be rather put out at the idea of your stealing their heritage." She met his gaze directly. "Have you ever been in an Egyptian jail, Daniel?"

Harry choked. The reporter paled.

"I have it on very good authority that it's not especially pleasant."

"So are we to trade my silence about your writing for silence about all this?" A hopeful note sounded in Daniel's voice. "Which does seem reasonable to me."

"To you perhaps. Goodness, Daniel, did you think I was offering you a bargain? I wasn't." She smiled and looked at Harry. "How moral of a man are you, Harry?"

"It depends upon what you mean by moral." His brow furrowed. "Are you speaking of murder? You did tell me to shoot him yesterday."

"Justifiable really as I was annoyed at the time." She waved off the comment. "And I knew you wouldn't. Although he was about to do very much the same thing to us. Not shoot us, of course, but abandon us in very precarious circumstances."

"I am not predisposed to murder either," Walter said.

Sidney glared at both men. "Did either of you honestly think I would advocate the taking of a life? Even his?"

"Not me," Daniel said quickly. "I had faith in you."

"I am both offended and appalled." Sidney crossed her arms over her chest.

"Our apologies," Walter said.

"Our abject, unhesitating apologies," Harry added.

"Accepted." She nodded. "I was thinking since Mr. Corbin wanted a good story, we should give him one. One that does not deal with the veracity of my writing, anything to do with his lordship and myself or the miraculous survival of Mr. Pickering."

"That is a good story. I hadn't thought of that one." Daniel frowned. "But if you eliminate all those possibilities, there's nothing left."

"On the contrary, I think a month in the desert with a Bedouin tribe—better yet six months—would give you a great deal to write about. Why, you might end up being called the King of the Desert. If, of course, Mr. Pickering is willing."

"Could I sell him?" Walter said in aside to Harry.

Harry shrugged. "Doesn't matter to me."

"I have no choice, do I?" Resignation sounded in Daniel's voice.

"Oh, but you do," Sidney said pleasantly. "A grand adventure that might make your career or an Egyptian jail."

Daniel huffed. "Not much of a choice."

Sidney smiled. "I never said it was a good choice."

"That was rather brilliant, Miss Honeywell," Walter said. "Corbin, my men will see you to your quarters and then we'll have a long talk."

Daniel muttered something under his breath then sighed. "Very well." He turned to Sidney. "I can't say it's been a pleasure but…" He smiled wryly. "It will be a good story. Sidney, Armstrong." He nodded and followed Walter's men.

"I was afraid you were going to offer him Walter's story," Harry said in an aside.

"Oh, I don't think he should be rewarded. Now, if he

wants to be part of the story, he'll have to work for it. Besides, I think if anyone should write Walter's story, it should be you."

"That's an interesting idea," he said thoughtfully.

A half an hour later, Sidney and Harry were ready to depart.

"Thank you for rescuing us, Walter." Sidney cast him her brightest smile. "I do hope to see you again someday."

"That would be a very great pleasure." He turned to Harry. "I assume you'll let Ben know."

Harry nodded. "I intend to send a telegram the moment we return to Cairo." He paused. "Will I see you again?"

Walter shrugged. "Who knows what life will bring next, Harry old man. Someday your butler might announce you have an unexpected visitor."

"Or I could ride back into your camp." Harry grinned but there was the tiniest hint of regret. "Take care, Walter."

"Travel safe, my friend."

Sidney was helped into her saddle. Harry mounted his horse and they headed toward Bedrachin where they were just in time for the next train. Harry was remarkably silent all the way back to Cairo but then so was she. Apparently he too had a great deal of thinking to do. After all, it wasn't every day one's good friend was resurrected and the reason for one's guilt vanquished.

They had barely stepped foot in the hotel when Mr. Nazzal appeared to take possession of the pectoral, adding his apologies for not telling Harry that Walter was alive but he had only confirmed it a few days ago. He assured Sidney the ladies knew she was safe and said he would let her know if the pectoral proved as interesting as they all hoped it was. She was grateful her friends weren't waiting in the lobby for them. All she wanted at the moment was a bath and a change of clothes.

"You scarcely said anything all the way here," she said as they approached the lift.

"I was waiting for you." He shrugged. "I figured it was your turn."

She nodded. "Yesterday, you said we needed to talk. Of course that was before Daniel turned out to be a cad and your dead friend came back to life."

"I did but you know everything now."

"Yes, but you don't."

He raised a brow. "Are you going to confess all?"

"More than you suspect." She drew a deep breath.

"There you are." Effie swept toward them, Gwen and Poppy a step behind.

Harry leaned in. "I expect to continue this later."

She smiled weakly. "I thought you would."

Effie threw her arms around Sidney as did the other ladies. For a few minutes, she was bombarded by questions and declarations and everyone talking at once.

"We were so worried about you." Effie sniffed back a tear.

"But that nice Mr. Nazzal assured us you were fine," Poppy added. "Did you find what you were looking for?"

"Unfortunately, we seemed to have lost Daniel." Gwen frowned. "Although, we are confident he can take care of himself. Still, one does hate to misplace a member of one's party."

"We have a great deal to tell you." Sidney glanced around. "Where's Harry?"

"He muttered something vague about lady travelers

and no privacy. Then he left," Effie said. "He might have mentioned something about a bath."

Poppy sniffed delicately. "Might I suggest you avail yourself of one as well?"

"I intend to." Sidney nodded. And then it was indeed time for her confession. Time to clear the air and tell him everything.

Whether she wanted to or not.

CHAPTER TWENTY-FIVE

SIDNEY BARELY HAD an hour to bathe and dress before the ladies appeared at her door. She was lucky to get that much time as her friends claimed to be dying of curiosity. She quickly filled them in on everything from the finding of the pectoral to Daniel's betrayal—at which point Effie said she would have shot him and would have enjoyed it—to Walter's resurrection and Harry's deception.

The ladies sat on the sofa like an odd sort of jury. They hadn't interrupted her once. It was not at all like them and rather disquieting. Sidney studied them closely. "Aren't you going to say anything?"

"My, that was an adventure." Poppy smiled uncertainly. "Millicent Forester couldn't have done better."

"There is one point that I find confusing." Gwen thought for a moment. "Correct me if I'm wrong, but didn't you say Harry sent a telegram to Mr. Cadwallender conceding defeat?"

She nodded.

"So victory is yours." Effie beamed. "Well done, Sidney."

"I haven't done anything. He let me win."

Poppy brightened. "And wasn't that sweet of him?"

"Sweet?" Sidney's voice rose. "He only did it to get us out of Egypt."

"He did it to save us from possible harm." Gwen shook

her head. "Unwarranted, of course, but terribly thoughtful of him nonetheless."

"I wouldn't call it thoughtful." Sidney stared at them. "I'd call it cunning and clever and calculating."

"Well, dear, you may call it whatever you want," Effie said, her gaze meeting Sidney's. "But you would be wrong."

Sidney shook her head. "Oh, I wouldn't think—"

"Then you need to start thinking," Gwen said in a no-nonsense tone. "This is a man who has set his own pride aside, pride that got him into all this in the first place, to do what he thought necessary to keep you safe. It might not have been the best action he could have taken but you can't fault him for being an idiot."

"All men are idiots to a certain extent," Poppy added. "Why, I'm not sure one who wasn't would be any fun at all. It really does give us an advantage they never suspect."

"And it does seem to us, a man who would voluntarily lose at anything in order to save a woman, whether his actions were misguided or not—" Effie shrugged "—is a man worth keeping."

"But he lied to me."

All three ladies gave her identical chastising looks.

"Yes, yes, I know but I lied to everyone—not just him. It wasn't personal. Furthermore, I did not intend to lie. There is a difference, you know."

"And one should probably consider the difference as well between a man who has a title and fortune and conceals it and one who claims to have a title and fortune and doesn't." Poppy grimaced. "In the scheme of things, one is eminently forgivable and the other isn't."

Sidney stared in disbelief. "You're on his side. All of you."

"No, Sidney." Effie pinned her with a firm look. "We are on your side. Always."

"As odd as it may sound, we have simply come to the conclusion that you and Harry are somehow on the same side now. Those sorts of things often happen when one falls in love." Gwen studied her curiously. "And really, Sidney, we'd be shocked if you didn't already know that."

"It's possible I suppose." They were right and Sidney did indeed know it.

"Tell us, Sidney," Poppy said briskly, "what are you going to do now?"

She shook her head. "There are still things he doesn't know."

"Then you should march right down to his room and tell him." Gwen gestured toward the door. "I would suggest at once."

"Millicent would." Poppy nodded.

"Millicent is fictional, dear." Effie eyed Sidney thoughtfully. "Perhaps it's time you stopped considering what Millicent Forester would do—"

Sidney opened her mouth to protest but Effie narrowed her eyes and Sidney reconsidered.

"—or what Mrs. Gordon would do. Perhaps it's time to consider what Sidney Honeywell would do."

"Sidney Honeywell has never done anything," Sidney said sharply.

"Sidney Honeywell created Millicent and Mrs. Gordon." Gwen ticked the points off on her fingers. "She cared for her mother, became an expert on Egypt as well as a successful writer and she finished her grandmother's work."

Sidney shook her head. "That was not why I came here."

"Regardless." Poppy smiled. "The end result is what matters."

"The Sidney Honeywell we know had the courage to leave her very safe world of words to come to Egypt in the first place." Effie's voice softened. "It seems to us, she should have the courage as well to trust the quite wonderful man who is so clearly in love with her."

Sidney stared at the trio for a long moment. It was easy to talk about courage, gathering it was a different matter. Did she have the courage to tell Harry everything regardless of the consequences? Did she have a choice?

"If you will excuse me, ladies." Sidney nodded and left her room before the resolve she'd managed to muster vanished. She strode briskly down the hall and knocked on Harry's door.

He opened it at once and she had the distinct impression that he was about to leave. His hair was still damp from his bath and for a moment, desire threatened to overcome apprehension.

"Harry," she said firmly and marched into his suite. "It's time we talked. Past time really."

"Exactly what I was thinking," he said cautiously and closed the door behind him.

"Do you want to sit down?"

"Not especially." He crossed his arms over his chest and leaned against the door. "Go on. Talk."

"Very well." She clasped her hands together—she didn't know what else to do with them—and drew a deep breath. "It's become apparent to me that I've been so busy keeping the truth about my writing from you, I have not told you much of anything about myself."

"I don't need to know," he said coolly. "Anything in your life that happened before you met me doesn't concern me in the least."

"Very noble." And really quite nice. "Nonetheless, I don't want any more secrets between us. And you deserve the truth."

"The truth? That will be a change." He bit back a grin. Wise of him. "Do go on."

"There's really little of interest to tell. I attended a well-respected school for girls. When my father died I took care of my mother until her death some four years ago now. I've had a passion for Egypt ever since I first met Aunt Effie and learned about my grandparents. After my mother died I started writing. I thought I had had been quite clear in stating my stories were simply based on true events— I never claimed they were my experiences but apparently people didn't notice."

"People see what they want to see or what they need to see." He paused. "Is that all?"

"You were right about me from the beginning."

"Oh, I knew that." He smirked. "I am usually right."

She ignored him. "I never realized I was competitive but apparently I am. Or maybe it's because I could go anywhere and do anything as Millicent. I was not willing to allow someone else to take that away from me."

He nodded. "Understandable."

"You're very clever, Harry Armstrong, and it was apparent to me it was only a matter of time before you denounced me so I chose to end my stories."

His brow furrowed. "You what?"

"I mailed my final installment of *Tales of a Lady Adventurer in Egypt* to Mr. Cadwallender a few days ago. Millicent Forester has at last decided to give her hand to

Richard Weatherly. And they are off to have new adventures together. None of which are for publication." She braced herself. "I couldn't allow you to win—to take my stories away from me. So I chose to end them."

His eyes narrowed. "So this game between us was a draw?"

"Exactly." She paused. "Well a tiny bit more of a victory for me but I think we can consider it a draw."

"You thought I'd be angry about this?"

"You are terribly arrogant, Harry. Not at all the type of man who likes to lose."

"No one likes to lose. And I would consider it a compromise rather than a draw." He chuckled. "I've never been especially fond of compromise either."

"So, this doesn't bother you?" she said slowly. "The fact that I beat you at what was essentially your own game?"

"When you put it that way…" He shrugged. "No, not really. I didn't lose after all. Anything else?"

"Nothing of significance." Although it was probably best to tell him everything. "Your writing is terrible."

"Ah yes, I could have done without that bit of truth but thank you."

"You have entirely too many sand fleas and vermin."

"I've heard that."

"But, from what little I read, I suspect you have wonderful stories to tell. And I intend to write them, with your assistance, of course."

"It doesn't matter." He shook his head. "Walter is alive and apparently content. With any luck at all, he'll have a long life ahead of him. There will be people who will remember him. He doesn't need my help now. And I don't need to tell our stories anymore." His gaze met hers.

"You did this, Sidney. You brought me back to Egypt. You redeemed my soul."

She raised a brow.

"I know it sounds stupid, reeking of overwrought words and, well, *feelings*." He threw up his hands in surrender. "But that's what you've done to me. And I must say I resent it." He shook his head. "And I'm glad."

"You should know, I intend to continue writing, not just your stories but others as well. And I intend to keep any income I receive from writing. I shall want papers drawn up stating that."

He shook his head in confusion. "Papers?"

"If I decided to marry you, not that you have asked but I'm assuming you will—"

He held up a hand to stop her. "Now there's something you should know. You were not my first unexpected visitor today. Less than an hour ago, I had an interesting chat with Lady Blodgett who wanted to know what I intended to do about my obligation as I had so obviously taken advantage of you." He was clearly trying not to grin but the corners of his mouth quirked upward. "I told her who took advantage of whom was in question."

Sidney gasped. "You didn't."

"My next visitor was Mrs. Fitzhew-Wellmore who also wanted to discuss my responsibilities in regards to marriage as well as extoll your virtues." He eyed her curiously. "You are apparently quite remarkable."

Her face heated. "You know how all three of them are prone to exaggeration."

"On the contrary." He straightened and moved toward her. "I agree with them."

"Oh?" She swallowed hard at the look in his eyes and resisted the urge to step back.

He nodded. "And then of course, not to be outdone, my last caller was Mrs. Higginbotham."

"She thinks you're wonderful."

He grinned. "I am. She too wanted to know if I intended to do the honorable thing—"

"I am not an ob—"

He pressed his finger to her lips to quiet her. "Do you want to hear the rest of this?"

She nodded.

He removed his finger and continued. "She pointed out how foolish it would be to at last find the one woman in the world meant for you, the woman who made you think about feelings you never expected to have, the woman who stole your soul, and then not do something about it. Because surely someone else might."

She stared up at him. "There is no one else."

"Good." He smiled. "Papers, eh?"

She nodded.

"I must be mad." He shook his head. "Papers it is." He took her hands, drew a deep breath and gazed into her eyes. "I love you, Sidney Honeywell. Do not leave me at the mercy of those old ladies. Do me the very great honor of spending the rest of your life driving me mad. Be my obligation and my wife."

"I love you too, Harry Armstrong. Aside from that—" she grinned "—I'd prefer not to be at the mercy of those old ladies either and I would be if I said no. They would say I was a fool and they'd be right. I can't think of anything I'd rather do for the rest of my life than drive you mad."

"Well, you did say we made an impressive team." He pulled her into his arms. "So you see—I really did win after all."

Her heart thudded in her chest. "You should also know the first story I intend to write is ours."

He grinned. "A love story, then?"

She nodded.

"Interesting except that ours is never going to end." His lips brushed across hers.

"Why, Harry, I thought you knew." Her voice was once again breathless. The things this man did to her. "The very best love stories never do."

The Earl of Brenton and Miss Sidney Honeywell, both of London, were wed at the Cathedral Church of All Saints on Wednesday last. The newlyweds plan to continue their tour of Egypt before taking up residence in London.

—*Egyptian Gazette*

A new series of lectures by our honored founders will be scheduled for Spring. Lady Blodgett, Mrs. Fitzhew-Wellmore and Mrs. Higginbotham are currently continuing their extended tour of Egypt.

—notice on the wall of the Lady Travelers Society

Mrs. Gordon thanks her readers who have embraced *Tales of a Lady Adventurer in Egypt* and hopes they will enjoy her new literary adventures, to be written under the nom de plume of Mrs. Armstrong.

—Literary Notes, *Cadwallender's Daily Messenger*

Cadwallender's Daily Messenger is pleased to announce the promotion of Daniel Corbin to special correspondent for Egypt. We anticipate the publication of his *Tales of a Gentleman Adventurer in Egypt* sometime next year. We trust he is even now compiling his adventures although his whereabouts are currently unknown.

—*Cadwallender's Daily Messenger*

EPILOGUE

Six weeks later

"I DARESAY WE will have a lot to talk about when we return home," Gwen mused idly. But then idleness was difficult to avoid from the deck chair of a tourist steamer moving slowly along the Nile.

"Who would have ever imagined the three of us seeing all the wonders of ancient Egypt." Poppy heaved a sigh of contentment. Thus far, they had seen pyramids and ruins, temples and tombs. They'd been to Karnak and Luxor and the Valley of the Kings. It was all the more extraordinary given they'd never expected to set foot outside of England. "And we have his lordship to thank for it."

"Or blame as he started all this." Effie chuckled. "Regardless, it was indeed generous of Harry to fund the rest of our tour of Egypt. He really is rather wonderful."

While Mr. Cadwallender had been thrilled at Sidney's victory, he had also seen fit to cut off his financial support—with the exception of their return fares home—as he pointed out the purpose of their trip had been accomplished. Still, it did seem a shame to have come all the way to Egypt and spend only a week.

"I do feel rather guilty though." Poppy grimaced.

"Nonsense." Gwen scoffed. "The man has more money than he can spend in a lifetime."

Poppy shook her head. "Oh, I don't feel the least bit guilty about that."

"I daresay Harry never imagined he'd be spending his honeymoon with three *old ladies* in tow." Effie grinned. "Although I suspect Harry never imagined himself married either."

"I don't feel bad about that either," Poppy said. "It was not our idea after all." She paused. "But I do have the tiniest bit of remorse about keeping everything we knew from Sidney."

"It was not our story to tell, Poppy," Gwen said mildly.

"Regardless of how you feel, even though it has all worked out quite nicely, Sidney would not be the least bit happy with us if she were ever to find out that we knew of Harry's years in Egypt and his new title nearly from the beginning." Effie paused. "His father's quite charming."

"It seems to me this is one of those secrets the three of us should swear to take to our graves." Gwen's gaze shifted from one friend to the other. "Agreed?"

Poppy and Effie nodded.

"I must admit, I rather envy Sidney." Poppy smiled. "I believe Harry is the beginning of a magnificent adventure."

"Goodness, dear." Effie adopted a serene smile, settled back in her chair and gazed out at the Egyptian countryside and the feluccas floating by. "The right man always is."

* * * * *

AUTHOR NOTE

Lost for nearly four thousand years, the royal city of Itjtawy was finally located in the 21st century through the use of NASA topography data and satellite imaging.

The name of Amenemhat II's queen consort is still unknown.

Get 4 FREE REWARDS!

We'll send you 2 FREE Books plus 2 FREE Mystery Gifts.

FREE
Value Over
$20

Both the **Romance** and **Suspense** collections feature compelling novels
written by many of today's best-selling authors.

YES! Please send me 2 FREE novels from the Essential Romance or
Essential Suspense Collection and my 2 FREE gifts (gifts are worth about
$10 retail). After receiving them, if I don't wish to receive any more books,
I can return the shipping statement marked "cancel." If I don't cancel, I will
receive 4 brand-new novels every month and be billed just $6.74 each in the
U.S. or $7.24 each in Canada. That's a savings of at least 16% off the cover
price. It's quite a bargain! Shipping and handling is just 50¢ per book in the
U.S. and 75¢ per book in Canada.* I understand that accepting the 2 free
books and gifts places me under no obligation to buy anything. I can always
return a shipment and cancel at any time. The free books and gifts are mine
to keep no matter what I decide.

Choose one: ☐ **Essential Romance**   ☐ **Essential Suspense**
                   (194/394 MDN GMY7)   (191/391 MDN GMY7)

Name (please print)

Address   Apt. #

City   State/Province   Zip/Postal Code

Mail to the **Reader Service:**
IN U.S.A.: P.O. Box 1341, Buffalo, NY 14240-8531
IN CANADA: P.O. Box 603, Fort Erie, Ontario L2A 5X3

Want to try 2 free books from another series? Call 1-800-873-8635 or visit www.ReaderService.com.